Hot Mother

Nancy Peach is a writer of women's fiction, a mother of three, and an owner of various ridiculous-looking pets. She is also a practicing doctor working for the NHS and a national cancer charity, and has been writing (in a terribly British, embarrassed, secretive way) for as long as she can remember. Nancy's debut, *Love Life* was published in 2021.

Also by Nancy Peach

The Mother of All Problems
Hot Mother

hot mother

NANCY PEACH

hera

First published in the United Kingdom in 2024 by

Hera Books
Unit 9 (Canelo), 5th Floor
Cargo Works, 1-2 Hatfields
London SE1 9PG
United Kingdom

A CIP catalogue record for this book is available from the British Library.

Print ISBN 978 1 80436 735 3
Ebook ISBN 978 1 80436 733 9

Look for more great books at www.herabooks.com

Printed and bound in Great Britain by Clays Ltd, Elcograf S.p.A.

1

For Hayley.

And all you Hot Mothers out there.

Chapter One

'What the hell did you think you were doing, you stupid woman?'

The man waving his arms around in the road probably had a point, but his expansive gestures were on the verge of causing more traffic chaos as the gridlocked queue behind us became restless. Some of these drivers seemed to be mistaking his feverish and entirely random arm movements as the signals of a traffic policeman. The Mini behind me, following his lead, started to move into the opposite lane, whereupon a white van commenced a furious orchestra of honking as it swerved into the lay-by.

'I'm so sorry,' I shouted above the squeal of tyres and blasts of various horns that had now joined the medley. I find the best way to deal with these scenarios is absolute contrition from the outset. Men whose cars have been rammed from behind by middle-aged women drivers in wheelchair-compatible vehicles rarely seem agreeable to the alternative approach of aggressive denial of responsibility. You've got to have a lot of confidence to pull that off, and the only person I know who can successfully achieve it is my friend High Powered Joy. You wouldn't argue with her unless you were suicidal. Besides, apologetic timidity is a personality trait that has served me well in the past.

And it was my fault, this accident. No point in pretending otherwise.

Patiently, I started to explain the circumstances that had led to the situation, partly out of a compulsive need to defend my own actions and partly out of a desire to bore him into submission, another useful technique I've previously deployed.

'This isn't even my car,' I said, smiling in the face of his mounting incredulity. 'It's my dad's – that's why it's a disability vehicle. For my mum – and her wheelchair. I'm not actually disabled myself.' He looked as though he might argue with that so I pushed on. 'It's just that I got distracted – I'm terribly sorry. I thought I saw my son's girlfriend snogging someone else and I panicked. I've got a board meeting in five minutes – well, less of a board meeting and more of an informal chat with friends – and I've only just finished walking the dog. He was an absolute nightmare, rolled in something horrific, had to change my outfit twice! And I slept dreadfully' – I finished with my trump card, knowing he'd be unable to mount a response – 'due to my hot flushes.'

Boom! Mic drop, et cetera.

Angry gesticulating man was broken.

Note that this is a highly effective way of shutting down an escalating conflict. Mention the perimenopause – or anything gynaecological, really: heavy periods, ovarian cysts, pelvic floor instability – and even the most agitated individual backs off. I recommend it to hostage negotiators, armed police responders and UN diplomacy teams – instead of chucking a grenade into a roomful of terrorists, simply shout the words 'vaginal dryness' and watch them scatter.

No part of the above slightly garbled explanation was untrue, by the way. My day really hadn't begun well. Waking at three in the morning bathed in a pool of your own boiling sweat is rarely conducive to a positive outlook, so I was already alert to the likelihood of impending woe, which is some consolation, I guess, given the Monday that followed. My husband Sam was of course snoring beside me when I woke, blissfully unaware of the now drenched creature he had married, and as the moisture evaporated from my skin, leaving me shivering like a newborn lamb, I pondered the term *hot flushes*.

In my early forties, when people still spoke of such things as vague and distant concerns, I thought they sounded fairly innocuous. After all, what kind of woman born and raised in one of the chilliest and dampest countries on the planet would mind being a little bit warmer from time to time? Friends made occasional jokes about saving on heating bills, which, given the cost-of-living crisis, seemed quite useful. But what nobody tells you about hot flushes is that any money you save on fuel in those feverish nanoseconds between roasted and frozen, is immediately consumed by the cost of washing your bedding and attractive pyjamas (breathable cotton, floral print in case you're interested) on a much more regular basis. Because as everybody (barring tramps, teenage boys and a certain breed of sporty adult man) is aware, revisiting fabrics that have been repeatedly saturated in your own sweat is not the most pleasant experience.

Thankfully my own brand of hot drowning was still a relatively infrequent occurrence, and not one that had taken place during a business meeting or dinner party.

Not like High Powered Joy, whose transformation from competent businesswoman to aquatic leviathan occurred in front of an audience of middle-aged men while she was presenting the current shortfall in the Parker account, a story she related to the rest of us with a certain degree of relish. Apparently, in classic Joy fashion, she had immediately insisted that all the windows in the building be opened to their maximum extent (only two inches, to avoid workplace suicides – not that Joy is particularly bothered), and the office heating system turned off at the mains, despite it being February. She then told every single employee and board member who had the temerity to complain that they should consider the environment, heat the person not the building, and that if they didn't like it they could piss off.

But that's Joy. I know that if I had a hot flush at work I'd be in much more of the *trying to pretend it isn't happening* brigade, dabbing at my forehead with a moistened tissue to distract from the torrents pouring from every other inch of my body – not just the armpits, you understand, oh no. Underneath the boobs and the backs of my knees are my own particular favourite places to find paddling pools of sweat as I lie there shivering in the small hours of the morning, dragged from sleep like a newt in the torchlight of a biology field trip.

Once I had freed myself from the swamp and shuffled stiffly to the airing cupboard (my joints are still fully functioning, but three in the morning is not the time to be breaking gymnastic records – the last time I tried a brisk walk I cricked my neck), I wrapped myself in a towel and returned to bed. The towel I chose was one of the 'threadbare, no fabric conditioner, stiff as cardboard' variety. Ancient, well-used and slightly soiled, much like my good self. These towels have been placed on the children's beds during vomiting bugs; they have mopped the floor when Sam let the bath overflow and when the washing machine died; they have formed the tablecloth for rainy-day picnics (when the kids were still small enough to believe that eating a packet of Wotsits and an egg sandwich on the playroom floor was an adventure); and one of them was even commandeered as an informal banner, hung from the windowsill bearing the legend 'Meat is Murder' in garish red paint by my eldest daughter Grace when she was going through a particularly militant phase of her Damascene conversion to veganism. But nowadays these venerable items of household linen are generally used only by me or the dog. In fact, they are informally known as 'dog towels', and are kept on the lower shelf of the cupboard as opposed to the 'guest towels' kept on the top shelf, fragrant and fluffy, waiting to be used by our infrequent guests who probably aren't that bothered by the luxury pile anyway.

Thus armed, I returned to my bed and tried to persuade my febrile body to return to sleep through the medium of mindfulness, despite the fact that my mind is already full — packed to capacity, crammed with useless information and a continuous running commentary of inane proportions. This morning's attempt was thwarted by the following thoughts:

> *Is that high-pitched squealing outside my window the sound of two foxes shagging or someone being murdered?*

> *Why is my left toe so itchy? Is it athlete's foot? Would that be possible when I am so evidently not an athlete? Is it cancer?*

Duran Duran — 'Hungry Like the Wolf' — assorted verses

Would renationalising the railways actually lead to an improved train service, and why do I find trade union spokesmen so strangely attractive?

What was the name of the actor the woman from last night's detective series was married to?

Did I sign the permission slip about Maisie's school trip to Pirate World, or did I use it as an informal shopping list when we needed bread, Sellotape and toilet roll yesterday?

Did I remember the Sellotape? Where did I put it?

Did a mosquito just fly past my ear? Are mosquitoes even around in January? Is this due to global warming, or am I simply creating a tropical micro-climate with my body heat?

Is that itchy lump on my neck a mosquito bite? Is it cancer?

Peppa Pig theme tune

Of course, at four in the morning what one actually needs is mind-emptiness, and this appears to be an impossible state for me to achieve. Instead I got a grand total of zero additional hours of sleep, and lay staring at the ceiling while Sam snored until the radio alarm went off at seven. My husband isn't a terrible snorer — his nasal breathing is not the congested trumpety orchestra of some fifty-year-old men (and having spent time on a camping holiday with four other families a few years back, I feel I can

6

say this with some confidence – we won't be going on holiday with Robin Vickery again anytime soon). But when you're wide awake in the middle of the night, even the most inoffensive snoring can make you feel homicidal. So it was that I emerged from my bedchamber unrefreshed, damp and utterly furious with my husband (who, thankfully, remained oblivious to how close he'd come to never waking up again).

I packed two of my children off to school. Maisie is in her final year of primary school and therefore can walk there unassisted, thank you very much – if I ever accompany her now I have to remain four paces behind and pretend I don't know her, much like a royal footman or a spy. The rules obviously change when there's additional luggage – if I'm tasked with carrying a junk sculpture or items for the Christmas tombola, as I was a few weeks ago, then I am allowed within a metre radius but must remain silent at all times. Nothing is more embarrassing when you are eleven than having an actual mother, it seems.

My middle child, Tom, had to get the bus this morning because his girlfriend, the lovely Lauren, was unable to drive him in. Despite Tom turning seventeen last month he hasn't been able to start driving lessons due to my car (also known as The Learner Car – somewhat erroneously in the case of my eldest daughter, Grace, who still can't reverse off the drive without hitting a wheelie bin, pedestrian or part of the masonry) being in the garage for reasons unknown. I'm sure they're known to the mechanic (something to do with a 'damaged sump' following an altercation with a pothole), but from my point of view repairs fall into one of two categories: expensive and extortionate. I fear my little Toyota's recent misdemeanours may fall into the latter group and that's about as much information as I need to take on board.

Children thus dispatched, I took our psychotic mongrel (mainly terrier crossed with idiot) out for his morning walk. Within moments he had rolled in fox poo, humped an unsuspecting spaniel and torn across an open field with me following in hot pursuit, hollering and swearing ineffectually as per standard. I hadn't put up much resistance when Grace had insisted on naming the dog Montmorency a couple of years back – I was probably still in mourning for Colin, our beloved and ancient Collie cross – and Grace, studying *Three Men in a Boat* for A level, suggested we bestow the moniker 'ironically'. Unfortunately, it doesn't matter how bloody ironic that naming process was when you find yourself stranded in the middle of a windy field shouting, 'Montmorency!' at the top of your voice and basically looking and sounding like a massive dick.

Eventually the bastard dog returned, and by some feat of superhuman strength (and treats), I managed to get the lead secured to his fox-poo-encrusted collar and we made our way back to the house where I got ready for work. This involved a shower and two complete outfit changes, the first having to be abandoned when I realised I'd missed a patch of something unspeakable still clinging to Montmorency's coat that needed immediate hosing. I don't tend to worry too much about what I wear to work; Bob's Place has quite a relaxed vibe, being a care home and day centre specialising in dementia, but we, the trustees, like it to feel special – a cut above your standard care facility. Rocking up in filthy jeans smelling like a farmyard would not have been appropriate.

Also, I'll admit it, I like 'dressing for work'. Pulling on a pair of trousers that aren't coated in food, mud and dog hair is tangible evidence of me having a role outside the home, something I've struggled for many years to achieve. With three kids, ageing parents and a well-intentioned but often absent husband to feed, clothe and generally keep alive, it used to feel that I was tethered to the house on a short leash of domesticity. My uniform during those early years of childcare was limited to stained tracksuit bottoms and baggy jumpers. There was no point in even pulling a pair of sharply creased linen trousers from the wardrobe; they'd need washing within about four seconds, and if there's anything I've learnt it's that I really don't need more soiled clothing to clean. Friends and loved ones may come and go, but there's one constant in my life, one thing that'll always be there for me, come rain or shine. And that thing is laundry.

To be honest, the tracksuit-and-T-shirt combo still features heavily in my wardrobe to this day, but I do try to make a point of keeping certain outfits just for work. Nothing fancy; a passably clean top is enough to make me feel purposeful and corporate, even if the only thing being discussed at our business meeting (three of us chatting over coffee) is whether our newest client would like to have sessions with the art therapist, or whether Derek's dodgy hip is still restricting his movement in Zimmer Zumba, or what's happened to the order of dementia-friendly cutlery that's been stuck on a lorry in Calais for the past four months. We do *do* businessy stuff at Bob's Place, of course – we have spreadsheets and policy documents and employment contracts to review – but our priority is always the clients and their families, which means our meetings are informal and occur on site so that we don't lose touch with what's going on at the coalface. Not that there's much danger of that for me, because my mother has been attending the day centre for the past five years, ever since Bob's Place opened its doors as the world's first and finest dementia hotel.

Mum's Alzheimer's has advanced significantly during that time, but I still remember those heady days of starting the business as if it was yesterday – the hours Tina spent ensuring that her late husband Bob's legacy money was spent wisely; the weeks Veronica and I spent navigating the planning regulations, recruiting the staff and registering with the local authority. And once Bob's Place was open, the work kept on coming – we barely had to publicise the business, such was the need for a quality care establishment with the client truly at its heart. Initially we started off as a day centre with occasional overnight respite stays, but more recently we've opened up to longer-term residents, extending the accommodation and providing nursing care where needed. In fact, I have been wondering recently about moving Mum there on a more permanent basis, just as soon as I can pluck up the courage to have that conversation with my father.

When Mum first came to stay with me, early in her 'dementia journey' as the therapists say, I was completely against the idea of long-term residential care. I'd investigated the local options, dragging her along with me, trying to put a positive spin on various dilapidated institutions who were all doing their best on very limited resources but who weren't exactly achieving a 'state-of-the-art home-from-home' vibe, if you know what I mean. At that point I knew Mum would be isolated and miserable, and I'd be racked with eternal guilt if I 'put her into care'. But this was seven years ago. Things change. Mum no longer really knows where she is most of the time, and besides, Bob's Place didn't exist then. Now we've got the best care home in the world right on our doorstep. I've been thinking for a while that she might actually be *safer* there too, particularly since the incident with the hairdryer and the washing machine. Anyway, I digress...

Once I'd squeezed into outfit number two (the zip on my trousers straining in a way that was frankly offensive given that I'd had no breakfast), I sent a quick text to Tom to check that he was safely in school. It's a bit kamikaze, the local bus, just as likely to sail past a group of waiting children as to bother stopping and collecting them – and Tom is now a towering hulk of a sixth-former, not like some of the tiny year sevens who presumably have priority. When Maisie starts secondary school next year, she'll have to run the gauntlet of the bus like her siblings before her. I would suggest that Tom drive her in, once he passes his test, but if he's still journeying to sixth form with the lovely Lauren come September, then it's likely there will be enough snogging and heavy petting going on in that car to make it a child protection issue if I were to allow a minor such as Maisie to witness it. The school bus is also a rite of passage – Grace and Tom have spent many happy years surfing the aisle as Bernard the driver takes a corner too aggressively; ducking to avoid the hail of projectiles lobbed by the seniors from the back seats; or squished four abreast into a double seat along with their sweaty gym bags, a broken umbrella and the inevitable biohazard of a neglected lunch box. So it's important that I allow Maisie to enjoy the experience too, lest I be accused of favouritism by the older children.

Tom replied with a single 'Y' that I assume was intended to convey '*yes, I successfully boarded the bus and have now arrived at the appropriate educational establishment, thank you for your concern, Mother'*, and I popped two doors down to borrow Dad's car, in much the same way as I did aged eighteen, except that nowadays his car is wheelchair-accessible and has the shape and echoey interior of a Royal Mail van. I've contemplated the idea of cycling to work, the wind fresh in my hair, the pleasant ache of exercise in my muscles, but I tried it once and nearly had a cardiac arrest on the ring road, so this, along with many of my environmentally friendly projects, remains a work-in-progress (i.e. unlikely ever to occur). Most of the time when I'm borrowing Dad's car I'm taking Mum over to Bob's Place with me anyway, so it feels legitimate rather than taking advantage, but today they were expecting a visit from the occupational therapist, and given that those visits are harder to arrange than an audience with the Pope, my parents were under strict instructions to stay under house arrest until he or she had been. I raised my hand to Dad, who was peering anxiously through the window at the sleet gathering in the grey clouds above and he mouthed 'Drive carefully' at me, using the expression that only an eighty-year-old man can get away with – a face that says, *it's mere moments since you learnt to drive, young lady, and don't you forget it – a car is a lethal weapon*, et cetera.

I nodded reassuringly at him. 'Hope it goes well with the OT,' I mouthed back before getting into the car and pulling away, leaving my father peering anxiously through the murky window.

Bob's Place was only the other side of town, and although the traffic was crawling along I was confident I'd be there for ten when the meeting started. Veronica, the other board member, was on holiday in Egypt visiting the pyramids with her partner Gee, so it was only going to be me and Tina going through the books and this week's rota. I was pulling up to a stop at the traffic lights, idly wondering whether Tina would have baked her usual banana muffins, when my attention was drawn to the bus shelter across the road where a group of kids were vaping so copiously that they appeared to be on fire. Emerging from a doorway behind the scented fog was a blonde, willowy girl who looked a lot like Tom's girlfriend Lauren. She was talking to a smart young man in a suit – he appeared to be in his early twenties. They were deep in conversation, sheltering in the doorway next to the curry house, and I was just wondering why Lauren would be using a free period to loiter around the High Street when the pair of them started snogging – vigorously.

Lauren!

Tom's Lauren?

(Not that he *owned* her, but WTAF?)

I was so distracted by the possible sighting of my son's dedicated long-term girlfriend sucking the face off an older man that I missed the driver of the Audi in front braking harder than expected and promptly went straight into the back of him.

Hence the current, less than ideal situation.

Chapter Two

Monday, 9.30 a.m.

Once I'd dropped my hot flush bombshell, angry Audi owner backed off, as well he might. God only knew what kind of haggish witchy voodoo I might hex him with otherwise. We exchanged numbers and he tried very hard not to have an aneurysm about the fact that this wasn't my car and therefore I had no idea of the insurance details (to be fair, I'd have almost no notion of the insurance details if I *had* been driving my own car; the last paper certificate I had from an insurance company was in 2016, and since then I've just clicked on the automatic online renewal. Driving4U has probably had several rebrands during this time and may even have ceased trading – who would know?). I breezily informed him that I would be in touch and apologised again for the fact that his bumper was now hanging off. I then stood, arms crossed, legs slightly akimbo, eyeing up said bumper and informed him (with no qualification whatsoever) that it was likely to be perfectly safe for him to complete his journey and that whiplash only tended to kick in a few days after an accident, so he should be fine for the foreseeable.

He muttered something under his breath, got back in the car and we both went on our merry way. At least, he did. I got through the traffic lights, avoiding the eyes of all the other drivers who'd been waiting patiently behind us, and pulled immediately into the Tesco's car park, where I rested my head so hard on the steering wheel that the airbag nearly activated.

'Calm, deep breaths,' I said to myself, trying to remember my yoga teacher Bendy Lydia's advice about mindful breathing. Slow and steady. Find your happy place. That sort of thing. Short inhalation and a looong exhalation, like the sides of a rectangle – or was it the other way around? Was I actually now hyperventilating? Best stop. I sat back upright and contemplated the sleet that was pelting my windscreen. Had that really been Lauren? Could I have been mistaken? If it *had* been her, kissing someone other than my son, was there any possible innocent explanation? Had she and Tom split up? I exited the car, into the sleet, and ran back to scan the scene of both my collision and Lauren's potential infidelity, but finding nothing other than an old lady with a tartan shopping trolley, I returned to the car and decided to phone Grace.

'Whaastmimishmum,' she answered blearily.

'Sorry, darling, did I wake you?'

'Mmm. A bit.'

'No lectures this morning?'

'No. What is it?' She sounded a bit more awake although I could hear a grunting noise in the background.

'Is that Seamus?' I said, thinking the grunting sounded male. 'Or Caroline?' I'm totally cool with the fact that my daughter is bisexual, something I try to demonstrate on a regular basis to the point where, as Grace has informed me, it completely undermines the coolness. Anyway, she didn't answer as to the provenance of the grunting, so I was left to draw my own conclusions.

'What it is, Mum? Are you OK?'

'Just wondering,' I said, casual-like, 'if you'd spoken to Tom recently?'

'Tom?'

'Your brother. I'm just wondering whether he'd mentioned splitting up with Lauren at all?'

'Who?'

'Lauren,' I said patiently. 'You know, Lauren, who your brother Tom has been going out with for eighteen months? His first ever girlfriend?'

'Mum, what's going on?' Grace's voice bore the trace of impatience I recognised from her teenage years, which makes sense given that she's only recently left those years behind.

'I don't know,' I sighed. 'I thought I saw her just now, kissing someone else – and I'm sure Tom would have mentioned if they'd split up. He was talking about how she couldn't drive him today because she was over at her dad's... He'd have told me if there was something wrong, wouldn't he?'

'Was it definitely her?'

'I thought so, but...' There was more than a seed of doubt in my mind now I came to think of it. 'I mean, visibility wasn't great.'

There was silence at the end of the line as Grace digested the information (or potentially fell back to sleep).

'Grace?' I tried again. 'What do you think? Have they broken up? Should I say anything?' Should I hunt the two-timing, scheming minx down and slap her in the face, was what I wanted to ask.

Grace made that little noise at the back of her throat, the exasperated one. 'Tom wouldn't call me to like, tell me about his love life, Mum. We don't "chat" on the phone.

That's just for parents and the student loan department. Old people, basically.'

I nodded to myself. 'OK, yes. Should have thought. But did he mention anything to you in person over the holidays then? I mean, you did speak to each other during those four weeks?' Grace had only been back at university a few days – surely it wasn't too much of a stretch to think she might have both communicated with her brother *and* remembered the salient points of the conversation over the intervening time period.

'Yes, we did speak to each other but not like *that*.' She made it sound as though I'd asked whether she'd explained to her younger brother how babies are made, or the steps involved in a cervical smear test. 'I'm not being funny, Mum, but I'm probably the last person Tom would want to talk to about, like, *relationships*. Other than maybe you. No offence.'

'None taken,' I said, feeling mortally offended. 'How about online then? Has he said anything on social media? Maybe Facebook?'

'Mum, nobody born in this millennium uses Facebook.'

'Of course. Yes.' I knew that. 'Maybe on Instagram then? Has he got one of those Rinsta accounts?' I was quite proud of myself for knowing the lingo and the difference between Rinsta, which stood for Real Instagram (where the youngsters do their chat) and Finsta, or Fake Instagram (where they post pictures for their parents to see) – but my balloon of pride was pierced by the needle of my eldest's withering superiority, as it so often is.

'Mum,' she said, using the tone one would take with an imbecile. 'Again, if Tom had gone to the trouble of setting up a fake account for the purpose of clarifying his relationship status, which I think is highly unlikely, then he almost certainly would not be inviting his older sister to follow it. He'd be more likely to share it with Maisie!' She laughed at the improbability of such a scenario.

'Good thinking,' I said. 'I'll ask her to have a look.'

'Maisie doesn't have an Instagram account,' she said. 'She's eleven. You're supposed to be thirteen.'

'Oh, right.' I was sure I'd seen the app on Maisie's phone. 'And would she be able to open one without my say-so? Theoretically speaking?'

'Well, she shouldn't be able to,' Grace sighed. 'But God knows, where Maisie's concerned.'

'Hmmm,' I said.

'I mean, I don't want to get sidetracked from our fascinating conversation here, but sometimes I feel the need to point out inequalities. Tom and I weren't even allowed a *phone* until we were like halfway through secondary school.'

'Oh, now, that's a bit of an exaggeration,' I scoffed. It's amazing to me, now the children are older, that Grace and Tom align themselves much more tightly as a unit compared to when they were both under the same roof and spent most of their time trading insults, shouting obscenities and hating each other's guts. Now it's all 'life was tough in the trenches for us, the older generation of siblings – everything is easier when you're the spoilt little baby sister'.

'It's not an exaggeration,' she said. 'And even when we got our ancient handsets we weren't allowed anything other than basic text messaging functions. You were worried Instagram would make us depressed, or that we'd be groomed by criminal gangs or something.'

'Yes, well – just because I don't mention that as an ongoing concern doesn't mean it's no longer occupying my headspace. Anyway, to clarify – you've not spoken to your brother in person, or seen anything on Instagram to indicate that he might have split up with Lauren?'

'Correct.'

'So, basically you're just as clueless as I am?'

'It would appear so. Can I go back to bed now?'

'Hmmm,' I said, frustrated by the lack of resolution. 'Remind me why we're paying your tuition fees again?'

'You're *not*. I'm paying for them, remember? When I start earning all my postgraduate millions?'

'Well, your living expenses then.'

'I dunno – maybe so I can afford to *live*? I mean, I'm sorry to be such a burden and all.'

'I'm just saying, I'm surprised that you're not currently in lectures or a tutorial or something. Shouldn't you be working towards your finals or your dissertation, or...' As I said this, I had a brief flashback to my student days and the proportion of my final year that was spent watching daytime television wrapped in a duvet with Sam. I realised that I maybe needed to dial back on the moral outrage. Grace clearly felt the same.

'Mum! Give me an actual break! It's January – my finals and my dissertation are months away. Anyway,' she said, 'this phone call isn't exactly productive use of my academic time, is it? Trying to work out whether you may, or may not, have seen someone who may, or may not, have broken up with my brother?'

'OK,' I said. 'Sorry.'

She softened immediately. 'Do you want me to make some discreet enquiries? I could message him.'

'On the family group chat? He won't like that.'

'No,' she said. 'Tom and I have got our own chat. It's called "Neglected Older Siblings".'

'Would you?' I said, my throat tight with gratitude. 'Don't mention that I think I might have seen Lauren kissing someone else.'

'I'm not stupid, Mum,' she said gently. 'Of course I won't.'

'And let me know if you discover anything.'

'Will do. Within reason.'

'Thanks, darling. I love you. I'll keep you posted if I hear anything as well.'

'Please do,' said Grace in the voice of one who doesn't really wish to be kept posted at all, someone who in fact wishes to tie up the conversation and get back to bed. 'Love you too. I'll see you Friday. Are you OK to pick me up from the station?'

I sat for a moment after Grace had disconnected the call, feeling the painful absence of my eldest daughter. It's been a couple of years since she left for university and I'd like to say that each time she returns home, the gaping chasm between a mother and her absent child becomes a little easier to cross, but it doesn't really. She was home for the holiday until only a few days ago, and she's back again this weekend for the belated Christmas celebrations with my brother Rory and his family, but there's always something temporary about her visits now. Her life no longer revolves around us – her parents and siblings. Her mind is always at least half occupied with student life and the friends she has in Reading. And so, by extension, you'd think that my life no longer revolved around her. That I would have refocused my attention on a slightly smaller household, leaving the part of my brain that was previously filled with thoughts of Grace to just float around the periphery of my consciousness. But it doesn't work like that. Thoughts of my eldest daughter pop into my head at the most incongruous moments. When I'm brushing my teeth, I always think of her weird aversion to other people's toothbrushes. When certain songs come on the radio or a familiar theme tune comes on the television, I am reminded of evenings singing in the kitchen or hunkering down in the sitting room to watch a favourite show with her. In the supermarket, if I see a new item added to the own-brand vegan range I always go to put it in my trolley, thinking *I'll cook it for Grace*, before remembering, *Grace isn't home for supper tonight, and by the time she does come home that mushroom couscous will have gone off* (although to be honest, who would know with mushroom couscous?). It doesn't seem fair, this imbalance – the part of me that will always be set aside for her, like a chunk of my heart has been specifically designated and labelled GRACE BAKER, when in all likelihood her heart is entirely consumed by Seamus or Caroline or whoever.

Having said that, Grace is not the type to be completely consumed by any romantic liaison. Not like my Tom. My lovely boy, who guards his heart far less fiercely than his sister. He's completely smitten with Lauren, has been going out with her for ages. They'd spent the whole of last summer revising together, had gone arm in arm to collect their GCSE results, and kept an eye out for each other at Boardmasters Festival while I had nightmares about them both being stabbed, overdosing on various drugs or drowning. He'd even accompanied Lauren and her mum on a camping trip to Devon (separate tents, although I did make sure that Sam had *that* conversation with him beforehand). Speaking of Sam, I wonder what he'd say about my possible sighting of Lauren? I knew he was busy at work, and this didn't constitute a genuine emergency, so a text would have to suffice. 'A bit worried about one of the kids but nothing urgent' was all I said, although this was a message I could in all honesty have sent on any given day of the year.

Never mind; I'd stew over Tom's love life later, along with the damage to Dad's car and the insurance claim for angry Audi man. Now I had to get to work.

Chapter Three

I arrived at Bob's Place a mere fifteen minutes later. My neck was sore but whether this was due to whiplash from the collision, a poor night's sleep or the result of me holding the steering wheel with such an iron grip as to render me incapable of movement, I don't know. A recent accident focuses the mind somewhat and I couldn't risk any further incidents, so I hadn't lifted my eyes from the road at all, despite an almost overwhelming desire to search for Lauren on each street corner I passed. The tension in my neck reduced significantly, though, as I pulled into the long, sweeping drive up to the main house. Bob's Place has always had this effect on me, even before it was a care home.

The first time I visited, it had been Bob and Tina's family home. I say family home, but they didn't have any children of their own, just this glorious mansion set among multiple outbuildings and gardens. Bob's kids from his first marriage had long grown and flown, but they also hated Tina and held her responsible for the break-up, so they rarely visited. As a result, once Bob was diagnosed with dementia, there was little that he and Tina could do other than rattle around their cavernous house while the party invitations and expensive trips abroad dwindled to nothing. Bob's wealth was no protection from the relent-less assault of Alzheimer's, or the isolation of Tina, his wife turned full-time carer, and as the trappings of their luxury lifestyle became increasingly meaningless, they searched for ways to adapt to their new situation, activities that involved social interaction with people facing the same challenges. One of these activities was the Singing for the Brain choir, which is where I met them. I too had been looking for an escape of sorts. A place where Mum could be herself – or at least, the new version of self that dementia had gifted her – and I could breathe for a few moments of freedom from the strain of caring for her alongside the kids.

We became firm friends, Tina and I. Separated by twenty years and several million pounds, but both tied to the same affliction and weighted down by the grief of watching a loved one being slowly pulled into dementia's vice-like grip. We supported each other, along with other members of the choir, and came to see one another as family. When our choir leader, the inimitable Fizz, fractured her jaw following a motocross accident (don't ask) and I stepped in to help, we relocated the singing sessions to Bob and Tina's house. Every time Mum and I pulled off the main road, meandering our way through the leafy lawns to the house, I felt a sense of well-being, knowing that my community, my little dementia family, were already in the building: Tina baking something deli-cious in the Aga; Clive warming up his rich baritone voice while his father Ernest swore at the pigeons through the window; Marie singing in a range that only small dogs could hear while Edith practised her high kicks and Gertie rattled her maracas.

I know the others felt the same back then, and when Bob died leaving Tina sole executor of his legacy fund with specific instructions to spend it all on dementia care, she knew that the best thing she could do with his money was to fling open the doors of their home and extend the feeling of well-being we all experienced there to a multitude of other families affected by dementia. Within weeks of the renovations Bob's Place was a huge success. We had recruited a range of therapists, and were offering a wide variety of activities suitable for people living with dementia who didn't just want to sit staring into the middle distance while reruns of *Knots Landing* blared from the television (although they were welcome to do that if they wished). Our reputation spread and we were inundated with requests, having to start a waiting list for most of our classes within the first month of opening (some of the sessions were less popular – mushroom cultivation with Graham on Wednesday morning only ever had a handful of attendees).

We offered spa treatments, massage and physiotherapy packages, pedicures with a trained chiropodist, music therapy, art therapy, embroidery and textiles, gardening and cooking. We set up a petting zoo with four chickens, a grumpy duck, two ancient Labradors and Noreen the donkey all on site. People could come for an hour a week to attend a particular class, or stay all day and treat the place as a home-from-home. They could bring their carers or attend alone, meet grandchildren for a swim in the pool and a walk around the grounds, or book an overnight room to provide respite for those at home. And now, we have all that, plus the addition of our long-stay guests, who feel just as much a part of the family as Marie, Ernest and Gertie did back when we opened. It's probably fairly evident but just for clarity, let me say: I love Bob's Place. This isn't just a job for me. I *really* love it.

I parked around the back of the main house and gently shooed one of the chickens away from Tina's prize rose-bushes, emerging through the heavy fire-safety door of the staff entrance next to what used to be the dining room and is now one of our physical therapy areas. I could hear the murmured voice of our new Armchair Pilates teacher gently encouraging Doreen to engage her core, and the subsequent confusion as Doreen struggled to interpret the instruction, thinking perhaps it was something to do with fruit. Brian had arrived early for the singing group and was sitting in the living room sharing a plate of toast with Gloria, one of our long-stay residents, and easily the most glamorous. Katya our art therapist was unloading a huge tub of poster paint from the back of her van and wrestling it through the door as I held it open for her.

'Tina looking for you, Penny,' she said. 'She is in – hmmm – flusters?'

'She's in a fluster? Her and me both,' I said. 'I think I've just caught my son's girlfriend *kissing someone else* on the High Street.'

For some reason I emphasised the words 'kissing someone else' using the voice that women of a certain age use to say the word 'hysterectomy'. The way that my mother would have mouthed it, exaggerated but almost silent. As in, 'Margaret's been in hospital – she's had a *hys-ter-ecto-my*' – looking about herself as if worried she might be arrested.

'Ah well,' said Katya, hefting the tub of sunshine orange against her substantial bosom. 'At least it was not blow job for money.'

I suppose she has a point.

Tina met me in the hallway as I was shrugging off my damp parka and finding a spare hook to hang it on.

'Penny!' she hissed. She looked ashen. 'We've got a visitor.'

'Oh, is Gloria's son, Malcolm, here?' I was looking forward to meeting him – he lived in South Africa and hadn't been able to visit since Gloria arrived, but she spoke about him so fondly.

Tina pulled a sad face. 'No – turns out Malcolm died a few years ago.'

'But – she talks about him all the time… Ahhh, OK,' I said, everything suddenly clicking into place. I suspected that, like many of our clients, Gloria had been informed about her son's death on a regular basis but always returned to the illusion that he was alive, and it was often much less distressing for our residents if staff simply joined in with the make-believe. Constantly reminding Gloria that her son was no longer with us would likely result in fresh grief every single time. Very occasionally I found myself slightly jealous of the interior life of our cognitively impaired residents. When the alternative reality conjured by the damaged brain was an upsetting one then there was nothing worse, but sometimes we saw people who had been gifted a more benign version of dementia where they wholeheartedly believed they were a famous film star or minor royal. Other people returned to a happy moment in their earlier life. One of our residents, Denis, had been an eminent cardiologist before dementia had grabbed him by the neurones, and loved nothing more than poring over the old cardiac traces and ECGs that Vishnu, our health care assistant, brought in from the hospital archives.

'It's not Malcolm,' Tina said, snapping me out of my daydream.

'Well – evidently. Seeing as he's dead.'

'It's the… *CQC*,' she said, using the hysterectomy voice – God, we were all at it.

'What?'

'The CQC. The Care Quality Commission. They're here.'

'Fuck!'

'Quite.'

'Why?'

Tina explained that the CQC had emailed her last week to announce an imminent inspection. For some reason she hadn't seen the email. 'I think it went into ham,' she said in alarm. I didn't have the heart to correct her. Anyway – the CQC seemed to feel that an unanswered email was sufficient warning to drop forty tonnes of regulatory bullshit into our laps this very morn, and lo, Tina had been met on the doorstep by Lorraine, the smiling assassin.

'She's terrifying,' warned Tina as we made our way through to the kitchen. 'I've already tripped myself up about fourteen times. I wish Veronica was here!'

'Hey, don't worry,' I said, slightly stung that Tina didn't feel my presence was reassurance enough. Veronica was the third member of our executive team. She was a colleague of Sam's in London and her business acumen had been invaluable when we were setting up Bob's Place. She had lost her father to dementia many years ago and the spectre of how diminished her dear old dad had been by the illness had stayed with her. She wasn't involved in the day-to-day running of Bob's Place to quite the extent that Tina and I were, still working most of the week in London with my husband (knee-deep in pensions rather than pensioners), but her commitment to the care home was just as resolute. Whatever spare time she had in her busy schedule of high finance and trips abroad to sites of cultural interest she gave to us, and when she'd been laid up recovering from pelvic surgery last year (not just the *hyst-er-ecto-my* but a whole load of other *ectomy*s besides), we had missed her enormously. She was part of our holy triumvirate, and we didn't really function the same without her.

However, there was no need to add to Tina's panic about the three musketeers being whittled down to two on a CQC inspection day.

'We'll be fine!' I said breezily. 'We sailed through our last one, didn't we? Just take a look at the Outstanding rating proudly displayed on our website!'

'Yes, but that was pre-Covid,' said Tina, chewing her lip, 'and pre-Brexit. Lorraine said that…'

But it was too late to hear what Lorraine had said. Because here she was, the woman herself, materialising from behind the door with a stiff little smile and a proffered hand. Her hair was moulded into a beige helmet of waves, held rigid by some sort of industrial-strength product. It seemed to move with a few seconds delay to the rest of her head. She had thin, nondescript features, and her face was completely expressionless as our hands met, my palm clammy against hers.

Right, Penny! Charm offensive required! I thought to myself, just as I had with Audi man after I'd crashed into him an hour earlier. Again I launched into my own version of death by charm overload, involving self-abasement, flagellation and offering my prostrate form as a sacrifice on the altar of someone else's good opinion.

'Lorraine!' I pumped her hand enthusiastically. 'How lovely to meet you. I'm Penny. Penny Baker. One of the trustees.' I gave her the smile that I keep in the jar by the door – like Eleanor Rigby, but hopefully much less depressing.

She retracted her hand as soon as she was able. 'It's Ms Rowbotham,' she said. 'Lorraine Rowbotham. But you can call me Lorraine. Which is lucky, seeing as you have already.' She smiled thinly – was she joking? I wasn't sure. Best to err on the side of optimism.

'Ah-ha-ha-ha, yes, of course.' I must have sounded slightly manic because Tina shot me a worried look. 'Sorry,' I said, pausing the strained laughter. 'Would you *prefer* it if we called you Ms Rowbotham?' I stressed the *th*. Heaven only knows what she'd do if I said Row*bottom*.

She waved away my concern with her clipboard. 'Whatever's easiest for you,' she said. Which, in itself, wasn't an easy message to decipher. I decided to avoid naming her altogether for the remainder of the conversation. I gestured to the kitchen table and we all took a seat.

Lorraine made an annotation to her clipboard – likely something bad about the kitchen chairs. 'So, Mrs Baker,' she said.

'It's Penny,' I said, determined to make this easier for her than she had made it for me.

She frowned slightly. 'Penny,' she said. 'As I was explaining to your colleague, Ms Carling…'

'Tina,' interjected Tina. 'Sorry.' She looked down at her hands.

'As I was explaining to your colleague, Tina' – she sounded pained – 'we have fulfilled our contractual obligations by alerting you to the inspection with a full week's notice. The CQC work on the principle that the contact information given by the provider is up to date, and that any important notifications sent via these channels are actioned promptly and effectively. I understand that on this occasion it appears that neither you nor Ms Carling received our email?'

'That is correct,' I said, knowing I'd checked the Bob's Place email account only last night.

'Curious,' said Lorraine Rowbotham. 'Because I have the confirmation right here.' She produced a printout. (I mean, who does that?) 'And it clearly states that an email was sent at nine forty-two on Monday the fifth of January addressed to a *Penny-at-madhouse-dot-me-dot-com*.' She raised her eyebrows.

'Oh, that's my personal account,' I said as realisation dawned. 'Your message almost certainly disappeared into the Bermuda Triangle of updates from school about SATs and changes to the PE kit, and slightly worrying post-Christmas emails from the credit card company!'

It was hard to tell from the expressionless face but Lorraine didn't seem amused. I crashed on.

'By the way, the *madhouse* doesn't refer to here! Just in case that's what you were... It's not like I think Bob's Place is a madhouse. It's my own house. You know, manic household, lots of kids and...' I trailed off, cursing my ancient email that had seemed so innocuous when I set it up years ago. I clearly needed to update the CQC with my much more professional-sounding business address.

'No matter,' said Lorraine in a voice that suggested it did matter and was clear evidence of my moral bankruptcy. 'Despite the email being sent a week ahead of the scheduled inspection to both yours and Ms Carling's given addresses, it seems neither was received and you were therefore unaware of our visit?'

'It appears so,' I said. I was quickly learning that it was best not to qualify Lorraine's statements with any extraneous information. Much like being on the witness stand.

'And Ms Fearnley-Scott…?'

'Is in Egypt,' I said. 'Veronica Fearnley-Scott is another of our trustees, but she's on holiday so she won't have been checking her emails. She's very strict on that. She knows that if there's anything serious we'll call her, but she doesn't want to be bothered by work issues when she's on holiday with Gee, so – I mean, work issues from her main job. She works in the City, in finance. With my husband.' *Honestly, Penny, how was that necessary information?*

I carried on valiantly. 'She doesn't really see Bob's Place as "work" – not "*work* work".' *Stop saying the word 'work', for God's sake.* 'Although of course, she does take it seriously. Very seriously. I just meant that the emails she's trying to avoid are not ours, or yours. She'd never deliberately avoid the CQC, it's more about…' *OK, just shut the fuck up, you raging lunatic.*

I took a deep breath. 'She's supposed to be getting in touch via Zoom in a moment for our board meeting.'

'Well, that's something, I suppose,' said Lorraine graciously. 'Would you like to connect her in?'

Tina and I exchanged a panicked look. We had both become more adept at online meetings during the pandemic, but we had been starting from a low base in terms of technical prowess and we'd not had to negotiate an international Zoom before. No matter. I reached across Lorraine, plugged in the laptop, logged in through the various embarrassing screensavers that Tom had installed (invariably photos of me looking utterly ridiculous) and clicked on the link to see the message 'Veronica is in the waiting room'. I wished there was some way of alerting her to our guest's presence before the call connected, but such is life. Veronica was well used to dealing with tricky people. She was like High Powered Joy. She'd eat Lorraine for breakfast, I thought smugly to myself as I admitted her from the virtual holding bay.

A fuzzy outline of a red blob appeared on-screen, surrounded by the white-hot glare of presumably an Egyptian sun. There was a crackling noise of static.

'Veronica,' I said. 'Are you there?'

More crackling.

'Can you hear us?' Tina leaned across the table towards the laptop. 'Can you hear us, Veronica? Are you there?'

I'm not the first person to have been struck by the similarities between a Zoom call and a seance. Perhaps Tina and I should join hands and close our eyes – throw a tea towel over the lamp. Perhaps Lorraine would go into a trance or the laptop would move slowly across the table and knock over a glass of water…

None of these things happened, but after about twenty minutes of trying to get Veronica to confirm her existence, including two attempts to log out and sign back in again, it dawned on all of us that this wasn't going to work.

'Let's just crack on without her,' I said gamely as I closed the laptop. 'What do you need from us?'

'Ohh – it really shouldn't be too onerous,' said Lorraine in a voice that sounded quite onerous. 'I'll want to have a look at your policy documents, check things are up to date. And then the inspection itself should only take a week – obviously I'll need to interview the staff, the clients, their families.' She gave a humourless laugh. 'The usual.'

Tina and I exchanged a look.

'Do you *normally* interview the clients?' I said, thinking that some of our residents might not be able to provide Lorraine with quite the level of feedback she was after. Particularly Daphne, who usually just swore at everyone. 'I don't remember that happening last time.'

'My approach is perhaps more thorough than some of my colleagues,' she said, smiling benignly. 'But I am sure you will find it fair. This isn't supposed to feel like a punishment.' She gave another little laugh that made me want to punch her in the face.

'Would you like an almond macaroon, Lorrai... I mean, Ms Rowbotham?' Tina said, getting to her feet. 'They're homemade. A big favourite with the residents.' She crossed to the oven. 'You'll have one, Penny, won't you?'

'I will!' I said brightly, and then to Lorraine, 'They really are delicious. Tina is an excellent cook. She oversees all the catering at Bob's Place. You won't find anywhere with a better menu.' This was true. Tina personally recruited every member of the kitchen staff and planned the residents' meals weeks in advance, working with a specialist dietician to take account of individual preferences and any issues people might have with swallowing.

'Is this facility hygiene standards-approved?' said Lorraine, glancing around Tina's beautiful kitchen, her eyes fixing on Mr Bingley, the elderly cat curled up in a basket near the range. 'I assume this isn't where the majority of meals are prepared for your clients?'

'Our main kitchens are in the block just across the courtyard,' I said, interjecting before Tina (or Mr Bingley) could feel the sting of offence. 'And they conform to all of the appropriate hygiene standards. When Tina says that various cakes and biscuits are the residents' favourites, she

34

is referring to the occasions when we make them within those facilities.'

'I am?' Tina saw me nod my head. 'Oh. Yes,' she said. 'I am.' She filled the teapot and brought it over on a tray with three china cups balanced precariously next to the plate of macaroons. Lorraine accepted a cup of tea but pulled a face at the offer of biscuits, whereas I'd shovelled half my almond macaroon in before the plate had even hit the table.

'Mmm,' I said inarticulately. 'Delicious, Tina.'

'Do any of your residents have nut allergies?' asked Lorraine, her pen poised over her clipboard like a circling vulture.

'No,' I said quickly. 'And none of their visitors do either.'

Lorraine gave a tiny snort and laid down her clipboard, removing two sheets of paper from its teeth and sliding them across the table towards us. I scanned the pages, which were covered in a font so tiny as to be almost illegible.

'Really do need to get some reading glasses,' I muttered to myself as I held the sheet at arm's length, an action that Tom and Maisie have started mimicking in recent months with merciless accuracy. It was a bullet-pointed list. A very long list.

'I'm sure all these policy documents will be familiar to you,' said Lorraine. Her smile was so thin it looked as though it had been drawn onto her face by a tattoo artist who had fallen on hard times. She gestured to the offending list in my hands. 'You've been through this process before?'

'Oh, yes,' said Tina eagerly. 'We got an Outstanding last time.'

'You did?' Lorraine's eyebrows lifted imperceptibly. She may as well have laughed in our faces. Of course we bloody did, Lorraine, I wanted to say, it's on your bloody top sheet of notes. *Outstanding*. Read it.

'And Gareth, the inspector, was so impressed with the set-up here that he moved his dad to Bob's Place as soon as a spot became available.'

'So, you gave his family member preferential treatment,' said Lorraine thoughtfully. 'And was that before or after the outcome of the inspection was revealed?'

'Oh,' Tina faltered, 'well, afterwards, obviously.'

'Hmm.' Lorraine scribbled something on her notepad that looked ominously like *Possible corruption/bribing a public official*.

'He was very happy with our procedures and policies,' said Tina, unable to leave it alone. 'He said at the time he couldn't give us any more ringing an endorsement than using our care service for a beloved family member.'

'Other than an Outstanding rating,' said Lorraine. 'He couldn't give any more ringing an endorsement than an Outstanding rating. Which is what he chose to give you.' Lorraine was clearly itching to add 'astonishingly' to the end of that sentence.

'But it's much like Penny with her mum,' said Tina, gesturing to me as my heart sank. 'She uses the care facilities for Mary, her mother, and she wouldn't do that if she thought...'

'She does what?' Lorraine interrupted with another little laugh, this one more ominous-sounding. 'You do what, Mrs Baker?' She turned to me.

'My mum,' I said, mind furiously whirring as to how I could stop Lorraine from turning yet another positive aspect of our care organisation into something negative. 'She has dementia. She attends the day centre here.'

'Your mother,' repeated Lorraine slowly, 'a member of your *immediate family*, is a service user?' She scribbled down something that looked like *Conflict of interest/glaring oversight/immediate closure* (although it was difficult to read the exact wording, to be honest, due to being middle-aged and in denial about the need for glasses). I felt a trickle of sweat pool beneath my bra.

'It's just a practical solution since I'm working here. She's not moving in permanently.' *Yet*, I thought to myself, because I knew Dad couldn't cope with looking after her full-time for much longer.

Still, that was a drama for another day. Which was lucky, because given the sleep deprivation, runaway dog, potentially heartbroken son, car accident and CQC grilling, I felt like I'd had enough drama today – and it was still only eleven o'clock.

Chapter Four

Monday evening

Despite Lorraine Rowbotham's Spanish Inquisition continuing long into the afternoon, I got home in time to collect Maisie from Kids Aboard, her after-school club. Being an ancient year six student with a whopping eleven years of life experience under her belt, Maisie is predictably lukewarm about the need to be detained in an after-school club, particularly when her fellow students are mainly from the lower age ranges and have usually broken down in tears, wet themselves or stabbed today's designated best friend in the eye with a wax crayon come four o'clock. However, she knows that if she can hang on in there till a little closer to five, then she'll likely get a slice of school toast and jam (completely different to home toast and jam – not sure why), and this bizarrely seems to make up for the indignity of having to play Giant Jenga with the little ones. If only all of life's weary vicissitudes could be dealt with so simply.

The trouble is, Maisie has reached the stage that comes to us all. She has grown out of her current environment a few months ahead of schedule. It's no bad thing. I'd prefer her to be complaining about primary school being babyish and boring than clinging desperately to its reassuring walls, fearful of the future, but it's a bit sad, if I'm honest

– all the things that used to hold her spellbound have now just become 'so lame'. No more breathless anticipation at the prospect of Miss Sanchez reaching the final chapter of this week's class storybook; no clenched fists of excitement about Forest School Friday, where the main objective is to get as damp and muddy as possible before being allowed to regain normal body temperature with a hot chocolate and two mini-marshmallows; not even a flicker of interest about the impending visit to Pirate World. The magic of childhood is trickling away and she, like her brother and sister before her, is itching to join those high-rolling movers and shakers, the youths of secondary school. Even if they don't have toast and jam.

She was already waiting by the door when I arrived through the gates in a screech of tyres. The one advantage of picking up after hours is the justifiable use of the Teachers' Car Park – a more hallowed turf you couldn't imagine. There's most likely a deed of covenant for every square metre, and parental use is limited solely to the collecting of children after hours. Dropping off colossal art projects, bringing clothes for the recycling depot or recent major surgery are no excuses for requiring this level of vehicular proximity to school. There are good reasons for this, of course; I distinctly remember Maisie nearly going under the wheels of some enormous four-by-four when she took a corner a little enthusiastically on her bike and ended up in another mummy's (or daddy's – let's face it, probably a daddy's) blind spot. Cars can't be going willy-nilly in and out of a primary school gate during the busiest times of day. But the little thrill of terror I feel merely pulling into a space marked TEACHERS ONLY in fluorescent capitals with additional signage on the adjacent wall is on a par with smoking a spliff in a convent. I imagine.

Mrs North – who, after fifteen years of teaching all my children at various stages of their primary school journey, is finally retiring due to exhaustion this summer – was stood tight-lipped alongside Maisie, looking pointedly at her watch.

'Mrs Baker,' she said. 'We were beginning to wonder where you'd got to.'

I sighed, used to this familiar line of conversation. It would probably save both me and Mrs North a great deal of time if I simply recorded it on my phone and played it back at each pick-up.

'Here I am,' I said, as per the script (imagine the stage direction states, *in a jaunty tone*).

'The younger children have all been collected by their parents, so Maisie has been helping me with the photo-copier, haven't you, Maisie?' Mrs North smiled fondly at my youngest daughter and I remembered why I didn't really dislike the woman. She'd always been lovely to the children. Her issues arose when talking to adults – the main problem being that she forgot they were, in fact, adults.

'Sounds like fun,' I said, jingling my keys as I stood freezing in the outdoor wet play area.

'And we've had a little bit of toast, haven't we, Maisie, to keep us going!'

You had to hand it to the woman – she knew how to keep the workers sweet.

'Excellent – no need for supper then,' I said brightly. 'I'm joking, I'm joking. A nutritious meal is moments away' (perhaps not *entirely* true). 'Come on, Maisie, where's your book-bag?'

In the car for the two-minute drive home, we managed to cover quite a lot of conversational ground. Maisie is not one of those children who holds back when discussing her day. It's not like being with Grace or Tom; the former would only think to mention it if a meteor had hit the school, and the latter would tell me about what he'd had to eat at breaktime, and lunchtime, and perhaps snacks between classes. Ask about lessons, and they would both stare at you, blank as a page of an unused exercise book. Ask about friends, interactions with the opposite sex, points of gossip (pupils who'd been suspended or excluded for various misdemeanours – basically the interesting stuff), and if you were lucky you might get a shrug and a 's'OK' or 'dunno'. Maisie, however, likes to relate her day in both lurid tabloid technicolour and microscopic detail, and to be fair, she seems to have a lot of material to work with; the politics playing out among the year six girls' friendship groups in a single week would be enough to fill an encyclopedia.

'So, Eva was being really mean again,' Maisie began without prompting. Most school stories started this way – Eva was previously known (to me, at least) as The Terrible Evangeline – High Powered Joy's daughter and source of more than her fair share of drama and small-girl tears. 'And she made Molly cry because she said she wasn't her friend any more. And then she said she was only joking and asked Molly if she'd like to come to her party, and then she said that *that* was a joke and she *didn't* want her to come to her party at all because it was going to be at Splash Down Mega Park, and ten-year-olds couldn't come. And Molly said that was OK because she was eleven, but then Eva was like, people who need glasses also can't come unless they've got like waterproof contacts or something, because they might hurt themselves on the water slides and anyway Molly probably wouldn't want to come because some boys might be coming and there might be kissing and stuff, and Molly probably wouldn't like that. And then Jasmine said that if people were going to be kissing then she didn't want to come to the party because her parents wouldn't let her kiss boys until she was like twenty or something because she might catch hepatitis, I think. And then Eva said that was OK because she hadn't really wanted Jasmine to come and had only invited her because her mum was friends with Jasmine's mum.' She paused to draw breath. 'And then Jasmine went to go and cry in the toilets and Eva said she didn't care because Jasmine was really annoying anyway, showing off about having a bra and she knew that Jasmine stuffed socks down it to make it look like she has boobs and that if she went swimming then everyone would find out. And so she asked me if I'd like to come to Splash Down Mega Park instead. And I said yeah, OK.'

My brain struggled to keep up with the detail, fatigued as it was by the events of the day. 'So – you're going to Evangeline's party?' I said as I indicated left into our lane.

'Yeah. And we're doing a project about family trees,' said Maisie, switching topic as easily as a daytime television host ('thanks for that harrowing report on knife crime, Danny. Coming up next: have you ever found a worm in your wellington?').

'Family trees,' I said. 'Sounds fun.' I didn't really mean that. It sounded tedious, but it is part of the parental contract with school that each project must be met with a modicum of enthusiasm. I think I signed something to that effect along with the photography consent forms in reception year.

To my surprise, Maisie agreed. 'Yeah, it does. Mrs North helped me start it, she said it will be good for us to understand how we're all mixtures of loads of really, really old people. Like you and Daddy. It's about diversity and shared hedges.'

I puzzled this over for a moment. 'Shared *heritage*?'

'Yeah, that too.'

–

Tom was sitting on the ancient, faded sofa playing something on the Xbox when we got home. His headphones were on and he lifted his hand from the controller briefly to acknowledge our presence. The rest of the house was pitch-black. Obviously Tom hadn't thought to turn any lights on before getting straight down to gaming – either he was keen to reduce our fossil fuel consumption, or he was oblivious to the fact that other people lived in this house and might appreciate an illuminated entrance hall on their return. Unfortunately, in the blundering darkness of the corridor we discovered (tripped over) evidence of Montmorency's most recent acts of destruction. Left unattended he had chewed through a pair of my trainers, some swimming goggles and four of Maisie's paint pens, which were now lying in shards on the stone floor. The paint from these pens had been trailed through the hall in a variety of neon doggy pawprints, leading us directly to the perpetrator, who was sitting proudly on his technicolour bed with a scarlet muzzle. He looked as though he'd been involved in a killing spree, and I cast my eye around the kitchen for signs of eviscerated rodents or dead pigeons, but it was simply that Montmorency's colour palette for the day had been taken from the red side of the spectrum, and on later inspection the pens he had chewed were a combination of Magenta, Cherry Blush and Flamingo Pink.

'Maisie,' I said through gritted teeth. 'Could you ask your brother for a hand, please?'

She dropped her book-bag in the middle of the doorway along with her abandoned school shoes, as per standard. '*Tommm!*' she hollered.

'He won't hear you,' I said wearily, wringing out a dishcloth from the side of the sink and approaching the dog with trepidation. 'Go into the sitting room, lift up one of his headphones and ask him politely to come into the kitchen. And mind the paint pens…' Too late. I heard Maisie yelp as she impaled her foot on a particularly spiky shard.

Twenty minutes, one phone call to the vet's, one helpful but fairly inept teenage son attempting to clean the floor, one tearful daughter with an elevated and bandaged foot, two ruined outfits and one colourfully unashamed dog later, I started on preparations for supper. Tom had already made himself four rounds of sandwiches an hour earlier on his return from school and as a result we were out of cheese, ham, tomatoes and bread. What we always have industrial levels of in our house, though is pasta.

'I'm so hungry,' Tom muttered weakly from where he was wiping the last trace of paint off the floor with what seemed to be one of the guest bath towels. 'What's for supper?'

'Pesto pasta,' I said, removing the fluffy but ineffective towel and replacing it with a damp cloth repurposed from one of Sam's old T-shirts. 'Tom, I'm not being funny but do you actually know how to clean up after a spillage?'

He looked hurt. 'I'm trying to help.'

I sighed. 'I know, poppet. You go and have a sit-down. I'll sort this.'

'I might not make it to the sofa,' he said, dragging himself along the floor in the direction of the sitting room. 'Might. Faint. From. Hunger. Before. I. Get. There.'

'That's a risk you'll have to take,' I called after him. 'And don't rugby tackle your little sister. She's hurt her...'

Maisie let out a wail from the sitting room.

'Foot,' I said wearily as I returned to the kitchen and poured half a metric tonne of pasta twirls into the saucepan.

Chapter Five

Once I'd fed the dog, dished out the pasta, laid the table and poured everyone a glass of water, we finally sat down to eat. Tom and I let Maisie's instructions regarding accurate documentation of family trees wash over us.

'So if someone's died you can colour their spot black,' she said, shovelling in a mouthful of pasta. 'And if you marry your cousin you have like two lines between you or something. And Noah said it's illegal. But Eva said it's not illegal and that the royal family do it and that's why they get diseases. And Noah said, that's high treason, and that Eva might be put in the Tower of London and have her head chopped off, but he was only joking. And Eva punched him in the arm when Mrs Mabuse wasn't looking and told him to shut up. And then Molly said—'

'Where's the cheese?' Tom asked suddenly. 'We can't have pasta with no cheese.'

'We can't,' said Maisie, visibly alarmed by the prospect, despite the fact that both children very evidently could eat pasta with no cheese and were currently doing so with gusto.

'There's none left,' I said wearily.

'There must be,' he said, as if this were the most ridiculous notion he'd ever heard.

46

'You ate it all, sweetheart. In your sandwiches.'

'But I hardly had any!'

'There was a five-hundred-gramme pack in the fridge,' I said, my voice as mild as the absent cheddar. 'And the wrapper for it appears to now be in the bin. Well, not in the bin obviously, but near the bin. Empty save for a few cheesy crumbs. The only logical conclusion I can come to is that someone ate it. And the only person here,' I said, looking at my son, 'was you.'

'Montmorency was here too,' he said, eyebrows raised in outrage at the accusation.

'Montmorency, despite being a thieving delinquent, is not big enough to get onto the kitchen counter. He does not have the manual dexterity to grate a portion of cheese, and he's definitely not intelligent enough to leave the empty wrapper next to an abandoned knife and plate, arranged in such a way as to imply recent sandwich construction and consumption,' I said. 'Plus, he was busy eating the paint pens. *Plus*, if Montmorency had scarfed that volume of cheese he'd have been sick by now. But nice try.'

'Well, you need to buy more, Mummy,' said Maisie sternly. 'Because we're growing children and Mrs Mabuse says we need to eat dairy stuff for our bones to be strong.'

'Yes, I'm not entirely sure that consuming half a kilo of cheese in one sitting is essential for optimum bone strength,' I said. 'But thanks for the information. I'll upscale the next cheddar order accordingly. In the meantime, you seem to be managing to force the meal down fairly well.'

'Evening all!' Sam gave the front door a hefty slam behind him. The wooden frame is warped and at this time of year it sticks terribly. We tend to have two months in the summer when our doorway functions like an ordinary portal and the rest of the time you risk shoulder dislocation with each attempt at opening or closing. 'Mmm! What's this?' He pointed to the dish on the table where Tom was helping himself to thirds.

'It is – well, it *was* – pesto pasta,' I said as Tom tipped a few sad-looking twirls off his spoon into the now empty dish. He grimaced up at his father.

'Sorry, Dad, I didn't know you'd be...'

'Wanting to eat?' said Sam, one eyebrow raised. And then he laughed and shucked Tom around the head. 'Don't worry, mate. I'll have a protein shake before I head off to the gym, and then I've got some of the salmon and kale left over from yesterday. I'll be fine.' He dropped a kiss on my forehead and ruffled Maisie's hair. 'How are my girls?'

'Few things to chat about later,' I said under my breath as I joined him over by the fridge. 'Do you want a glass of wine?'

'With my protein shake?' He laughed. 'No, I'm fine. Anyway, Pen, I'm still on Dry January.'

'Oh, yes. Of course.' I slid my empty glass of red along the countertop behind my back. 'So am I.'

He peered over my shoulder at the glass and gave me a grin. 'Sure you are. Anyway, what's been going on? What was the message about?'

'Don't worry – we'll talk later, when you get back from the gym,' I said, thinking that the unexpected CQC visit, the car accident and the possible imminent heartbreak of our only son were topics that should probably wait until we were alone. Anyway, Sam was already eyeing up the empty pack of pasta twirls lying on the kitchen surface next to what had been my glass of Merlot.

'Did you use my pasta?' he said, a frown crinkling his forehead.

I turned to follow his gaze. '*Your* pasta?'

He picked up the empty packet. 'Yes, it's a high-protein one. Made from yellow peas, I think.'

'We've been eating peas?' said Maisie, with the kind of horror usually reserved for sprouts and broccoli.

'Well, pulses, yes,' said Sam, looking forlornly at the empty pack. 'This was the stuff I bought to go with the butternut squash and kimchi.'

'Kimchi being fermented cabbage?' I clarified, wondering whether this explained the smell of farts coming from the fridge. I had been blaming Tom – it seems, perhaps, unfairly. He nodded and I paused for a moment to gather my thoughts and wonder what on earth had happened to the man I married.

Sam's new-found attentiveness to his health and fitness can be traced back to an ill-advised comment about his paunchy tummy a year ago (blame my brother Rory for that one), and the more recent hospital admission of an old school friend who'd had a heart attack. My husband seemed to feel that Kebab Nick's angina (the clue is in the name) was a klaxon announcing his own mortality and he responded accordingly. Needless to say, the evangelical zeal with which he was embracing this lifestyle change was pissing me off no end, and paradoxically made me much more inclined to reach for the wine and biscuits myself.

'Well, sorry about that, love,' I said now about his special bloody pasta. 'I'll add some more to the online order along with the cheese, shall I? Can you just use regular twirls instead?' *Like the rest of us mere mortals*, I wanted to add.

'Suppose I'll have to,' he said without a trace of irony. 'It's just that pulses and legumes are much better for... never mind.' He could see he'd lost me – to be fair, I was making no attempt to hide my glazed expression. Having spent two decades trying to persuade my husband of the benefits of a diet rich in pulses, legumes and root vegetables only to be roundly laughed at while he consumed his processed meat and refined carbs with gusto, it now felt a bit rich to have the same foodstuffs mansplained back to me.

'Wait,' said Tom, his fork in mid-air. 'Do you mean pulses as in, *lentils*? This is made *of lentils*?' He looked horrified.

Sam and I both laughed, breaking the tension. 'Pretty much,' I said. 'And the pesto contains basil. Also a plant. You're practically a vegan now. Just like Grace.'

He grimaced but was evidently still hungry enough to finish off the rest of his plateful. Mention of Grace reminded me of our limited phone conversation this morning and my hopeless attempts to pump her for information. Better to go directly to the source.

'Lauren not coming over this evening?' I said, trying to keep my voice casual. I can't have done a very good job because Sam gave me a very strange look.

'No, she's revising.' Tom picked up his plate and carried it *almost* as far as the dishwasher.

'Oh? You've got exams?'

'Kind of.' Tom shrugged. 'Nothing major. Lauren's subjects are a bit more full-on than mine.'

I collected the now empty pasta dish and put it in the sink to soak. Our dishwasher is highly temperamental and likely to explode if we put anything other than completely clean items in it (either that, or it coats every single plate and glass in a fine grainy residue of baked-on particles, depending on how resentful it's feeling).

'I thought I saw her this morning.' The words spilled from my mouth before I'd had time to plan the sentence to sound appropriately spontaneous. 'Lauren. By the bus stop on Kingston Road.'

I risked a sideways glance at my son. Tom looked nonplussed as if unsure whether a response was required. I tried again, aware that I was tipping into pushy mum territory. 'I was surprised because it was past nine. But maybe she was on a study period?'

'Maybe.' Tom shrugged. 'She was at her dad's this weekend. She might have been running late. Is there anything for pudding?'

'Probably something in the fridge.' I swirled the soapy suds around the sink contemplatively. 'Is he still with the au pair, her dad? Did they actually move in together? Must be hard for Lauren – having to go and stay with them both.'

'S'pose.' His voice was muffled as he rummaged in the back of the fridge. 'We don't really talk about it since her parents got divorced. Lauren says the whole thing just grosses her out.'

'She knows she can talk to you though – if she needs to?'

'Well, yeah.' He shrugged, half his body still in the fridge.

'And everything's all right with you and her? No problems or anything?'

'Don't think so,' he said, pulling out a family pack of yoghurts. 'Can I have the raspberry one?'

Later, when Sam was back from the gym and piously preparing his omega-rich salmon and kale supper, he asked why I'd been interrogating our son.

'It wasn't an interrogation,' I said. 'I thought I was being quite subtle.'

Sam laughed into his inferior-quality pasta. 'About as subtle as a kick in the bollocks,' he said. 'Come on. Spill the tea. What's your beef with Lauren?'

'If you promise to stop with the youthspeak, I'll tell you,' I said, dropping my voice to a whisper. Now that the kids are older and seem to have outgrown bedtime, there's no predicting where or when they might appear. 'I saw her kissing someone else this morning. Properly snogging. Some guy in a suit. Not a sixth-former. A proper suit.'

'Oh?' Sam raised his eyebrows and I instantly wanted to reassure him.

'I'm not completely sure it was her though,' I said. 'I was in the car. And it was sleeting. And she was on the other side of the road. Behind the bus stop.'

'Oh, right,' said Sam, visibly relaxing. He chewed on a piece of kale for a few moments, ruminating like a cow in pasture. 'Did you get around to making that appointment at the optician's?'

I pursed my lips in annoyance. 'What if I *was* right, though?'

He shrugged in much the same way as his son had done an hour earlier. 'If she dumps him for someone else, you mean? He'll be all right, Pen. Shit happens. It's not like he's going to be with her forever – they're seventeen, he's got plenty of years of sowing his wild oats ahead of him.'

I wrinkled my nose up in distaste at the expression. 'Yes, but I can't bear the thought of *her* dumping *him* –

especially for some, some *older* man. What would that do for his confidence?' I said. 'And anyway, I don't want him feeling like he's been made a fool of. He ought to know, so that he can prepare himself…'

'Pen.' Sam's tone was a warning. 'Don't get involved. You remember how pissed off Grace was when I told her she could do better than that idiot she was with a few years ago?'

'You were right though. That Dillon was a dickhead.'

'Yes, but she didn't thank me, did she? Nobody thanks a parent for being *right*. Nobody wants a parent commenting on their relationships, in any capacity. Stay out of it.'

I pursed my lips again. 'Are you sure you're not just trying to avoid any drama?'

'In this household?' he said, eyes wide. 'Heaven forbid.'

'Hmmm.' I grumbled to myself.

'I think just try not to worry about it. And try to act normal next time she comes over. It's likely it wasn't even her anyway. Sounds like the poor girl's got enough on her plate with her own parents at each other's throats.'

'Maybe you're right,' I said. 'She's a nice girl. She wouldn't be messing about behind my Tommy's back. Not when we've practically adopted her into our family.' I pulled out a chair opposite him and sat down. 'Anyway, that was just the start of today's adventures.' I told him about the car accident (I might have implied that the Audi driver had more to do with it than in fact had been the case) and then about Lorraine Rowbotham from the CQC.

'She's back tomorrow,' I said, my fingers drumming on the table with agitation. 'So I'll need to leave early. Help Tina get things prepped. The woman's a complete nightmare. I've already had fourteen emails from her since I got home.'

Sam winced. 'Sounds like a right jobsworth.'

'Yeah. It was a little unsettling, to be honest. It's like she's actively trying to find fault with us.'

He reached across the table and placed his hand over mine. 'Pen, don't take it personally. This Lorraine won't find anything wrong with Bob's Place, no matter how hard she looks. It's an amazing achievement, what you've done there.' He smiled proudly and I felt a warm glow in my chest.

'It is. But that's why I do take it personally,' I said. 'It feels personal. To me and Tina especially.'

'But you run a tight ship. It'll be fine, Pen.'

'Hmmm. About that tight ship...' I poured myself another glass of red, any pretence at Dry January abandoned. 'Tina said something a bit worrying just before I left. Apparently the finances are looking a bit precarious – post-Christmas, and everything.'

I told him about Tina's comments, whispered urgently to me as Lorraine packed up her messenger bag earlier that evening. It seemed that we'd gone into our overdraft a little sooner than expected and she'd ended up needing to use her own credit card to pay the touring theatre company we had performing *A Christmas Carol* for the residents last month.

Sam raised his eyebrows. 'You're not even two weeks into the month,' he said. 'That does seem a bit early to be going into the red. I thought the overdraft was just for emergencies.'

'It is,' I said. 'Well, it was.' I didn't want to admit that we have been dipping into it more frequently over the past year. 'It's just that cash flow is harder to predict at the moment – you know what it's like, we're a small business; there's a cost-of-living crisis… Anyway.' I made my voice cheerful. 'I'm sure it'll be OK. I mean, Bob left us so much in that legacy fund. And once Veronica's back from holiday we can take a good look at the books, maybe arrange a meeting with the accountant…'

Sam put on his deliberately reassuring face, the one I know he uses to cover up an underlying niggle of anxiety. 'That sounds like a good idea,' he said. 'Once you've got the inspection out of the way I'd give Graham a call, get him to do you a projection.'

'Will do,' I said. 'But first we've got to make sure Lorraine's happy. Honestly, today was an absolute joke. We got no actual work done at all, just tearing around the office looking up old documents and answering increasingly random questions about the staff. She wanted to know why Nula had a three-month gap in her CV from thirty years ago. She also wanted to know why Eddie, the gardener, didn't have an up-to-date certificate of manual handling, even though he's never been so much as within three metres of our residents. Tina and I were just increasingly baffled by the things she was coming out with… She wanted to know why there were no extra-large non-latex gloves on site, despite there being no extra-large people with extra-large hands, or anyone with a latex allergy – sorry, I'm doing a Maisie,' I said as I ran out of breath.

Sam is used to the women in his life rambling on and just continued to tuck into his fairly unappetising dinner. 'Don't you worry, love, you crack on,' he said between mouthfuls.

'Well then—' I said, and went on with my minute-by-minute account of the whole day. Which I'm sure he enjoyed no end. 'The trouble is, Sam,' I said, about an hour later. 'I have the horrible feeling Lorraine's just getting started.'

'Bloody hope she's not there much longer,' he said. 'I feel like I know far more about Lorraine Rowbotham's preferences and irritating habits than I do about my own children. Maybe we should just get her to move in.'

'She would, you know,' I said grimly. 'Given half a chance she'd be there in the bathroom while I'm brushing my teeth before bed. "Do you have the appropriate toothbrush-handling certification, Mrs Baker? Have you attended the relevant courses? May I see copies of the certificates from 1983 onward to indicate that you have in fact been flossing in accordance with the guidelines as stipulated in the *Manual of British Dental Hygiene...*"'

'All right, you,' said Sam, patting my hand in a slightly patronising way. 'Don't stress about it. Just be your usual charming self, answer her questions as best you can and don't let her wind you up. After all, she doesn't have to love the place.'

'You're right,' I said, taking his plate to the dishwasher. 'I'll just tell her, this is Bob's Place. It's amazing. And if you don't like it, Lorraine, you can shove it up your Rowbotham.'

'Attagirl,' said Sam.

Chapter Six

Thankfully there was no recurrence of the tropical monsoon in my bed last night, but I still didn't get much sleep. I was up until two in the morning responding to the multitude of Lorraine's emails and updating our medicines policy. Maisie had also informed me that the payment for school dinners hadn't gone through so she needed a packed lunch for the rest of the week, and it took me a good twenty minutes to rustle up anything approaching edible from the remaining ingredients in the kitchen, given the fact that Tom had eaten enough fresh produce to feed a small Pacific nation between arriving home and bedtime including ALL THE BLOODY CHEESE. I had hoped that Sam might nominate himself in charge of the packed lunch, given my very obvious busyness (which I was quite vocal about), but sadly he had to immerse himself in an ice bath for half an hour followed by an intensive session on his hamstrings with the vibrating physio gun that looks like something from a pornographic version of *Avengers Assemble*. There was no point in questioning the ongoing trauma being done to a fifty-year-old body in the interests of health and fitness, so I just let him get on with it.

Lauren came to collect Tom at around eight this morning, summoning him from the driveway with a beep. There didn't seem to be anything untoward going on, although it's hard to tell whether someone has been unfaithful just by looking at their car through a murky window. I walked Maisie in the general direction of school, keeping my distance while carrying her belongings as a good sherpa should, and then took Montmorency to his favourite field where he proceeded to stick his still-magenta muzzle into a literal pile of shit – animal or human origin unspecified.

Once I'd managed to catch up with the self-satisfied stinker, I frogmarched him home, where he leapt onto every soft furnishing and upholstered item in the immediate vicinity, covering them all in a fine camouflage of brown streaks and pawprints before finally coming to rest on the sofa that he knows he's not allowed on. The trouble is it's too late to tell him off by the time he's sat there, tail wagging adorably, and my shouts of 'Down, Montmorency! Off! Off!' sailed over his fluffy head. I scooped him up, careful to avoid the enthusiastic 'play-biting' mouth given his recent choice of meal and hauled him into the kitchen where he could do marginally less damage. And then, armed with a dubious aroma and sheaf of hastily prepared notes, I set off to face Lorraine Rowbotham at Bob's Place.

On the way I went to collect Mum for her session of Singing for the Brain. Don't be misled by the fact that this comment only takes up a single sentence. Collecting Mum is a lengthy and time-consuming process, especially when you are having to do it while simultaneously explaining a recent car accident to your father, an accident that occurred while driving his vehicle and one that he has spotted evidence of from half a road away.

'Is that a new scratch on the bonnet?' He pulled back the net curtain, eyes laser focused as he peered through the gloom at a microscopic nick on the Vauxhall's paintwork.

'Yes, sorry, Dad.' I paused in my winching of Mum up and out of her easy-riser chair (something of a misnomer). 'I nudged into an Audi at the lights on the High Street yesterday. Nothing to worry ab...'

'Whereabouts? That junction by the bakery?'

'Uhm, no,' I grunted, taking the strain of Mum's weight as I held her hands and pulled her towards me. She was now suspended at a jaunty forty-five degrees and her bottom was almost out of the chair. This was a critical point in proceedings and she could easily lean too far forward and topple us both. 'It was just down from the zebra crossing.'

'Easy does it,' called Dad as he swivelled the wheel-chair alongside. 'This way, Mary. Your carriage awaits.' We gently encouraged Mum to shuffle sideways. 'Near Tesco?'

'What?' I said. 'Oh yes. Just before that turning.'

He nodded sagely as we lowered Mum into the wheel-chair. What the nod was supposed to signify I had no idea. Dad has always been a details man, which must relate to his past career in military logistics. I think if he can work out the timing and geographical terrain of any given incident, it gives him a better grasp of the situation, which I understand. But with age, this previously useful habit has become somewhat less endearing and he has a tendency to fire very specific and minutely detailed questions at you in the manner of a *University Challenge* host.

'What model was it – the Audi?'

'Really not sure, Dad. Anyway, I'll sort it – please don't worry. How did things go with the occupational therapist yesterday?'

'Hmmph,' Dad grumbled in a dissatisfied way, indicating that there would be minimal further discussion.

'Did they suggest any home aids? A hoist maybe, for getting her in and out of the chair? A ramp for the doorway?'

He pursed his lips. 'We'll talk later,' he said, pointing discreetly at Mum.

I gave him a confused look.

'Out of earshot,' he mouthed.

'I don't think she can...' I stopped myself. Dad still clung to the belief that Mum understood every word of every conversation uttered, and while I thought this was unlikely, given her total lack of engagement and her tendency to start humming at odd intervals or fall asleep in the middle of the most strident debates, it was possible that she was processing more than she let on. 'OK,' I said. 'But we *will* talk later.'

I crouched down next to Mum's chair. 'Ready for singing?' I said brightly.

She turned her face in the direction of my voice but didn't make eye contact. 'Passport?' she said, looking down at her lap and plucking anxiously at the blanket I'd placed across her knees. I glanced at Dad and he shrugged.

'You don't need a passport, Mum. We're going to Bob's Place,' I said, and she smiled faintly, her worried expression gone. There was a little dusting of powder on her cheek from where Dad had clearly tried to put her make-up on, and one of her earrings was askew. 'You look pretty this morning, Mum. This colour suits you.' I discreetly fixed her earring while plumping her pale blue scarf more snugly around her. 'Cold out,' I said, and she raised a querulous hand into the air in a way I recognised as a gesture of concern. 'But I'll get the blowers on in the car. We'll soon be roasting!' I grimaced in a cartoon fashion and fanned my face with my hands.

She laughed. She doesn't necessarily understand the content of what you say any more, but she does respond to the tone and she enjoys a bit of visual comedy – which is where my face comes in, evidently. I was once told by a beautician that I had a very expressive face. That was before she told me that they had a special on dermal fillers that month, and did I want a two-for-one on my crow's feet and my frown lines. I'd only been in there to get my eyelashes tinted. I didn't go back.

By the time we got to Bob's Place the choir was already in full swing. Fizz, our Singing for the Brain leader of the past seven years, long since recovered from her fractured jaw, was wafting her trusty scarves and maracas around the studio that had been Tina and Bob's old drawing room. Lorraine Rowbotham, the smiling assassin, was hovering in the hallway with a clipboard, and although I was determined not to let a pesky CQC inspector rush me or my mother, it was nice to be able to demonstrate our accessibility policy with Mum as a living example, gliding through the widened doorway and taking a leisurely turning circle across the smooth lino (narrowly missing Lorraine's feet – the element of jeopardy was not entirely accidental).

Everywhere in Bob's Place is accessible, not just for wheelchairs but Zimmer frames, rollators and even ambulance trolley stretchers. It's always such a relief when Mum and I arrive here. I know that I can easily take her to the bathroom if I need to. I know that we can roll straight from the back of the car into the sheltered area and through the main doors without encountering a single drop of freezing rain. And more importantly, I know that if there was an accident, if she toppled out of her chair or became particularly distressed, I'd have multiple pairs of robust, willing and qualified hands to help me. I don't have that sense of reassurance and security anywhere else, because in most scenarios my only available helper would be Dad, and while he is very willing, he is no longer what you would describe as robust. The anxiety I've started to feel when I walk through my parents' front door is not just about Mum; it's Dad, too. How would he be able to physically help me if something happened to Mum – and how would I feel if something happened to him as a result of looking after Mum – like a fall or putting his back out? He's not as strong as he used to be. He's recovered from the hip fracture and stroke in his early seventies that precipitated Mum's moving in with me, but he's never been quite the same, and the trouble with ageing and frailty is that it only goes one way. Down. Being a carer for Mum for the past seven years – even with Sam and I virtually on their doorstep – has taken its toll. He's exhausted. He's isolated. And he's also completely in denial.

Chapter Seven

Tuesday, 8 p.m.

'It's funny,' I said to my friends, Caz, Zahara and High Powered Joy, in the pub later that evening, 'I have these conversations all the time with families at work. I see spouses, siblings and children, even grandchildren, refusing to acknowledge that the person they love is deteriorating, or admit that they are fearful for the future, and I can have a rational discussion with them in a way that I simply can't with Dad.'

'I think that's true for all of us,' said Joy, leaning across to pour me a glass of wine. 'I have conversations with people at work that I wouldn't dream of having at home. My colleagues tell me I can be quite intimidating in an office setting.'

Zahara, my oldest and dearest friend, snorted into her Sauvignon. 'I can't imagine that for a moment, Joy,' she said. 'Interesting that you feel you rein it in so much outside of work.'

Caz and I both laughed along with Zahara, all three of us realising how utterly terrifying working with, or more likely *for* Joy must be. I still remembered the trepidation we used to regard her with when the kids were small. High Powered Joy would basically bully us and the other mums into looking after her (then terrible) daughter Evangeline, picking us off like carrion as we dropped our own children at the preschool door, or sending demanding emails about which days we could choose to have the pleasure of Evangeline's company (choosing *not* to have that pleasure was never an option). Of course, this was all before we witnessed her softer side and brought her into the fold – but I suspect that High Powered Joy's softer side is very rarely witnessed in the workplace.

She threw Zahara an imperious look. 'I just meant that it's not so unusual to find these conversations difficult with people who are close to you,' she said. 'Especially parents who've been in a position of authority for most of your life. It's hard to challenge that hierarchy.'

'It's not like I want to force Dad into accepting that Mum needs to go into residential care,' I said. 'It's that we can't even discuss the possibility. He must see that her care is compromised at home, but I can't broach it in case he feels it's a slight on his ability to cope.'

'Yeah, your dad wouldn't be happy at all with that suggestion,' said Joy.

'Maybe it's not just about pride,' said Caz, swirling her glass of Diet Coke. 'Maybe he feels guilty. Maybe he promised your mum he'd never put her in a home.'

'Oh God, yes,' I said. 'We see that all the time at Bob's Place. Families who've made promises they simply can't keep, and then they cling onto that promise like a talisman while their relative deteriorates to the point of crisis. I think once the hospital steps in, then families feel the decision's taken out of their hands and it's OK to let go – because the doctor tells them they have to. That's what Rory says, anyway.'

'I'd probably do whatever Rory told me to,' said Joy, referring to my brother. 'And not just because he's a doctor. He does have a natural authority, doesn't he? Maybe *he* should talk to your dad.'

I scrunched up my mouth at this. I'm used to playing second fiddle to my older brother in all things, but it still rankles. Zahara spotted my expression.

'I think Penny is best placed for this conversation,' she said firmly. 'She sees the set-up in her parents' house on a daily basis. And she literally works in a care home, the very best of care homes, in fact. Rory's not the expert here, Penny is.'

I smiled at her gratefully, aware of what she was trying to do.

'Yeah, yeah, I know your Rory can be a pain in the arse,' said Joy, turning back to me with her understatement of the century. 'But that's the perfect reason to delegate the difficult jobs to him.'

'You've got a point,' I conceded. 'Dad will still feel guilty though, whatever we say. He'll feel like he's abandoned her.'

'Do you have anyone at Bob's who *is* pissed off about being in a home?' asked Caz. 'Like, people who *do* feel they've been abandoned and are furious about it?' She shrugged. 'I met a woman like that on the breast unit once. Ninety-two and sharp as a tack, but she'd been told by social services that she couldn't continue to live safely on her own at home. She was absolutely fuming. But then, she was pissed off with everybody and everything. I'm not suggesting that your mum would feel like that, by the way. Just interested.'

Caz has become fascinated by the 'patient's experience of care' since she had breast cancer a few years ago. So much so that she retrained as a counsellor and now works for Macmillan, helping women who are going through a similar process. Her youngest son, Alex, is in the same school year as my Tom, and they have been friends for as long as we have, meeting way back in the mists of time on the pitches of St John's after-school football club (Little Kickerz – the 'z' makes it even more cool, you see, as Tom once explained at great length). Caz is one of the kindest people I know and would be horrified to think she'd ever offended anyone (unlike Joy, who's fairly sanguine about it), but her nosiness paired with an occasional lack of filter is often quite entertaining. The majority of her clients appreciate her relaxed attitude, although one woman did not respond well to being asked whether she really was happy with her choice of nipple tattoo following breast reconstruction, feeling that this was a little too intrusive.

I shook my head in answer to her latest question. 'Not really,' I said. 'I mean, sometimes people are distressed when they first arrive, but usually they've been with us for respite before so it's familiar and anyway, there's always so much going on at Bob's Place – everyone settles in eventually. I do tell families that. And it's the truth.'

'I bet it's like preschool,' said Caz. 'When the kids save their really tearful outbursts for drop-off and collection.'

I nodded. 'Absolutely. But I don't think it's a deliberate thing. Like, it's not a calculated emotional blackmail—'

'Not like it is with toddlers then,' said Caz, laughing. 'It was definitely deliberate with Alex. He'd be bawling his eyes out, clinging onto my coat like a deranged limpet, and if he saw me wavering, even for a moment, the screaming would ramp up few notches. But according to Miss Janice, as soon as I left the doorway he'd be charging off to the painting table or the story corner and barely give me a backward glance.'

We murmured our agreement and shared a nostalgic collective sigh, having all been through similar with at least one of our kids.

'Do you remember when our children needed us to be with them all the time?' said Zahara fondly. 'Every waking moment. Like there was total panic if you even left the room – and when you came back they'd snuggle up so close to you that their skin stuck to yours and...'

'It was completely fucking exhausting,' said Joy. 'And I only had the one. *And* I went back to work pretty much as soon as was physically possible after Evangeline was born. Once the car crash of my nether regions was in a basic state of repair I legged it out of there as fast as I could, without pissing myself over the floor, obviously. And yet...' Her gaze drifted into the middle distance before she snapped to. 'No,' she said. 'I can't pretend that was a phase I feel enormously sentimental about. I think a combination of nannies and preschool leaders saved my life – I probably ought to have told Miss Janice that, but I always found her a sanctimonious bitch, to be honest.'

'She was, a bit,' I said, remembering my own experience with Miss Janice the time Maisie declared that the new Smurfs film was a 'total bag of shite' in the hearing of numerous three- and four-year-olds. I had tried to explain to a fuming Miss Janice that growing up with two older siblings meant Maisie was sometimes exposed to inappropriate adult language and that I would ask her brother and sister to be more careful in future, all the while knowing that she'd heard it directly from me, her potty-mouthed mother. But to this day I stand by my assessment of that film. *Smurfs: The Lost Village* is two hours of my life I'm never getting back.

I look around the pub table with a warm feeling this evening. I've got a lot of shared history with these women, and they have been there for me through some challenging times. Zahara I've known ever since I moved to the village seventeen years ago, back when Grace was an adorable three-year-old (and not one who said things like 'total bag of shite'), Tom was a babe in arms, and Maisie was just a twinkle of pounds sterling in the IVF consultant's eye. Zahara was pregnant when we first met, and by the time Sam and I had celebrated our first Christmas in our new home, she had given birth to her eldest, Rex, using the power of essential oils and yogic breathing alone (I kid you not – still think she must have hidden a kilo of heroin in the birthing pool without anyone knowing). We've shared the trials and tribulations of raising our families alongside each other ever since. Zahara supported me through the years of repeated miscarriages and failed IVF rounds, and she was overjoyed when I finally felt safe to admit to being pregnant with Maisie (I was already twenty weeks gone and approximately the size of a garden shed, so I think she'd already guessed). The fact that this pregnancy coincided with her second one, and that Maisie and her daughter Darcy were born only months apart, further cemented the friendship and I know that she's always in my corner.

Zahara is truly one of the most perfect people I've ever met, and yet she's funny and self-deprecating in a way that ensures you can't possibly dislike her or envy her perfection. When her (now ex) husband Hugh cheated on her a while back, I was ready to tear out his eyes with my bare hands because honestly, how dare he think for one minute that he's found someone to match this paragon of womanhood? But in retrospect Zahara has had the last laugh. Where Hugh now seeks out younger and younger women like an aged Hollywood lothario let loose in the Playboy Mansion, Zahara is in a wonderfully happy relationship with Rajesh, a computer programmer five years her junior who she met online. In fact, Rajesh was ostensibly the reason for the four of us gathering in this slightly impromptu fashion on a chilly Tuesday in January.

'I was too excited to wait for the weekend to tell you all,' Zahara said, eyes sparkling like some kind of teen heroine. 'Raj has asked me to marry him!' She extended her left hand across the table and we all gasped appreciatively at the hefty but tasteful square-cut diamond perched on her ring finger.

'Congratulations!' I squealed. To be honest, I already knew because she'd called me from the airport on their way back from Italy, but I didn't want Joy and Caz to feel left out. Also, squealing about the engagement helped quash the selfish part of me that felt a tiny pang of envy at my best friend's good fortune. I was thrilled for Zahara, obviously. But it's sometimes hard not to also covet the flush of new love when it's right there in front of you – even if the person currently experiencing it deserves a burgeoning romance in her life more than anyone else you know.

'Oh, babe! That's brilliant news,' said Caz, pulling her into a hug. 'Tell us all about the proposal.'

Joy was already up at the bar ordering champagne. 'I think we've wiped them out,' she said, returning with two bottles and four flutes. 'I've apologised to Mandy for using up her stock but it looks like these two might have been in the cellar long enough to have become vintage.' She ripped off the foil with a flourish, easing the cork out in a matter of seconds, but then she always has had the air of a woman used to opening champagne at speed.

'Congratulations, gorgeous,' she said to Zahara as she filled a flute and passed it to her. 'You deserve all the good stuff, including a hot toyboy who worships the ground you walk on. Especially one who's dynamite in the sack, and doesn't mind your tendency to adopt waifs and strays.'

Zahara took her glass. 'Thank you,' she said. 'But they are not waifs and strays.'

'They absolutely are,' said Joy with an indulgent smile. 'And if you keep mopping up Hugh's ex-girlfriends and their offspring for all eternity, you'll never get that house back to yourself. But I'm sure Rajesh knows what he's taking on. Marry me, marry my many social projects, et cetera.' Joy was referring to Nadia, the woman who Zahara's ex, Hugh, first cheated with (at least, the first she knew of). Any rancour Zahara felt towards her for bringing about the eventual divorce was washed away when Hugh dumped Nadia and their six-month-old daughter, Summer, for a waitress called Astrid. Zahara took in Nadia and baby Summer for a few months while they found somewhere permanent to stay, and has kept in touch with them ever since, attending Summer's recent nativity play when Nadia was working, donating every item of clothing that Darcy has grown out of to her younger half-sister and generally being on standby when Nadia wants to complain about Hugh's lack of moral fibre or delayed maintenance payments. The woman is universally acknowledged as a soft touch and sometimes we (mainly Joy) have to rein in her kindly urges lest she make herself bankrupt and her own children homeless, but it is also one of the reasons we love her.

'I just know how it feels,' said Zahara, not for the first time. 'Basking in the glory of Nice Attentive Hugh only to have it ripped away.'

'When they discover that he's Sexually Incontinent, Vain and Conceited Hugh,' said Joy.

'Exactly. Anyway, I'll be inviting them both to the wedding, so you'd better not be mean about them, Joy,' said Zahara warningly. 'God knows they've been through enough without you picking on them.'

'You're not inviting Hugh, surely?' I said, thinking that I'd have to tamp down my murderous urges if I saw him again.

'No way,' said Zahara. 'I'm not fucking mental.'

'And cheers to that,' said Caz, raising her glass.

Chapter Eight

As if Friday the thirteenth weren't ominous enough, today was the last day of Lorraine Rowbotham's visit and the start of an indeterminate waiting period as she weighed up the positive and negative aspects of our organisation. Today's instalment of Lorraine's Tortuous Inspection Process included Tina and I being treated to a minutely detailed account of our shortcomings, both as care providers and business managers. Lorraine is so very thorough that she has managed to find fault with the company of decorators we used four years ago (one corner of peeling wallpaper was declared an immediate infection control risk, despite it being behind the desk in Tina's office); our catering supplier (Norman Shilling, purveyor of the finest meat products including our bacon, apparently has a history of eczematous dandruff, and Lorraine thinks she's seen him handling a frozen leg of lamb without wearing a hairnet); and our online security (thanks to my leaving a password-protected laptop open in the kitchen for twelve seconds while I put the kettle on, despite there being nobody else in the room other than Lorraine). She has also been roundly dismissive of our 'little extras' – all the things Tina, Veronica and I are so proud of, like the personalised birthday cards for our day centre clients, the Memory Book sessions, the line dancing class we arranged for Edith, and the Grandparent Days, where we invite families over for tea and cake (plus optional Giant Dominoes in the garden).

There hasn't been a single acknowledgement of a job well done, no recognition of the effort we put into making this care home a cut above the rest, or a moment where that woman has cracked a genuine smile, not even when one of our oldest residents, Arnold, said we were the loveliest people he'd ever known (although his comment was somewhat undermined by the fact that he thought I was his great-aunt). As this week draws to a close, I don't think I've ever felt quite so exhausted or demoralised – and I've come last in the PTA Family Fun Run twice (Fun and Run being two words never destined for inclusion in the same sentence, unless it's a prison sentence).

But my Friday the thirteenth horrors were not over once I'd seen the back of Lorraine; oh no. No sooner had she disappeared on her broomstick in a puff of evil green smoke than Tina handed me the most recent bank statement. Sobering reading, I can tell you. We both stared at the pages for what felt like an eternity, desperately hoping that the figures would magically transform into a positive balance.

'We haven't paid the gas bill yet,' I said hoarsely.

Tina shook her head. 'It was that or the staff,' she said. 'And we can't afford to lose any of them.'

'But we can't afford to have our heating and hot water turned off either.'

She shrugged. 'I know.'

'How – how has it…' I didn't know where to start. 'How have we got to this point without realising?' I said eventually. 'What does the accountant say? Why didn't they alert us?'

Tina looked sheepish. 'They did,' she said. 'Do you remember our last annual meeting, Graham said the cost of living is going up, staff costs were escalating. I mean, our outgoings have always exceeded our income by some margin. We knew that, the accountants knew that. It's what Bob's legacy money was for. To top up. To make Bob's Place more than just an average care home. Every month I've shifted money across from the trust fund to the business account, and the previous projections indicated that we could carry on like that for about ten years.'

'Well, yes,' I said. 'That's the sort of time frame I was working to. And we've talked about what we're going to do at that point.' It had been a bleak conversation. The only choice if we didn't find another legacy fund or additional income stream was cutting back on all the features that made Bob's Place special; or else charging people an extortionate amount for the service. Which had never been the intention. We wanted this level of care to be available to everyone, irrespective of income.

'But that means we've got another four or five years before we have to look for additional funding,' I said. 'And just before she had her operation, Veronica was making enquiries about those social investment projects, the ones the big corporations get involved with. She definitely felt we had options…' I trailed off, sensing that perhaps I hadn't fully appreciated the impact of losing our finance director for six months while she underwent major surgery last year.

'The trouble is,' Tina said, 'that every month, the amount I have to transfer has increased. Everything's so expensive. And I want it all done properly – how Bob would have wanted it. But it all costs so bloody much.' (I knew things must be bad if Tina was swearing. She was pretty old school when it came to bad language.) 'I've had to increase the direct payments,' she said. 'But I've also had to take bigger chunks for renovation costs, and all that work we did to the house, it cost a lot more than I'd budgeted for.'

'But you said it was OK to spend that money on the renovations,' I said, confused. 'You said the fund could easily support it.'

She gave a long exhalation through her nose. 'I miscalculated,' she said eventually. 'I fell into that trap. I got so used to having money that I forgot it can run out. Bob always looked after the finances. I never had to worry about it when he was alive, and that fund always felt like a never-ending supply. Until David had his skiing accident and we had to pay the kids' school fees, and then Caroline wanted money for her catering company, and…'

'Wait, what?' David and Caroline were Bob's children, Tina's stepchildren. They had been horrible to her when Bob was alive, refusing to spend time with their father if Tina was even in the building. But since their father had died and left a small fortune behind him, they had been remarkably attentive to their once detested stepmother.

Tina looked sheepish. 'They have a right to that money,' she said quietly. 'He was their father. If anything, they have more right to it than…'

'No!' I said. 'They have no more right to it than you. More importantly, Bob wanted the fund spent on providing dementia care – that was his dying wish.' (Bit strong from me, but needs must – and it *had* been his dying wish.)

'He did. But he also wouldn't want his children to starve,' she said.

I snorted in exasperation. David and Caroline were far from starving paupers. A more venal, brattish, undeserving pair of spongers you couldn't imagine. But I may have been slightly biased. At the end of the day this was not my money. I was not the executor of Bob's will, and I was not the one having to tell his own flesh and blood that they couldn't have a hundred grand to invest in an artisanal meringue company.

Tina sighed, the weight of responsibility written into her drooping shoulders. 'Anyway, various deductions have been made over the past few years. Some anticipated, others less so.' She took a deep breath. 'I had a letter from the investment bank last month and they said reserves are dwindling. I thought I'd see how we would manage without Bob's money for a month. Probably shouldn't have done it over Christmas, but...'

'So this is just a temporary exercise,' I said in a rush, the relief washing over me as I indicated the bank statement in my hand. 'This was just to illustrate what would happen when the money *does* run out – like a trial run?'

'Ye-es,' said Tina slowly. 'But a trial run with a purpose.'

'Oh, I know,' I said. 'But we can pay the gas bill this month at least?'

'We can. This month.'

I picked up on her tone. 'This month,' I repeated. 'How many months have we got left?'

Tina tilted her head. 'About twelve,' she said. 'If we're lucky, we'll make it to the end of the year.'

Fuck.

Chapter Nine

Thankfully, to distract me from impending bankruptcy, my perfect brother Rory, along with his perfect family including fiscally responsible Australian wife, Candice, have come to visit for the day. Rory isn't quite as much of a twat as he used to be (but the bar was never high to begin with). Since he met Candice, who is his equal and then some, he's become a little more understanding of how it feels to be a normal flawed human in the shadow of a god (or goddess, in this case – and one he worships appropriately). Their decision to move back to the UK has helped with logistics as regards our parents (although Rory being an hour away means that the default child to call if help is required continues to be me, what with being virtually next door). Fatherhood has improved him, too. For a man used to excelling at every activity he turned his hand to and being in control of all aspects of his life, the chaos of parenthood has been an education, and I am absolutely here for it. Witnessing my brother attempting to wrestle a swim nappy onto a vocal and outraged toddler while a teething baby wails and vomits on his shoulder are moments of my life I shall treasure to my dying day. And I don't care if that makes me a bad person. I've been in my brother's shadow for forty-odd years. The fact that the balance has shifted slightly now, and that my parents see us in more equal terms at last, has helped to undo some of my resentment, but not all of it. And Rory is still a smug bastard, no getting away from it.

'Of course, Madison-Jane has been flagged up for the gifted and talented programme,' he said today over lunch, referring to his five-year-old daughter.

'Has she now?' I replied in dutiful Aunty Penny fashion. 'MJ, that's exciting!' I dished out a helping of peas onto the plate of the child prodigy in question.

'Yes, Aunty Penny,' she said seriously as she moved her peas to a separate segment of the plate, away from the turkey breast which itself had been distanced from the roast potatoes by a couple of inches. 'Daddy said it was exciting.'

'And you have a new reading book,' Candice prompted from the other side of the table, where she was trying to convince two-year-old Callum about the merits of parsnips. I'd gone for the full festive menu given that this weekend was our belated Christmas family gathering, Rory and Candice having spent the end of December in Australia with the in-laws so that Candice's parents could enjoy some quality time with the grandchildren.

'A new book,' I said. 'Sounds like fun?'

MJ shrugged. 'I don't like the people in it,' she said. 'They're stupid. And it's about magic. Which isn't real. Mrs McCarthy said I needed to use my 'magination more better, but I don't like stuff that's pretending.'

'Fair enough,' I said. My niece is nobody's fool. She's deeply sceptical of everyone and everything in a hilariously endearing way. You won't catch her wandering off with a stranger to go and see some puppies. She'd have given any potential kidnapper or child molester a thorough DBS check and handed them over to the appropriate authorities before she even said hello. In fact, maybe she should go and work with Lorraine at the CQC when she grows up.

'I think instead of dragons they should have crocodiles and real animals, and it should tell us about how they lay their eggs and how many teeth they have and real fings 'stead of made up fings,' she said.

'There you go, J. K. Rowling,' said Rory, smiling fondly at his daughter. 'More reptile facts in your books, please.'

'I think I've got a book on newts at home,' said Dad from the far end of the table. He and Mum had managed to avoid the fate of Rory, Sam and my kids, who had been relegated to the camping chairs and patio table, hastily wiped clean of garden debris and covered with a paint-spattered oilcloth. Mum was in her wheelchair, which we'd managed to squeeze through our doorway with only minor damage to the architrave, and Dad was on a proper chair – still ancient but slightly less liable to collapse than the camping version, as Tom had already demonstrated twice. The result of there being two tables crammed into the space of one was that nobody, once seated, could actually move. A point of contention for the majority of fidgets in my family but particularly Callum, who seemed intent on proving that a plastic picnic table could bear the weight of a small boy. The trouble is that our house usually feels only just big enough for the four of us. I think Tom was somewhat smaller when Grace was still living here, and now when she comes home from college it feels that we are bursting at the seams. Low-beamed ceilings and tiny crooked doorways are all well and good until you're trying to host and feed a group of eleven that includes a woman in a wheelchair, three men of six foot (although I suppose Dad may have shrunk a little), one hulking teenager who is in danger of overtaking both his own father and his uncle in the height stakes, and one headstrong two-year-old boy who has recently learnt how to hurl himself off items of furniture. Still, it was lovely to have everyone under the same roof, if only for a few hours, and even Grace had returned home for the day, although Sam was dropping her at the station this evening so she'd be back in time for some demonstration or other tomorrow.

'I like noots, Grandad,' said MJ, fixing her grandfather with her serious gaze. He smiled as he offered Mum a spoonful of mashed potato and peas. 'Why does Granny have baby food?' she asked him, watching with interest.

'It's not baby food, MJ,' said Rory. 'Some grown-ups need soft food too. Granny has problems swallowing. Big bits of food make her cough and splutter.'

'Does it make her be sick?'

'Sometimes. So we have to be careful.'

'Grandad is good at doing feeding,' she said. 'Better than when you gived Callum rice pudding when he is a baby.'

'True, that,' he said. 'Well remembered.'

'Not really sure that we've got the hang of it now he's a toddler,' said Candice as a large chunk of parsnip sailed past my ear. Callum had smeared the remainder into his hair and Montmorency was hoovering up the debris from the carpet beneath him. He's not as stupid as he looks, that dog. He knows that toddlers at mealtimes equals raining snacks.

'Baby,' said Mum suddenly.

'Yes, Mary,' said Candice, who was sat the other side of her. 'He is still a baby really. Aren't you, my gorgeous chubs?' She directed this at Callum, squeezing his cheek while he gurgled in delight.

'He is not a baby, Mummy,' piped up MJ. 'He is starting at preschool soon and preschool is not for tiny babies.'

'No,' said Candice. Her voice carried a trace of sadness and I could see that she was already nostalgic for the months of tiny babyhood.

'How were your parents, Candice?' I asked, leaning across the table to offer her another roast potato as compensation for the loss of her growing children, and almost decapitating myself on the pendulum lamp in the process.

She took a potato and cut it into small pieces, handing them to Callum absent-mindedly. 'They were good, thanks, Penny. It was – it was—' Her eyes suddenly filled with tears, and Rory reached across and put his hand over hers.

'They were on great form,' he said. 'And they loved seeing the kids. They were quite sad when we left.'

'Granny Australia said I was a princess,' said MJ. 'But I told her it wasn't true because Mummy and Daddy aren't a queen and king.'

'Sorry, Penny,' said Candice quietly to me. 'I just miss them, that's all. It's always worse when I've just said goodbye. I never seem to get used to it.'

I nodded and offered her another roast potato, this time to compensate for her distant parents. I'm a great believer in eating your feelings, especially where roast potatoes are involved.

'I know a lot about princesses and kings and queens from my school project,' said Maisie loftily from the head of the patio table. She had been uncharacteristically quiet for the past five minutes, and clearly felt that she had conceded sufficient air time to her younger cousin. 'We're doing family trees, Uncle Rory. And Mrs Mabuse said that royal families are good examples of jeanology because they have lots of records written down about who is related to who.' Maisie has taken to pronouncing gene-alogy in this way; I think she assumes denim is involved somewhere in the process.

'That does sound interesting, Maisie,' said Rory. 'Of course the British monarchy has one of the best examples of inherited gene mutations with respect to haemophil—'

'My project's not about them,' Maisie cut in quickly, aware that Uncle Rory liked the sound of his own voice just as much as she did and could potentially go on for hours. 'It's about *our* family. I'm making a family tree with *everyone* on it.' She glanced around the room as she said this, making it sound more of a threat than a privilege, but there was a general nodding of heads which she took to be majority consent.

And so, after we'd opened our presents (excellent Aunty gifting from me as MJ unwrapped her encyclopedia of amphibians and reptiles; less excellent Uncle gifting from Rory, who had bought Tom a whoopee cushion and a Beer Monster T-shirt from Australia), we spread a large sheet of wrapping paper out on the floor and Rory helped Maisie sketch out the details of the Baker—Andrews family tree. Maisie accepted Uncle Rory's assist-ance because he was a doctor who knew about jeans and jeanology, although he was only allowed a pencil crayon. She was in charge of the felt-tips, natch. Candice went to put Callum down for a nap and when she rejoined us, Maisie added her parents and siblings to the sprawling picture. The tree was now starting to stray over the edges onto different sheets of wrapping paper, to the point where Sam's second cousin ended up being written across a pair of antlers and Dad's estranged Uncle Bartholomy was ascribed to a cartoon elf. Sam caused much hilarity when he asked why Grace's entry wasn't marked with a snowflake, but she got her own back by showing him a rotund, bewhiskered Father Christmas and suggesting a strong physical resemblance.

Of course, Dad was the ultimate star of the show because he was the only person who knew any names from the higher end of the tree (the trunk? The canopy?) and by the time we finished, we had six generations of Andrews, with Sam promising to contact Nana and Grampy for information to even up the Baker side of things as soon as possible. Maisie stuck the three sheets of wrapping paper to the wall of the sitting room with Blu-Tack and insisted that it remain there until her project was completed, which appears to be the summer term. Great. It's going to look beautiful come spring, and the festive red and gold are very in keeping with the duck-egg colour scheme. It also rustles every time Montmorency runs past it, which proved a little disconcerting this evening when Sam and I settled down to watch that old winter favourite, *A Quiet Place*.

By the time the family tree was complete, Tom's girl-friend Lauren had come over and the two of them disap-peared upstairs. MJ asked earnestly whether they would be playing with the whoopee cushion together in Tom's bedroom.

'They might be,' said Rory, his mouth turning up at the corner. 'It's a great present, after all.'

'Why is Uncle Sam laughing?' MJ asked, confused.

'It's a grown-up thing,' said Maisie in a voice that suggested she got the joke but couldn't be bothered to explain it to someone in year one.

Callum's wail drifted down the stairs and Candice darted up to get him.

'Do you want a hand in the kitchen, Penny?' Rory inclined his head towards MJ who, unsatisfied with the response to her whoopee cushion query, was once again engrossed in her amphibian and reptile book. 'I don't think my presence here is required, and we've got a bit to catch up on.'

That sounded ominous. I steeled myself for some terrible revelation but it turned out that Rory just wanted to talk about Mum, who had been dozing peacefully next to the fire throughout our family tree discussion.

'She seems less and less engaged,' Rory said as I passed him a tea towel. 'And I haven't seen her mobilising out of her chair the whole time we've been here. How does Dad manage getting her out and about?'

'They don't get out much at all any more,' I said. 'I still take Mum over to Bob's Place every other day but the process of getting her in and out of the car has been taking longer and longer. And transferring her to the wheelchair is more of a challenge. I think Dad uses the days I take her out of the house to get the practical things done, the shopping and cooking and whatever. But he doesn't get out much, often no further than popping next door to us.'

'She's lost weight, hasn't she?' he said, wiping carefully around the roasting tray.

'I do try and make sure they're stocked up with meals.' My tone may have been a little defensive. It's a default response with Rory, even if he's not accusing me of any deficiency. 'I do extra batches if I'm cooking something big for the family, and Dad can do a basic lunch for the two of them. But I think she's just lost her appetite generally. You remember she went through that phase of eating everything we put in front of her? Like the off switch for self-restraint had just gone?'

He nodded.

'Well, now it's the opposite. Dad sits there so patiently, offering up tasty morsels while his own food goes cold. But she turns up her nose at most of it.'

'I guess her calorie requirement has reduced. If she's as immobile as you say. The problems swallowing can't have helped. Probably put her off eating.'

'Yes, it can't be the most appealing prospect if you feel like you're choking on the smallest bite,' I said, wondering idly whether this might be a way to reduce my own rapidly expanding waistline, simply develop a poor swallow reflex and risk asphyxiation every time I nibbled at a biscuit.

'Has she had any more of those absence episodes?'

'Hard to say.' I dredged a baking tray out of the sink. 'Sometimes she's so vague I don't know whether she's even conscious. I have to check to see if she's breathing. I'm never sure whether that's an absence seizure or a snooze.'

'And falling?'

'All the time,' I said gloomily. 'Mostly it's OK because Dad can just call Sam and the two of us can physically lift her up. She hasn't hurt herself falling so far, it's more just a gradual slide onto the floor – it's not like she's moving anywhere at pace, so no fractures or bruising or anything. She never even seems to notice – certainly doesn't appear to be troubled by it. I just worry that one time Dad won't be able to get hold of us and he'll try and lift her himself.'

Rory looked thoughtful and we stood in silence for a moment, washing and drying in sibling solidarity.

'It seems as though Dad's struggling to look after her at home,' he said eventually. 'I can't help but feel that maybe it's time we considered—'

'Residential care,' I finished for him. 'I know. Me too.'

Rory looked surprised. 'I thought you'd be dead against the idea,' he said. 'You were always so…'

'Intransigent? Bloody-minded?' I offered, and he smiled. 'I think working at Bob's Place has helped me see the possible benefits. I mean, it wouldn't take much to beat some of the awful places Mum and I looked at seven years ago when she came to stay with me. You know – when Dad broke his hip.'

'Oh yes!' He took the baking tray. 'Wasn't there one home you looked around where someone had shat in a chair and nobody had cleared it up?'

'Moreton Springfields,' I said, a grim smile on my face. 'Still haunts me now, the sight of that turd perched jauntily on the vinyl upholstery, all those really old, frail people staring vacantly into space or crying out to us as we completed our tour, me trying to persuade Mum we were simply checking out boutique hotels.'

Rory grimaced. 'It was pretty awful for you, wasn't it? That six months when she was living with you and the kids were still little. I don't think I fully appreciated it, what you went through.'

I paused, scouring pad still dripping suds into the bowl. It wasn't often that my brother admitted he'd been wrong. 'Do you know what?' I said eventually. 'It wasn't all bad. The whole experience made Mum and I much closer. And we found the dementia choir, which led to me getting back into music, playing the piano again and meeting Tina, establishing Bob's Place… There were some good times. And it made me more resilient, less likely to take other people's shit.'

'So it was character-building.' Rory gave his characteristic bark of a laugh. 'That's what Dad would say.'

'Yeah,' I said. 'I guess it was. Phantom crapper and all.' I drifted for a moment in memories of that time – the chaos and anxiety about how I would cope with caring for Mum and the kids, tinged from this distance with the rosy glow of nostalgia.

'So now we've got Bob's Place as an option, you're thinking it might suit Mum better than the Moreton Springfields of this world?' Rory said, grabbing the roasting tin I was wafting in his general direction.

'It's partly that,' I said, leaning against the sink, 'and partly having seen Mum withdraw so much. You know, I used to worry that she'd be sad about leaving home – and leaving Dad? I used to think that we could care for her properly in her own house forever. Well, I don't think she even notices her surroundings now. And when I see her tottering about as Dad tries to move her into the bathroom or just stop her sliding out of her chair, I think maybe she'd be safer at Bob's. Much as it pains me to say that.'

Rory looked relieved. 'That's how I feel,' he said. 'But I thought you'd think I was a total bastard if I suggested it.'

'Don't worry,' I said. 'I'll always think you're a total bastard. Nothing's going to change that.'

He flicked the damp tea towel in my direction. 'I'm a lot better than I used to be.'

'Marginally,' I said. 'But it's all relative.'

'Fair point.' He smiled as he carried the dry roasting tins to the cupboard. 'So now that we're in agreement about Mum,' he said, trying to cram a dish back into the

Jenga stack of pots and pans. 'I guess the only thing we've got to do…'

'Is convince Dad,' I said, and we both grimaced.

Chapter Ten

Veronica is back from Egypt – thank God. Someone to share the money worries with, if nothing else. Although actually she feels terribly responsible for the whole thing.

'I'm the one with the financial background,' she said, rubbing at a small patch of peeling skin on the bridge of her nose. 'I should have interrogated the accounts more thoroughly. And interrogated the accountant, come to that.'

'It's not your fault, Veronica,' said Tina. 'You couldn't help being off sick last year – it's just one of those things, isn't it? You can't predict how long the recovery period is for something like that. Besides, the business account has been fairly stable while Bob's money has kept coming in. Increased costs, yes, but all gradual and manageable. It's the legacy fund that's drying up. And it's my responsibility to keep on top of that. So this is *my* fault, nobody else's.' She rested her elbows on the table, her face drawn. She looked exhausted, and I was suddenly reminded that Tina's connection with dementia had been the result of her spouse having the condition, not a parent, like Veronica and I. Admittedly she had been much younger than Bob, but I sometimes forgot that she was closer to my parents' generation than mine. She was now pushing seventy and, let's be honest, probably didn't need this hassle in her life. Maybe she'd rather jack it all in and settle into a well-deserved retirement. She seemed to be having the same thoughts.

'I have been wondering about looking for a care home manager,' she said. 'Someone to replace me in the future, someone with a bit more energy. Trouble is, I suppose we can't afford to recruit someone new at the moment.'

Veronica looked thoughtful. 'Hmmm – you might be wrong there, Tina. This may be a case of, can we afford not to? If we want to make this business financially secure for the future, then we are going to have to make some changes. We always knew we wouldn't have the legacy fund forever, and we've treated it like Santa's grotto, knowing that we could go high-end with the refurb, bringing in little luxuries for our clients.'

'That's what Bob would have wanted though,' said Tina sadly. 'He'd have preferred a few years of the high life to a longer period of utilitarian functioning.'

'Oh, I know,' said Veronica. 'What I mean is that we've executed that part of his will according to his wishes. Now we need to think differently. We need sustainability. How do we make Bob's Place viable for the future?'

'Securing more funds,' I said. 'But how?'

'What we need is someone who knows how,' said Veronica.

'Like a fundraising expert?'

Veronica nodded. 'Someone who can sniff out new revenue streams for us. We need a campaign manager – a head of fundraising. And we need them quickly.'

'Is that not part of my marketing and publicity remit?' I said, feeling a bit worried I hadn't been pulling my weight.

Our roles had changed within the organisation over the years, and the boundaries between our jobs had blurred and merged more than once, so it was occasionally difficult to keep track of who did what. Some aspects of the business were more clearly defined. Veronica had always been in charge of finances, although she had little control over the direct income stream coming from Bob's legacy fund (or not, as now appeared to be the case), and Tina and I tended to look after the invoicing. Tina was in charge of the day-to-day running of the home, the buildings and wider estate, and my main role was focused on the day centre activities and events, planning the timetable, finding therapists to run the sessions, alongside managing governance, safeguarding and compliance (which is why the CQC inspection weighed so heavily). My marketing knowledge was limited to a single module of a business studies degree completed almost thirty years ago, but I was quite proud of how quickly we always managed to sell tickets for our Bob's Place events and had taken that as an endorsement of my brilliant publicity skills. Seems maybe Veronica didn't share this opinion.

'I'm not really talking about marketing,' she said. 'Bob's Place markets itself to a certain extent. We're certainly never short of clients or residents, and our waiting list is at a record high.'

I allowed myself a small smile of relief as she continued.

'I think it's more about a targeted fundraising campaign. A separate role. We've always run on a small management team which means we're nimble and adaptable, but also very overstretched. And that means balls get dropped. CQC compliance, financial oversight, big stuff that needs our full attention.'

'And if we're focusing on that then it's difficult to find time for fundraising,' I said, understanding better where she was going.

'Exactly.'

Tina looked doubtful. 'I'm not so sure that expanding our executive team is the answer,' she said. 'It sounds expensive and, if I'm honest, a bit unnecessary.'

Veronica shook her head. 'I think it *is* necessary. We've got to change. And in order to do that we've got to spend a little up front. Speculate to accumulate.'

'How about if it's a part-time post and a fixed-term contract,' I said, warming to Veronica's idea. 'A year? And then if it doesn't work out, we haven't lost anything other than their salary.'

'And how about,' said Veronica, 'we make a plan to advertise for a care home manager by, say, the end of the year? That way there's an end in sight for you, Tina, without us having to pay for two new roles immediately. And then hopefully next year, when things are a bit more financially secure, there'll be some breathing space. Someone to take over the day-to-day running, as you've suggested, while you stay on in maybe more of a non-executive director role?'

'I'm not sure that we should conflate the two issues,' I said. 'It's not an either/or situation, Tina. We can still aim to recruit a manager even if you don't agree to a fundraising lead.'

'Of course.' Veronica's expression was firm. 'And I don't want you both thinking that I've just swooped back from my holidays and come up with this harebrained scheme on a whim. I've been thinking we need to shake things up for a while.'

'So have I,' I admitted.

Tina glanced down at the two pieces of paper she held in her hand. One was the business account balance, now perilously close to our overdraft limit. The other was Bob's legacy fund statement. Beside her on the table was a gold-framed photo of her and Bob in happier times, both of them smiling into the sunshine.

'OK,' she said. 'Let's do it.'

–

We didn't finish our meeting for another two hours, by which time Veronica had to leave to catch her train for London.

'I'll be back later in the week,' she said, pulling on an immaculate three-quarter length charcoal-grey coat and swinging her Kelly handbag onto her arm. 'But I'll email when I get to the office – we'll get the job spec finalised as soon as possible.'

'Dress,' piped up Mum, who had been sitting quietly in her wheelchair up to this point. She'd finished her hydrotherapy session half an hour earlier and the carers had kindly brought her through to sit with me in the kitchen while we finished our meeting. Hydrotherapy usually left Mum fairly exhausted, so it was a surprise to see her respond enthusiastically as she reached out to touch Veronica's coat.

'Do you mean *coat*, Mum?' I said. 'It's beautiful, isn't it?'

'Beautiful,' Mum agreed, still rubbing the luxury fabric between her thumb and fingers. She smiled up at Veronica. 'Beautiful,' she said again.

'Thank you, Mary!' Veronica appeared genuinely flattered. 'I love it too. Max Mara.' She pulled a mock grimace, presumably to indicate the exorbitant cost. 'But I picked this one up in the January sales.'

I regarded Mum curiously. She was leaning forward in her chair, examining every inch of the coat, checking the lining, peering at the stitching detail, with a huge smile on her face. I hadn't seen her so animated for months.

'Do you want to try it on?' Veronica shrugged it off her shoulders and held it out for Mum, who looked absolutely delighted.

'Oh, no, I – are you sure?' I said, faltering as Mum eagerly slipped her arms into the sleeves and Veronica scrunched this hugely expensive coat in around her, the fabric rucking up in the back of the wheelchair.

'There,' she said. 'It really suits you, Mary.'

'How much was it?' I asked, noting Mum's radiant expression as she wrapped the side panels of cashmere around her front, resting her cheek on the soft faux fur of the lapel.

'Two fifty,' said Veronica. 'Give or take.' We both watched on as Mum hugged her arms around herself, hands tucked up into her armpits.

'Cosy,' she said with a wide smile. 'Beautiful.'

'Here, Mary.' Veronica propelled Mum's wheelchair out of the kitchen, across the hall and into the studio, where the outer wall was lined with full-length mirrors. 'Have a look.'

Mum's response to seeing herself reflected back while wearing this glamorous coat was enough to bring a tear to my eye. I was suddenly reminded of watching her getting ready to go out for the evening when, as a little girl, I was allowed to perch quietly on her bed, handing her scarves and hairspray and blusher brushes while she twisted and turned in the mirror, checking her outfit from every angle. It had been so long since I'd seen that expression on her face; the critical eye assessing how a garment fell, whether it flattered her shape or exaggerated areas she wanted hidden; the smile of satisfaction that came from seeing a quality piece of tailoring doing what it was supposed to do. Even though the coat was bunched up behind her the overall effect was transformative. For a moment she was her old self, 'the prettiest girl in the room' as Dad used to say.

'Which shop was having the sale?' I muttered to Veronica as I got my phone out of my pocket.

–

'You spent *how* much?' Sam said later that evening. 'On a coat?'

'You should have seen her face, Sam,' I said as I handed him his protein shake. 'She was so happy.'

Mum had eventually returned the coat to Veronica after patting it for a lengthy period, but she had talked about it in her funny little way of isolated words until we got home – and even then the first thing she said to Dad as I wheeled her through the door was, 'Coat. Beautiful. Mary.'

'And I know it's frivolous. A massive extravagance. But I thought, it's like a belated Christmas present. The past few years the things I've bought her have all been so functional and practical: new slippers, zip-up fleeces, cotton nighties. I wanted her to just have a present for a present's sake. Something lovely.'

'I get that. I really do. And it sounds as though she'll love her new coat. But I thought our household budget was pretty tight at the moment,' Sam said, not unreasonably.

'If this is about me suggesting that you shouldn't spend two thousand pounds on a Peloton bike, then I'm not interested,' I snapped back. I was already feeling guilty about the purchase, worrying whether I'd miscalculated the impact of a single garment – no coat, however gorgeous, was going to bring Mum back to me, and what if, when it arrived, she simply ignored it or thought it was a rug? What a colossal waste of money it would be. But the best response to feelings of guilt, as we all know, is deflecting them onto a spouse. 'We've got nowhere to put an exercise bike, for a start.'

'But it was in the sale,' Sam said sadly between gulps of his shake. 'And Martin's got one in his garage.'

'Our garage is already full of crap,' I said. 'Your crap, mostly. The rowing machine from last year? The weights? The punchbag?'

'Well, you use that,' he said. 'Don't pretend you don't. I've seen you lamping the shit out of it in the past. Nearly broke the garage window.'

'Yes, well, that wasn't really fitness-related,' I said huffily, recalling a time following a conversation not dissimilar to this one where I had become so incensed that I had indeed marched out to the garage and knocked the shit out of said punchbag, almost breaking both my wrists in the process.

Sam put his drink down on the counter and wrapped his arms around my shoulders. 'Sorry, Pen,' he said, his voice muffled by my hair. 'I know we haven't got space for a bike as well. And I know Pelotons are expensive. I was just surprised that a coat would cost that much, that's all.'

'You and me both,' I said, softening immediately. 'But honestly, Sam, it's so hard to get through to Mum now, so hard to get any reaction at all, let alone one of over-whelming delight. I just couldn't say no.'

'I understand,' he said, pulling back so he was looking at me. 'And you do know that if you ever wanted to use any of the gym equipment, you can. I don't want you to see it as "my thing". I'd be very happy to get you started on the weights or the ergo if you wanted to improve your fitness.' His hands slid to the sides of my waist, where a number of fat rolls were gathered at the top of my jeans. This was unfortunate timing given his next sentence. 'It wouldn't be a bad idea, you know. With a good balance of lifting and aerobic exercise you'd probably shift some of the weight you've put on since the menop...' He trailed off, the look of horror on his face similar to a man who has condemned himself to death.

'The weight I've put on since the *what*, Sam?' I said acidly.

He gulped. 'The weight that – the weight— I just meant that you've been talking about feeling fat, and...' He knew he was getting into deeper water. I could see the signs of panic. 'And – and not being as fit as you were. And I thought...'

I folded my arms across my chest and glared at him.

'You said – YOU said – you'd put on a couple of stone, and that was why you were doing Dry January.' He broke off to look pointedly at my almost empty glass of Merlot on the kitchen counter. 'And I just thought it might help if— Oh, never mind.' He sighed, admitting defeat, threw his hands melodramatically into the air and left the room, muttering to himself about 'only trying to help' and 'what's the bloody point'.

It wasn't until he was completely out of earshot that I started to cry, sitting at the table as hot, angry tears of shame plopped into my wine glass. I'd been worrying about my weight, and more generally how I looked, for a while now. The wrinkles, the grey hair, the general sagginess of everything from my knees to my jowly cheeks. Sam's fitness regime and subsequent gym-toned body, while extremely pleasing to the eye, only served as a counterpoint to my own wobbliness, and even though I thought I was reconciled to ageing gracefully, I was finding the reality harder than I had anticipated. Every time I caught sight of myself in a mirror these days I did a double-take, thinking that my great-aunt Dora had popped round to say hello. And Dora, bless her, hadn't even been much of a looker in her youth if the photos were anything to go by.

The only saving grace for me had been the knowledge that my husband still loved the way I looked. There had been one occasion in the entirety of our marriage where I had questioned his fidelity and wondered whether he was attracted to a junior colleague at work. This had been seven years ago, and I had been proved completely wrong in my suspicions. Since then I'd had no reason to doubt his commitment or worry about him straying, but now even *he* thought I was overweight. How humiliating that my own husband had resorted to nudging me into an exercise regime both of us knew I'd never commit to. And how depressing that he clearly no longer found his fat, unfit, borderline alcoholic wife remotely attractive.

Chapter Eleven

Sam and I didn't directly discuss my weight again (I think he realised that wifely obesity was as far down the list of acceptable spousal conversational topics as you can get, somewhere between 'other women in the village I'd like to shag' and 'how cool I imagine my life would have been if we'd never met'. But the subject of my general health reared its ugly head this evening as I cleared up after supper.

I wasn't in the best of moods to begin with. Our CQC report following Lorraine Rowbotham's visit had arrived in my inbox at six thirty that morning, sitting there like a smug toad until I got to Bob's Place and could open it with Tina and Veronica present. We had been awarded a 'Good' overall, but this was a far cry from our previous 'Outstanding', and some domains, including safety and leadership, had been marked as 'Needs Improvement'. This was a bit of a blow, I'm not going to lie. We'd bust our arses trying to jump through all the hoops Lorraine had strategically laid in front of us, and the minor discrepancies she'd pulled us up on (such as not locking the residents' own nail varnish and toothpaste in a secure cabinet) felt unfair in the extreme. But more importantly, criticism of our leadership felt particularly personal to the three of us who had invested so much time and energy in this project. Bob's Place was a part of us, and up until the recent financial difficulties, it was everything we'd dreamed it could be. We were used to receiving compliments and praise for our facilities. Maybe we'd become complacent, or maybe Lorraine was just a vindictive bitch, but either way her report had well and truly pissed on our bonfire.

'Never mind,' said Veronica, gamely clapping her hands together as Tina and I sat there, glum-faced. 'Onward and upward. We have a plan in place and most of these, these ridiculous' – she waved her hand dismissively in the direction of the report on the laptop screen – '*recommendations*, can be easily dealt with, even if it is incredibly frustrating to reduce care to a tick-box exercise. Next time Lorraine Rowbotham comes to visit, she won't know what's hit her. Every single item in this whole goddamn house will have its own secure locker, and even the postman will have had a thorough DBS check.'

'Now.' She turned to address me. 'Penny, have you finished the advert for our new fundraising manager?'

'I have indeed,' I said, opening this document while closing the CQC report. Veronica was right; we needed to move on. I was quite pleased with the job description and role specification I'd managed to pull together, and Veronica agreed it needed minimal additional work. We agreed to launch it on the various online recruitment pages immediately.

–

Driving home, I felt surprisingly sanguine about the CQC report. It wasn't great, but at least we weren't being closed down. Likewise, the finances were secure for a year – that was more stability than a lot of small businesses had at the moment. I was just in the middle of congratulating myself on a positive mental attitude when I pulled up at the lights where I'd rammed the Audi coming the other way two weeks ago. Dad's echoey mobility vehicle had been returned to him last week, complete with minor scratches, and I had paid the excess on my insurance for Audi man's repairs. I had also paid the extortionate costs for my own car to be returned from the garage with a new sump, and was reflecting on the fact that Sam's dreams of Peloton ownership were even further out of reach than previously, when I was again distracted by the goings-on in the doorway behind the bus stop.

It was the same man I'd seen on the previous occasion – same suit, same hairstyle. He must live in the flat above the estate agents, I thought idly. And he was engaged in the same vigorous heavy petting that he had been two weeks ago. With the same girl. And this time, with no vape fumes and no sleet to contend with, the visibility was clear. The girl he was snogging was definitely Lauren.

Luckily there was no Audi to crash into this time, and although I delayed my fellow road users' progression through the green light by remaining stationary for a full three minutes until they'd changed back to red, I didn't incur any further motor-related expenses, only the ire of the drivers behind me. I went to collect Maisie from school unsure of how to proceed, but decided that the best thing to do was absolutely nothing until I'd spoken to Sam.

Maisie was full of beans as she often is when there is no after-school kids' club (or babysitting, as she now refers to it). I work a shorter day on a Wednesday, and don't tend to bring Mum over to Bob's Place, so my usual itinerary once I've collected Maisie is to pop in and see my parents on my way home. This way they get the dubious pleasure of their granddaughter's company for a full two hours before supper and she gets to regale them with stories of Eva's misdemeanours, Archie's verrucae, Jasmine's fear of earwigs and Darcy's recorder solo that went wrong and sounded like a series of farts. Today there was more chat about the family tree project, and of course some smart arse classmate had to go one step further, didn't they.

'Leon's parents have had swabs taken,' Maisie announced unexpectedly over her glass of squash.

'I'm not sure Leon's parents' swabs are any of our business, Maisie,' I said, although I was a little intrigued. Had they been to the STD clinic and then, in a spirit of candour, informed their children?

'It's for the project,' Maisie said. 'Leon found out he's related to some Vikings and a man called Genghis Khan.'

'Heavens,' I said. Because what else can you say in that situation?

'Can we do it?'

'What, find out if you're related to Genghis Khan?'

'No. Well, maybe. Can you and Daddy do swabs? You have to do it in your mouth and send it off in a little envelope and Leon says you get a report and he brought his in and it was really interesting and Mrs North *and* Mrs Mabuse both gave him a gold star for research skills and he hasn't even got as good a family tree as our wrapping paper one and he said it's only seventy pounds and Mrs North said it provides a fascinating insight into inheritance.'

'Uhm – perhaps,' I said faintly as I caught up with the key bits of data in that extraordinarily long sentence.

'Seventy pounds is a bargain,' said Maisie with the tone of one who has no understanding of the value of money.

'And just think what we'll learn about ourselves. The possibilities are endless.'

'Have you been watching YouTube adverts again?' I said.

'I have. Leon showed me the one for Ancestors dot com which is where his dad got their swabs from. Look, I'll show you.' She pulled my phone out of my handbag and with alarming speed, had unlocked it and found the website.

'Please, Mummy,' she said. 'It will be so much fun, and I can get a gold star for research as well.'

Later, I was relaying the conversation to Sam. I'm in no way the natural salesperson my daughter is and was finding it hard to justify why I wanted to order a DNA swab from an online company (and I do seem to be spending an awful lot of January having to defend various purchases to my husband).

'What harm can it do?' I said. 'It's nice that she's so invested in this project – it's really captured her imagination. Anyway, it's just under a hundred quid' (hundred and twenty, actually) 'and we'd easily spend that on a family trip to the museum or some other educational activity.'

'A hundred quid each?'

I looked sheepish.

'No, Penny. Absolutely not. We haven't got that kind of money to throw away on – on ridiculous projects.' (I could see he wanted to also say, *or Max Mara coats for old ladies who have dementia and don't know a coat from a polar bear.*)

'You don't think it's worth it? To encourage a bit of self-directed learning? To make her happy?'

'Two hundred pounds, Pen? No. To be honest, I don't think it's worth it. Maisie would be perfectly happy with a bag of Haribo, and she can get her gold star for research some other way. Our family is interesting enough as it is.'

I sighed as I brushed some crumbs off the kitchen counter. 'Trouble is… I've sort of implied…'

'You've said yes?' He had his back turned to me while he was fussing with his trainers, but let's just say he was not doing an excellent job of keeping the frustration out of his voice. 'Well, tell her you've changed your mind.' He turned back to face me.

'But I sort of promised…' I gave a plaintive grimace, palms held upward in a 'what can you do' gesture.

He huffed through his nose. 'Pen,' he said gently, 'you've got to stop letting our youngest daughter run rings around you. She's in danger of becoming a spoilt brat.'

'I don't think that wanting to investigate her heritage or immerse herself in a school project is being a spoilt brat,' I said, slightly outraged on Maisie's behalf. 'It's not like she's asking for a pony or a sports car.'

'Yet,' he said ominously, arms folded, legs akimbo.

'Well, I'll just tell her Daddy said no, shall I?' I said, adopting his stance. 'I'll tell her that you feel it's not worth it – spending money on a project that her school has endorsed and…'

'No,' he said through gritted teeth. 'Don't say that, because it wouldn't be fair. You'd be painting me as the bad guy,' he added under his breath, 'again.'

'Well, sorry,' I said, fired up with righteous indignation. 'But it's just telling the truth. You *are* the one saying no.'

'Pen—' He obviously wanted to say something else but then seemed to think better of it. His head dropped as he adjusted his knee support.

'Just tell her whatever you want to,' he said wearily. 'I'm heading off for a run.'

'In the dark?'

He gestured to the headlight and back reflector attached to his person. 'Yep.' He paused by the fridge. 'Do you fancy joining me?'

'Sam,' I said warningly. 'Don't start.'

'You might like it,' he said, easing down into a series of frankly alarming squats. 'Just a gentle jog to start off with. And it would be good for reducing your blood pressure and cholesterol. After what happened with Nick…'

I sighed, adopting the same posture of weary resignation my husband had taken seconds earlier. Sam and I seemed able to segue seamlessly between contentious topics at the moment. No sooner had we de-escalated the Ancestors.com DNA swab argument than we were straight back in the middle of this old chestnut.

'You told me that Nick smoked liked a chimney, drank a bottle of vodka on a night out and thought the gherkin in his Big Mac was one of his five-a-day,' I said. 'I understand that his heart attack has frightened you, Sam, but he wasn't exactly a paragon of health to begin with. And he is not *you*.'

'Yeah, but Pen,' he said, bouncing lightly on the balls of his feet as he rolled out his shoulders, 'neither of us is getting any younger, and the risk of heart disease only goes up. Strokes, cancer, all these things are associated with poor diet and lack of exercise. And high blood pressure's a silent killer.'

At least he knows to avoid talking about weight and fat distribution now, but honestly, does he not think I have enough things to worry about regarding my health without adding heart disease and cancer into the bargain?

'To be honest, Sam,' I said (quite loudly), 'I think there are plenty of other things causing my blood pressure to go up what with the CQC inspection results, the financial issues at Bob's Place and the fact that I'm now certain Lauren is cheating on Tom. I don't think that jogging in the January rain is likely to address any of…' I trailed off, following my husband's now stricken gaze to the doorway, where Tom was standing, ashen-faced, having heard everything I'd just said.

Chapter Twelve

Friday 27 January

So. The perfect end to a Wednesday evening.

There was no styling it out. I had to tell Tom what I was referring to while Sam stood there aghast at my parenting fail. He took it fairly well. Sam, that is. Not Tom. Tom took it terribly.

'Lauren said we needed to talk when she came over on Saturday,' he said hoarsely. 'But it was mainly about school and plans for next year and thinking about uni and stuff. It didn't sound – I didn't think – I didn't realise she was breaking up with me.' His eyes filled with tears and I went to put my arm around him. He just about tolerated it. Tom is a great one for cuddles, even now at the ripe old age of seventeen, but I guess being cuddled by your mum when you've found out you've been dumped by your long-term girlfriend is a bit conflicting, especially when it was your mum who provided evidence of the crime. I was the messenger – and you know what happens to messengers.

'Maybe she's been thinking about the future. Whether she wants a boyfriend when she's concentrating on her A levels,' I said. 'And it's very hard to keep a long-distance relationship going if you both head off to different universities.'

He pulled back from me. 'But that's ages away, Mum! It's like, two years' time. We don't need to split up now just in case it's difficult in two years!'

He made a good point, but then it wasn't me he had to convince.

'Anyway, if she wanted to concentrate on her school-work then why is she copping off with some random guy in the street?'

This was another strong point. Any argument I was trying to make on behalf of Lauren fizzled to nothing in the face of my anguished son.

'I think you should talk to her, mate,' Sam said. 'Find out what's going on.'

Tom nodded sadly and pulled his phone out of his pocket as he made his way out of the kitchen.

'We love you,' I shouted after him. 'You're lovely. And handsome. Any girl would be lucky to have you.' I could hear the heavy thudding of his feet on the stairs and the low rumble of his voice as the call presumably connected to Lauren.

I was itching to follow him and eavesdrop, but Sam knows me too well. He shook his head. 'Leave him,' he said. 'Let him come to us. He knows we're here.'

I crumpled into a chair. 'My poor boy,' I said sadly.

Sam was easing out his hamstrings. 'Is it OK if I still go for a run?' he said.

I nodded. Not because it was OK, but because I couldn't articulate why it wasn't.

-

Tom spent much of the remainder of the evening sat in his room with his headphones on while I fretted and paced the floor, occasionally making it halfway up the stairs to go and see him and then forcing myself to turn around and go back down. As Sam had said, our son knew where I was if he needed me. Lucky Tom didn't need his father, who was out pounding the damp pavement in his body lights and Lycra, headed God knew where. Still, I didn't sleep a wink that night, and it wasn't just because I felt like a boil-in-the-bag chicken. I simply couldn't switch off the internal monologue, this time flooded with thoughts of impending doom regarding my son's future relationships with women (as well as the usual climate concerns, health worries and random theme tunes from Eighties cartoon series).

By Thursday morning I was convinced that none of my children would ever meet people with whom they could have a meaningful relationship – which prompted me to phone Grace, who was in no mood for my bullshit (she didn't actually say that out loud, but she conveys an awful lot through nasal exhalations). Tom had come down to breakfast as usual and told us that he and Lauren had split up. Maisie said it was a bit annoying because Lauren had promised to do her a gel manicure, but then showed surprising empathy by spontaneously giving her older brother a brief but heartfelt hug.

'All of my friends think you're sublime,' she said earnestly. Maisie has been obsessed with the word 'sublime' since she watched the Barbie movie and heard Ken say it. She uses it liberally and often inappropriately. This time however I felt it was justified and gave her a fond squeeze around the shoulders before she told me that I was messing up her hair.

Grace when I phoned her was on her way to a lecture and in a rush. She did sound a little upset on Tom's behalf, but it's hard to fully engage in the relationship troubles of your younger siblings when you are forty miles away and absorbed in your own independent life. I've just about come to terms with the fact that my eldest daughter sees herself as separate from us now. This acceptance has been hard-won. For the whole of her first year at university I felt as though I had lost a limb. I wept uncontrollably from mid-September to mid-December and only managed to put my game face on a few days before she came home for Christmas. I even came close to seeing a counsellor – what I was experiencing felt like grief – but then Caz got her breast cancer diagnosis, and what felt like grief suddenly faded in the face of more pressing concerns about a condition that might result in the genuine bereavement of someone else I loved. Luckily, Caz made it through surgery and chemo like an absolute legend and is now in remission – which is code in this instance for 'out on the piss with her friends on a Friday night'.

We met at our usual haunt, The Cock, beloved pub of the village (read, the only pub in the village) and by half past nine we had covered the updates regarding Zahara's wedding (mainly a circular conversation about the merits of marquee receptions versus rustic barns), toasted the CQC rating for Bob's Place (because, as Joy said, a 'Good' is still a 'Good'), commiserated with Caz about her eldest son James still not understanding how a washing machine works, and moved on to the hot (flush) topic of the moment. As per usual, we were barely onto our third bottle of wine (between the four of us – we're not animals) before Joy and Zahara ended up in one of their rows about the menopause. The argument boils down to whether it's a medical condition that needs treatment or simply a phase of life to be celebrated and ameliorated using only mindfulness and herbs. It won't surprise you to know that Joy is in the former camp and Zahara firmly in the latter, with both women having strong opinions (although one of them is significantly more vocal about those opinions than the other – I'll leave you to work out who). Their conversation inevitably starts well but deteriorates rapidly into accusations of denying one's biological needs, propping up the pharmaceutical industry and ultimately enabling the patriarchy – so, you know, light and relaxing topics.

This time it was my fault. Without thinking, I mentioned last night's recurrence of the hot drowning that had kept me awake between one and three, and immediately I felt the beam of Joy's laser-focused attention fall upon my naivety.

'Have you got a prescription yet?' she said. The question was innocuous enough. Beside me Zahara stifled a tiny sigh, barely audible to anyone other than me.

'Uhh – no. Not yet,' I said. 'I'm still not sure whether...'

'It's really important that you get this sorted, Penny.' Joy's expression was set, her well-defined brows angled like a hawk about to swoop on the harmless vole that was me. 'Every day you're existing in this low-oestrogen state is another day of damage to your bones, your heart and your brain. You need to get your levels topped up – stay in the game.'

I could almost feel Zahara squirming in the seat beside me. She took a large gulp of her Sancerre, presumably in an effort to quench her own retort.

'I don't necessarily feel like I'm out of the game currently,' I said. 'I mean, I'm not entirely sure I was ever noticeably *in* the game. I'm just finding it hard to sleep, that's all. I don't have any symptoms during the day.'

'I find it utterly baffling that so many of my friends are happy to exist in this state of inertia about their own health,' said Joy, lifting her hands in the air. She didn't look baffled. She looked furious, like a teacher whose student has handed in a piece of inferior-quality homework. Not for the first time I imagined the life of an underling in Joy's business empire. The idea of having to report back to her on some minor error or human failing was enough to bring me out in a sweat of the existential rather than the hormonal variety.

'I'm in a state of inertia about most things, Joy,' I said affably. 'Nothing new there.' I don't rise to her provocation any more. I know it comes from a good place. She is genuinely worried about my bone density.

But Zahara could contain herself no longer. 'Not everybody needs HRT, Joy,' she said, her voice mild but firm. 'Menopause is no more a medical condition than puberty or pregnancy. We don't all need to be on patches for it.'

Joy pursed her lips, settling herself in for the familiar argument. 'But Penny *has* symptoms,' she said, gesturing to me as I shrank back in my seat. 'She's not sleeping. She's waking up in a pool of freezing sweat every night. Surely you wouldn't deny her treatment for that if it's available?'

'It's not every n…' I began, but Zahara cut in over me.

'I'm not saying I want Penny to feel unwell, Joy.' I could hear an edge creeping into my best friend's voice. 'But I also don't feel that she should be bullied into taking unnecessary chemicals if she doesn't need them.'

'Ladies, please don't weaponise me in this conversation,' I said, holding my hands up in the air. 'I'm not your pawn.'

Joy laughed. 'You're definitely not my porn,' she said. 'I can't speak for Zahara, but I generally prefer more cocks in mine.'

Caz spat her wine back into her glass, snorting her amusement as I almost choked on a roasted peanut. 'Jesus,' I said, my eyes streaming. 'I think it's stuck in my throat.'

Joy nodded sagely as she thumped me on the back. 'Yeah, they say that in most of my favourite films, too.'

By now Zahara was laughing along as well. Joy always does have a way of defusing tension, although to be fair, it's usually her who has ramped up the tension in the first place. And the pair of them were kind enough to wait until they were sure I'd fully recovered from the peanut incident before they relaunched the debate.

'Have you tried any of the plant oestrogens?' Zahara said as she poured me another glass of wine, most of mine having been used for the medicinal purpose of clearing my airway. 'I find that a combination of black cohosh and agnus castus fruit extract works for me.'

Joy rolled her eyes so hard I worried they might never return from the back of her skull. 'You sound like bloody Lindi,' she said, referring to one of the school mummies whose obsession with homoeopathy and all things alternative was bordering on cultish.

Zahara momentarily closed her eyes, taking a deep breath in through her nose and out through her mouth.

'Don't tell me,' said Joy, giving her a nudge. 'That was you practising mindfulness in order to neutralise the rage?'

Zahara's lips narrowed into a thin line for a moment and then she shrugged. 'Yes,' she said. 'It was. And no. It's not especially effective.'

Joy gave her a fond smile. 'It might be easier to just punch me in the face, babe?'

'Don't tempt me,' said Zahara, flicking a crisp in Joy's direction. 'Anyway, listen, we're supposed to be helping Penny. What did you do, Caz, when you had all those hot flushes starting the Tamoxifen?'

'Hmm?' Caz lifted the pub cat, Lardie, onto her lap and gave him an absent-minded stroke. 'I've just learnt to live with them I guess. I know I'm not allowed any oestrogen.'

'Well, obviously having breast cancer puts a different slant on it,' said Joy briskly. 'Although Dr Rodriguez says there are still some situations where targeted HRT is helpful even then.' She inclined one eyebrow.

'Definitely can't have it,' Caz said, still smiling. 'What with my genetic history. Doctor says no. To be honest, it's quite helpful having someone tell you exactly what to do now and again. Makes the whole thing a lot easier – if having half your family blighted by a cancer gene can be said to make anything easier.'

We all fell briefly silent at this, humbled as we often were by Caz's robust attitude. Although her surgery and subsequent chemotherapy had finished two years ago, it was easy to forget how difficult that period had been, and how cancer's long arm extends into the rest of your life even when you think you've 'beaten' it. Still, we knew better than to dwell on those darker days, and as is often the case, there were more women's health-related topics to cover before this night was through.

-

Much later on, when significant quantities of alcohol had been consumed and the remaining regulars had left the bar, pushed out by our noisy middle-aged cackling, no doubt, a curious expression crossed Caz's face.

'You know what you said about porn,' she said, as Zahara topped up Joy's glass with the dregs of the bottle.

'Yup.' Joy leaned back on her bar stool, swaying slightly. She didn't seem in the least bit perturbed by the non sequitur (we had been discussing the best garden shrubs for a clay soil).

'Do you watch a lot of it?'

Joy nodded. 'A fair amount,' she said. 'More than I used to.'

A small frown line creased Caz's forehead right between her luxuriantly regrown eyebrows. 'I can't imagine wanting to do anything less,' she said honestly. 'The idea of even having sex is pretty unappealing, but the idea of watching other people do it...' She grimaced. 'My libido's bombed in recent years. I don't know whether it's my hormones or just the fact that I'm so knackered the whole time. Nige says he doesn't mind, but...' She shrugged.

'Yeah, things have calmed down a bit between me and Raj nowadays,' said Zahara, reaching across Caz to pick at the remaining crisp fragments that were stuck to the shiny foil of the packet. 'It was all a bit crazy when we first met but, five years on, we're more of a once-a-week couple. And that once a week is usually the weekend when the kids are with Hugh. I still feel a bit odd shagging someone other than their father when they're in the house.'

I felt duty-bound to offer my own modest strike rate to the overall batting average (although I'm not entirely sure I've got this cricketing metaphor quite right). 'That's better than me and Sam,' I said. 'We're maybe once a month – or two months – it's usually just a question of whether we remember to get round to it. Bit like the PTA charity clothing collection.'

I didn't voice my vague fear that the reason for our dwindling bedroom activity might be related to the fact that my husband thought I was fat and no longer found me attractive. Instead I watched Joy take a thoughtful sip of her drink as Vince behind the bar tried desperately to pretend he wasn't eavesdropping. (We knew that what was discussed in The Cock stayed in The Cock though. It was like a Catholic confessional with Barman Vince our beery, chain-smoking priest and Landlady Mandy our stern Mother Superior.)

'We've got the opposite problem at home,' Joy said. 'My sex drive's gone through the roof now I'm on the testosterone gel. Simon can't really keep up. He does his best, poor love, but since he hit sixty he's not really into swinging from the chandeliers. More worried about slipping a disc than slipping me anything. Usually I have to take matters into my own hands, as it were.'

Vince promptly dropped a stack of beermats into the Boddingtons drip tray and I giggled in the way of a small child overhearing a grown-up saying a rude word. I'm well used to Joy's direct conversational approach on a myriad of topics, ranging from bowel habits to Brexit. But despite years of friendship, sometimes her naughtiness catches me unawares – and she's terribly easy to encourage. Now, for example, playing to her eager audience she lurched forward over the table, a smirk on her lips.

'In all seriousness,' she said quietly. 'Sometimes it's all I can think about. Simon took Evangeline to the theatre on Saturday for a matinee performance of *To Kill a Mockingbird* and I spent most of the afternoon masturbating furiously while watching the Star Wars original trilogy.' She cackled with laughter. 'I'm surprised I didn't do myself an injury. "Cause of death, my learned colleague?" "We believe the deceased wanked herself into a coma over Harrison Ford, Your Honour. She never regained consciousness." "Dear God, not another one. Hand Solo over Han Solo. Case dismissed."'

There was a moment's pause while Vince made an indeterminate noise behind the bar, and then Zahara spoke.

'Erm — I don't *think* that's how an inquest works, old chum,' she said, and we all fell about laughing.

Chapter Thirteen

Tuesday 14 February

Valentine's Day, and not a card in the house. Well, that's not strictly true. I did have a flyer through the door enquiring as to whether my gutters needed cleaning, but unless that's a particularly niche double entendre then my dreams of romance and passion are once again shattered. Sam and I have been married for twenty-three years now (which makes me feel absolutely ancient – I can definitely remember my parents' silver wedding anniversary and thinking at the time that they were a mere sniff away from death), and in the near quarter-century of our union, we've paid occasional attention to the appropriate celebrations and rituals – anniversaries of the day we met, when we got married, and of course, the consumer behemoth that is Valentine's Day. But it's not a big deal if someone forgets one of those. Not as if I was feeling sad and a little bit neglected this morning as my husband caught the early train for work without so much as a peck on the cheek. No siree.

More disturbing was coming home from Bob's Place yesterday to discover Tom feeding a teddy bear into the wood burner, his eyes blurry with tears (Tom's – although the bear's plastic eyes were a little foggy, what with the melting and all).

'Tom!' I screeched, just about managing to stop myself from adding, *what the fuck are you doing, you total arsonist?* I grabbed the weird iron prong things that usually sit redundant in the grate, serving no discernible purpose, and pulled the stuffed creature out onto the hearth just as its nylon fur began to smoke purple. (Maybe that's what those prongs were invented for – rescuing unwanted love tokens from their untimely cremation.)

'No point in keeping it.' Tom shrugged sadly as he watched the lumpen mess coagulate on the flagstones. 'I'd only bought it as a sort of joke – an ironic thing. We'd always said we wouldn't be one of those couples who gave each other lame presents on Valentine's Day. Now we're not even a *couple*.' His voice broke a little on the last word.

I sighed. 'I understand that you wanted to make a gesture with this,' I waved my hand in the general direction of the fireplace and the charred teddy bear, 'this – ceremonial burning. But setting the house on fire is not the way back into Lauren's heart.'

'I don't want to be back in her heart. I don't want to be anywhere *near* her,' he said, the sentiment somewhat belied by the sob at the end.

I put my arm around him. 'I just mean, maybe think these things through, Tommy, OK? Basic facts. The wood burner is for wood. Synthetic materials release noxious chemicals when they're on fire. You could have trashed the burner and poisoned the rest of the family into the bargain. Maybe next time you want to make a ritual sacrifice, give the teddy to Montmorency?'

He nodded miserably. 'Sorry, Mum,' he said, every inch the little boy of six who had broken the greenhouse window with his football. 'I was being stupid.'

I looked at him properly. There were dark circles under his eyes. 'Are you OK, Tom? I know you're sad, but are you managing? Like, with your schoolwork and keeping on top of things?'

I saw the hurt register in his expression. 'Schoolwork?' he said, incredulous. 'Give me a break. Is that all you and Dad are bothered about?' He shook his head in disappointment. 'I've split up with my *girlfriend*,' he said as he got to his feet and crossed to the door, emphasising the last word as if it was synonymous with 'wife of sixty years'.

'Yup,' I said quietly to myself after he'd left the room. 'We were aware of that fact.'

It would be hard for anyone in the family to have missed his suffering during the two weeks of separation from Lauren; even egocentric Maisie, who charged through life accompanied by the constant soundtrack of her own voice, had noticed that her brother was 'being a bit weird – like Miss Jackman when her house was burgled and Leon said she had a storker which is a bit like a heron but nastier and follows people around and makes them cry'. (Another one of Maisie's comments that required some unpicking.) And the reason for my gentle yet badly received enquiry as to whether Tom was OK, was that he did *not* seem to be on top of things. Initially, he'd missed two days of school pleading a sore throat, but since being restored to education he's been coming home from school and sitting glued to the Xbox for four or five hours at a time. No homework. No conversation. No slouching around the kitchen hunting for food and company. The lack of homework for two weeks isn't completely out of character, but the lack of foraging and engaging with other members of his family is. Tom is a social animal. He's nothing like Grace was as a teenager, confined to her room for days on end, semi-nocturnal, only observed at peculiar hours when she might scuttle across the landing to borrow your hairbrush before declaring it 'extra' or 'bougie' or something equally incomprehensible. Tom wasn't like that. Usually he'd stroll into whichever room someone was in, even if you were in the bath, and just stand there chatting away and spraying crumbs as he demolished a pork pie or half a loaf of bread. Except now he had taken a leaf out of the 'Grace Baker Aged Fifteen' playbook and turned it into his magnum opus.

I tried to speak to Sam about it last night, but he was so knackered by the time he returned from the gym that he crawled into bed and was asleep before I'd even got as far as 'so maybe you could have a little man-to-man chat about the importance of getting his life back on track, and...'

Instead I lay there beside my snoring husband, fuming and ruminating over the injustices of life, namely:

How could Lauren have dumped my lovely boy (this particular question has been on a perpetual loop in my brain)?

How long was it going to take for Tommy to pick himself back up?

What would happen if he didn't – would he become one of those resentful misogynist types?

How could I protect him from all the macho posturing bullshit I knew was out there on the internet – the cage-fighting, cigar-smoking, 'treat 'em mean, keep 'em keen' brigade, lying in wait, eager to drip poison into the unsuspecting ears of spurned young men with hurt feelings?

Why couldn't I stop scenario-building and cata-strophising?

Why couldn't Sam see that a conversation with his son was necessary and that he was the one who had to initiate it?

Why was Sam always either at work, or out running, or out at the gym, or literally doing any fucking thing other than being a husband and parent?

Why was I always so angry with Sam?

Why was I always so angry?

Why was the Peppa Pig theme tune in my head again?

However, insomnia, lack of Valentine's acknowledgement and general disappointments aside, today was a good day. The scent of spring was in the air as I drove across town in the mobility car (mid-February is too early for the scent of spring, but that's global warming for you), Mum was secured in the wheelchair behind me, wrapped snugly in her new coat which had arrived last week (and which she'd pretty much refused to be parted from since – money well spent, if you ask me), so I turned up the radio and we sang along to the tunes with the windows down and fresh air blasting through our lungs. We arrived at Bob's Place, the driveway lined with bluebells and late snow-drops peeking through the undergrowth at the base of the beech trees, and once we'd parked up I steered Mum into the lounge so she could have a chat with Edith, another inaugural member of the dementia choir, who has been with us since the care home opened. I then went through to the office (i.e. kitchen – you know this by now) to greet Tina and our newest member of staff (drum roll)... Joe!

Joe Devlin is our brand-new fundraising campaign manager, and he's hit the ground running. Veronica, Tina and I were pleasantly surprised by the shortlist of candidates who responded to our advert, and the interviews went well for almost everyone (apart from a chap called Malcolm, who made a point of telling us he didn't believe in social media and thought that branding was something you did to cattle). But Joe really shone from the moment he applied for the job. His CV was impeccable, with a background in fundraising for companies ranging from the Royal National Lifeboat Institution to Goreston Ladies' College. He also made a point of introducing himself to the residents, and to the clients who were attending the poetry session that day, and the questions he asked us about the operational side of things were insightful and intuitive from the start. Luckily he'd just finished on a large contract and was therefore available to start immediately (which, while not being the main reason we hired him, was still a definite bonus). Yesterday was his first day in post and today he'd already made me a cup of tea by the time I arrived in the kitchen.

'Thanks, Joe.' I took the mug and pulled up a chair at the table where Tina was sitting, chewing on a flapjack as she peered at the screen.

'I hope it's OK,' Joe said, his voice apprehensive as he tried to gauge Tina's reaction. 'I've been working on an outline strategy. Just pulling together some rough ideas. I thought it would help to make sure I'm heading off in the direction you're all happy with – checking we "share the same vision".' He made air quotes and pulled his face to indicate that while he was using corporate jargon, he was also appreciating that it sounded a bit wanky.

Tina was nodding as she read through his notes. 'You've put a lot of work in, Joe,' she said kindly. 'Penny, take a look.' She pushed the laptop over to me and I scrolled through the document. There was a comprehensive breakdown of our current situation – what Bob's Place stood for, the community we served, and also ideas for target groups, people who might be interested in investing in the company or being associated with the brand.

'It's pretty basic,' Joe said over my shoulder, 'and essentially it's just building on the excellent marketing work you've already done, Penny. Your brand is already well established, and that's testament to a really good initial strategy. I'm assuming you've got a lot of experience doing this sort of thing?'

'Oh, well, not much,' I said, my cheeks a bit pink with pride. 'Business studies degree many years ago, but nothing much since then.'

He looked impressed. 'Well, you've done a great job,' he said. 'It makes my life a lot easier in terms of fundraising if we have a clear underlying message.' He was looking directly at me, which was a little disconcerting. His eyes were a very dark shade of blue, I noticed. Almost navy. Like the deepest parts of the ocean. Anyway.

'I guess I always just thought, why make it complicated?' I said, gathering my thoughts like a normal human being. 'The simpler the message, the easier it is to establish the brand. I mean, we just want people to immediately associate Bob's Place with quality care. Everything else is…' I shrugged.

'A bit "extra",' he offered. 'Sorry, that's just what my kid says all the time.'

'Mine too! Everything's "sooo extra",' I said, and he laughed.

'Right up until it's "sooo lame",' he said.

'Exactly.' We smiled at each other. I remembered from his interview that he'd mentioned a teenage son. 'Anyway.' I returned to the screen. 'This looks really good – and I think it definitely chimes with our thoughts. Some of your ideas around events could work really well. When we first opened, I used to organise little concerts and things, quite small-scale, but they were fun. I just haven't really had the time over the past few years.'

'Well, you've got me now,' he said, still smiling his slightly wonky but also quite handsome smile. 'That's what I'm here for.' He turned to include Tina in the conversation. 'I'm thinking we probably want to have two parallel workstreams. Maybe a sort of background programme I can set up that just becomes business as usual: your coffee mornings, raffles, family quiz nights, that sort of thing. And then we maybe look at a bigger, standalone event – a ball, gala dinner, auction of promises, that sort of thing?'

'Or another concert?' I said. 'Just bigger?'

'Our choir is a big feature of Bob's Place,' said Tina. 'Penny's done an amazing job with the music programme. Seems sensible to capitalise on that somehow.'

'Absolutely,' he said, his eyes suddenly alight with excitement. 'A musical event would be great. We should think about more promo on various social media outlets too – a few reels on Instagram and Facebook featuring some of the activities...'

'You'll be asking us to post Edith's dance routines on TikTok next,' I said, sounding like I was ninety.

'You'd be surprised, but honestly, videos of pensioners go viral just as much as those ones of cats falling off radiators do.'

'Have you been trawling my internet history?' I said, and he laughed.

'Seriously,' he said. 'Your dementia choir – Tina showed me the recording of your first concert – that kind of thing could really play out well on YouTube, or even the dreaded TikTok.'

I gave a shudder. 'Every time I look at the home screen for that site, it's like a bad acid trip,' I said. 'Don't make me put pensioners on there.'

'I won't make you do *anything* you don't want to, Penny,' he said, his eyes meeting mine again. His mouth turned up at the corner and for a fraction of a second I felt a flicker of something in my stomach – something I hadn't felt for years. Was he flirting with me? But then he laughed in such a relaxed way I knew I'd been mistaken – that was workplace banter, if it had indeed been anything.

'Well, live video streaming aside,' I said, returning to the screen to cover my blushes, 'this is good work. Really comprehensive. I'm not sure how you found the time. You only started yesterday.'

He held his palms up. 'What can I say? I'm keen to get going. That, and I need to distract myself from bingeing episodes of *Below Deck* on Netflix of an evening.'

'Oh, God! Me too!' I said. 'Sam hates that show, so I'm always having to sneak episodes in when he's out at the gym – which is quite often, these days...' I trailed off, trying to remember the last time my husband and I had sat down to watch any form of television programme together.

Joe gave me a curious look. 'Well, I love it,' he said. 'It's my guilty pleasure – not that I think any pleasure should be a guilty one, really… Anyway.' He pointed towards the screen. 'I was thinking in terms of ongoing events. I could work up some ideas around the choir, but also the multitude of other activities we offer here at Bob's Place…'

I felt a bit conflicted by Joe's sudden ownership of the place in that sentence. He'd only been here for two days; who was he to describe it as 'ours'? But on the other hand, Bob's Place did inspire that sort of feeling in a person. And it was exactly that shared feeling of ownership, that sense of collaborative working, that we wanted to promote.

'Clearly our USP…' said Joe (*unique selling point* I mouthed to Tina over Joe's head. *I know*, she mouthed back). He gave us a quizzical look. 'Our USP is the fact that this is a collective exercise,' he continued. 'You treat your clients like guests. And you treat them like adults. When I used to go and visit my aunt in her nursing home, I hated the way she was infantilised. It was all "Maggie's really enjoyed her ice cream today, haven't you, love?" or "Maggie's been a bit naughty, wandering off again," in a disappointed parent tone. And the staff were always talking to the family members, the people who paid the bills, like they were in charge. They didn't include the residents in their decision-making – even when the decisions were about them. You guys don't do that. It's one of the first things I noticed when I came for the interview. You treat people with respect – and dignity.'

'I don't know as it is always terribly dignified,' I said, thinking of Irene, one of our residents, who liked to flash her knickers at the plumber whenever he came to fix the boiler, but inwardly I was beaming. Joe saw the heart of Bob's Place. I knew we'd been right to hire him. Tina was smiling too.

'So, if you're in agreement, I'll carry on working through these ideas this week. Get some plans in place for a larger event, maybe over the summer?' He looked at me again. 'It makes sense, Penny, if you and I work pretty closely together on this. I don't want to add to the rest of your workload, which is significant, but given your experience with both marketing and running previous events, I expect I'll need to tap into your expertise fairly regularly.'

'Sure,' I said, feeling purposeful and important. 'Whatever you need.'

'And I don't want to tread on your toes,' he said, those blue eyes latching onto mine. 'I really want this to work out, so if I'm doing anything you're not absolutely happy with, just say.'

'Oh – yes, OK,' I said, stuttering a little for some reason. There was something about the way Joe phrased things that seemed to imply a subtext, but maybe that was just me overthinking it.

'And we need our focus to always be on the brand,' he concluded, shutting the laptop down decisively and smiling at us both. 'Nothing fancy – just knowing our USP and threading it through all of our fundraising events, all our media coverage, whether that be mainstream or social media. It all has to come down to our core message – Bob's Place is different: it provides exceptional care with the resident at its heart.'

'Certainly sounds better than Tina's original tagline when we first opened the place,' I said.

'Hey!' She laughed. 'I thought it was quite catchy.'

'Her initial suggestion,' I said, gesturing to encompass an imaginary sign, 'was "Bob's Place – you don't have to be mad to visit here, but it helps".'

Joe looked momentarily horrified and then his face collapsed into laughter. 'OK,' he said. 'I think I can probably improve on that.'

–

He promised to come back to us with a definitive plan by the end of the week. Given the fact that he's part-time (he does freelance consultancy projects for the remainder), I feel a bit bad about how many hours he's already spent on this, but I guess it's up to him – he knows we can't pay him any extra. He says he'd prefer to get the job done properly even if it means going over his contracted time, and he seems to be enjoying it. It's early days, but I'm glad we've got him on board. We needed some new blood, and it makes a change to have a man around; alters the dynamic, in a good way. Because Joe doesn't seem to be one of those blokes who throws his weight around. He knows that Tina, Veronica and I are in charge, and he seems entirely comfortable with that – no toxic masculinity or 'grumpy little boy' complex noted so far.

And if he was complimenting me earlier, or possibly even flirting – well, what's the harm? It's a world away from the response I get from most men nowadays. I've hit that age that people describe in hushed tones – the one where you become invisible to the opposite sex. And much as I previously dismissed it as 'old lady nonsense', I can see now that this shit is real. Most men *really* don't see me any more. Their eyes simply glaze over while they wait for the young, hot totty to arrive. It's not like I was ever what old geezers would describe as a page three stunner, but I had, up until recently, been of reproductive age (technically speaking – I'm not sure as I would have been enormously happy about being pregnant at forty-five, but it was at least theoretically possible), and it seems that in this world where we are defined by the male gaze, fertility is key. Maybe it's the pheromones, maybe it's the fact that my face has caved in on itself or that my body has ballooned, I don't know. But when I went to the garage to get the car looked at last week (the second time I've had to go back because that sump sure ain't fixed), the young lad taking my details genuinely didn't seem to register my presence.

I'm used to being dismissed, familiar with the patronising, 'Have you asked your husband about the car, love? Does he know you're out here alone with his credit card?' schtick. But what I'm not used to is being invisible. And if I told myself that this particular mechanic was just a bit socially inept, and that maybe he was like this with everyone, my theory was roundly disproved when I saw his response to the next customers, a middle-aged man followed by a woman in her thirties. Neither of them was on the receiving end of what you'd call spectacular service, but their presence at least registered. They didn't have to resort to a comical hopping about in order to achieve eye contact. They didn't have the mechanic walk off halfway through their explanation of the problem, or answer his phone while they were describing the odd clanking noise the car makes when changing gear. No. They were seen. I was not.

And so, as I say. If working alongside Joe for a few hours a week makes me feel a bit more visible, where's the harm? He's a colleague. He's going to do a great job, I have no doubt about that, and he puts a smile on mine and Tina's faces. I know a great many young, attractive women who have been hired for a lot less.

Chapter Fourteen

Tuesday 21 February

Pancake Day today, and at Bob's Place there was quite the carnival atmosphere. While we don't tend to go big on Lent, feeling that losing one's cognitive function is penance enough for anyone, we do try to make the most of other national celebrations and festivals. And the Festival of the Pancake is particularly jolly. We don't encourage our more frail and elderly clients to have too much contact with hot oil and cast-iron cookware, but many of our residents and day guests are pretty handy with a frying pan, and by the end of the session almost everyone has had a go at flipping a measure of batter, even if the end result looks less like a French crepe and more like something the cat threw up. Derek used to work as a sous-chef in a high-end London restaurant, and has been known to flip pancakes in both hands simultaneously, whereas Dolly, a retired sports teacher, usually tries to break her own annual record for number of flips in a single toss (I believe those are the correct technical terms in the world of pancake-making).

It's a chance for everyone to let off a bit of steam, and even the most withdrawn of our residents enjoy the end result: a mid-morning snack garnished with lemon and sugar (or anything the eater wants, really; we've had some strange requests over the years, and we generally try to accommodate) and made using batter according to Tina's secret recipe. It is almost foolproof (I say almost, because whenever I take the batter mix home and try to fry it up in my own pan it becomes fairly evident that a culinary fool is perfectly capable of ballsing up the entire enterprise), and I found today's session particularly therapeutic as Mum and I lobbed batter into the air. I was feeling the need for a bit of aggressive flipping because Sam and I had had another minor disagreement last night when I discovered that he had signed up for a triathlon in Scotland over the summer.

'It's a sponsored one,' he said, thrusting the laptop under my nose to show me the completed enrolment form. 'And it's a high standard of competition – more of an iron man, really. Look, you can see the different event categories – I think I'd have a good chance in the senior section as it's fifty to sixty, so I'd be younger than the majority. And the training schedule looks manageable.'

'Hmmm.' I managed to convey limited enthusiasm without saying an outright no.

'I was thinking maybe I could raise money for a dementia charity,' he said, pleased with himself for being so thoughtful.

There was silence for a moment as I digested this. 'That's a nice idea, love,' I said eventually. I peered at the screen, mainly to buy myself time and modulate my voice because I didn't really want to let on how irritated I was about what seemed to be an entirely self-indulgent suggestion, charity or no charity. 'Uhm, so it's over a long weekend?'

He nodded, still smiling widely.

'And, probably a day to travel up and another to travel back?' I said. 'So, five days total? Presumably you'd be paying for accommodation while you're there?'

He nodded, the smile faltering slightly. 'And the entrance fee,' he said. 'I'd have to pay that as well.' He angled the screen back towards himself so I couldn't scroll down to check out the likely exorbitant cost of almost killing yourself through exhaustion and/or drowning.

'And how much training would you need to do for it?'

'Uhm – probably quite a bit…' His panicked expression meant he knew he was trapped. 'I mean, it is a really significant physical challenge, Pen. There's no point in asking for sponsorship for just a little run.'

'No. I can imagine,' I said.

'So – I'd need to put the work in.'

'And just to clarify, that "work" would take you away from the house, away from me and the kids, for significant periods of time?'

'Yes, but although I wouldn't be *here*, I'd be doing it for *you*, sort of. For your mum? For Bob's Place, maybe?'

'That's really kind of you, darling,' I said, keeping my voice neutral. 'I can really see how this is going to benefit me.'

He didn't pick up on the sarcasm. 'Yeah, and I thought maybe if I did well in this one then I could look at competing in the Norseman, maybe next year.' He opened up another tab on the laptop to show me. 'It's in Norway. You jump off the back of a ferry into an ice lake and then swim…'

'Norway?' I said faintly.

'You have to be selected,' he said, the excitement palpable. 'There's no way I'd get in now, but maybe after the Lochside Challenge, if I did well, who knows?'

'Who knows,' I repeated. 'Certainly not me.'

'So, it's OK that I've signed up then, yeah? It's the end of July.'

'You've already signed up,' I said. 'This "asking my opinion" is merely a formality, then?'

He faltered. 'I thought you'd be excited about it,' he said. 'Because of the sponsorship.'

'Well, maybe you thought wrong,' I said, finally snapping. 'The prospect of you disappearing for days on end, risking injury and possible death in order to indulge your hobby, fills me with horror, quite frankly. And Bob's Place won't benefit because we're not a charity. I don't think you've necessarily thought this through, Sam.'

He was predictably crestfallen, and a part of me felt bad for raining on his parade, but honestly, he wasn't a child. He was a grown-up fifty-year-old man who seemed to require a sort of boarding school house sports competition in order to achieve meaning in his life, while the rest of us had to just get on with the daily grind. As midlife crises went, an iron man triathlon wasn't the worst, but to dress this event up as some sort of treat for me was a bit much.

'Well,' he said, 'I've signed up for it now, whether you support me or not.' He pulled a classic grumpy face, one that I'd seen Tom wearing a lot in recent times. His parting shot was about me going away for Zahara's hen weekend next month, and how that would probably cost a similar amount, but that was obviously *fine* because it was *my* thing.

'I am well aware that my going away for Zahara's hen *night* is an indulgence, Sam,' I said, stressing the singular. 'And that's why I asked you about it first, checked we could afford it and made plans for you and the kids for when I'm away. You'll be pleased to know that I do not

135

need to take additional evenings and weekends out of our packed schedule in order to train for a hen party, and neither would I dream of pretending that the weekend will somehow be of benefit for you. I acknowledge that this is something I want to do and that you are being kind in facilitating this for me. But let's just contrast that with how you've presented the Lochside Off-road Challenge, shall we? Can you see the difference? Hmmm?'

He stomped off and a few moments later I heard the front door slam as he slid out into the night, doubtless to begin the first of many tests of endurance, both his and mine.

I mentioned it to Tina this morning while we were preparing the batter. I say mentioned, when really I meant 'ranted for half an hour'.

'It's just so annoying,' I said, furiously beating the eggs together in the stainless steel bowl. 'And it's just such a masculine thing to do — indulge your hobby and ask people to pay you for the privilege. I don't ask people to sponsor me to read novels, do I? I don't say, "Hey, how about you give a hundred pounds to a charity of my choosing every time I go to the bloody cinema with my friends," do I?'

'No, you don't, Penny,' said Tina gently as she stilled my hands and picked some eggshell out of the mix.

'And I don't expect everyone to bend over backwards to accommodate me, not just bend over backwards, but actively cheer me on, despite the fact that this activity is going to cause enormous disruption, and it's bloody dangerous, and...' I trailed off, aware that Joe had entered the kitchen. Slagging off one's husband in front of the new, attractive male member of staff was pretty poor form (slagging him off to Tina was completely standard).

'What's bloody dangerous?' Joe said, all warm smiles and nice-smelling aftershave. 'Are you talking about you with an egg whisk, because you look pretty lethal to me.'

I laughed despite myself. 'Nothing,' I said. 'Just whingeing. Although some of this conversation relates to you.'

'It does?' said Joe.

'It does?' said Tina.

'Yes. I was wondering whether we should look again at charitable status for Bob's Place. Someone I know is hoping to raise money for a dementia charity and he had suggested donating here, which obviously isn't currently possible, and I think maybe we need to revisit the decision we made when we first set up the business. Given your fundraising expertise you must have worked with many charities, I thought you'd be in a good position to advise.'

'Yeah,' he said. 'Absolutely. Can I ask why you didn't consider it at the outset? Did all the paperwork put you off? I know it does with some businesses.'

'A bit,' said Tina. 'When we were getting started we had the legacy money and I guess it already felt like we had the benefits of a charity, just one that had received a massive donation up front. Veronica looked into it, and we didn't really seem to gain financially from charitable status at that point. There were other issues with it, weren't there?' She turned to me.

'It just seemed like a real ball-ache, to be honest,' I said. 'Loads of regulatory pressures, mountains of paperwork and no flexibility once you've been approved. When we first opened we didn't really know what Bob's Place was going to become, how it was going to develop. It was all a bit of a leap of faith. And I think we were worried that committing ourselves to our early governing statement might have restricted us in terms of how we could grow the business – we maybe wouldn't have been able to start offering residential care, for example.'

'Ahh, OK, yeah.' Joe nodded. 'Makes sense. I know other organisations I've worked for have felt the same. But the parameters have changed now?'

I nodded. 'I think so. We're more defined as a business structure, and I think our governing statement wouldn't change radically from this point. Also,' I grimaced, 'our initial "massive donation", the legacy fund, has pretty much been spent.' I wasn't sure how much of our current financial difficulties to reveal to Joe – he was our employee, and a fairly new one at that. But on the other hand, he needed to understand the dire situation we were in if he was going to be able to help us. 'Let's just say it's no longer massive,' I said. 'We really need to start attracting charitable donations. And we need the tax breaks, the gift aid, all of that.'

'Understood,' he said. 'I'm very happy to look into it for you. It sort of falls within my remit, and as you say, I've worked for both types of organisation. I can maybe present the options and see what you as the executive board decide?'

'That would be really helpful, Joe,' said Tina. 'As long as you're sure it doesn't interfere too much with the fundraising itself?'

'Of course,' he said. 'I'll make sure it doesn't. And to be honest, I think making a decision about charitable status might influence the kind of fundraising options you want to consider. I understand the initial reservations but as you say, the landscape has changed, and this would mean we could tap into other revenue streams. There are a lot of corporate options, big players who like to be seen to be helping various philanthropic endeavours. And while dementia isn't a particularly sexy subject, the rise of dementia choirs such as your Singing for the Brain one, has given it some traction.' He paused. 'Sorry, I'm running away with myself.'

'No, no, honestly. It's great,' I said, genuinely impressed. 'I like the fact that you're thinking so broadly.'

'Yes,' agreed Tina. 'This is exactly what Veronica meant – a fresh pair of eyes on the situation really helps. We're happy to be open-minded.'

He looked relieved. 'Oh, that's really good to hear,' he said. 'Sometimes clients can be quite wedded to the status quo, especially when there's a personal investment like there is with Bob's Place.'

'Luckily I'm not *that* wedded to Status Quo,' I said. 'Other than "Rockin' All Over the World", obviously.'

'Well, quite,' he said, laughing. 'And who wouldn't be?'

Chapter Fifteen

Sam and I didn't really discuss the triathlon again. It has just become an unspoken given thing. He's doing it. I'm a bit annoyed about it. He's hurt by my lack of support. There we are.

On a more positive note, the conversation about charitable status has proved to be really productive. Even though Joe's done all the legwork himself, he still refers to it as 'Penny's idea' – which is particularly gratifying in the world of business, where women's suggestions are almost always snaffled up by men who then present them as their own. He shared all his findings in a very professional presentation and gave us a breakdown of the factual data without trying to influence us one way or the other. The possible downsides of becoming a registered charity remain, but the benefits now seem to far outweigh them, and we voted unanimously to go ahead with the application. Joe says he's happy to fill in all the appropriate paperwork, and once we're happy with the governing statements, he can go through the details to make sure we're compliant with the various requirements. As he pointed out, I've already got my hands full on the compliance side of things, what with reviewing every single bloody element of Lorraine Rowbotham's CQC report and trying to make sure we jump through every one of her hoops like some kind of deranged care-providing acrobat. Luckily there's a lot of overlap, so Joe and I have been able to work closely, merging different policy documents so that they hopefully please both Lorraine and the charity registration board.

I had wondered, after such a long time working as a tight little team of three, whether the arrival of someone new within the management structure would rock the boat, or whether I would find it hard to work with someone other than Tina and Veronica. But Joe is just very easy to be around. He's committed to the project, and brings boundless energy to each element of what might otherwise be quite dry subject matter (recruitment guidelines and medicine management policies, for example). And each time we get a bit bogged down with the CQC or charitable trust application, he'll suggest we break and look at ideas for events instead (which is much more fun). He's also very good at thinking laterally – asking about the range of outbuildings on site and whether we have ever thought about renting them out, either to private therapists or linked businesses. His idea to run a café from the old stable building has real potential, and I could see Tina flicking through recipe books for ideas before he'd even finished talking.

He doesn't always get it right. I'm not entirely convinced by some of his other ideas, particularly the choir sponsorship. The first company he approached were continence aid manufacturers who wanted the singers to wear T-shirts that said: 'Don't Let Bladder Weakness Stop Your Power Ballad', which seemed questionable, although better than the pharmaceutical company specialising in enemas who offered to pay for a new conservatory if we put up posters emblazoned with 'Rectoblast – Regular Motions are Music to Our Ears' – which we all felt was a bit too graphic. But he takes our feedback on board, he listens, changes course when needed and shuts down the options we don't like without any grumble of discontent. He has managed to completely overhaul our website (under the guise of adding a separate events page), which now looks much more professional, and the increase in the dementia choir's online presence through various social media channels has definitely boosted interest. Once we're a charity we can start looking much more widely – Joe's been talking about second-hand clothing shops, online auctions and even sponsorship sites where people (like my husband) who want to run a marathon, abseil down the Grand Canyon, jump into a den of starving tigers or simply hold a nice fundraising coffee morning can do so while raising money for Bob's Place.

Speaking of coffee mornings, today was my very last Mother's Day breakfast. Hopefully not the last time I ever eat breakfast on Mother's Day (that would be a particularly specific and ineffective diet regime), but the last one at St John's Primary School attending in my capacity as a parent. When I add up the number of years I've been coming to celebration assemblies, Easter bonnet parades, nativity plays, sports days, PTA fundraisers and indeed Mother's Day breakfasts held here, I think I should probably have my own bronze plaque on the wall – or perhaps a comfy armchair with my name emblazoned across it. Seventeen years of continuous unbroken service from me and St John's. For that entire period of time there has been at least one little Baker in attendance, and for all key events, that one little Baker has been accompanied by me.

While every year is scattered with milestones, this one in particular reads like a catalogue of parenting finality. We've already had the last nativity play. Maisie was in the chorus of villagers because, to be fair, nobody wants to see an eleven-year-old Mary – they want a four-year-old Mary with a slight lisp, one who looks angelic and does something unspeakably cute like offering the baby Jesus to her daddy in the audience, or sweetly chastising Joseph for falling over the donkey. Year six are always relegated to choral duty at Christmas, and there they stand, looming over the reception year like ancient oaks in a field of tiny saplings – unspeakably cool and world-weary, eye-rolling hard as they chant their way through 'God Rest Ye Merry Gentlemen'.

Similarly, the Mother's Day breakfast presents differing challenges according to the age of the child one is currently mothering. When Maisie was in reception (feels like the blink of an eye – albeit a lazy eye) the goal was to get through the class rendition of 'I Love My Mum' without anyone bursting into tears (grown-ups or children) or wetting themselves (mainly children). 'I Love My Mum' is a song primarily designed to cause maximum distress to both performers and audience as rows of terrified four-year-olds (accompanied by Mrs North and Mrs Mabuse on percussion) stumble their way through lyrics like 'I love my mum and she loves me – more than I'll ever know. She gave me life, she cares for me – she is my superherooo', while gazing in fixed adoration, not at their mums but at Miss Arnold, the reception teacher, who is mouthing the lyrics with the exaggerated action of a sign language interpreter at a rock concert. The whole thing is emotionally exhausting and leaves everyone feeling like they need a lie-down. Even Mrs North has been known to weep copiously over her glockenspiel, and a few years ago one of the teaching assistants was crying so hard she fell off her chair.

By year one we progress to artwork, and watery-eyed mothers are presented with Cubist-style portraiture of the highest standard. Here the challenge is not taking visible offence at how you've been portrayed (because nobody, not one single person, has ever looked at a portrait of themselves painted by a five-year-old and thought, yeah, I look pretty hot). Spider eyes with colossal spikes of eyelash bleeding down purple cheeks, tiny foreheads, crazy clouds of hair, huge balloon noses, leering grins, crooked boulder teeth and fierce monobrows all feature, and all have to be met with a delighted smile and effusive praise for the little Picasso. An additional challenge comes through keeping a straight face while observing the other mothers' valiant efforts to look pleased at their poster-paint like-nesses. I distinctly remember having to look away to avoid pissing myself laughing when Tiggy, one of the uber-mummies, was presented with a picture of what looked like an eighty-year-old man, her daughter beaming with delight as Tiggy took in the balding head, hairy nose and bushy grey moustache adorning a portrait clearly labelled 'My Mum', just in case there had been any doubt. Even Lindi (Tiggy's subordinate uber-mum chum) had allowed herself a tiny smirk as Tiggy slid the painting under her chair, face down 'to keep it safe, darling'.

Year two brings the poetry — rhyming couplets composed by six-year-olds to express their innermost thoughts and the extent of their filial love. My particular favourite being Zahara's son Rex delivering the immortal lines: 'My mum can use a rake. My mum laughs like a snake', which we all felt was a lovely sentiment. Year three is craft (clay coil pots that have invariably broken into separate grey rings by the time you get home but *maybe you could wear them as bracelets, Mummy?*) and the year four students have the dubious honour of a talent show, where they are given the opportunity to perform short sketches of their own composition. Inevitably there will be a small army of little girls doing what is loosely referred to as 'gymnastic routines'. These involve kamikaze roly-polys, human pyramids that topple precariously close to the audience, and usually at least one child losing their temper because Amber was supposed to catch her legs in the handstand but instead stood there paralysed with fear as Molly's feet sailed past her ears. There are also several children playing pieces on the piano or vocally murdering current chart hits in the musical section, at least one boy doing keepie-uppies with a football and a couple of confident nine-year-old wags performing a comedy sketch about farts.

But by years five and six the children are deemed old enough to actually help with the eponymous breakfast itself, and so it was that Zahara, Joy and I were met at the entrance to the school hall by Darcy, Evangeline and Maisie, who ushered us to our table complete with jam jar of wildflowers (mainly dandelions), paper roll tablecloth, melamine plates and teeny-tiny chairs. Caz wasn't with us – she no longer has any kids at primary school – her youngest, Alex, is in Tom's year, and her eldest, James, has just 'left home' to start an apprenticeship without actually leaving home because it's just too bloody expensive to rent anywhere. Zahara's son Rex is at secondary school, and once Darcy leaves St John's at the end of the year she, like me and Joy, will have no children left in primary education. However, seven-year-old Summer (the result of Hugh's affair with Nadia) will still be here, and given that Zahara has pretty much appointed herself unofficial stepmum fairy godmother to her ex-husband's offspring, it's likely that her involvement with the school will continue (indefinitely, perhaps, as Hugh continues to hump his way round the county like an uncastrated dog, impregnating everything in his wake). Today, for example, Zahara was having to leave immediately after her croissant to go and watch Summer, currently in year two, recite her Mother's Day poem because Nadia was at work and didn't want Summer to feel left out by not having a mother present during the reading.

This of course highlights the other main challenge of the Mother's Day breakfast. It's a lovely event for the school to run but it does, as is so often the case, penalise the mums who work full-time. I know that Caz often had to miss the breakfasts when her boys were at St John's because she couldn't get someone else to cover her shift. Joy has more control over her timetable, being one of the chief execs in her company, but she would argue that the reason she is still at the top of the tree is precisely because she didn't take days off willy-nilly to sit on small chairs eating stale patisserie. Having said that, I think she was determined not to miss this final Mother's Day breakfast. It's not that Evangeline isn't perfectly capable of striding through her school life sans parental input – she'd most likely be ambivalent about Joy's presence at any school event – but on this occasion even Joy is a bit sentimental.

'Well, it's the last time we'll do this, ladies,' she said as we took our tiny chairs and perched our buttocks uncomfortably upon their rigid plastic. She dabbed at a sticky patch on the tabletop. 'Is this jam?'

'Stickiness in a primary school setting could literally be anything,' said an acerbic Mrs North, gliding past on her way to the canteen. 'I would not suggest any further investigation, Mrs Rossi.'

'Understood.' Joy withdrew her hand sharpish – she knows the score. Mrs North is the absolute undisputed boss within the walls of St John's, and if there is one thing that Joy respects it's a defined power structure with a woman at the helm.

'Girls,' Mrs North called imperiously over her shoulder. 'Have you taken the orders for your table yet?'

'There are still some people missing,' said Evangeline, gesturing to the empty seats. 'You said to wait for the year five mums before we took the orders.'

Mrs North nodded graciously. 'You are right, Eva. I did say that. Good of you to remember. I think some of them might have been held up at the PTA bookstall.'

Joy beamed proudly at her daughter for knowing the correct protocol (and being fearless enough to call Mrs North out on it).

'I wonder who's manning the stall this morning,' said Zahara, folding her hands in her lap (the easiest way to heed Mrs North's advice about avoiding table stickiness). 'I thought maybe I should offer to lend a hand.'

'Oh God, no,' said Joy, rolling her eyes. 'The best thing about the kids leaving primary school is not having to help out at PTA events ever again.'

'Joy, you were never actually *on* the PTA,' I reminded her.

'No – too bloody right,' she said. 'It was bad enough hearing you lot banging on about it. God help me if I ever have to spend another night out on the beers worrying about who's in charge of bringing the float for the fete or who had forgotten to book the circus performers or how many raffle tickets had been sold. You've both done your time. You especially, Penny. There should probably be some sort of lifetime achievement award for those who've put in a decade or more. Like a Victoria Cross. Anyway, everyone knows that year six mums are exempt from PTA duty.'

'Hmmm.' Zahara didn't seem convinced. 'I'll take a little look on my way over to Summer's poetry reading,' she said quietly, and then glanced in the direction of the entrance door. 'I wonder which year five mums are on our tab... Oh.'

It was clear from her expression, without me even needing to turn in my chair, that the year five mums soon to be joining us were none other than Tiggy and Lindi, led by their youngest offspring, Rhiannon and Aurora respectively.

'Hello, ladies!' Tiggy greeted us with a brittle smile as she scanned the rest of the room surreptitiously. 'Are you certain we're on this table, darling?' she enquired of her daughter. 'I felt sure that Mrs North said we'd be sitting with Tabitha Gray and Annabelle Green?'

'The year six and year five parents have to sit mixed up,' said Eva sternly. 'So you can, like, mingle and stuff.' Her voice, like that of her mother's, brooked no room for discussion.

'Wonderful,' said Tiggy, pulling up a tiny chair. 'Your daughter's very' (slight pause) '*confident*, isn't she?' she said to Joy.

'Thank you,' said Joy, well aware that Tiggy hadn't intended this as a compliment. 'I think it's very important for girls to feel able to speak up.' She arched an eyebrow.

'So that they can grow into strong young women who know their own minds.'

Joy was the only person I'd ever met who could return serve with Tiggy, and observing the rare occasions that these two women came into each other's orbit was both highly entertaining and excruciatingly tense. I could feel Zahara next to me almost bubbling over with the need to pour emollient on the situation.

'Well, this is exciting, isn't it?' she said once the girls had squabbled over taking our orders, all of them eventually conceding to Eva's natural authority as she was the one wielding the notepad and pencil.

'I don't know about exciting,' said Lindi ominously. 'A communal breakfast is more like Russian roulette for us, given Aurora's allergies.'

'Oh, that's a shame,' I said. 'Have you asked whether she can be excused from handling the food?' Aurora had clearly inherited the non-specific multiple food intolerances of her sister Chloe – allergies that had been diagnosed by a naturopath but never confirmed by an actual doctor, and that astonishingly seemed to vanish as soon as Chloe reached secondary school and was able to choose her own food.

'I have, Penny.' Lindi sighed heavily. 'But I don't want her to feel ostracised from her peer group. It's very important that school activities are inclusive of those with special needs and not just geared towards the dieticonormative majority.'

'Dieticonormative?' I said as Joy coughed *bullshit diagnosis* quite indiscreetly.

Lindi didn't hear her. 'Thankfully her symptoms don't appear to be triggered by skin contact,' she said. 'It's purely related to ingestion. I've given her some pulsatilla and bioflavonoids earlier. That should provide her with some degree of protection against the various toxins in the croissants.'

'Oh, so she *is* able to eat them then?'

'Yes – as long as she's careful.'

'Does she have an EpiPen?' I asked, a little alarmed that we may be required to deal with a full-on paediatric anaphylaxis.

Lindi looked horrified. 'No, Penny – I wouldn't want her injecting anything like that into her system. They're full of heavy metals like mercury and aluminium.'

'And the doctor said she didn't need one,' Tiggy interjected, 'because she's never had a confirmed reaction to anything.'

Lindi rolled her eyes. 'Well, that's doctors for you,' she said.

Luckily the children returned with our breakfasts before Lindi could expound on any more of her conspiracy theories.

'You can give them the pastries,' said Eva authoritatively to the two younger girls. 'We'll do the hot drinks. Mrs North said year fives are not allowed to touch the coffee pot.'

Tiggy's daughter Rhiannon looked as though she might be about to protest, but one glance from Eva and she closed her mouth.

'Well, you've done a super job, girls,' I said as the teapot slid worryingly close to the edge of Eva's tray. I lifted it off. 'Shall I pour?'

'Yes, Mummy, you pour,' said Maisie, clearly feeling that Eva was hogging the year six limelight. 'Do you want your croissant?'

'Uhm – well, I haven't had a chance to...'

'It's just that the teachers said we can have anything our mums don't finish,' she said, eyeing up the baked goods that had barely been on my plate for fifteen seconds.

'It's hard, isn't it, Penny,' said Tiggy with a little moue of concern, 'teaching them about healthy choices and controlling their appetite. I always say to Rhiannon, you don't want to end up getting fat like Mummy!' She laughed as she plucked at an invisible inch of flesh on her skinny thigh.

'But you're not fat,' said Maisie.

Tiggy gave a tinkling laugh. 'And *that's* because I know when to stop eating,' she said, jokily poking her finger towards my daughter. She turned to me, and I swear she was staring at my waistline that was admittedly bulging slightly over my jeans. 'It's all about setting an example, isn't it?'

I opened my mouth to say something, but Joy beat me to it. She'd had a brush with anorexia in her twenties and was particularly sensitive to this kind of conversation (insofar as she was sensitive about anything).

'I think it's an absolute tragedy that we allow our girls to be body shamed before they've even hit their teens,' she said. 'It's no wonder we have such high rates of depression and anxiety among our young adults when we indoctrinate them with these completely unreasonable and unachievable standards from such an early age. We should be teaching them how to eat healthily. Not how to be thin.'

Tiggy looked as though someone had slapped her. 'Well, of course that's what I meant,' she said huffily. 'We're terribly body-positive in our house. We all enjoy Lizzo's music, and think she's so brave for…'

Joy stared her down and Tiggy didn't dare continue. The girls all stood around watching closely – aware that a power play was unfolding but not sure where their allegiances lay, or whether it would affect their chances of scoring pastries.

'So, because we're body-positive, does that mean I can have your raisin swirl?' Eva said innocently.

'Nice try,' said Joy as she took a bite out of her pastry. 'But no. This is a Mother's Day breakfast, Evangeline, and I am your mother.'

Eva rolled her eyes. 'Yeah – like I don't *know* that,' she said under her breath. Maisie giggled and the group of them strode off, the year five girls in the wake of the year sixes.

'You just wait, ladies,' said Joy to Tiggy and Lindi. 'By this time next year your two will have hit the tweens. And suddenly they'll have more attitude than a group of militant Climate Crusaders – no offence, Penny.'

'None taken,' I said, although internally I was cursing her. Why give Tiggy any more ammo?

'Climate Crusaders?' she piped up, evidently relieved to have Joy's critical beam shifted away for a moment. 'You're not a part of that, are you, Penny? I never had you down as the supergluing-yourself-to-motorway-bridges type.'

'Not me,' I said wearily. 'Grace. My eldest. I don't know whether you remember her, Tiggy? She's at uni now, but she was here at St John's ten years ago, maybe when your Reuben was in reception?'

Tiggy shook her head. 'Goodness, no,' she said. 'I can barely remember anything that far back. How funny, Penny, to think that you've got a daughter that old!'

'Hmm. Hilarious,' I said.

'And she's the militant one, is she?' Tiggy wasn't about to be deflected from this new development.

'Well, I don't know, she – she has strong views on a few things. And I'm very proud of her for that.'

'But you don't condone the tactics they're using? These climate protesters. I mean, I'm all for the environment and everything, but John was queuing on the motorway for four hours on his way back from orchestra rehearsal in London a few weeks ago. Did I mention that Reuben was performing at the Albert Hall in the spring?'

'No,' I said brightly (about to employ your basic parenting diversionary tactic). 'That sounds amazing. Is he still enjoying the trumpet?'

Tiggy proceeded to witter on about Reuben's prodigious talent, all thoughts of my ancient and likely criminal twenty-year-old daughter forgotten. I always felt on much safer territory when discussing Tiggy's children and their various achievements, but to be fair, I also had a great deal of respect for the musically gifted, whatever their parentage. Music had been a release for me in my youth, and I knew how much comfort came from ridding oneself of teenage angst in the form of singing or playing an instrument. And from what I'd heard, Reuben had a fair bit of teenage angst to rid himself of. One imagines with a mother like Tiggy you'd need to blast out some aggressive top notes on the brass every now and again.

'Will he be there around the same time as the French spelling bee finals?' Lindi asked Tiggy politely. 'We found out yesterday that Chloe got through.'

It was like watching two professional card sharps, each one making an opening bid and then taking turns to trump each other. Of course the outcome was always the same, but as long as Tiggy ended up with the winning hand, everyone was happy and the earth remained on its natural axis.

'Oh, that's lovely news,' said Tiggy, all bonhomie and warmth for her friend. 'Of course, Reuben never really took to French. Being virtually fluent in Spanish he never felt the need, and you know what boys are like!' She rolled her eyes in my direction, as if Tom was the gold standard of lazy boy behaviour.

'Do you think your girls will pursue languages?' Lindi asked the three of us. 'Because if they do it might be worth getting some additional tutoring in over the school holidays. They stream for most of the subjects from year seven.'

'Eva won't need to worry at Goreston Ladies' College,' said Joy dismissively. 'The amount we're paying in fees, I'd be pretty pissed off if she needed additional tuition.'

'She's going to Goreston?' said Tiggy, her mouth gaping open with envy for a moment before she remembered to close it.

'Yes. Simon and I felt she'd benefit from the smaller class size. And academic standards are far higher in single-sex schools.' Joy spoke with the certainty of one who has a bit of cash and only one child to send through private education.

'Well, I think it's terribly important that my children go to a mixed-sex school,' said Tiggy, immediately taking back the moral high ground. 'And also that they experience life outside the rarefied atmosphere of a private school.'

'So, we're both happy then,' said Joy.

'Yes,' said Tiggy through thin lips, arms folded across her scrawny bosom. 'Very happy indeed.'

Zahara and I glanced at each other. Although neither of us had discussed it, I suspected that she shared my feelings about Eva's education. I wasn't entirely convinced that Goreston would play to her strengths and she struck me as the kind of child who needed a bigger playing field, quite literally.

Either way, it was nothing to do with us. I'd already warned Maisie that Eva was likely to feel nervous about going to a different school to her friends, and that as a result she might resort to escalating levels of showing off. This advice has been borne out – Maisie asked me only last week whether Goreston really did have its own on-site cinema complex and water park as per Eva's latest proclamation (Joy later confirmed that there was a widescreen television used for nature documentaries and a large pond).

'It's funny, isn't it,' Zahara mused, dabbing at her remaining flakes of croissant. 'They're such a tight little unit at the moment, these kids of ours, aware of each other's foibles and failings. They know who's good at maths and who's scared of spiders, whose parents drive which car and where everyone in the class goes on holiday. And they all know their teachers so well. And it's all going to change.' Her mouth turned down slightly at the corners.

'Oh, Zee,' I said, patting her knee sympathetically. 'I remember when Grace first started secondary school and she couldn't get her head around the fact that her subject teachers didn't know her at all. She came home in tears that first day. Although that was partly because she lost her bus pass and her lunch money.'

'Well, I think it's great that they're all coming of age,' said Joy. 'It's a chance to reinvent yourself, isn't it, secondary school. Same as university. I bet you've seen it with Grace, Penny. That transition, child to teen to adult – it's exciting to see who they become, isn't it?'

'Kind of,' I said. 'But it is also a bit sad that they don't need you any more. You lose that sense of being continually involved in their lives – ultimately you just *see* less of them.'

'I read somewhere recently that by the time your child reaches the age of twelve you've already spent seventy-five per cent of the time you're ever going to spend in their company,' said Tiggy, unable to stop herself interjecting. 'And that when they reach eighteen, you've hit ninety per cent.'

'Thanks for that, Tiggy,' I said. 'I feel loads better now.'

We all inadvertently glanced across the hall to where our girls were gathering plates and carrying trays piled high with pastries and hot coffee. They were still so little, still just practising being grown-ups, but it wouldn't be for long. And I knew that better than my friends.

–

I thought about this later as I walked back from school, the spring sunshine bright in my face and the pollen count high in my nose (the only reason my eyes were watering, thank you very much, nothing to do with being a bit emotional). There was only Caz in our immediate circle who understood the strange semi-bereavement of a child leaving home, and for her the situation had been so emotionally charged, given her ongoing treatment, that the 'eldest son moving out' grand gesture had been somewhat lost, not least because James had been studying at a tech college nearby and had moved back home about a week after term started. Nobody else in our group of friends had a child of twenty who lived in another part of the country. And nobody else fully understood the permanent sense of disconnection, always feeling as if you'd left something really important behind but couldn't remember what or where. The only other significant woman in my life was my sister-in-law Candice, and she was a long way off worrying about children leaving home. Her immediate concerns were how to get some sleep and how to get some bloody sleep – I remembered those days well.

No. The one person I knew who would understand, the one person who had been through the same experience, who knew how it felt to be a mother watching your children grow up, leave home and make families of their own, would have been my mum. She could have helped me navigate this emotional terrain – in fact, she would have insisted on being there to support me through this. She'd be able to say, 'It's all going to be fine, Penny, dear. You'll look back on this and feel proud of the human beings you made, and I can guarantee you'll experience fulfilment and happiness in other ways. I have been there. I know what you're going through.' And I'd believe her because she's my mum.

Trouble is, Mum can't tell me it will all be all right – she can't even articulate how she feels about yesterday's lunch, let alone share insights regarding her emotional experience of thirty years ago. And that loss feels particularly acute at times like this. My relationships at both ends of the family age spectrum are changing, becoming more fragile. Sometimes it feels as though I am a tree whose roots have withered prematurely with Mum's dementia. The thing that has kept me tethered to the earth has weakened, leaving me vulnerable to the winds of change. And now that tree is losing its branches as they snap off and head out into the wide world. Pretty soon there'll be nothing left of me but a trunk. As I said to Sam when he came back from his run and found me in tears over my protracted metaphor this evening, 'I'm just a log, Sam! Just a rotting log covered in moss and mushrooms, waiting to decay!'

Fair play to the man; this statement made no sense whatsoever and I'd given him absolutely no context for it, but he hugged me and told me he was sure I'd be a lovely log nonetheless.

Chapter Sixteen

Sunday 19 March

Mother's Day

Mothering Sunday was upon us, and in the traditional manner of the season I awoke to the sounds of Sam pulling on his knee support and running shoes.

'Morning,' he whispered. 'Didn't want to wake you. Just popping out for a quick 5K.'

I grunted attractively and rolled over in bed, hoping to get back to sleep. Last night had been another one of those disrupted by hot sweats, and I knew I'd spend the rest of the day feeling exhausted as a result. I made a mental note to go and see the GP to discuss it. I couldn't think of the last time I'd been to see a doctor about anything concerning my own health; it was always either the kids or Mum, but I really did need to start being proactive – just as soon as I'd sorted out everyone else.

An hour later I was awoken by a combination of Sam's return, the dog barking (why Sam hadn't taken Montmorency out on a run with him was anybody's guess – something about interrupting his running flow) and Maisie enquiring whether I would like toast as part of my breakfast in bed. She told me she was organising it *all* and I was left in no doubt that this would be a significant undertaking. I warily agreed, while knowing that breakfast in bed invariably means crumbs in the sheets and stressing over potential spillages, no matter how careful you try to be. As predicted, twenty minutes later I was sat bolt upright, a tray precariously balanced on the hilltop of my duvet-clad knees while I scooped soggy cereal into my mouth and sipped at a lukewarm cup of stewed tea. Still, it was a lovely thought and I thanked Maisie profusely. She wasn't to know that I hated Marmite on my toast. Or that I didn't take any sugar in my tea, let alone three spoonfuls.

I had a homemade (school-made) card from Maisie ('probably the last one I'll ever make you,' she said cheerfully as she handed it over), and when Tom finally woke up he and Sam disappeared on a trip to the supermarket shrouded in mystery, only to return half an hour later very pleased with themselves as they presented me with a bunch of wilting carnations and box of half-price chocolates that had passed their sell-by date. By this time Grace had phoned.

'Did you get the e-greeting thing?' she said. 'I couldn't justify going down the dead tree traditional card offering, but I wanted you to know I was thinking of you. Happy Mother's Day.'

'Thanks, darling,' I said. 'That means a lot.'

We proceeded to discuss the usual weekly topics: how her course was going, how close she was to finishing (or perhaps starting) her dissertation, whether she had any ideas about future job prospects when her degree ended in two months' time ('God, like, I know! All right, Mum! Stop stressing me out!'). I also managed to inject some cool parent banter around her current love interest, Claude, gender unknown (I'm sure you can imagine quite how cool I was), and asked the routine questions about drugs, alcohol, cigarettes, vaping, Rohypnol and other date rape products ('because there's things they can just inject you with now, Gracie – you could be standing up at the bar one minute and tied up in the back of someone's van the next'). She loves these chats, my daughter. I can tell from the lengthy pauses and deep, steadying breaths she takes between my questions.

I wasn't sure whether to mention my concerns about Tom being so down, but when I'd last spoken to Sam about it he'd been fairly dismissive, and although I knew my daughter was perfectly capable of the same reaction, I just wanted another female opinion on the subject.

'Grace, have you heard anything from Tom?' I said. 'I'm just a bit worried about him.'

'Since he split up from whatsername? No, nothing. Probably even less than usual, actually. I sent him a message about four weeks ago saying sorry to hear he'd been dumped. I did sort of imply that it was astonishing he'd ever had a girlfriend in the first place, given the fact that he's a complete nobber...'

'Oh, Grace!'

'No, but that's completely standard chat for us, so I was surprised he didn't reply.'

I told her about the roasted teddy bear on Valentine's Day and about him becoming more withdrawn. 'You know how he'll usually follow you around the house just to have some company?' I said.

'God, yeah.'

'Well, he just shuts himself in his room now. We barely see him.' I paused. 'I miss him,' I said, a little forlorn-sounding. I only just managed to stop myself adding, 'I miss you, too.'

'Oh, Mum,' she said. 'Don't worry. He'll be back to his usual idiot self before you know it. I'll talk to him, OK?

Don't worry about it, please. Especially not on Mother's Day. Enjoy yourself, yeah?'

'Oh, OK,' I said, surprised. I didn't normally receive this sort of instruction from Grace. 'Thanks, darling. And thank you for your, er, e-greeting.'

'No problem. I'll try and pop home sometime in the next few weeks. There's a demo on Saturday, but I could maybe get the train over after that?'

'OK,' I said, feeling that panicky sadness I always got at the end of one of our calls. 'That would be lovely. I love you, Gracie. So much.'

–

For lunch we took my parents to the local carvery, which freed me up from cooking. I bought Mum a new cashmere scarf and a patterned cardigan. I know from experience that it's easier to get her into front-opening garments than over-the-head ones (she gets a bit distressed when her face is stuck in the neck hole and she can't see anything – understandable) but her current wardrobe, aside from her coat, is very functional, all fleeces and elasticated-waist joggers, and I wanted her to have something pretty. She spent so much of her life before the dementia enjoying fashion and making herself look nice, it's important (to me at least) that we keep some semblance of the person I hope she still is inside. In the same spirit, when we'd finished our colossal but surprisingly lacklustre roast, we returned to my parents' house and I painted Mum's nails with the new varnish I'd bought. She tolerated it fairly well, only wincing occasionally when I got the emery board out.

By the evening I was starting to feel the sleepiness that comes with daytime drinking (if you can't have a bottle of warm Chablis with your pork and gravy on Mother's Day, then when can you?) so I sat on the sofa eating my chocolates and scrolling through my phone in unintentional imitation of my children. First was my e-greeting from Grace, which was a series of dancing characters with the faces of all my children copied and pasted to look as though they were singing 'Dancing Queen'. It was actually pretty funny – Grace knows my sense of humour and the fact that it veers towards the lame end of the spectrum. Next I made the mistake of glancing at Facebook, and was sucked into the vortex of Tiggy and Lindi's daily musings. Tiggy's is usually the best account if one wants to laugh at some of the delusional bollocks she comes out with – she is an enormous oversharer, posting on a regular basis about her wonderful life. Lindi is more circumspect – I think she uses social media to engage with the alternative lifestyle community more than to show off (although there's a fair bit of that too). Both had been on excellent form since Friday's school breakfast. Tiggy's post from that morning showed an angelic Rhiannon posing with a plate of pastries, accompanied by the comment: *Mother's Day Breakfast at St John's Primary – our lovely local village school. So glad that both my children have access to the best state education rather than propping up elitist institutions #KeepingItReal #Education #SchoolOfLife #KeepClassOutOfTheClassroom.* Nice, I thought to myself. I'll have to alert Joy to that not-so-subtle dig.

Today's posts were less political and infinitely more nauseating. A photo of Rhiannon and a sulky-looking Reuben dressed in their Sunday best with the caption, *Off to church #MotheringSunday #MothersDayService.* This was followed by several close-ups of the posies of flowers they'd clearly been given in church with a comment,

Flowers for all the mums in church today, and then my two angels offered to distribute posies to the women in the village without children, so they didn't feel left out! (blushing with pride emoji) *#SoThoughtful #CountingMyBlessings #Flowers #ChildlessWomen #BarrenButNotForgotten* (I did properly laugh out loud at the last one).

It didn't end there. We were treated to several shots of the gifts Tiggy had received from her *#SoGenerous* offspring and the Mother's Day lunch they had allegedly prepared unassisted – although the julienne of vegetables looked suspiciously like the prepackaged version from Waitrose, and the foil tray holding the baked Alaska dessert was just visible peeking over the rim of an earthen-ware pot Reuben was holding in his gauntlet-clad hands (*#ThisBoyCanCook*). Finally, we were treated to a photo of the queen herself: Tiggy, buffed, filtered and high-lighted and flanked by her two children *#LittleDarlings #SoLucky #MumsLife #TheGreatestGift #Motherhood*. As always, Tiggy's husband didn't feature in a single post. It seems he's just not photogenic enough.

Lindi's page had a single post from Friday (photo of the pastries with the hashtags *#GlutenFreeMums #Stop-SulphitesInSchools #AllergyActivism* and *#Dieticonormative* (which she's clearly determined to see trending), and then a post from today with a fairly standard photo of Aurora and Chloe looking anaemic and murderous respectively (*#MyBeautifulGirls #MustTakeAfterTheirMother* laughing emoji). Joy had posted some GIF about gin and periods, which I liked, and Zahara hadn't posted anything because she's essentially a normal human being who rarely treads the Facebook boards.

I have also not posted for many months (I'm more of a skulker than a poster), but Sam has taken to recording daily photos of his training schedule, which I'm sure is a delight for all those out there who live to see sweaty fifty-year-old men in Lycra looking like they're on the cusp of a cardiac arrest. There are links to his charity donation page ('Sam's Dementia Challenge – Part One: The Highlands', which makes it sound as though he is personally planning on wrestling the disease into submission and throwing it off a Munro peak, while also making it clear that he plans to take on more epic challenges in far-flung locations) and regular updates on his nutritional intake, vital statistics, steps taken and calories burned. It's enough to make you feel exhausted just looking at it.

I did give the page an obligatory like, but couldn't bring myself to add a *#SoProud*. I'm not *#SoProud*. I'm *#QuitePissedOff* while also aware that this makes me *#SoUnreasonable*. As soon as we'd returned from the carvery (where he'd made such specific requests regarding his roast dinner as to make it virtually inedible, while also sitting there piously with an empty plate as the rest of us tucked into crumble and custard for pudding), he went out for a 10K run. I'd seen him briefly as he made himself a protein shake before throwing his sweaty clothes in a pile on the bedroom floor. He then showered and emerged wearing a different Lycra outfit (this time with built-in wired support, a corset for the modern man) and went straight to the garage to lift weights, which apparently warranted grunting so loudly that it made Montmorency bark (not that it takes much, granted). By the time I'd put the second load of washing on (smelly gym kit is no respecter of Mother's Day), emptied the tumble dryer of the first load and cleaned the kitchen, I was knackered, so I hauled myself off to bed and left him to it.

Chapter Seventeen

Monday 20 March

This morning was the usual crazy rush to get everybody ready for school, work and, in the case of the dog, another day of sleeping, barking, farting and general destruction. I was keen to got to Bob's Place because Joe and I were currently researching options for an Easter family fun day and a pop-up charity shop, and there was a lot for us to discuss. However, the fun day and pop-up shop would have to wait because Maisie's hair needed immediate attention. She had slept in plaits, hoping to awaken with a perfectly crimped set of curls, but unfortunately one side had rucked up and stuck to her face overnight. It was now as matted as the pelt of a long-dead animal and stuck together with some gloopy substance that she eventually admitted she'd pinched out of Grace's bedroom thinking it was a hair product. I genuinely dread to think what she might have uncovered, but I put my game face on and set to work with a gallon of conditioning detangler spray and a heavy-duty brush. Sadly during this intensive rescue mission I discovered more than I had bargained for, specifically more wildlife than I'd bargained for. Maisie had nits. Not just a couple but a whole community encompassing all the generational stages of nittery from juvenile egg to hefty adult – the population of lice looked to be moments away from significant infrastructure and developing a functional democracy. I retrieved the fine-toothed comb from the upstairs cabinet and mined Maisie's scalp until I was confident the majority of the buggers were out, before tying her hair into a firm plait, pinning it to her head and making her promise that she wouldn't sit too close to anyone at school today. I then looked at my watch. Trouble was, if Maisie had nits then it was likely the rest of the family did.

'Tom,' I said, approaching my son gingerly. 'Has your head been itchy at all?'

He looked at me, nonplussed. 'What?'

I brandished the comb. 'I'm going to have to check your hair, dude,' I said. 'Sorry. Nits in the house.'

He gave me a look laden with tragic despair, but I had no time for teen boy drama today.

'Sit down,' I said, pulling out a chair. 'There's no way I can reach your head way up there.'

Thankfully Tom's head seemed to be lice-free – I guess locking yourself away in your room and avoiding all contact with your family has some advantages – but he evidently found the intrusion on his personal space unbearable, wincing and yelping with pain every time I so much as glanced the comb in his general direction.

'I can't help feeling that Maisie bore that a bit more stoically,' I said, holding the comb up to the ceiling light to check for any signs of life. 'I'll buy some of the shampoo today and we'll all need to use it this evening. *None shall be spared from the cull.*' I'd put on an ominous tone hoping to make him laugh, but no joy.

He nodded, as if this confirmed all his worst suspicions about life, slung his bag on his shoulder and loped out of the house, slamming the door behind him without so much as a kiss goodbye.

Maisie raised her eyebrows as far as her tight hairline allowed. 'Tom's sooo moody at the moment,' she said. 'And he doesn't even have nits! Is he still doing puberty?'

'Maybe.' I bustled her into her coat and gathered her belongings.

'Will I be like that?' she said. 'When I get boobs and everything. Will it make me grumpy?'

'The boobs themselves don't make you grumpy,' I said. 'Most of the time. But some of the other stuff can.'

'Periods.' She nodded wisely as she picked up her rucksack. 'Scarlett Jackson started hers last week and Mrs North said she didn't have to do PE *or* canteen clear-up. I can't wait to start mine.'

'Hmmm. Careful what you wish for, darling.' I wrestled Montmorency into his halter lead and we set off into the torrential rain and gale-force winds of a March morning.

Once I'd dropped Maisie and walked Montmorency (I use the term walked in the loosest sense, given the weather; it was more of a sprint home dragging the dog and an inverted umbrella behind me), I collected Mum for choir practice.

'How was your lamb yesterday?' I asked Dad as we manoeuvred Mum into the wheelchair. 'I thought they'd overdone the pork a bit but the pudding was lovely, wasn't it?'

'What?' he gave me a distracted look, wincing slightly as he straightened up.

'Have you hurt your back?' I asked.

'No, no,' he said. 'It's nothing. You get along now.'

'Da-ad,' I said, using my highly effective warning tone (admittedly I rarely needed to use it on my father). 'What is it? What's happened?'

He shook his head, clearly irritated at having been caught out. 'Oh, no, nothing,' he said. 'Just something silly. Your mum had a bit of a wobble last night when I was trying to help her into bed. She sort of slid out of her chair and was on the floor before I could catch her.'

I put my hand to my mouth. 'Oh, God! Was she OK? Are you OK?'

'Pfft.' He waved his hand dismissively at me. 'It's fine. She was fine. Not bothered at all, were you, Mary love?' He raised his voice for Mum's benefit and she stared blankly back at him. 'I managed to get her back up eventually. No harm done.'

'You should have called us. Sam would have helped. He was already lifting weights in the garage – you could have added to his workout, Mum!' My tone was more jovial than I felt. I could see from Dad's face that he was in some discomfort and that the events of last night had been more stressful than he was letting on. But in true Dad fashion he wouldn't let me question him further.

'It's all fine,' he said. 'Don't fuss. Now, you two need to get on. Your mother's been so excited about singing today, haven't you, Mary?' He beamed at her as she gazed into the distance of the corner of the sitting room.

'It's pretty wet out there, Mum.' I wheeled her towards the door.

'Finland,' she said.

'No. We're not going to Finland. We're going to Bob's.'

'Bob's,' she said. 'Hmmm. Yes.'

–

Joe was in the kitchen working on the website when we arrived. He informed me that Tina had just gone to the bank but would be back in an hour. 'I said I'd cover until you got here,' he said. 'Maggie and Dinesh are both on shift, so I thought it'd probably be… Are you all right?'

I opened my mouth to utter the usual *yes, fine*, but then shut it again and before I knew it a tear had squeaked its way down my cheek. Joe went to put an arm around me, thought better of it and put the kettle on instead.

'I wasn't sure whether a hug would be – uhm – you know, appropriate,' he said when he returned to the table with a box of tissues he'd found on the windowsill. 'But tea's always appropriate, so I thought that would be safe territory.'

I snorted a little laugh through my nose. 'Sorry,' I said. 'I'm – I'm uhm…'

'Take your time,' he said. 'Here if you need me, and all that.' He went back to the kitchen counter and plated up two slices of Tina's lemon drizzle cake. 'She told me I could start it before she left,' he said, gesturing to the cake in case I thought he was taking liberties.

'Thanks.' I took a mouthful and dabbed my eyes with the tissue. 'I'm sorry,' I said. 'It's nothing really. It's just my mum. Well – it's her and Dad. I'm not sure how he's coping, and he's too stoic to give us the full picture, but she's getting worse and… and he needs more help, and…' I trailed off. 'I just don't know what to do.'

Joe listened quietly as I warbled on in this circular fashion for about ten minutes (probably felt like hours to him). I ended up telling him about Mum's initial diagnosis and how she's deteriorated since then, how I feel like I've almost lost her completely, how it's a slow, tortuous bereavement that nobody else really understands, and how now my worry is transferring back onto Dad in much the same way as it did when Mum first came to stay with us.

'He broke his hip,' I said, between mouthfuls of my second slice of cake (Joe had very nobly indicated I could have his piece). 'And then he had a stroke on the operating table while they were repairing it. So Mum came to live with us for six months. It was quite the eye-opener, as you can imagine. I had no idea what living with someone affected by dementia was like because Dad had done such a convincing job of brave-facing it.'

'Jesus. That must have been really tough,' said Joe, chin resting in the palm of his hand as he listened to my tale of woe. I caught myself thinking that it was nice to have someone's full attention for a change. It's extremely rare for Sam or the kids to hang on my every word at home, and even when I'm out with the girls there's usually someone who's got a funny story to tell or a morsel of gossip to offer up. We all love each other, but we're also aware of our place in the conversational queue and often itching to share our own anecdotes from the week, or interject with a differing opinion. Sam often comments on the parallel conversations I have with Joy, Caz and Zahara and the fact that they all occur simultaneously. We speak over each other but seemingly manage to success-fully communicate significant amounts of information, despite our conversation sounding like a massive cloud of pointless noise to an outside observer. Anyway, it was nice to be listened to and I took full advantage.

'He made a full recovery, my dad, in true *Commanding Officer Gordon Andrews*-style, but it still took it out of him. He's never been quite the same. And now he's seven years older, but he's still trying to provide the majority of care for a woman who is barely mobile and who, when she is up on her feet, can fall forward, backward or sideways without a moment's notice. Well, you've seen what she's like when I bring her in for sessions.'

Joe nodded but he didn't seem in any desperate hurry to interrupt my flow, so I carried on.

'We do have carers coming in to help get her washed and dressed in the morning – although it was like pulling teeth to even get him to accept that help – but everything else falls to Dad: feeding her, getting her to bed, all of the – you know – *personal care*.' I blushed a bit at this point, which is most unlike me. 'I just think it's too much for a man nearing eighty to cope with, physically or emotionally.'

'And what happens when you talk to your dad about it? About your worries?' Joe's voice was kind, his expression enquiring, as if he was genuinely interested in the complicated knots of my wider family dynamic. Again I was struck by how rarely I had this amount of unimpeded air time and attention.

'He's – uhm – he hates the conversation,' I said, bluntly. 'He just makes it really obvious that he'd rather not talk about it. So you end up having to be the bully, force the issue, knowing it makes him uncomfortable. It's not fun.'

'And does Rory help?'

I was surprised that Joe remembered Rory's name. I'd only mentioned him in passing. 'Yes, Rory's quite effective at the bullying tactic when required,' I said with a watery smile. 'But he's got young kids – you know – there's a lot on his plate at the moment.'

'And there isn't a lot on your plate?' Joe looked at me pointedly. 'C'mon, Penny, you've just told me that you took on the role of full-time carer for your mum when she came to live with you, and by my reckoning you had two kids at school and probably a preschooler to contend with at that point in your life. Where was your brother then?'

'In Australia,' I said quickly. 'But that wasn't his fault. And he's been much more helpful since he and Candice moved back to the UK.' There's always that perverse part of you that needs to defend a sibling, irrespective of what an arse he is. Despite the numerous times I've wailed and gnashed my teeth about Rory's pompous ineptitude, I couldn't let anyone else imply that he was anything other than perfect.

'Yes, but part of that help should be taking some of the burden of worry off your shoulders,' said Joe, not unreasonably. 'Does he live nearby?'

'About an hour away. But he's a doctor and his hours are erratic. He works really hard...'

'I'm sure he does. But presumably his being a doctor means he's really well-placed to have these conversations with your dad?'

I nodded. 'Yes.'

'Sooo,' Joe said slowly. 'You need to get him on board. Assuming he agrees about your dad not coping?'

'He does. We talked about it a couple of months ago.'

'And did anything happen as a result of that conversation?'

'No.' I sighed. 'That's the trouble with Mum's dementia – the situation evolves so slowly that each time there's a flashpoint and you think, right, we *must* do something, then a few more weeks go by and you find that you *haven't* done anything, but nothing's really changed. It was the same when we were trying to stop her driving – there would be an incident in the car, something minor, just losing her way to the supermarket or forgetting where the indicator was, and I'd think, shit, maybe she's not safe to drive any more, but then time would pass and she'd get from A to B without incident and I'd let myself forget about it. Until it came up again.'

'And presumably you eventually managed to stop her driving?'

'Yes. In the end it was easier than we thought – Dad just made sure he drove everywhere and eventually she stopped asking. No dramatic showdown like some people have. Certainly, listening to some of the stories from the residents here I think we got off pretty lightly.'

'And your dad was on board with that decision – to stop her driving? So there must be a way of getting him to acknowledge this new deterioration? Ideally with the same non-dramatic resolution? The times I've seen him here with Mary he seems like a practical guy – someone who you maybe need to present things to in a factual manner, who maybe responds better to logical argument than emotion.'

I laughed. 'Absolutely. You've pretty much nailed him there.'

'So, you just need to come up with a few evidenced points to illustrate why you're concerned.' He ticked them off on his fingers. 'One, last night's fall where he hurt his back by lifting her. Two, whatever it was that triggered the conversation with Rory a few months ago. Three, I don't know, whether the carers have mentioned anything?'

'God, yes, Steffi said only last week that they might need to get a hoist in and that the agency would recommend having two carers for lifting. Dad's been taking on the role of second carer up until now, but I get the impression that the girls are starting to worry about the safety of that scenario.'

'Exactly. OK, so you've got your evidence-based argument that there's a problem. Now you need to present him with possible solutions. One, get more care at home, like, pay for two carers each visit, more visits, whatever. Two, look at increasing your mum's respite stays here – I know you said she's had the occasional overnight stay, but maybe you want to look at a week – suggest your dad has a proper break? Three, considering more permanent residential care...'

'Shit, you are really good at this,' I said, slightly awed by this methodical breakdown of what I considered to be a highly emotive topic.

'Thank you.' His cheeks went a bit pink. 'I guess encouraging people to do things is one of the main parts of my job. Usually it's putting their hand in their pocket for a good cause, but I'm fairly accomplished at persuasive language.'

'You are!' I laughed. 'You could probably talk me into doing anything!'

There was a peculiarly charged silence for a moment before Joe cleared his throat. 'Yes, well, anyway – does that give you a starting point, of sorts?'

I stood to clear away our plates. 'It does,' I said. 'It really does. Thank you so much. For listening, and for coming up with a plan of action.'

'Well,' he said, smiling. 'I love it when a plan comes together.' He mimed puffing on a large cigar, Hannibal Smith-style.

'I still ain't gettin' on no plane, fool,' I said, responding in my best B. A. Baracus voice, which gratifyingly he laughed at. When I try and do impressions at home the kids just look at me like I've lost my mind – although, to be fair, none of them have watched *The A-Team*. 'Anyway.

We need to crack on with some work. I feel like I've been banging on for hours about my domestic situation.'

'You haven't,' he said, clicking on the keyboard of his laptop to reopen the tab. 'Do you want to see what I was doing just before you got here?'

I nudged my chair up against his and peered at the document in my usual long-sighted-but-in-denial way.

'I've been thinking,' he said, 'about building on the amazing musical offering here at Bob's Place. That, and the concerts and events you've already held. Like we discussed.' He glanced across at me to check I was happy. 'And I think that we should go much, much bigger this year. Really open it up. Big venue. Big city. We could look at Birmingham if London's just too expensive, although we might get more investment if we stick to the capital... I'm thinking choir performance followed by gala dinner, followed by auction. It would be a lot in a single night, but if we made sure we had some corporate sponsorship for the event itself, we could keep the ticket price fairly reasonable so it doesn't stop your average punter from attending. Then hopefully we make money out of the high-rollers during the auction.'

'Are we likely to have many *high-rollers* in attendance?' I said, raising an eyebrow.

'Sorry. That sounded a bit grannyish. You know what I mean, though. Big spenders. And yes, I think we can definitely get some very wealthy firms to buy up a table or two. As you've pointed out, dementia is an almost universal experience. It's touched countless people's lives and it's not a disease of the poor, it doesn't discriminate. There's a lot of rich people out there who feel as desperate about the disease as the rest of us normals. And they want to do something, they want to spend their money on something good and worthwhile.' He paused, putting on an angelic smile. 'And that's where I come in.'

'With your persuasive language,' I said.

'I'm pretty well-connected, as it goes.'

'Are you now?' I laughed. 'OK, Joe Devlin, friend to the rich and famous. Sounds like a great plan. What do you need from us, from me, to get this going?'

'Not too much. Don't worry, I can sort all of the logistics. I can target the sponsors, all those bits.'

'That's a relief,' I said.

'But what I can't do...' He regarded me gravely. 'Is anything remotely musical. I am tone-deaf. My singing voice makes children cry and small animals run for shelter. The idea of formulating a musical programme, of choosing songs and working out the right running order, of marshalling the residents here into a cohesive, melodic chorus – well, the very thought of it brings me out in hives.'

'Whereas that's the bit I absolutely love,' I said. 'It's like, one of my favourite things to do, get our brilliant choir geared up for a big performance.'

'And that,' he said decisively, shutting the laptop, 'is why we're the perfect team.'

Chapter Eighteen

Wednesday 22 March

Joe and I discussed his idea with Tina and Veronica yesterday, and they are happy for us to proceed with the gala performance and auction. The plan is definitely ambitious but somehow Joe makes it feel achievable. I'd never be confident enough to pull off an event this size without having a nervous breakdown, but I guess this is what we were paying him for – to think big. And it's nice to have an exciting project to look forward to. The CQC compliance work is tedious box-ticking, and for me, the sheer volume of pointless bureaucracy was in danger of taking the shine off being at Bob's Place. Likewise, the charity status application would have further added to the 'trapped in an office' feeling that the three of us had so long strived to avoid. But Joe has been as good as his word. He can't do the CQC stuff, that has to be me, but he's taken the charity paperwork completely off our hands, keeping us updated and copying us in to all correspondence while ensuring that every form is completed, every email responded to and each requested document sent in a timely fashion.

As a result, after a few hours of clinical governance and policy review each morning (I make sure I do the really dull stuff first), I can get on with choir practice and working on the running order for the musical perform-ance. About half the choir members are day centre clients and half are residential, so when Fizz is here for the formal singing sessions, or our music therapist Aleesha is here for the Rhythm and Movement class, we can pull together a larger chorus. But between these times I can lead smaller group sessions. Today, for example, I brought all of our altos and sopranos together in the drawing room studio for a freestyle session, playing a whole range of tunes and encouraging our day clients and long-stay residents to sing along to whatever took their fancy. Some songs have a much wider appeal, unsurprisingly, and it's really important for the quality of the final performance that our choir actually enjoy singing the songs we end up with. I've made the mistake before of choosing a set list with the audience in mind, as you might do with a more conventional choir or band. Our choir is anything but conventional, and the result of this poor planning was a group of disinterested pensioners staring at the walls and refusing to join in, or simply singing the song of their choice over the top of the one I was playing. Luckily that particular concert had been a small Christmas gathering and nobody really minded Ernest shouting his version of 'Don't Let the Bells End' over my 'Away in a Manger' keyboard melody, but I learnt my lesson. As with everything else, let the person with dementia decide what they want to do and just go with it – because they'll only go and do it anyway.

My one concern about the summer performance was how we were going to make it equitable for all of our performers. Many members of the choir are simply not able to get to Birmingham or London. Some would struggle to even make it off site. In previous years and for smaller summer concerts this had not been a major issue – we simply wheeled the beds and chairs of our less mobile choristers out into the drawing room, opened the huge double-fronted doors and arranged our stage on the veranda with the audience seated in a connected marquee (only a lunatic wouldn't plan for the possibility of torrential rain in that scenario – admittedly I *have* been that lunatic). We've adapted in other ways, too, in years gone by. For the Christmas concert in 2020 (Covid Christmas, that cheery old time) we set the whole choir up in the drawing room but this time we livestreamed the performance to all the families and friends who'd purchased an online ticket. The residents who had been in isolation due to testing positive in the preceding days were all able to contribute because I'd taken the opportunity of recording a solo performance from each singer in the months leading up to Christmas, and we simply added these to the feed dotted between the ensemble pieces. There was one particularly poignant moment when the recording of Gwen, our oldest resident at 103, singing 'Oh Little Town of Bethlehem' played out over our screens, because sadly Gwen had died a week earlier, but we all felt that she would have wanted her final performance to go out posthumously. 'The show must go on,' she had said on numerous occasions, often unrelated to discussions about the choir and seemingly apropos of absolutely nothing.

The Covid concert ended up being one of our biggest-selling events because everyone (it felt like the whole bloody world at the time) just wanted to watch some old people having fun without having to leave the hermetically sealed safety of their own homes. And from the staff point of view, we all needed something to cling to after the trauma of losing so many. That small concert,

180

recorded over Zoom, really showed me that music can be healing in almost any scenario.

I discussed my concerns with Joe today, and the steps that we had taken in previous years to ensure equal access to the performance, and between us we came up with a brilliant plan (if I do say so myself). We've decided to do the same thing we did for the Covid concert but combine it with the best bits of the live performances. In other words, every singer who is able to travel to the venue and perform live on stage will do so, but those who can't will be recorded and their solos (or contributions to the chorus) will play on a bank of huge screens flanking the stage. I'm thinking Taylor Swift at São Paulo with the enormous projected images for those in the seats at the back – except most of our performers will have a few years on Taylor, obviously.

–

Flush with the enthusiasm of a new project and the success of another joyful singalong with Mum this afternoon, I decided that today was the day to tackle Dad about plans for her future care. I left Bob's a little earlier than usual, having worked through my lunch break for the past three days, and Dad gave me a concerned look from the door of their bungalow as he saw me wheeling Mum towards him.

'Is she not well?' he said. 'Has something happened? The carers aren't due until five, so you might have to give me a hand.' He looked towards Mum. 'Are you all right, Mary, darling?'

'Mum's fine,' I said, 'aren't you, Mum?' I bent to look at her face as we approached the door. 'She really enjoyed today's session. Katya the art therapist said she could hear Mum's harmonies above everyone else's.' (What Katya had actually said was, 'Your mother, she enjoy Oasis, yes? I think she sound happy like a loud goose,' but I interpreted this as a good thing.) 'The reason we're back early is that I just wanted to have a bit of a chat,' I said, hefting the wheelchair over the lip of the ramp. 'A bit of a forward planning…'

'I'll put the kettle on,' said my father wisely as I wheeled Mum into the sitting room.

Between us we managed to move her back into her chair, although I noticed that Dad was still wincing when he straightened up. I helped Mum to a few sips of cooled tea accompanied by bite-size pieces of digestive biscuit (her current favourite, as long as she sucks them rather than swallows them whole – if that happens, she's coughing for about forty-five minutes), but I knew I had to launch into The Chat before I lost my nerve.

'So, your back is still hurting a bit, Dad,' I said, stating it as fact rather than asking (he'd simply have denied it). 'And I know that moving Mum is becoming more of an issue.'

He went to protest, but I held my ground. 'I *know*, because the carers have mentioned it, Dad. And I can see it with my own eyes every day at work.'

My father chewed his lip for a moment and then seemed to admit defeat, taking a seat beside the electric fire, which was belting out heat in its usual fashion. The room always smelled faintly of hot dust mingled with Mum's lavender perfume. He stayed silent while I voiced my concerns although I could see his mind, still as sharp as ever, whirring over the information as I tried to stick to some of the principles Joe had suggested: keeping it brief, sticking to factual rather than emotional information, presenting solutions. I talked about increasing the respite care as a starting point, appealing to his practical nature with common sense. Advising that a trial run of perhaps a week at Bob's would allow both of them to see the potential benefits. I kept looking at Mum to see if there was any flicker of recognition or understanding, but it seemed not. She just stared out of the window, watching as the drops of rain coalesced and then divided into tributaries trickling down the pane of glass – she was smiling, but entirely lost in her own little world.

Eventually I ran out of steam and Dad leaned forward in his chair, his hands resting on his knees. 'Understood,' he said. 'Have you discussed this with Rory?'

'I have,' I said. 'And I think he's going to try and give you a call sometime this week. Or maybe pop in with Candice and the kids on Saturday. Not that you'll be able to chat much in that scenario!'

'Indeed.' His face broke into a smile. I knew how much both he and Mum loved seeing their youngest grandchildren, despite the fact that Callum could be a bit tiring.

'It's not that either of us thinks something has to happen immediately, Dad,' I said, keeping my voice low. I didn't think for one minute that Mum was paying attention to what I was saying, but on the other hand, it didn't feel right talking about her as if she wasn't there. 'We just feel it's important to have a plan. And that plan is likely to involve outside help. Now and in the longer term, we need to think about Mum's safety and your health, both of which are starting to be compromised.'

'I'll have a little think about it, Penelope,' he said, pushing down on his knees to give him the momentum to get out of the chair. I knew he was in a serious reflective mood as he'd used my full name. 'I suppose your idea about respite might mean I could go to Devon with Rory and the family for a few days when they're on holiday in June?'

'You could,' I said, eagerly. This was definitely a good sign. 'Or you could look at one of those river cruises you've always talked about. The ones that Mum always said looked deadly boring.'

'Bor-ing,' said Mum, speaking to the window more than either of us. 'Ugh.' Dad and I looked at each other and smiled.

Chapter Nineteen

Saturday 25 March

Zahara's hen party

'A toast!' said Joy, holding her glass aloft. 'To the most gorgeous bride-to-be and all-round goodest of good eggs: Zahara!'

'Zahara!' Caz and I shouted gleefully while the woman herself blushed and tilted her sparkly tiara at each of us in turn. Joy took a long slurp of her Bollinger. We were on Zahara's hen do, and Joy was taking her mini-break duties of getting absolutely leathered very seriously.

'What time are we due at the spa?' Caz asked.

Joy looked down at her phone. 'Three o'clock. I've got an alert set up for everyone's treatments. And lunch is booked for a quarter to one, so we should probably get a move on.'

Between the three of us we'd managed to arrange the main components of the hen do with minimal involvement from Zahara, and had essentially stuck to the brief of, 'Please, please, please, no strippers, no penis straws or L-plates.' We'd kept things small – just the four of us – because the wedding itself was going to be small ('an intimate gathering – i.e. as cheap as possible', Zahara had said), and you can't really invite people to a hen party when they're not invited to the main event. You probably could with a stag do, but that's boys for you – less FOMO and much more motivated by any excuse for a piss-up. Sam would likely attend the stag do of Attila the Hun if he thought there was a decent chance of a beer, a kebab and a chorus of 'Sweet Caroline' in a dodgy nightclub at the end of it. At least, he would have in the days before his body became a temple. Anyway, Zahara had been given a tasteful tiara and a tiny 'bride-to-be' enamel pin to wear as her only accoutrements indicating the impending nuptials. We all agreed with her stipulation about L-plates – as Joy pointed out, a provisional driver P-plate would have been slightly more appropriate for a second marriage, a practical acknowledgement that the bride had been down this road before and knew to proceed with caution.

'Not enormously romantic,' I said.

'But true,' said Joy firmly. 'That's the excellent thing about second marriages – you go into them with your eyes open.'

'Even if those eyes are slightly jaundiced,' said Zahara, knocking back the rest of her glass. 'As a result of previously being wedded to a total shit.'

'You're the least jaundiced person I know,' said Caz, who had moved straight on to the mojitos, claiming that champagne gave her a headache. 'Hugh might have been a total shit, but you've emerged from that marriage like a phoenix from the ashes.'

'Like a Valkyrie,' I said. I was halfway through my own glass of champagne and nowhere near as used to the effects of daytime drinking as Joy. I already felt like I might need a snooze. 'We're all so proud of you. And so, so pleased that you've found someone so special – not as special as you, obviously – but almost.'

Joy helped herself to another glass. 'Are you welling up, Mrs Baker?'

I nodded. 'I might be. What of it?'

Zahara's brow creased in concern. 'Tears of happiness though, right?'

'Of course!' I said. 'What else would they be?' *Jealousy*, I thought to myself, the word popping into my head unbidden. At least a few of these tears currently swimming in my lower lids were ones of envy and self-pity. Why am I such a rubbish friend? How can I be envious of Zahara after all she's been through?

Caz was eyeing me curiously as if intuiting my thoughts. She has a habit of doing this since she trained as a counsellor – always wanting to explore everyone's hidden hopes and fears. I had a horrible feeling she was about to ask a classic Caz question. Sure enough.

'It makes you think about your own marriage, doesn't it?' she said, addressing the room but still looking at me. 'Re-evaluate it.'

'Oh, I don't know,' I said, aiming for a casual tone as if I'd never given it a moment's thought. 'Maybe.'

'Of course it does,' scoffed Joy. 'I for one am hideously jealous of this,' she gestured to Zahara sitting next to her, '*love's young dream* thing we've got going on here. No offence, darling.'

'None taken,' murmured Zahara, pouring herself a second glass of champagne.

'It's bollocks to suggest otherwise,' Joy continued, looking sternly at me. 'Of *course* you see what's happening to friends and reassess your own life choices. It's completely natural. Doesn't mean you're not ecstatic for their good fortune…'

'Exactly,' said Caz, who was now on her second mojito. 'We all do it. Any life event affecting those close to you impacts on you as an individual, too – we're all egocentric, at the end of the day. Even with big global news events the natural human reaction is to think, what does this mean for me, or what would I do if this was happening to me? I bet you all had similar thoughts when I was having my chemotherapy – it's completely natural to feel sympathy for someone close to you while still being grateful that the shit they're going through isn't happening to you.'

'Yeah, or your mum's dementia, Penny,' said Joy. 'When you tell us about the latest development, I feel ghastly for you, but to be honest there's always a tiny part of me feeling relieved that I'm not going through the same thing – I'm not proud of myself for that, but there it is.'

'So essentially, Caz and I have got the lives that you don't want, while Zahara has the one you do,' I said, slightly annoyed with Joy for putting it all so starkly, even though she had essentially just given voice to my own envious little green-eyed monster.

Where Caz was in the business of asking the nosiest and most pointed questions, Joy had a habit of answering them with brutal honesty. Although it was an approach that often forced me out of my comfort zone, it was also one of the best things about this group of women – I never had to worry about causing offence or someone misinterpreting something I'd said and going on to harbour a deep-seated resentment about it for years to come. If Joy disagreed with me or felt slighted in any way, she'd simply come out and say it, no judgement, simply acknowledging her own emotional response. Equally, Caz had long abandoned all the polite, superficial niceties and just went straight for the jugular with her questions, although her main motivation was to make people feel better through talking and getting things off their chest. Joy's main motivation was simply that this was the way she was, take her or leave her. Either way, there was nowhere to hide once the pair of them swung into action.

'It's not as simple as that,' said Joy now. 'I'm happy with my life. I don't have many regrets. But you see some major life event happening to someone else and it does make you question your own choices, of course it does.' She turned her laser focus back to me. 'I bet you sometimes wonder what would have happened if you'd never met Sam, or if you *had* still met him but decided to end the relationship when some other interested party started sniffing around.'

'Daniel Rowley,' I said, smiling dreamily. 'He sniffed around for a bit.'

'There you go,' said Joy, triumphant. 'Do you not wonder from time to time what life would be like if you'd ditched Sam for Daniel Rowley? What did he end up doing?'

'I don't know,' I said, poker-faced.

'Liar,' said Joy. 'You've googled him since, surely – looked him up on Facebook or LinkedIn? I do it with my exes all the time. Just to keep tabs on what they're up to.'

I laughed. 'OK, you got me. Daniel Rowley is now running a health and well-being retreat in Cambodia with his Swedish wife and adopted daughter. He's in a heavy metal band and still looks pretty hot, to be fair.'

'Bingo!'

'Although I'm sure he's never really got over losing me.'

'Of course,' said Joy. 'And our thoughts and prayers are with Daniel at this difficult time.'

'It's true,' said Zahara, who was getting ice from the minibar for Caz's mojito. 'When I found out about Hugh I couldn't help but compare my situation with all of your happy marriages. I remember wanting to stomp around the house shouting "it's so unfair" like the kids do when you say something completely unreasonable like they can't be on the Xbox until four in the morning.' She took a swig from the bottle of Bollinger as she crossed the plush floor of the hotel suite back to the sofas and dropped a handful of ice into Caz's glass. 'But I remember you saying to me, Penny, that you'd always assumed I had the perfect marriage with Hugh. And of course, it really wasn't. It was far from perfect. Sometimes it was awful. Just goes to show you never really know what's going on in someone else's relationship. None of us do. Even brilliant friends like us.'

'I'm feeling a bit worried about my marriage,' I said suddenly, the words out of my mouth before I could stop them. Everyone turned to look at me, varying degrees of concern on their faces. 'Sorry. I don't really know why I said that – just ignore me.'

'What is it?' said Caz. 'What's the problem?'

I sighed. I didn't really know where to begin. 'It just feels like we've lost something, something's missing,' I said. 'Like we still live in the same house and parent the kids and share the same bed, but we don't spark off each other in the way we used to. When I see him, like, when he walks into the room, I'm annoyed. And I don't know why. And don't say it's the menopause' – I turned to Joy fiercely – 'because I refuse to have all my emotional responses and relationships defined by my hormones. I'm just not sure how to get that connection back again. How to feel excited when I see him rather than the default, slightly pissed-off feeling I have now.'

Joy, whose eyebrows had lifted slightly at my uncharacteristic snippiness, nodded. 'I feel the same,' she said. 'Certainly, from time to time I feel like things are a bit stagnant with me and Simon. But then we've been married for seventeen years. I figure it's probably normal. And perhaps very slightly related to me being menopausal – not that I'd dream of implying it was the same for everyone.' She gave me a tiny smile of acknowledgement.

'It's a partnership, though, isn't it,' said Caz. 'Marriage, especially long marriages, sometimes they're just about going through the process together, sharing the practical aspects of life even when you're not all blissed out with the romance, or at it like rabbits, like our Zahara and Raj are.'

Zahara had remained quiet through this part of the conversation, and I suddenly felt terrible.

'I don't want to take over the entire hen do with this,' I said. 'It's Zahara's special…'

'Oh, bollocks to that,' said Zahara, taking another large swig from the bottle of champagne. 'You're my friends, and if you're having issues then I want to know about them. It's a big deal to me, Penny, if you're feeling low. And yes, so is my marrying Raj, but we can talk about that anytime. In fact, I'm sort of done with talking about my wedding plans, to be honest. It's starting to feel a bit dull revisiting all that "how much is this caterer charging, do I want Rex to have a buttonhole arrangement, which bloody flower petals do I want in the confetti" business. I don't want this trip to be all about me – that kind of thing always makes me feel a bit awkward. It's a girls' weekend. We should be able to talk about girls' things.'

'OK,' I mumbled, looking down at my lap and still feeling a bit wretched. Not only was I an awful friend for feeling jealous, I also seemed to be hijacking an entire bloody hen party to talk about my marital woes. *Not cool*, as Grace would have said (a few years ago when saying *not cool* was a cool thing to do – it's probably not cool to say it now). 'I don't know if there's an actual solution here. It's not like I want to leave him or anything...'

'So, what do you want?' asked Caz.

I sighed again. 'I don't know. Things to go back to the way they were, maybe?'

'How they were *when*? When your kids were little?'

I shook my head. 'No, God no. When the kids were young life was even harder and Sam and I barely saw each other. It was probably worse then than it is now.'

'So, before you even had kids?'

'But then we wouldn't have our family,' I said. 'And that's sort of the cement that keeps us together... Maybe I don't mean going back to how things were, because there is no *perfect* time. And we couldn't go back anyway. I guess the problem is I can't really envisage my life, my marriage, in the context of the children leaving home – I worry that one day the house will be empty and Sam and I will turn around and look at each other and realise we have nothing in common, there's nothing there. And by then I'll be in my mid-fifties and completely set in my ways and there'll be no way of changing direction. It's like the older you get, the more your options close down.'

'So, you want change?' Caz was in full flow.

'Yes. No. I don't know. With the children I want to freeze time and for them never to leave home and never to leave me. For me I want things to move on and to feel like I'm progressing through life, making my mark on the world, achieving stuff.' I paused, it suddenly hitting me that maybe this was what Sam was doing with all his exercise – giving himself targets to achieve, creating a sense of purpose, however trivial I felt that purpose was. I floofed back into the deep seats of the sofa. 'So if you can just arrange that, Caz, a simple combination of freezing time and progressing it, then that would be great. Get back to me when you've changed the space-time continuum.'

'Will do.'

'I think what you're describing,' Joy began, a little tentatively for her, 'is some of the angst we're all feeling at the moment. Some of it's about our relationships with the men in our lives, some of it's about our relationships with our kids or our parents, some of it is about the legacy we want to leave, the mark we make through work or creative output. And some of it is about our relationship with ourselves, our bodies, and, much as I hate to say it, our hormones.'

'But you know, the biggest thing right now,' said Zahara, hiccuping slightly, 'the biggest, most important thing is our relationships with our friends, the women in our lives. That's one area where there's no angst.'

'Just to clarify, Zee,' I said, 'you mean us, right? We're the women in your life?'

'No, I meant Tiggy and Lindi, actually,' she said with a straight face. 'You lot are a massive pain in the arse.'

'Well,' said Caz, pouring herself another mojito. 'Sorry about that, because you're stuck with us. Forever and ever. Till death do us part.'

'I now pronounce you – the best bunch of babes,' I said, slurring a little as I held out my glass for a top-up. 'Shall we have one more teensy drink and then get some food, please? Because otherwise I'm going to fall asleep in this executive suite and never make it as far as my hot stone massage.'

'And that would be a real tragedy,' said Joy seriously.

Chapter Twenty

Saturday afternoon

After a delicious lunch, which hopefully mopped up some of the alcohol, and once we'd all taken a solemn vow to avoid heavy topics for the remainder of the weekend, we made our way to the hotel spa and managed to commandeer adjacent loungers by the heated whirlpool. Caz was briefly absorbed in adjusting the top of her swimming costume.

'It's one of those post-mastectomy swimsuits,' she said, foraging around beneath the shoulder strap. 'There's these flesh-coloured silicon pads I can pop into the pouches but I've lost one of them. I think maybe one of the boys thought it was a chicken fillet and tried to stir-fry it? Either way, this is not the best look.' She pointed to her breast area where one cup was pertly rounded and the other billowed emptily.

'Would it be better to take the other one out?' I said. 'Make it even?'

'Or we could find something else for the empty side?' suggested Joy. 'Like a – like a lime?' She pointed to the 'hydration station' where a glass chamber of citrus fruit flanked the water fountain.

'Or you could go for the Madonna early Nineties "Vogue"-era look?' I said, indicating the cone-shaped paper cups on the shelf behind the fountain.

'Fuck it,' said Caz. 'I'm not really bothered. What's the worst that can happen? Someone sees me and thinks I've lost a boob.'

'Exactly. And if they mention it, you can surprise them and say, "Actually I've lost both."' I did an exaggerated shrug.

'Just misplaced them down the back of the sofa,' said Caz. 'What can you do?'

'Anyway, if it's any consolation I'm not exactly feeling beach-body ready,' I said, pointing to my wobbling thighs. 'And I don't have any excuse.'

'You're fine,' said Joy, rolling her eyes.

'I know there's nothing *wrong* wrong,' I said, feeling immediately guilty for following Caz's post-mastectomy concerns with my own trivial tale of chubby woe. 'But sometimes I wish I didn't feel like such a whale.' I sighed, poking my protruding stomach. 'I've got to do something about it. The pounds just keep piling on.'

'You should come to the gym with me,' said Joy, her torso tight and compact in her zip-up one-piece. 'Power-lifting. That's the way ahead for women our age. You should try it.'

'Ugggh. You sound like Sam,' I said, cross with her for giving me solutions. Surely she realised I just wanted a whinge – I didn't want anyone actually telling me what to do about my predicament, or heaven forbid, giving me *helpful advice*.

'You look gorgeous, Penny,' said Zahara loyally as she extended her long, tanned legs on the lounger beside me. 'And I love that colour on you.'

'What? Industrial Navy?' I said, trying not to laugh (or cry). Zahara was always so keen for her friends to feel beautiful, but sometimes the depths she would sink

to in order to contrive a compliment were ridiculous —
and actually made you feel worse.

'Yes, it's a very – uhm – utilitarian look,' she said. 'And
slimming, too.'

'You are the *worst* liar,' I said. 'But I love you for trying.'

'Nobody here gives a toss what we look like,' said
Joy briskly as she dipped her toes in the water. I noted
her prominent calf muscles, the tendons visible as she
flexed her foot. 'It's not *Love Island*. None of us are on
the pull. And besides, nobody looks at women over fifty
anyway, negatively or positively. It's just one of those facts
of life – the patriarchy is only interested in fertile, fuckable
women. We've dropped out of the range of the male gaze
– like those eye tests where they check your peripheral
vision with those little flashing lights. Our lights are still
flashing but we're out of sight – stars in a distant galaxy.
It's quite liberating when you think about it.'

'What, being invisible?' Caz said.

'I prefer to think of it as being off-grid,' said Joy. 'Like a
stealth bomber. Or a silent assassin.' She mimed tiptoeing
along the pool edge holding an imaginary gun to her
chest.

'A silent assassin, drunk on Bollinger, with a voice like
a foghorn,' I said, laughing. 'Wait – is that MI5 on the
phone?'

'You're right,' she said, returning to the lounger.
'There's nothing stealthy about me.' She stretched out and
lay for a moment, staring up, wide-eyed, at the recessed
ceiling lights before popping back into a seated position.
'I'm shit at relaxing,' she said. 'Can we order drinks by the
pool, do you think?'

'Ssshh,' said Caz, nodding over to the lounger where
Zahara was sitting, eyes closed, breathing deeply.

'Ooohhh,' I said. 'Is she being mindful?' I watched Zahara's mouth turn up at the corners.

'Trying to be,' she said, opening one eye.

'Is she focusing on her core?' hollered Joy as two bemused twenty-somethings swam past our feet.

'Not currently,' said Zahara, both eyes now open.

'You should, you know,' said Joy, sagely. '"Neglect your pelvic floor at your peril," my menopause doctor said. We should probably be clenching at all times.'

'Yet another thing for us to be bloody worrying about,' I grumbled. 'Anyway, I'm not convinced that any number of Kegels is going to reverse the damage done by evacuating three human beings through my perineum.'

'Have any of you tried those pelvic floor weights?' said Caz. 'I saw them advertised in one of the Sunday magazines. Along with the elasticated trousers and comfortable slippers. They're supposed to help strengthen everything. Give you the vaginal muscles of a Thai sex worker firing out ping-pong balls, apparently.'

'That's an interesting marketing strategy,' I said. 'Did they actually say that in the Sunday supplement?'

'I haven't tried the weights,' said Zahara leaning in confidentially, all attempts at mindfulness abandoned. 'But I did try a jade egg a few months ago.'

'A what?' I said. 'Is that not a thing in *Lord of the Rings*? Was there a dragon guarding it?'

'No,' she said. 'Jade eggs. They're sometimes called yoni eggs.'

'Like Gwyneth Paltrow!' screeched Joy. 'With her candles that smell like genitals and her yoni eggs. On her website. Gloop, is it?'

'Ssshhh,' I hissed, grimacing apologetically to the two younger women who'd swum past a minute ago and were completing another lap of the pool.

'Goop,' said Zahara. 'Although I didn't buy one of those. She charges about two thousand pounds.'

'Hang on,' said Caz. 'You've stuck a two-thousand-pound egg up your chuff? Was it a Fabergé?' (We all winced in unison at the very thought.)

'It's not an actual egg, Caz. It's like a smooth stone,' said Zahara. 'A crystal. Similar to the weights you're talking about, but more natural. In Taoist teaching the jade egg is supposed to lift your energy inwards. The theory is that the crystal itself has healing properties, that it's better for your internal balance.'

'Your chakras,' I said knowledgeably.

'And how is your chakra now?' Joy asked, eyebrow raised.

'Traumatised,' admitted Zahara. 'It wasn't a great success. I'd been thinking, you know, wedding coming up, more specifically, the wedding night – I didn't want to let the side down.'

'With your saggy sides,' said Joy. 'Sorry – that should have stayed in my head.'

'When does it ever though, Joy?' Zahara laughed. 'So yes, that was the plan, build up a bit of muscle strength – it wasn't just for Raj, it's supposed to improve things for both parties, if you see what I mean.'

'Everyone's a winner in the jade egg game,' I said in a Bruce Forsyth voice.

'Hmm, well, not in my case,' she said. 'Probably one of my more expensive mistakes, although the one I bought was a lot cheaper than the Goop ones.'

'So what was the problem? Was it uncomfortable?' I said, crossing my legs at the thought.

'No, that wasn't the issue.' Zahara lowered her voice again, which was more than the rest of us had been doing. A couple in their thirties had already moved their bathrobes to a completely different area of the pool. 'The problem was more that it was *too* comfortable. I completely forgot it was in there. I'd put it in after dropping the kids at school and then I'd just got on with my day.'

There was a collective raising of eyebrows as we all imagined the slightly strange thought of our friend going about her day while incubating a gemstone.

'I went to the supermarket,' she said. 'Made dinner. And then it was Rex's parents' evening. And I was meeting Hugh there, you know how he likes to show willing when it comes to the kids.' I nodded; Zahara's ex-husband always insisted on presenting a united front when it came to his children's education. He was even magnanimous enough to refrain from bringing along whichever girlfriend he was seeing, although that may have been because they were getting closer and closer to being school age themselves.

'So,' continued Zahara. She had our full attention. 'I met him in the car park and we walked over to the school hall making a bit of small talk. He was asking Rex about homework and sports and whatever. I was rummaging around in my handbag for a tissue because I'd got this rotten cold.'

'Hadn't been taking your echinacea,' I said.

'Indeed. Anyway. We'd just reached the hall and I started coughing. Regular cough, nothing dramatic, but of course… the egg popped out.'

There was a dramatic pause as we gave a collective sharp intake of breath.

'Fuck!' said Joy in an uncharacteristic whisper. 'You *coughed* it out?'

'Yeah,' said Zahara, struggling to speak for laughing. 'One minute to go before the first teacher appointment and I laid the bloody egg!'

'On the floor?' I asked, horrified by the image of Zahara's crystal skittering across the polished linoleum of the school hall.

'No. Into my knickers,' said Zahara. 'But you know how they run these parent evenings at secondary school, where it's like speed dating and you just move from teacher to teacher with no time in between to pop to the toilets and...'

'...remove a rock from your nether regions?' I said.

'Yes, exactly. There's no time between appointments. So, I just had to walk like John fucking Wayne over to the first teacher, praying that this egg would stay within the confines of my knicker elastic and not drop to the floor. And then I had to sit down. Or at least, look like I was sitting down. In reality I was hovering about an inch away from the plastic chair because there was literally no way I could place my full body weight onto the stone without causing some significant bruising.'

'Oh. My. God,' said Joy, tears rolling down her cheeks. 'That is one of *the* funniest things I have ever heard. Did you seriously conduct the entire parents' evening with a crystal rattling around in your scanties?'

'I did.' Zahara nodded gravely. 'Eight different teachers. Accompanied by my fourteen-year-old son and my ex-husband. Neither of whom I could exactly confide in. My upper thighs were shot to pieces by the end of it, all that hovering. And I didn't listen to a word they were saying about Rex. I couldn't concentrate on anything at all. As soon as the last one, Mr Griffiths the maths teacher, finished speaking, I excused myself from the hall, found a quiet corridor and fished the thing out of my knickers.'

'What did you do with it then?' Caz said, eyes wide.

'I dropped it in one of the flower beds by the car park on my way out,' said Zahara. 'I feel guilty every time I see one of the gardeners doing the weeding there now.'

'I wouldn't worry about it, Zahara love,' said Joy, her voice wobbly with laughter. 'Better in their bushes than yours.'

Chapter Twenty-One

Sunday 26 March

Good God. Woke up feeling like someone had stuck my eyelids together with glue and sandpapered my tongue while hitting me over the head repeatedly with an anvil. I was like Wile E. Coyote in one of those cartoons from the Seventies. Rolled over and slung my arm across an unfamiliar body.

'Grawphngggllll?' I rasped. Which was hung-over code for 'what the holy hell has happened to me?'

Zahara shifted my arm off her shoulder. 'Sweaty,' she mumbled – I'm not sure whether she was referring to me or herself, but we'd obviously not got the memo about our hotel suite's air conditioning. Either that or a nuclear apocalypse had destroyed our atmosphere overnight and we were currently roasting in the unfiltered rays of an unforgiving sun.

'Help,' came a bleat from the adjoining room, where Caz and Joy were residing. I then heard the sound of footsteps making their unsteady way to the en suite. I fumbled on the bedside table for a glass of water – had three o'clock in the morning Penny given a thought to what ten o'clock in the morning Penny would need? Ah, yes, she had! I cracked my lips into a parched smile of gratitude to my former self as I felt the cool rim of a ceramic cup – it was a toothbrush mug but it held liquid and that was all I needed. Being unable to achieve a fully upright position at this delicate hour, I propped myself up on an elbow and inhaled the contents sideways through my mouth. Unfortunately, it was gin. I spat it out and tried not to vomit while contemplating a search for more appropriate hydration, but the distance to the now occupied bathroom felt insurmountable so I returned my head to the pillow with a whimper.

An hour later, and Zahara was shaking me awake. 'Penny,' she said. 'We've got to be out by midday and Joy's still being sick in the bidet.'

I sat up and took the proffered paracetamol and pint of water. 'Caz?' I said blearily, wondering whether all four of us were similarly afflicted.

Zahara smiled. 'She's gone down for breakfast,' she said. 'Felt it was a waste of a four-star buffet otherwise.'

I nodded. 'It is,' I said sorrowfully. Hotel breakfasts were the absolute best.

'We can still make it if you want?' Zahara looked at her watch. 'They're serving until eleven. You've got ten minutes.'

Miraculously I managed to pull on a T-shirt and track-suit bottoms, and the two of us made our way downstairs to meet Caz with a promise to Joy that we would try and smuggle out some carbs and a double espresso for her.

Caz was a little green around the gills but she's made of stern stuff and had loaded up her side of the table with a four-course banquet.

'There's pastries over there,' she said, gesturing to a circular table in the centre of the glass-domed dining room. 'All your kind of European nonsense like cold cheese and bratwurst on the table by the window. And proper cooked breakfast over there.' She pointed to the far end of the vast room where people in crisp white cotton with crisp white smiles were serving a small queue of late diners like ourselves. 'There's everything you could possibly want,' she said as she buttered a slice of toast. 'Black pudding, hash browns, sautéed mushrooms, eggs done any which way you want them' – she smiled naughtily at Zahara – 'didn't see any jade ones, though.'

'No egg jokes,' I said, pouring myself a tea from Caz's pot on the table. 'I can't cope. I feel nauseous enough as it is.'

'And definitely not once we get home,' said Zahara firmly. 'That egg story stays on tour.'

'But I won't be able to look at those flower beds by the school car park in the same way again,' I said.

'It's been enough of a struggle for me to even go back on site, let alone speak to any of the teachers,' said Zahara. 'Poor old Mr Griffiths. I keep wincing every time I see him. Anyway – let's get some food.'

I perused the dried fruit and muesli counter before finding myself drawn to the full English, and by the time I returned to the table I was carrying a grand total of three plates and a pot of tea – pretty impressive given that I appeared to have lost most of my basic coordination. Joy had made it downstairs and was sitting at our table wearing a kaftan and a pair of sunglasses. She looked like Sophia Loren, if Sophia had been doused in tequila and pulled through a hedge.

'Morning,' she rasped, raising her gaze from the coffee she was drinking in tiny concentrated sips.

I offered her a hash brown and she held up a hand to block it from sight.

'Too soon?' I asked, and she moved her head a fraction to nod.

'It's a huge hotel, isn't it,' said Zahara, looking around the vast breakfast area. 'Caz says there's a ballroom on the third floor, just above the spa. Is this the sort of place you'd be thinking of for the summer fundraiser, Penny?'

'Hmm, not sure,' I said, shovelling in a forkful of fried egg and baked beans. I was starting to feel a bit better as the caffeine and carbs hit my system. 'Joe's doing most of the research on that score. He thinks he might be able to get us a slot at The Carlton just outside of London. Got its own auditorium, and you can hire out the entire dining room.'

'The Carlton?' said Joy, eyebrows raised and therefore faintly impressed. 'How'd he manage to secure that as a venue? They have a two-year waiting list.'

'He says he's terribly well-connected,' I said, laughing as I remembered my conversation with Joe a few weeks ago. 'No, he's very self-deprecating really, but he does seem to be able to pull strings. He's got a couple of celebs lined up to introduce the choir and run the auction. It's all starting to feel quite exciting.'

'Quite the wonder boy.' Joy's voice was acerbic, so I knew she must be feeling a bit more like her old self. 'You want to make sure he's not overstepping, Penny. Keep him on a tight leash or he'll take over more than just the fundraising.'

'He's not like that,' I said, defensive of my employee. 'He doesn't overstep the mark or try and throw his weight around. Honestly, Joy, I know you're used to dealing with chauvinistic corporate types but that's not Joe. He fits right into Bob's Place because he gets that we're relaxed about workforce structure – it's a flat hierarchy.'

'No such thing as a flat hierarchy, babe,' said Joy, taking another minuscule sip of her espresso and breathing out slowly.

'Good point, but still, you've got it wrong,' I said firmly. 'He's been an absolute godsend. He's helped me with the charitable status application. He's done all the donkey work on that. He's come up with some brilliantly creative ideas for fundraising and…'

'That's what you're paying him to do though,' she said, unable to let it lie. 'It sounds like he's made quite the impression, but don't let it sway you. Once he's completed this project, he's gone. You've got to keep your business head on. You're the boss.'

I rolled my eyes. She was right, of course. Joe was with us on a fixed-term contract and it wasn't like he was doing it out of the goodness of his heart; we were paying him a decent amount to do all this work.

'He's quite the looker, according to Zahara.' Caz lifted her head from her plate where she had been busy devouring a stack of pancakes slathered in maple syrup.

'He is,' said Zahara. 'Charming, too. I've only met him a few times when I've been doing the textile class at Bob's, but he seems to have made a really positive contribution to the business. I know you're just being cautious, Joy, but I agree with Penny, he seems like one of the good guys.'

'He is,' I said, surprising myself with my fervour. 'He really is.'

'OK, OK,' said Joy, holding her hands up.

'And he clearly holds you in very high regard,' said Zahara, throwing me some side-eye.

'Ooh, does he now?' Caz's fork, loaded with pancake, paused inches from her mouth.

'He's a colleague,' I said, my cheeks suddenly burning. 'We get on well. As colleagues.'

'Doesn't always look at you like a colleague,' said Zahara naughtily. 'You've definitely still got it, Penny.'

Well, I don't think I've ever laughed so hard.

'Zee,' I said, once I'd cleaned up the tea I'd spluttered across the table. 'Look at me!' I gestured to my tracksuit and my ratty hair. 'Look at my face,' I said, indicating my caked mascara and creased cheeks. 'I think whatever I've *still got* isn't anything Joe would be in the market for. Come on. I'm six years his senior, and he's on a totally different level to me looks-wise. I've seen pictures of his ex-wife. She's your sort of territory, my friend. Not mine.' I held up a hand to silence her, seeing she was about to come in with a *nooo – what?* sort of comment.

'I'm not the type he goes for,' I said. 'And I'm his boss, as Joy has pointed out.'

'Power can be a great aphrodisiac,' said Caz sagely.

'I don't think that phrase necessarily applies to running a care home,' I said. 'My job doesn't really give me the level of sexual magnetism you're implying.'

'Fair enough,' said Caz. 'You've got a point.'

We moved on to discussing our plans for the rest of the day, which had originally involved a brisk country walk (it seemed less appealing when most of us felt like we'd already been trampled by a herd of cows), and eventually it was agreed that we would find a quiet corner of the hotel with some squashy sofas where we could read, sleep or try very hard not to be sick, depending on requirements. And although I dismissed Zahara's comments as pure nonsense and a likely indication that she was still drunk, I can't deny that the mere thought of someone thinking I still had it, whatever *it* was, was not completely unappealing.

Chapter Twenty-Two

Friday 31 March – end of term

Easter cake sale

The end of the spring term and the start of the Easter holiday beckons. Of course, one has to undergo the annual torture of the school Easter bonnet parade and bake sale, but like everything this year, I am feeling strangely nostalgic and rose-tinted about it. Gone is the performance anxiety of previous years when I either slaved away over a hot stove for days in order to produce something inedible, or admitted defeat and bought a set of Mr Kipling cakes only to break into an anxious sweat at the thought of sneaking them past the biscuit police of Tiggy and Lindi. This time I've made a cake (well, to be completely honest, Tina has made me a cake) and a bonnet ahead of time. Of course, Maisie has now reached an age where she refuses to be seen dead in my homemade bonnet, and so the papier-mâché crown bedecked with chicks and bunnies that I made in one of the craft sessions at Bob's Place (our art therapist Katya made most of it) has been given to Mrs North to offer to any child whose mum might have forgotten/been incapacitated/could really have done without this shit. Thus, I feel I am paying back. Or paying it forward? Basically,

I'm doing whichever is the best thing for a strong feminist and champion of motherhood to do.

Pick-up was at midday, so I left work early having spent most of the morning discussing how the application for charity status was going with Joe. He was also keen to know my thoughts about dates for the gala dinner and summer performance. It sounds as though The Carlton has a very small window, i.e. one possible date due to a cancellation, and Joe was keen that we book it before they gave the slot to someone else.

'July the twenty-eighth,' I said, flicking through the calendar on my phone. 'It's a Friday but it looks OK from my point of view. In fact, the kids will have broken up from school so I'll have more flexibility around weekdays anyway, so yeah, let's book it!'

He looked really pleased. 'Great. I'll give them a call. You doing anything nice over the holidays?'

'Well, apart from the carnage of the school Easter cake sale, which is always a highlight, we're seeing Rory, Candice and the kids tomorrow. We're aiming for a lovely, bracing family walk around Snapeshill Park. Not entirely sure how easy it'll be pushing Mum's wheelchair around some of those tracks, but she can probably wait in the café with Dad if it's too muddy.'

'How are things going... with your mum?'

'Uhhm. Okay-ish,' I said. 'I spoke to Dad a few weeks ago, used some of your phrases. Thanks for that, by the way. I haven't had a chance to say thank you, and it was really good of you to just listen and—'

'It's no problem, Penny,' he said quietly. 'Really. Anytime.'

'Well. After my initial burst of bravery we haven't discussed it since, but I know my dad. He'll be mulling it over. Mum's plateaued again, so there's no imminent crisis but, as I always say to clients' families, the time to plan for crises is when you're not currently in the middle of one.'

'That's a catchy phrase.'

'Isn't it.' I laughed. 'Point still stands, though, even if I can't make it into a soundbite. We need to act while things are quiet. I'll maybe get Rory to have a sort of follow-up chat tomorrow.'

'Good idea. Hope it goes well.'

I slung my bag over my shoulder and picked up my supermarket carrier, heavy with Tina's cake. 'And you?' I said. 'Any plans?'

He shrugged. 'Milo's with his mum for most of the holiday,' he said. 'So there's no point in me taking any leave, really. He's with me this weekend though.' He beamed. 'Snapeshill Park's not a bad idea, actually. There's a go-kart track over the far side of the wood, isn't there?'

'Uhm, yes. I think there might be.' I knew there was; Tom and Sam used to hurtle around it regularly a few years ago. But I didn't want to sound too definite. I realised I was at risk of engineering a scenario where Joe's family met my family, and I wasn't sure how I felt about that. But I didn't want to be unfriendly either. It must be tough for Joe only having Milo every other weekend; options for fun father-and-son activities might be limited.

'I guess I might see you there then,' I said cautiously.

He must have picked up on my tone. 'Ah no, don't worry. I'll probably take him to the skate park instead,' he said a little awkwardly. 'Happy Easter, if I don't see you.'

'You too.'

'And I hope the uber-mummies like your homemade cake,' he said, winking expansively.

Joe had prior knowledge of this particular cake's provenance, and the fact that it was indeed homemade, just not by me. But there was no way I was going to reveal this as I proudly brandished my carrier bag in the school hall.

'Have you brought anything for the bake sale, Penny?' Tiggy asked, pointedly ignoring the supermarket shopper where Tina's lemon drizzle cake was nestling in a double layer of greaseproof paper.

'I have,' I said, waving the bag in front of her nose. 'Right here.'

'Tesco?' she said, her mouth a moue of disapproval dressed up as polite enquiry.

'Only the bag, Tiggy,' I said proudly. 'The baked goods are homemade!'

'And labelled with…'

'Labelled with the full list of ingredients and potential allergens,' I said, cutting across her. Since the CQC inspection Tina has been all over our ingredient lists and has print-off sheets for every item produced in the kitchen. I hadn't made the mistake of taking one of those and revealing that someone else had been involved in the baking process to Tiggy though, oh no. Instead, I'd painstakingly handwritten it out on a wonky scrap of paper, which was much more in keeping with my brand and would therefore lure the Paul Hollywood of St John's Primary deeper into my world of bakery fraud.

I'd like to say she looked begrudgingly impressed, but if anything she looked disappointed that I had removed an opportunity for her to demonstrate her superiority. 'Great,' she said. 'Just the one cake, is it? Lucy's made three, including a gluten-free version for Lindi's girls.' She inclined her head in the general direction of Lucy, a new mum with a daughter in reception.

'Is it sulphite-free, though?' I said meaningfully.

A tiny indent of concern broke the Botoxed alabaster of Tiggy's forehead and she rushed over to grill Lucy.

'Penny,' admonished Zahara, who was standing beside me. 'What did you do to that poor woman?' We both watched Lucy now cringing under Tiggy's smiling interrogation, opening up one of multiple cake tins to allow detailed inspection as if she was going through the red channel in customs.

'It's character-building, Zee,' I said, feeling a bit guilty. 'Besides, those reception mums only need to put up with Tiggy for one more year after this. They've got away lightly.'

'There's always a Tiggy,' said Zahara wisely. 'Every generation of primary school has one. I think they respawn, like in that computer game.'

'She'll be bringing out the sniffer dogs next,' I said, nodding over to where Lucy was now annotating one of her many ingredient labels to doubtless highlight the possible presence of sulphites while Tiggy watched over her sternly.

'Don't talk about Lindi like that,' said Zahara, and I laughed loudly just as the woman herself approached me from behind.

'Penny,' Lindi said brightly. 'Aurora mentioned that Maisie's big sister was involved in the Trafalgar Square riots last weekend. How extraordinary. I imagine you were worried sick!'

Tiggy was back. 'What's this, Penny?' she said, all smiles (while seething that this morsel of gossip had escaped her).

I silently cursed Maisie for not keeping her mouth shut, but I suppose Sam and I had been arguing quite loudly about it a few days ago. The fact that Grace had been cautioned by the police on the same day that I was getting pissed in a hotel spa with Zahara seemed to have added more fuel to my husband's irritation. I now weighed up the various merits of lying through my teeth versus dangling a titbit of intrigue for these women to scrap over and finally devour.

'Yes, she was involved,' I said. 'But no harm done. She's absolutely fine – I'm picking her up from the station in a few hours.'

'The police station?' said Lindi, in hushed awe. Tiggy's mouth fell open at the prospect of conversing with the mother of a convicted felon.

I allowed the pause to drag before I put them out of their misery. 'No – the train station,' I said eventually, feeling Zahara shaking with silent laughter beside me. 'She's keeping a low profile for the week. You know how it is.' Lindi nodded fervently. 'Look,' I said, dropping my voice to a low whisper. I was enjoying the feeling of being the *really bad mum* rather more than I should have. 'We're trying to keep it quiet at the moment – it's rather a sensitive issue, so I'd prefer not to talk about it, if that's OK. I know I can trust you.'

'Of course, Penny, our lips are sealed,' exclaimed Tiggy, her eyes wide with sincerity. She was clearly enjoying the frisson of danger, ecstatic to have the information and slighted by the implication that she might blab (of course she would blab – I gave it approximately four minutes before the news reached PTA Central and almost wished I could be there to witness the reaction).

'I am the soul of discretion as regards family secrets,' said Lindi, giving me a meaningful look. 'I have a few of my own.'

'Oh, stop trying to be enigmatic, Lindi!' Tiggy gave an annoyed half-laugh. 'We *all* have secrets.'

'Ain't that the truth, ladies,' I said, which effectively closed the conversation.

–

The cake was an enormous success (sold and consumed within ten minutes of going on sale), and I spotted my Easter crown perched atop the head of a year four pupil on the other side of the hall where it was being much admired (I may have invented the last bit). I duly gathered up the belongings of both Maisie and Eva (Joy was at work) and untied Montmorency from the fence post to which he had been tethered for all of twenty minutes, although the way he greeted me, you'd think I'd been lost to civilisation for several decades. I then escorted the entourage back to our house, carrying a total of seven different bags (PE kits, book-bags and bin liners full of craft, all in duplicate, plus a carrier of sweets that Eva had apparently 'won' in the end of term raffle, although I think perhaps *bullied the other children into letting her win* would have been a more accurate description of events), while manoeuvring around a dog with separation anxiety who evidently felt he couldn't bear to be more than ten inches from my ankles for the remainder of the journey lest I chain him up and abandon him again. Once home, I made the girls some sandwiches and deflected questions along the lines of:

'Why aren't we allowed to listen to songs with explicit lyrics?'

'Why can't you drop us off in town, give us some money to go shopping and pick us up at some unspecified time from some unspecified location?'

'Why can't you drive us over to Eva's boyfriend's house, and why can't I have a boyfriend who's already at secondary school?'

'Why can't I get some fake tan/shave my legs/buy these crop tops from a fast-fashion website for £1.50/have my nose pierced?'

I have learnt over time that there is no point attempting a logical discussion around these topics with someone who is still at primary school. A firm, 'No – because I say so,' eventually becomes sufficient. I deploy the sentence liberally and with a formulaic tone so that after the fifteenth time of asking Maisie usually realises the answer will not change. Unless of course I'm distracted by the prospect of awkward conversations with my eldest about staying on the right side of the law. And so it was that Maisie came to purchase ten of the crop tops, have her nose pierced and get herself a boyfriend who went to secondary school, all within the space of a few hours (not really).

Joy came to collect Eva at around the time Tom returned from school, and after I'd made him two rounds of toast and scrambled four eggs (his appetite has picked up a little in recent weeks), I set off for the train station. I wasn't sure how long Grace was planning on being home for but I always want her to feel she can stay as long as she likes, so I tend to make sure I have plenty of vegan food options in. The downside of this planning is that if she's only staying for a night, the fridge becomes a fermenting compost of pulses and tofu that nobody else will eat. Not even Sam on his health drive. This visit seemed likely to last more than a week, though, as I thought she'd probably want to be with us for Easter (for the oat milk chocolate eggs and hot cross buns if nothing else), and I also secretly hoped she'd be using some of the time at home to write up her dissertation and/or revise for her finals.

Grace's dissertation is looking at the effect of movement and song on mood – whether dancing and singing can have a positive impact on mental health and cognitive function. She's been interested in the practical applications of using music as a therapeutic tool ever since Mum joined the Singing for the Brain choir, and she proved extremely helpful joining Granny in the very first concert we staged – not something I had originally anticipated from a grumpy fourteen-year-old who rarely strayed beyond her bedroom. But despite my reservations, she loved being involved with the choir and her interest led ultimately to this degree course in music psychology.

I'm obviously thrilled she has a chance to study a subject she's passionate about, particularly as I feel a smidgen of resentment about how I was ultimately forced away from studying music and persuaded into a business studies degree myself, but now I'm a parent of an undergraduate, I have started to appreciate what my mum and dad were banging on about in terms of future career prospects. So far, there has been no mention of what Grace is planning on doing when she graduates in a few months' time. And I haven't been brave enough to raise it since the last time, when a few tentative enquiries led to an accusation of stifling her creativity and undermining her self-worth. As an aside, it seems that the self-worth, inner confidence and general mental well-being of your average student are much more delicate and precious commodities than they were in my day.

Today, my concerns were less about her course and more about her possible police record. On the drive over I contemplated how to play the conversation and realised I had no idea where to begin. Sam and I hadn't even been aware that she'd been present at the riots until Monday when she'd called us, and so I thought I'd make that my opening gambit.

'It was good of you to let us know about the police caution,' I began as we set off back towards home. (This is not necessarily a sentence I ever thought I'd utter to one of my children.)

She shifted in her seat and something glinted in the corner of my field of vision. 'Is that another piercing?' I said, thankful it was at least in her ear and not her lip like the other one.

'Had it done a few weeks ago,' she said, fiddling with the loop. 'It's a bit sore. Might be infected. Or maybe it was knocked about on Saturday.'

'Yes. About that,' I said. 'What exactly happened in London?'

There was a pause and I realised that my usually fearless and feisty daughter was on the verge of tears. I put my hand out to rub her knee. 'Oh, sweetheart,' I said. 'Talk to me.'

'It was horrible, Mum.' Her voice caught in her throat. 'It was just supposed to be a peaceful protest. None of us wanted any trouble. We never do. We just wanted to raise awareness, open people's eyes. It was supposed to be a slow, silent march along Whitehall, maybe stop some traffic, but that was all. No vandalism, no damage to property, no obstructing of emergency vehicle access, nothing. In the grand scheme of things, considering the damage we're already inflicting on ourselves through climate change, it really was *nothing*. There have been calls within the group for us to be a bit more militant, but so far nobody's really got the stomach for it. And it always seems to be the Tarquins and Tabithas who suggest the hardline tactics, knowing their parents can buy them out of any trouble if needed. But like I say, Crusaders' current policy is peaceful protest. We don't go looking for trouble. At all. You've got to believe me.'

'I do, Gracie, I do!' I meant it. None of Grace's previous demonstrations had ever ended in violence as far as I was aware (which admittedly might not have been that far). The group of friends I'd met from Climate Crusaders all seemed lovely. Leaf, with her green hair and lactose intolerance, Seamus with his sensible jumpers and Shay with their soft-spoken voice and polite enquiries after Grace's siblings. These weren't people who should be in prison. They were kids, deeply frightened for the future of the planet. That was all.

'So how did the police end up getting involved?' I asked cautiously. 'If it was peaceful, as you say.'

'Word had got out somehow,' she said bitterly. 'Someone had posted about the protest and it had been picked up by some bunch of thugs looking for a fight. We were all getting ready to march, there were hundreds of people, all sorts, some even as old as you.'

'Imagine that,' I said.

'Mums with babies in slings and dads with pushchairs, people in wheelchairs – we didn't have anything with us other than the banners and the odd megaphone. We were all chatting, it was a nice atmosphere. There were a couple of normal police officers around in their high-viz, but probably just the usual levels of security for Whitehall.'

I wondered briefly how my daughter came to have any knowledge of what was considered 'normal security'. 'And then?'

'And then, these bastards turned up. Sorry, but they were. Angry bastards, already pissed by ten in the morning and itching to kick a few heads in. Some had baseball bats. One of them had a bloody petrol bomb!'

'Jesus.' I took a deep breath as we waited at the lights.

'And it just all went downhill from there,' she said sadly. 'We tried to get moving, start the march, but they sort of had us penned in and then the riot police turned up – horses, pepper spray, water cannon, the lot. It was carnage.'

I nodded. I'd seen the footage on the news, watching it with a dawning sense of unease as we waited for a call from Grace. I think I knew she was there even before she confirmed it. Whenever something like that comes on the television I find myself searching for my daughter's face in the melee, even if the protest is in Chile or somewhere.

'And were you hurt?' I asked as the lights turned green and we pulled away.

'No. Not badly. Some guy pushed me around a bit, called me a woke bitch – like that's the worst thing they can come up with – shouting about what he and his mates like to do to girls like us...' There was real anger in her voice now, back to the fearless little warrior I knew. 'So I started shoving back, threw my banner at one of them and it caught him in the eye, got hold of one of the megaphones, you know...' She shrugged.

'And that's when you were arrested?'

'Not *arrested*. Cautioned. Civil disobedience. They told me I was lucky not to be charged with inciting violence. Inciting violence?! I said to the officer, you must be really bloody stupid if you think I'm the problem here, which didn't exactly help the situation.'

'Oh, Grace.'

'And they bundled us all up into a riot van while they tried to get control of the situation. A whole bunch of us – some protesters, some far-right Nazis... So that was fun.'

I winced, imagining the scene and wondering how on earth my tiny little girl, who surely was only five years old a few moments ago, could have ended up in a police van with a load of psychopaths.

'Anyway,' she said, leaning back into the seat. 'Next time we'll be more careful. Plan a route with more exit points, try and keep it off the socials until the morning of the demonstr...'

'Next time,' I interrupted. 'Are you sure you want to do this again?'

'I won't be bullied by people like that, Mum,' she said, turning to me, her expression fierce. 'I *won't*. This is too important.'

My heart sank. I recognised that tone from teenage arguments over topics such as curfew times, full-sleeve tattoos and the inappropriateness of kicking one's brother even if he's *being a total knobhead*. Resistance was futile, as I had learnt to my cost. 'But your father and I – we were worried about you,' I said, trying my best. 'We're worried about your safety, worried you'll end up with a criminal record and the impact it'll have on the rest of your life, Grace. You won't be able to travel to certain countries or work in certain professions, you won't be...'

'There's no travel on a dead planet, Mum,' she said, arms folded in front of her. 'There are no jobs, no safety, no society if the world is on fire.'

'Yes, I get that, but—'

'I can't just do nothing, Mum. You understand that, surely? I don't want to look back and think I should have acted, I should have made a difference while it still counted...'

I nodded. As I said, resistance is futile.

Chapter Twenty-Three

Saturday 1 April

April Fool's Day

'So I told her that I understood, and that she had my blessing,' I said, pushing a bramble out of the way of the footpath.

'You said what?' Sam's voice was muffled beneath his scarf.

'I said I supported her, Sam. Grace has my full support. I might even join her sometime.'

'You!' he spluttered. 'You, on a protest march?'

'Yes,' I said, my voice calm as we navigated the puddles after last night's downpour. 'Grace said there are all sorts of people involved. Even some as old as me!' I was hoping to get a little laugh out of him at this comment, but no luck. His brow furrowed in consternation under his beanie hat.

'Is it not enough that I've got a criminal niece,' said Rory coming up behind us and clapping me around the shoulders, 'without my little sister being locked up, too?' I could tell without looking at his face that he was much more amused by this than my husband, which was guaranteed to wind Sam up even further.

'You just wait, Rory mate,' he muttered darkly. 'You wait until MJ decides she wants to raise awareness about the plight of the Madagascan lemur and chains herself to the railings outside Buckingham Palace.'

'Are we going to Buckingham Palace?' said MJ. She had caught us up and was now trudging determinedly alongside her father, red wellingtons struggling for purchase. 'We'll see the King?'

'No, darling, not today.' Rory grabbed her hand to keep her upright.

'Oh.' She looked disappointed. 'I'd really like to see a king. It's nice visiting Aunty Penny, but...'

'I bet the King doesn't know where the fairy houses are, though,' I said enigmatically. 'He's probably never even seen them.'

'Fairies aren't real,' MJ said with a frown.

'Well, their houses are definitely real,' I said. This was a factually correct statement. 'Shall I show you?'

MJ considered my proposition with the level of gravity it demanded. 'OK,' she said, pulling her mittened hand away from Rory and slotting it into mine. 'But can you make sure I don't wobble? My wellies is slidey.'

'Absolutely,' I said as I skidded off the track in the general direction of the fairy village. 'Solid as a rock, I am. Nimble as a mountain goat.'

'You is funny, Aunty Penny,' she said seriously. We stumbled our way to the copse of trees that someone had been kind enough to turn into a tiny hobbit village, Montmorency pulling hard on the lead while I tried to look like I had some semblance of control over him.

'Do the fairies have garages too for their fairy cars, Aunty Penny? Is they having fairy school?'

'Not sure. We'll keep a lookout.'

'Will Montymossy eat the fairies?' she said, watching the dog with concern.

'No, definitely not. He doesn't like the taste of fairies, or elves, nymphs, sprites, anything of that nature. Besides, fairies know how to hide from dogs just like they can hide from us. But luckily they leave their acorn porch lights on and their tiny doormats out so we can at least see where they live.'

'Like on *Location, Location, Location*?'

'Very similar.'

'Am I doing good imagining, Aunty Penny?' MJ's brow was furrowed in concentration and I remembered her saying at Christmas that her teacher Mrs McCarthy had asked her to use her imagination a bit more. She was clearly troubled by the idea that she was not doing everything perfectly at school.

'You are,' I said. 'Spectacularly good. But do you know, there's no special clever way to do imagining, you can do it however you like. If Mummy reads you a story and you see a picture in your head then that's imagining, and if someone tells you about a funny thing that happened with a smelly dog and you feel like you can smell that smelly dog, then that's imagining, too.' We approached the first treehouse which had a turret formed from a branch and a tiny, curtained window lit by a solar panel. 'And if you see a fairy house and you can't picture the fairies hiding inside it doing their ironing, then that's OK too. You can just enjoy the pretty house and think it looks cool in the tree.'

'That's good,' she said. 'I'll tell Mrs McCarthy.'

I spent a much more enjoyable hour discovering hidden doorways and staircases in the trunks of ancient oaks with my niece than I would have done arguing with my husband about Grace's protest march, although I dare say that in my absence Rory was probably doing his best to stir the pot of discontent for his own amusement. He can't help himself. Sam hadn't really had a proper chat with Grace since her return. She'd done her usual trick of disappearing almost as soon as we'd reached home. *Out with friends*, her message read, which I guess was more information than we sometimes had.

'Would just be nice to know she's not in prison,' Sam had said gloomily when we received this particular text. But then he hadn't had the informative car conversation I'd had with our daughter and was therefore still in the *grumpy* phase of worried parent. I had moved into the *understanding* phase (or as Sam would put it, the *trying to be a cool parent despite being worried* phase).

Unfortunately, in addition to Grace and the riot police, there was another issue niggling away at our display of marital harmony this weekend. Over supper last night I'd been talking excitedly about the gala dinner and how amazing it was that we'd secured The Carlton.

'Whoa, The Carlton!' Sam looked impressed. 'I've been to a do there. When we were working on the Nationwide account. It's very plush.' He rubbed his hands together. 'Well done, Pen,' he said. 'That'll be a cracking night out. Can't wait.'

I didn't tell him that it was Joe who'd booked the hotel – there's no harm in taking the credit for someone else's work when it's just you talking to your husband, is there? 'So I think there was a cancellation,' I said. 'Because they only had availability for the last weekend in July. After that they were taking bookings for two years' time.'

He paused the gleeful hand-rubbing and gave me a strange look. 'End of July?' he said. 'Not the twenty-ninth?'

'No,' I said, 'twenty-eighth. Friday the twenty-eighth. How lucky is that?'

'It's the triathlon, Pen,' he said, clearly hurt that I didn't have it imprinted on my memory. 'The last weekend in July is the triathlon. I'll be in Scotland.'

'But it— What? Are you sure?'

'Yes! I've been training for the past two months – as you've pointed out many times. I think I'd know when the challenge deadline was.'

'But it's not on the kitchen calendar,' I said, guilt making me defensive. I could see he was upset but honestly, how was I supposed to keep tabs on all of his comings and goings if he didn't record the dates properly?

'Your calendar?' He sounded confused. 'You mean, the one you use for the kids' activities and the dog's trips to the vet, and when the cars need their MOT and when the dishwasher repair guy's coming?'

'The one I use to *organise the household*,' I said, witheringly. 'Of which you are a member. Do you not even refer to it? Did it not occur to you that it might be useful for me to have a record of your buggering off to Scotland for four nights?'

'I did refer to it!' he sulked. 'When I made the booking. I looked to make sure there was nothing important going on.'

'You. Did. Not,' I said, that ready anger bubbling just beneath the surface. 'You thrust the iPad under my nose, asked me if it was OK and when I begrudgingly said yes because I felt cornered, it turned out you'd already booked your space! Don't come at me with this "I took *your* schedule into consideration" crap when we both know that's not true. If you had, you wouldn't be doing the bloody thing at all!'

We both stood there fuming at each other for a moment.

'Well,' I said eventually, 'I'm sorry that I didn't remember the *exact dates* of your triathlon challenge – the one you hadn't written down on the calendar. But the fact remains that this is the only date the hotel can do. They have no other availability, and it was a massive coup to get the booking and I'm not going to change it just because you want to jump in a cold pond and go for a damp bike ride.' (I felt bad at this point; Sam's face was closed off and I knew I'd pushed it too far with that last comment – it was just plain rude.)

'OK.' He shrugged, deflated. 'I guess we'll just spend that weekend apart then.'

'Fine. I guess we will.' I made a big gesture of crossing the kitchen to mark out the weekend on the calendar in thick black pen. And then I put the kettle on. The anger was ebbing away as quickly as it had arrived.

'Do you want a cup of tea?' I asked politely – which was my way of saying sorry.

'No,' he said. His voice was quiet. 'Thanks, but no. I'm popping out.' And this was his way of saying he needed a bit of time to forgive me for my horrific cruelty.

I don't think our conversation today regarding Grace has exactly built any bridges, but luckily by the time MJ and I had finished looking for fairies (and debated how Phil and Kirsty might describe the structural elements of their homes), Sam and Rory had made it back to the café with Maisie, Candice and Callum and everyone seemed quite chipper. Mum and Dad were already there – the wheelchair was just too cumbersome for the footpaths, and after Rory had nearly turfed Mum out onto the gravel about four times (my brother's attitude to most activities is 'run at it fast', which isn't necessarily good when in charge of a pensioner) he'd wheeled her back round and up the ramp to the tearoom where they'd been sitting ever since, Mum staring at the table and eating occasional bites of gingerbread doused in tea, and Dad reading a copy of *Motor World Weekly* from last year.

Maisie was now helping Dad do the magazine crossword, having decided that the fairy village was just too babyish for an eleven-year-old. Candice was looking rosy-cheeked and outdoorsy although there were dark circles under her eyes if you looked closely (I couldn't help it – she's so beautiful that I have to seek meagre amounts of solace from her tiny imperfections when I can). And the likely source of those circles, Callum, had fallen asleep in his pushchair and was now snoring gently, a trickle of drool gathering on his downy little cheek. The café was stiflingly hot and condensation ran down the insides of the windows as the steam from the coffee-maker belched out from behind the counter, but after a chilly fairy hunt the warmth was quite welcome and MJ and I quickly divested ourselves of gloves and hats.

'Hi, Mummy,' Maisie waved from her corner of the table where she was still peering down at the crossword. 'How do you spell carburettor?'

'Uuuhhhm. I don't know. Ask me another.'

'Can I have an all-day breakfast panini?'

'Yes,' I said, peering at the menu.

'And a smoothie?'

I looked at Sam. 'Yes?'

'Whatever you want, poppet,' said my husband, not fully grasping the fact that this sort of invitation to Maisie would be taken to its literal extreme.

By the time the waitress brought the trays of food to our table it looked as though we'd ordered for a family twice the size of ours.

'Goodness. We need Tom,' I said. 'Where's a starving seventeen-year-old boy when you need one?' Tom was at home, ostensibly 'doing some coursework' but more likely playing *Call of Duty*. Surprisingly the prospect of a chilly walk in the park with his very small cousins had not been hugely appealing, but I was still a bit annoyed with him for bailing out. Some family activities just had to be undertaken regardless of whether you thought you'd enjoy yourself or not. I'd been put through all manner of visits to draughty old churches, military museums and stone monuments perched atop windy cliffsides in my youth, and it hadn't done me any harm (other than the fact that I still complained bitterly about it to this day).

'Do you remember that time you made us visit Billington airfield, Dad?' I said now. 'It was snowing. I thought my feet were going to fall off.'

'And we weren't allowed to buy anything in the gift shop,' laughed Rory. 'Because the novelty pencils were fifty pee and you said that was daylight robbery.'

Dad smiled indulgently. 'You loved that trip,' he said. 'I remember you found a funny-shaped stone, Penny, and you brought it home and kept it on the windowsill for years.'

'Funny-shaped stones,' I said to Maisie meaningfully. 'That was what counted as a souvenir in my youth. Think on next time you want a life-size foam replica of Taylor Swift from Madame Tussauds.'

Callum was stirring in his pushchair and our collective attention was momentarily diverted as he opened his mouth to wail before things took a dramatic turn at the far end of the table.

'Mummy,' cried Maisie. 'Look at Granny! She can't breathe!'

Chapter Twenty-Four

Saturday afternoon

Mum had decided she fancied a piece of Maisie's panini, and it seemed she had literally bitten off more than she could chew. To be honest, I'm surprised she still has the manual dexterity and coordination to get something into her mouth, but once in, the toasted crust had wedged itself in her airway. For a moment we all sat motionless, watching as Mum's eyes started to water and bulge, her throat bobbing ineffectually as she tried to clear the offending item. And then Rory shot into action, leaping up from the table and racing around to Mum's side. Within seconds he had pushed her forward in the wheelchair and was thumping her on the back, the thwacks of his palm between her shoulder blades clearly audible.

'Why is Daddy doing that?' asked MJ with a sort of worried but detached interest.

'Has my panini killed Granny?' shrieked Maisie, ever the drama queen.

'Mum?' I said, grabbing her hand and trying not to panic as her face took on a dusky hue. 'Mum, it's going to be all right. Rory's going to sort it all out. It's all going to be fine.'

'Call an ambulance,' shouted Rory. The woman with the pink-rinse hair behind the till pulled out her phone.

Callum was yelling his head off by now and Candice had moved to our end of the table.

'We're going to need to get her up out of the chair for an abdominal thrust to be effective,' she murmured to my brother and he nodded, gesturing for Sam to come and help. Between them they hauled Mum into a semi-standing position and Rory circled his hands around her middle. Oddly, one of my first thoughts was that her cardigan wasn't buttoned up properly, watching as she dangled there like a rag doll. Rory pulled his hands sharply back, inward and upward. Still nothing.

'Come on, Mum,' he said, as if he could dislodge the panini bolus by force of will alone. He repositioned himself and gave another almighty thrust under her ribcage.

There wasn't a projectile missile like some of the stories you hear about the Heimlich manoeuvre (which was a little disappointing), but something did seem to shift and Mum took in a raspy gulp of air, letting out a little moan on the exhale.

'Mum?' I said, watching her face. 'Rory, I think she's breathing.'

The woman with the pink hair was now standing at our very crowded end of the table holding a hard orange plastic case. 'Do we need the defibrillator?' she asked. 'I'm first-aid trained. Should we do mouth-to-mouth?'

Candice was watching Mum's breathing. It was now coming in shallow gasps but had some regularity. She nudged me aside to check her pulse.

'I think we're OK,' she said kindly to the pink-haired lady.

'Are you absolutely sure? I *am* first-aid trained.'

'She's a doctor,' I said. Candice gave an embarrassed little grimace. 'And so's he.' I gestured to my brother.

The woman with pink hair looked a little deflated. 'Well, just let me know,' she said.

'Thank you *so* much for calling the ambulance,' Candice said, her voice full of warm emphasis. 'Did they say how long they'd be?'

Rory and I meanwhile were trying to arrange Mum comfortably back in her wheelchair. I wrapped her coat around her shoulders, not because it was cold (it was anything but) – but it felt like something one did with a person who had been involved in a traumatic incident. That and the fact that her Max Mara coat was guaranteed to put a smile on her face. Since I'd bought it in January she'd worn it practically every day and I had no idea what would happen when summer eventually arrived; I'd probably find her bundled up in it on the hottest day of the year.

'Would you like a little drink of water, Mum?' I said, making enquiring eyes at Rory and Candice (and even pink-haired lady – anyone who looked vaguely medical or authoritative).

'Very cautious, I think,' said Rory. 'I'm not convinced that her swallow is great. She might end up aspirating.'

I didn't really know what aspirating was but it didn't sound ideal and I didn't want to be responsible for it. 'I'll let you,' I said, handing the glass to Candice.

Mum took a shaky sip but started to cough and splutter so Candice held off. A few moments later the ambulance arrived and a couple of burly paramedics clad in fluorescent yellow strode through the doorway full of practical bonhomie and chatter. There was a brief exchange of information between them and my brother while they checked Mum's oxygen saturations and respiratory rate.

'It was a panini,' I said helpfully. 'An all-day breakfast one. My daughter's, actually. She didn't finish it.' (With hindsight I realised this particular level of detail was not required.)

Once they'd listened to Mum's chest (and handed the stethoscope to Rory so he could have a listen too), they wheeled her into the back of the ambulance where Dad took a seat beside her and held her hand. Half the café were standing on the walkway to wave her off; many of them had their phones out and seemed to be recording the whole thing, which was a bit weird, but then I guess it's not every day you witness that kind of drama. Quite a few of our residents at Bob's have issues with their swallowing so it's not my first rodeo, ambulance-wise, but I've never seen the Heimlich manoeuvre performed before.

'God, I'm glad you were here,' I said to my brother as they closed the doors on my parents. 'I'd have been hopeless. I guess you must do this all the time.'

'Literally never done it before in my life,' said Rory cheerfully. 'Choking on a panini wasn't a common occurrence in the army, and my patients aren't usually eating during consultations. Only time you usually need to do the Heimlich is as a civilian – it's not really a medical procedure.'

'Guess not,' I said. 'Maybe it's just your natural air of confident authority that's reassuring then.'

'Probably.' He smiled. 'You couldn't tell I was bricking it?'

I shook my head. 'No! Not at all!'

'Quite scary having to do that to your frail elderly mother,' he said. 'I think I felt one of her ribs break.'

I raised my eyebrows. 'Yikes,' I said. 'But you know – you also saved her life.'

'Hmm.' He didn't look convinced. 'We'll see. You can get secondary complications in someone that age, particularly when she's got such a poor respiratory output. They'll definitely want to keep her in overnight for monitoring, and I expect she'll see the speech and language team, check her swallowing reflex.'

We agreed that Rory would drive Dad's car and follow the ambulance to the hospital while I went to the bungalow and gathered up a few of her belongings.

'At least she's got her best coat,' he said, smiling as he opened the driver's door.

Sam had paid the bill and updated the café staff and customers as to Mum's progress. A few people were still filming on their phones even now the ambulance had gone, so I suspect there'll be a couple of very boring TikTok videos of my husband doing the rounds, saying things like, 'she looked like she was breathing a bit more easily' and 'lucky there's a doctor in the family', with a comedy grimace and thumbs up. Unlikely to go viral, I imagine.

'Well,' he said once we'd parted ways with Candice, MJ and Callum. 'That was quite something. Are you OK?'

'I think so,' I said. 'I'll feel better once I know she's been checked over properly – in hospital. But yes, it was quite frightening, wasn't it?' My voice gave a little wobble that I tried to steady for Maisie's benefit. 'I genuinely thought for a moment...'

He nodded as he started the engine. 'So did I.'

'I hope Granny's going to be OK.' Maisie's voice was quiet from the back seat.

I turned to give her knee a squeeze. 'I'm sure she will be,' I said, knowing that Granny was never really going to be what most people would describe as OK.

'I did finish up the rest of the panini,' she said, more upbeat. 'So it couldn't do any more harm.'

'Good for you,' I said. 'That probably made all the difference.'

—

Later I met up with Dad and Rory at the hospital. I no longer feel the same trepidation about medical institutions and appointments that I used to. In fact, through a combination of working in the care sector, being related to a couple of doctors and looking after Mum, I've become quite the expert. Mum has been in and out of A&E on a fairly regular basis over the past few years with various funny turns, falls and infections. Sometimes she has to stay in for observation which she absolutely hates, because there is nothing more confusing to a confused person than an institution that does not distinguish between day and night. But most of the time the staff in A&E seem to understand that keeping an elderly woman with dementia in hospital against her wishes is less than ideal and they send her home on the same day. Sometimes it's me sitting with her, playing the waiting game as the casualty team deal with far scarier things behind noisily billowing curtains. Sometimes it's Dad. And occasionally, Rory makes an appearance. It's quite a rarity for all three of us to be there, though and the A&E nurse didn't look thrilled as we added to the congestion in the department.

'I'll head back to Candice and the kids,' said my brother after a cursory hug. He was evidently bored by just hanging around waiting, although after his heroic lifesaving antics earlier I couldn't really begrudge him some time with his young family. His job means that Candice is often on her own looking after the kids, and Callum can be a bit of a handful (I say that in a doting aunty way, when what most people would describe him as is a bloody nightmare). As he pulled on his jacket I felt the momentary panic of knowing our family expert was about to leave the building. I knew a lot about Mum's condition, about her day-to-day needs, but Rory knew the language of hospital. He was fluent in it. We non-native speakers were at a significant disadvantage when it came to making polite enquiries, as follows:

> 'Excuse me, staff nurse. Any idea how long we might be waiting? It's not a problem, of course, I can see that you're busy, but the parking is costing me the equivalent of a rental property in Chelsea...'

> or 'Did you say the doctor would be sending her for a scan, or to a different hospital? Not a problem, it's just we don't know anyone who lives in Leeds and I might need to organise a few things...'

> or 'Is there anywhere I can get a cup of tea? Not a problem, but I think I may just have sustained third-degree burns trying to get one out of the broken vending machine...'

> or 'That man has just vomited blood all over my shoes. It's not a problem, of course, I can see that you're busy, but where might I find a mop?'

or '*I think the lady in the corner might be dead. Not a problem, but should someone let the coroner know?*'

But it's a rarity, as I say, for Rory to be here, so I guess we just do what we always do in his absence – wait for information from an overstretched, under-resourced and absolutely knackered staff.

'They keeping you in, Mum?' I said, leaning over to kiss her forehead. I smoothed back the soft waves of hair from her face and straightened the collar of her blouse. 'You can probably take the coat off. It's quite warm in here.'

Dad shook his head. 'I've tried,' he said, smiling. 'She's not having a bar of it, are you, Mary?'

She turned to the sound of his voice but stared at him blankly.

'Are you all right, Dad? It's been quite an exhausting few hours already.' I pulled up a plastic chair and sat beside him.

'Might still be a long wait before they find her a bed,' said Rory, a half-guilty expression on his face. 'Should we take it in turns? I could come back in a few hours?'

'No, it's fine.' I gave him my most reassuring smile. 'You go. Give my love to the kids and Candice. We'll see you over Easter?'

'Yeah, lovely. Candy will be in touch about logistics.' He turned to go and then paused. 'Look, I can't imagine they'll get this far on a Saturday afternoon, but if anyone mentions her unsafe swallow and starts talking about artificial feeding, then let me know asap.'

'OK,' I said, a little uncertainly. 'Is that something they're likely to talk about?'

He sighed and lowered his voice so that only Dad and I could hear – not that Mum would have been listening; she seemed to be fascinated by the weave of the hospital-issue blanket. 'Because of the choking incident and her evident problems with swallowing, they might say that the only safe way to get food and drink into Mum is via a tube.'

'One that goes through her nose?' I asked. I'd seen those (mainly on TV, admittedly).

'Yes, initially. But NG tubes are mainly for fluids – they're a temporary solution. What they'd be aiming for is a PEG tube. Goes directly into the stomach.'

'Oh, right – yes, I think one of our residents, Brian, had one for a short while.'

'And did Brian have advanced dementia?' asked Rory.

'Yes.'

'And did he have a good quality of life with the PEG tube in?'

'Well, no. He didn't really have a great quality of life anyway, but after the tube he wasn't able to get to many of the activities and he obviously didn't come to the dining room for meals because... Oh, I see where you're going with this.'

'They work well for some conditions but they're a nightmare in the frail elderly,' he said grimly. 'It might prolong someone's life by a few months, but the gain is undermined by the recurrent infections, the blockages, the balancing of nausea and constipation and...'

'OK,' I said. 'No PEG, I get it.'

'I'm just saying I'd want to be present for any conversations about it,' Rory said quietly. 'I'm not trying to take over.'

'It's a relief, Rory,' said Dad, voicing my exact thoughts. 'It's good to have someone around to prepare us in advance of these sorts of things.'

Rory looked disproportionately pleased by this comment, but I guess Dad has always been sparing with his praise where his son is concerned. A situation mirrored with Mum and I in the past – until she developed dementia and became inordinately happy about the smallest things I did. Prior to a few years ago it felt like she directed all of her criticism at me and all of her pride (and forgiveness) at Rory. But since her diagnosis, and particularly since the period when she lived with me, she's much more demonstrative of her affection. It's a cruel twist of fate that it took the disinhibiting effects of dementia for us to reach this warm equilibrium, but, as my father says, it is what it is. I waved Rory off, squeezed Mum's hand and settled myself in for a long wait.

Chapter Twenty-Five

Tuesday 11 April

I was thinking about the peculiar twists and turns of my relationship with Mum today at work – the fact that her dementia has paradoxically brought us closer together. I know it can just as easily go the other way and a person can forget a spouse or child entirely. Many times I've had the sense of trepidation that I might walk into my parents' house and have Mum say, 'Who are you?' She'd done it with Rory when he first came back from Australia and it nearly broke his heart. I'd seen it here at Bob's Place, too. Family members in tears because their loved one no longer remembered them, or worse, associated them with something bad. One client's grandson had a terrible time of persuading Grandad that he wasn't some sort of malign force. And all this while Grandad had arbitrarily decided that both his granddaughters were an absolute pleasure to have around. 'It's so unfair,' the client's daughter had said to me. 'Dad always smiles when the girls visit, thrilled to see them, and then Josh arrives and it's all hard stares and "leave me alone". It's been really difficult for him. He's only fifteen. He doesn't understand that for whatever reason Grandad has confused him with someone else, someone he didn't like.'

We had at least been able to direct Josh and his grand-father towards one of our counsellors to talk through some of these issues. Having a family therapist come in for sessions three times a week was one of the best decisions we ever made as a business, although it was a decision that Joe was now questioning in our Monday meeting, albeit very politely.

'She's just very expensive,' he said, looking through Fatima's contract. 'If you need her, you need her, but I wondered whether in the interests of reducing your outgoings you could...'

'We need her,' I said firmly. 'And we need her three times a week. A lot of our clients have had absolutely no contact with a therapist or counsellor before they come here, and their spouses and families are even less likely to have had that sort of support. We all,' I gestured to Tina, and Veronica who was going through the post, 'felt that it was an essential part of the package we offer.'

He held his hands up. 'Fair enough,' he said. 'Absolutely fair enough. I'm just trying to help.'

'Good news, team,' Veronica interrupted. She was holding our most recent electricity bill in her hand and thumped it down on the table triumphantly. 'That fixed rate Penny managed to secure us last November on our gas and electricity has saved us thousands of pounds.'

'Yay, Penny!' Tina was beaming.

'Well, that was a stroke of genius,' said Joe. 'I bet there's a few companies who wish they'd done the same thing before prices went through the roof. Good call, Penny.'

'Why, thank you.' I nodded modestly, secretly very pleased with myself.

'This calls for a celebration,' announced Veronica. 'We need a team night out. Nothing flash – can't afford to blow the budget. How about dinner at The Thatched Inn this Friday?'

Joe and I both consulted our phones.

'I think that works for me,' I said. 'The kids are still off school but that shouldn't affect things, and Grace might still be around for her extended *reading week*.' I put heavy emphasis on this to demonstrate how little reading my daughter has actually been doing over the Easter period. 'Sam's away on another training weekend. The triathlon's only three months away, as he keeps reminding me.' I glanced at the rest of the table. 'Sorry, did that sound bitter?'

Tina laughed. 'No, not at all. How's he getting on with it? You must remind me to sponsor him. I keep forgetting.'

'Oh, don't worry,' I said. 'He'll remind you himself. Pretty much every time he sees you. It's all he bloody talks about.'

'Now that *did* sound slightly bitter,' said Veronica. 'Although I have to agree with you. He's the same at work. I've told him I don't want to hear any more about how many reps he's done or what he's benching, but if he's away for a training weekend then I expect I'll hear all about it on Monday.'

'You and me both,' I muttered.

Joe finished tapping things into his phone. 'There,' he said, having clearly shifted some arrangements around. 'Friday looks good.'

'Great,' said Tina. 'I'll phone them this evening, book us a table.' She turned to me. 'Now,' she said. 'We haven't really caught up about what happened with your mum.'

I filled them in regarding the drama of the previous Saturday. 'She was back home for Easter,' I said. 'Which was nice. But lunch on Sunday was a bit fraught. She's on thickened fluids instead of solid food because the speech therapists weren't happy about her choking risk, and it felt a bit cruel having her up at the table with us but not able to eat any of the roast. She kept reaching for bits of food from everyone else's plates and we had to stop her, and just offer her mashed potato and gravy instead. It's like baby-led weaning but in reverse.' I looked at Tina and Veronica's blank faces, remembering that neither of them had children of their own.

Joe was nodding. 'I remember that phase,' he said. 'Lisa was obsessed with pureeing things for Milo. Sweet potato, carrot, swede... Turned all the plastic fittings in the dishwasher bright orange after a while.'

'It does!' I nodded fervently. 'And the Tupperware.'

'Anyway,' said Tina, gently returning me to topic. 'At least she's out of hospital.'

I nodded. 'Yes.' There was a pause. 'But you've got to wonder, for how long? I can see Dad watching her the whole time now – he's riddled with anxiety, waiting for the next medical emergency. I don't think last Saturday did his stress levels any good.

'One thing that was helpful, though: the hospital had a word with him about Mum's care package, going forward. There was a lovely occupational therapist who spent time talking to him – they had a very considered conversation about where Mum would be safest, and when Dad said that his daughter ran Bob's Place, she said she'd heard only good things about us and that maybe it really would be worth considering us as a long-term option.'

'Which is what you and Rory have been saying, isn't it,' said Joe.

I nodded.

'I'm amazed you've held off for as long as you have,' said Veronica with a deep sigh. 'My dad had to go into residential care within months of his dementia diagnosis.

I just couldn't cope. He was a danger to himself and to me.'

'And did he hate you for it?' I said in a small voice. 'Sorry to ask, but...'

'No, you're all right. I don't mind.' She considered my question. 'I really don't think he did,' she said eventually. 'I might be deluding myself, but I think there was still enough of him left to know that it was the best option, to realise that living independently was no longer safe and that living with me was killing us both.'

'I'm going to have a chat with Dad tonight, I think. He might be more amenable to the idea following the conversation with the OT, and having been so shocked by that choking episode. It might have made him see that he can do what's right by Mum and still have some life of his own...'

'You OK, love?' said Tina, putting her hand over mine.

I brushed away a tear. 'Yes, thanks,' I said, grateful for her concern. 'It's just been an emotional couple of weeks, what with one thing and another. Having all the kids back home again, trying to work out what Grace is going to do after university and how to stop her getting into trouble with the law. Trying to mend Tom's broken heart and not lose my temper with him for mooning around the place like a wounded puppy. And everything with Mum. And Dad. It just feels like loads of big, heavy decisions to make.'

Joe let out a deep breath. 'God, it's tough for you guys,' he said, with feeling. 'You and Sam must be finding it difficult, working it all out.'

I shrugged, not willing to admit in front of Veronica that Sam had spent a lot of the past week running, lifting weights and cold-water swimming in the local flooded quarry. He and I hadn't really spoken about plans for Mum

– but then, it was mainly a decision for me, Rory and Dad. And, of course, the woman herself. Problem was, Mum couldn't articulate what she wanted. We were in the unenviable position of making a choice on her behalf without being able to consult her in any way.

Chapter Twenty-Six

Friday 14 April

I did manage to speak to Dad a few days ago and I was right: the fear of Mum choking, falling or having another funny turn, combined with the advice of the hospital team, have resulted in a bit of an epiphany. He is now more open to the idea of a semi-permanent residential placement for Mum. 'Not forever,' he was quick to clarify. 'But maybe just take it a few weeks at a time. See how it goes.'

'That's it,' I said. 'If she was unhappy and couldn't settle then we'd stop, she'd come home. That's one of the huge advantages of Bob's Place – we can be flexible about duration of stay.'

'And she knows everyone there,' said Dad, mainly seeking to reassure himself.

'She *does* know everyone there,' I agreed. 'And all the staff love her. And I'd be there almost every day. You could be there as much or as little as you wanted. You could stay over some nights, or not. Just play it by ear?'

'She has fallen a few times,' he said. 'As well as what happened last Saturday. Worried me a bit.'

'Yes,' I said, wanting to be very careful with this candid admission from my father. 'And Rory has said that medically it might be better for her to be looked after by qualified staff. Might be a bit safer in terms of her falling, and also the swallowing.'

He nodded. The safety aspect was a good card to play, appealing to his logical, reasoning side, like Joe had suggested last month. Dad was genuinely fearful for Mum's health now and it was starting to give him a haunted expression. And for me, the thought of Mum having a choking fit brought on by a mouthful of food delivered by Dad, and him having to sit and watch her spluttering to death and feeling like he'd caused it – that was the kind of scenario that kept me awake at night (along with all the other crap, like whether Grace was taking her multivitamins, whether I'd locked the back door, and whether my husband still fancied me, obviously).

'And I'd be able to come in and see her whenever I wanted?' He furrowed his haywire eyebrows at me.

'Whenever you wanted. Yes.'

'Hmm.'

I left it at that. He had to come to this decision on his own, which in classic my father fashion he did within twenty-four hours of the conversation.

'Do you have space for your mother?' he said when he called me this morning.

'Space?' I shouted at the phone. 'In the car? She doesn't normally come with me on a Friday, Dad, and I'm already halfway there.' I pulled off the main road and onto the quieter lane to Bob's Place.

'No, I meant *space*,' he said meaningfully. 'As discussed.'

'Oh, yes, of course. I'll see what the availability's like.'

'Is it a question of waiting for one of the current residents to die?' he said, clipped and matter-of-fact.

'Uhm, well, not always,' I said. 'Sometimes residents move on to a different place, geographically rather than spiritually. But yes, a lot of the time, it is.' I already knew we had a room free since Doreen had died a week ago. She was ninety-four and had been an avid collector of china figurines. Her daughter had come to collect her belongings a few days ago and had left with a carful of clanking porcelain milkmaids and shepherdesses. I winced every time she thudded over a speed bump on her way out.

'Right. Good. We'll get things organised then. Just for a trial run. OK. Bye, love.'

He doesn't do small talk on the phone, my dad. He doesn't really do small talk full stop.

I mentioned all this to Tina, Veronica and Joe this evening when we went out for our meal to rejoice about the 'could have been much worse' utility bills (not a traditional celebration in many cultures, but small wins and all that). Tina had booked The Thatched Inn which was just around the corner from Bob's Place, a venue we had frequented so many times that they had decided to lay on a 'Bob's Afternoon' once a week in the summer for any residents who wanted a half-price pint in the pub garden.

'Well of course we can find space for your mum,' said Tina immediately. 'There's the Corfu Room, now that Doreen's – uhm—'

'Died?' said Veronica, never one to beat around the bush.

'Yes, exactly.' Tina wiped a little tear from her eye. 'I'm going to miss her.'

'I know. She was a poppet, wasn't she,' I said. 'I don't think the cleaners will miss dusting all that porcelain though.' I held my glass of prosecco aloft. 'A toast – to Doreen. And her many china milkmaids.'

'To Doreen,' Veronica, Tina and Joe murmured, chinking their glasses with mine.

'I'll let Dad know,' I said. 'I think maybe we'll need a couple of weeks to get our heads around it but we'll aim for the start of May. That way Mum will be there in time for the "Spring into Summer" picnic fundraiser.'

I was trying to focus on the practicalities but occasionally I caught myself thinking, *this is it*, this is what we have all tried to avoid for so long but now it's finally here, Mum going into a care home. In these moments of doubt it didn't matter that the home was Bob's Place, or that I worked there, or that we'd held off for as long as we had. In those moments the only thought nibbling away at my brain was, *how could you put your own mother in a home*, and the only feeling was guilt. I tried to explain it to Joe a little later once Tina and Veronica had left (pleading age and Saturday-morning art gallery commitments as their respective excuses for needing an early night).

'It is hard,' I admitted, sinking my fourth or fifth glass of prosecco (that's the trouble with starting an evening drinking fizz: you end up sticking with it for the duration – often not the best plan). 'I know it's the right thing. Rory knows it's the right thing. Dad knows.'

'But it still doesn't make it an easy decision,' said Joe. 'I do get it. I remember when my aunt went into a home because of her Parkinson's. Everyone was racked with guilt for months. Even now my mum struggles with it, and it wasn't even her decision, it was my uncle's. He's always got this apologetic look on his face whenever he sees us at family events, like he let the side down by admitting defeat. But she was just too disabled for him to look after. She was in and out of hospital, one infection after another.' He looked sad for a moment.

'Were you close?' I asked. 'It sounds like a close family.'

'Yes, I guess we were,' he said. 'She and my uncle didn't have any kids of their own so they spoilt us rotten when we were little. They were always the cool ones – they travelled a lot, lived in France and then Canada for a while. My ex and I used to visit them for holidays when Milo was small.'

'That's nice,' I said, and then after a short pause, 'Why did you split up?'

He looked surprised, as well he might. We'd never had *that* sort of conversation.

'God, I'm sorry,' I said. 'I have no idea why that came out of my mouth. I must be more pissed than I thought. Sorry. Ignore me. It's none of my business.'

He shrugged. 'It's OK,' he said. 'I'm fine talking about it. Besides, you've just confided in me about how guilty you feel regarding your mum – it's clearly that kind of evening.'

Before I had time to wonder exactly what that kind of evening was, he was gesturing to the barman for another drink. I realised that he was probably pretty drunk too, given how much we'd consumed along with our meal. Luckily we were both getting taxis home, although we'd already worked out that we were in completely opposite directions so couldn't share one.

'Lisa left me for her personal trainer,' he said once he'd got another pint in front of him.

'Shit!'

'Yes,' he laughed. 'It was.'

I didn't really know what to say after that. If it had been a female friend confiding in me about the fact that her husband had left her for his personal trainer I'd have been able to fully embrace the righteous indignation, but somehow it felt a bit different this way round.

'It's just such a cliché, isn't it?' He shrugged. 'That was the worst thing about it in a way – feeling like people were laughing at me. Classic bloke reaction, I guess, worrying about the impact on my macho pride more than the end of a marriage, but I just felt like such a dick. I should have seen it coming.'

'Oh, I don't think it's unusual to feel that way,' I said. 'My mate Zahara, she discovered her husband was having an affair and she felt like she was the only person in the world not to have known. Whereas the truth was we were all completely gobsmacked. With hindsight the signs were there, of course…'

'Yeah, same. Plenty of signs once you start looking. Lisa was seven years younger than me, for a start. It doesn't feel like it's going to be an issue, that sort of age gap. And I know a lot of people manage with an even bigger gap than that, but I should have realised I needed someone who was more of an equal. Someone who knew herself and didn't expect me to constantly reassure her, validate her. Lisa had a lot of growing up to do – which I didn't see at the time – and there were sort of cultural reference points missing, too. My mate Dev always uses the KLF test. If she's never heard of the KLF then she's too young for you.'

I laughed at this. And felt a curious urge to explain that of *course* I knew who KLF were and had bopped along to many of their tunes in my teenage years. Although maybe I wouldn't have used the word *bopped*, because that sounded like something an elderly aunt might say.

'Lisa didn't really want to have kids that young either,' said Joe. 'I mean, of course she loves Milo now, adores him – she's a great mum. But she was twenty-four and we'd only been going out a few months when she found out she was pregnant. It wasn't long enough to get to know each other properly.'

'When did you separate?'

'Few years ago. The Covid lockdown didn't help. We couldn't get away from each other, and suddenly forced into each other's company for weeks on end, it was obvious we weren't as compatible as we'd thought. We used to sort of communicate *through* Milo, used him as a bridge or a barrier depending on how things were going. And that's not good for a kid. I think we both feel bad about that.'

'Is it amicable now?' I asked, intrigued in spite of myself.

He laughed sharply. 'I don't think you could call it amicable,' he said. 'We're civil. Just about. For Milo's sake. But to be honest, if I never had to see her again I wouldn't be too concerned. She's still with Phil, the personal trainer. He's all right, I suppose. I'm not thrilled about him being Milo's stepdad, but it could be worse.'

'And you're...?' Again the words were out of my mouth before I'd thought about it.

'Single,' he said firmly. 'I've had a few girlfriends since then but nothing serious.'

'Are you doing the whole dating app thing?' I said. 'Zahara tried it – eHarmony, Tinder, Fish in the Sea, or something?'

'Plenty of Fish.' He laughed. 'That's a bear pit – if I can mix my metaphors. No, I've been on there but it's all a bit...' He pulled a face.

'Yeah, that's how Zahara felt. She met Rajesh through the *Guardian* dating site which was a bit more civilised, I think. Soulmates. But that's closed now. Otherwise I'm sure she'd recommend it.'

'You don't need to fix me up, Penny,' he said laughing. 'I'm fine.'

'Sorry,' I said. 'Must be really annoying when people do that.'

He shrugged again. 'Most of my married friends have stopped trying to set me up,' he said. 'It's quite sweet when people try because everyone just wants me to be happy. But my requirements are a bit more specific these days – I want to be with someone who's done their growing up. If anything, I probably want someone a little bit older than me. A proper woman. Someone with a bit of life experience, who knows her own mind and is happy in her skin.'

I nodded. That made sense. After what had happened with Lisa.

'The trouble is,' he said, drawing a circle in the condensation on his pint glass. 'Women like that tend to already be taken.'

My thoughts immediately went to Zahara. That was the kind of woman he was describing. And, yes, Rajesh clearly felt that he had won the lottery when she said she'd marry him. But then Joe was right; women like her were few and far between.

'It's tricky,' I agreed.

'Anyway.' He looked up from his glass, caught my eye and smiled. 'Having had one relationship go sour, I think I'd rather be on my own than with the wrong person. I'm perfectly happy now.'

'Well, that's good.'

He gestured around the pub. 'What's not to like?' he said. 'I've got a great kid, I love my job, I get on really well with my bosses...'

I laughed and he leaned forward, propping his elbows on the table as he lifted his pint.

'Life is good,' he said.

'Yes. Yes, it is,' I agreed.

'And I'm quite drunk,' he said.

'Yes. Yes, you are.' I laughed.

'And so are you.' He smiled, a slow, lazy smile, and there was something in the look he gave me at that moment – it passed so quickly I almost missed it – that made me feel, I don't know, *seen*. Understood. Like my presence had been noted, and appreciated. Here we were, just two people enjoying each other's company, sharing stories, discussing things that I'd usually only talk about with close friends. Close female friends…

I swallowed hard and sat back in my chair. 'I'd better get home,' I said, hoping he couldn't hear the slight catch in my breathing. 'I've, uhm – I told the kids I wouldn't be late.'

This was a lie. Grace and Tom were both at home and Maisie would be fast asleep in bed by now. None of them would be remotely concerned as to my whereabouts. But I felt suddenly as though I needed to get out of there. Somewhere beneath the layers of warm, boozy fog and the 'life is good' chat, I felt odd. And I really did not want to interrogate that feeling. It was dangerous. That much I did know.

Chapter Twenty-Seven

Saturday 15 April

In the cold light of a new morning I realised I'd let my imagination run away with me last night. I think the weirdly charged atmosphere I'd initially perceived as some sort of sexual chemistry was probably just my body's way of saying I'd had too much alcohol and needed to get home to bed. Immediately after I told Joe I wanted to leave, he'd called us two separate taxis and ordered us both a pint of lime and soda each so we wouldn't feel too rough this morning. We'd moved straight on to talking about work, and it was as if that strange moment hadn't even happened. Which it probably hadn't.

Even so, I sent a message to Sam as soon as I got back last night. Just to let him know I was home safe. He had called before I left for the pub (he knew I was going out with people from work – there was no subterfuge – and I might not have specifically mentioned Joe but I hadn't *lied* about anything). Unfortunately, I'd been in a bit of a rush trying to sort my hair out and choosing the maxi dress that made me look the least like an ageing hippy, so I hadn't really been paying attention to his comments regarding his scheduled lake swim or his route from Kendal to whichever mountain he was planning on sprinting up. The whole thing sounded like madness. He'd gone on his own and I'd suggested he might be a bit lonely, but he told me he liked the headspace, found it relaxing – which is nice. I had pondered at the time what that might feel like. A whole weekend where the only person I needed to worry about was me. I can't think that I've had that sort of headspace in the past quarter of a century.

Anyway, point was, I messaged him and by the time I woke up this morning he had replied with a selfie of him wearing his tri-suit (like a wetsuit but more lightweight – and considerably more expensive, naturally) and his goggles, gurning into the camera like an idiot. I sent a heart emoji and a blue shivering face emoji and made the girls some breakfast before taking Grace to the station to go back to university for the last time. I still try and send her off with a food parcel of sorts. It's mainly fruit and veg, but I threw in a bag of pasta and some mixed grains she likes (but can rarely afford). I also snuck in a couple of bottles of wine but not so much that she'd be unable to carry it back to her student house.

'So, just concentrating on final exams and getting that dissertation handed in, yes?' I said as we loaded her ruck-sack and holdall into the boot. I managed to stop myself asking any questions about impending protest marches or demonstrations.

'Yes,' she said, using the tone that implied no further comment was necessary. She strapped herself into the passenger seat of the car.

'Did you manage to get much done – on the project?'

'*Yes*, Mum. Don't worry. It's all under control. I've managed to write up half my dissertation this week – despite Maisie coming into my room every seven minutes to ask my opinion on her outfit, her nail varnish, and whether she should try being vegan because it will be difficult when she likes bacon so much, and her friend Eva says vegans have no iron, and Leon at school, who is *not* her friend, says vegans smell of farts.' Grace always could mimic her sister perfectly.

'I can imagine she's not hugely conducive to quiet study,' I said, and we shared a smile.

'And any thoughts about afterwards?' I decided to risk it. Seeing as this was my last opportunity to ask the question. And seeing as she was captive in the car for the next twenty minutes with no means of escape. Car journeys as a parent are often tortuous affairs, particularly when the children are small and prone to screaming unless you sing back-to-back nursery rhymes or join in with their pointless game of 'what colour will the next lorry be', but sometimes they come into their own – and for inter-rogation purposes they are ideal. As demonstrated by the last time I'd been in the car with Grace and picked up all the useful information about her police caution (again, not a sentence I ever thought I'd be writing).

There was silence for a few moments and I resisted the urge to fill the space with chatter.

'I don't really know,' she admitted eventually. 'I've been looking online. Thought I might register with a recruitment agency.'

'Good idea,' I said.

'It's quite a tough job market,' she admitted. 'If I wanted to practise as a music therapist, I'd need extra training.'

My heart sank. More expense. 'Is that what you want to do? Be a therapist? Or is it the research side you're more interested in? And would the therapy qualification be like a diploma? Could you work while you were doing it?'

She sighed and I noticed she was doing that repetitive tapping with her fingers that showed she was anxious. I decided to leave it. She had enough to worry about getting to the end of her degree. 'Grace,' I said, placing my hand over hers to stop the fidgeting, just like I often had to do with Mum. 'Don't worry. It'll be fine. There's plenty of time to sort this out when you come home properly, when your degree's finished.'

'Yes, about that,' she said, suddenly changing tack (she's not so different from her sister after all). 'I was wondering... Rania's parents live abroad and she's got nowhere to stay once our contract with the student letting company runs out. I don't suppose she could come and live with us, could she? It would just be for a month or so.'

'Uhm...' I was a bit thrown. 'Is Rania the one who *was* actually arrested a few months ago?'

'Well, yes,' she said, sounding annoyed, 'but that's got nothing to do with it – she should never have been arrested in the first place.'

'But I thought she was the one who threw four litres of red paint over a statue of Christopher Columbus and then stood on the bonnet of a police car shouting, "Burn the establishment, not the planet", or something?'

Grace folded her arms across her chest in a huff. 'Well, if you're going to be prejudiced against a person because of a wrongful...'

'I'm not being *prejudiced*, Grace, for God's sake. You're suggesting someone comes to live in our house and I'm simply making enquiries into whether they have a criminal record – you don't think that's a reasonable ask, particularly given the context of your recent brush with the law?'

'I don't think she's got any formal convictions,' she said cagily. 'Anyway, she's lovely. She could stay in my room. She barely eats anything. You wouldn't even notice...'

'All right, Grace,' I said wearily. 'Don't push it, OK? I'll have a think.'

We drove on in silence for a few minutes.

'Has Tom talked to you at all?' I asked eventually. 'Does he seem any happier?'

She considered this for a moment. 'Not really, Mum. He's pretty morose. I know I can't talk. I was morose at his age too, but...'

'Do you think he's depressed?'

'No,' she said. I took solace in this because Grace has a lot of friends who are on antidepressants, or in therapy, or both. She'd be better at spotting it than me.

'I think he's just sad,' she said, matter-of-factly. 'He's been dumped. He'll get over it.'

'Will he, though?'

'Yes. And he'll get over it a bit quicker if you stop fussing around him asking if he's OK every five minutes.'

'Oh. Right.'

'Sorry, Mum.' She pulled an apologetic face. 'But I think maybe you've got to just stop treating him like a wounded zebra and let him get on with it.'

'He hasn't told me to stop fussing.'

'Well, maybe he quite likes being poor little Tom who needs extra hugs and snacks and lifts to places?'

I pursed my lips. 'Noted. Should I try and get your father to have a word instead?'

'What, if he's not busy *training*?' I could feel the roll of her eyes in perfect unison with mine.

'Maybe that's the key,' I said. 'Get Tom into triathlons with Dad for distraction from his love life. Although,' I indicated to pull into the station car park, 'when I think of all the additional sweaty Lycra I'd have to deal with, maybe not.'

I did try to talk to Sam this evening, but he was completely exhausted by the day's activities in the Lake District. He knows I'm worried, but Sam's default response when it comes to the kids is, it'll all be fine – right up to the point where it isn't. For example, he wouldn't think about pinning Grace down regarding this friend coming to stay with us until she's actually here and there's no food in the house and no hot water left and it'll be, 'who is this Rania anyway, and why are we harbouring a convict?' The implication being, 'how have you, Penny, allowed this situation to occur?'

There's a balance of course, but in any relationship one partner worries more than the other. And that partner is me. It's not that I'm a pessimist – I just worry about being too blindly optimistic, thereby overlooking some critical detail that results in abject failure or catastrophe, which will then be my fault. It's admittedly not a great state of mind to perpetually be occupying and is probably giving me a stomach ulcer, but I think a lot of mothers exist in this constant state of high alert.

When the fate of your future (in the form of your offspring) can be determined by the tiniest change in their surroundings – how much screen time they have, what they eat, how much they exercise, whether their parent (i.e. *mother*) is around at home or out at work, how they perform in their SATs, whether they smoke/drink/take drugs – then it's no surprise that we parents (again – *mothers*) are nervous wrecks, riddled with guilt and anxiety. If you do a good job, and everything goes well, and your child turns into a functioning member of society, nobody thanks you – that child just leaves home. And if it goes badly, they and every other judgemental fucker out there will blame you for the rest of your (and their) days. It's quite the responsibility, and almost enough to make one feel a tiny bit stressed.

Chapter Twenty-Eight

May the fourth be with you. A happy Star Wars Day to all who celebrate, particularly Joy, who likes to commemorate the occasion in her own inimitable way, preferably alone – with the lights down low, thinking of Harrison Ford. I imagine she'd find this particular habit difficult to indulge in at work, but she does love a challenge.

Sadly for me, no such personal enjoyment. Today is the day Mum moves into Bob's Place and, as I may have mentioned in passing, we are all feeling pretty guilt-stricken and gloomy about it. Dad and I have tried to tell ourselves that this is temporary, like a holiday. But Rory is more clinical in his outlook.

'Unless she really hates it,' he said, 'I can't see her coming back home. Can you? It's not like her condition is reversible in any way. It's not like she's going to get better, even marginally. So, if she needs round-the-clock care today, she'll definitely need it this time next year. Or even next month.'

'She *might* really hate it though,' I said, worried.

'I don't think she will,' he said. 'There's a lot more going on for distraction at Bob's. She'll have company whenever she wants it. It's not like one of those care homes where people have to stay in their rooms and can't mingle

– she'll be in the lounge with her friends whenever she's not at choir practice or art class or yoga or whatever.'

I nodded. I knew he was right. This is the right thing to do – the best thing for Mum. And I've repeated that mantra every day this week, right up until today. Dad looked grey and tearful when I arrived this morning to drive them both into work, along with some of Mum's belongings. We've spent hours agonising about what things she might need or want in her room, as if once she's gone there's no going back to retrieve other items.

The mood in the car was sombre once we'd strapped Mum's wheelchair in. Both Dad and I were thinking the same thing: although this might not be the last time we take her out in the car, it's probably the last time we'll start from anywhere other than Bob's Place. The last time I'll be knocking on their door just before nine, peering through the swirly half-glazing for signs of movement. The last time I'll feel that little stab of fear when Dad hasn't heard me knocking and I let myself in, worried about what I might find inside. The last time I'll see him bustling about with his stick, trying to make sure all of Mum's bits and bobs are in her handbag, and Mum sitting in her favourite armchair by the window, wrapped up warm for the journey, whatever the weather outside.

We took everything slowly – although it was technically a work day for me, everyone knew the significance of this particular visit, and I had no meetings scheduled or specific tasks to complete. Instead, I spent the morning hanging up Mum's clothes in what still felt like Doreen's wardrobe, issuing instructions regarding her medication and making up the bed with her own duvet cover and patchwork quilt, lifting it to my face occasionally to inhale and check that the smell of my parents' bungalow remained in its fibres. It's funny how scent, out of all the senses, is so closely linked to memory – how the aroma of coconut and rum reminds you instantly of that package holiday to Benidorm, or a waft of Lynx Oriental can whisk you back to illicit teenage evenings in the back of your first boyfriend's car. I wonder whether anyone has ever looked at aromatherapy in the context of dementia care – maybe we should build a sensory room in Bob's Place, somewhere with music, lights, tactile surfaces and different scents piped through to little 'smelling booths'…

Maybe I should concentrate on paying the bills and getting through the next financial quarter first.

Anyway, Mum had her usual Thursday art therapy session in the afternoon, so I got on with some work while Dad sat in the residents' lounge, read the paper and talked to Gloria. Joe had arrived at midday and we looked through his ideas for the format of the gala evening.

'Should we have a little look through the general schedule again?' I said. 'I feel like I want to get my head straight about logistics in terms of how we're going to get everyone to the venue, setting up the sound system, that sort of thing. Is there any way we can have a dress rehearsal?'

He looked dubious. 'Probably not,' he said. 'Not on site, anyway. But you could come with me sometime when I go and see Sonja – she's the events manager. I'll email her now, ask if we can have a nose around the auditorium – see what the sound and lighting is like.'

'Great,' I said, feeling relieved. Joe had taken on the significant burden of stress related to running an event of this size, but I was still nervous about my little portion of it. I wanted to feel like I had a handle on the elements that I could control (if coordinating a group of frail people with dementia to sing in harmony on stage in a vast auditorium could ever be described as under control).

'I know we've got months yet, but summer's always crazy in our house and this year, with all of Maisie's "last year at primary school" activities, that time is going to fly by. I just want to check through the details you've confirmed so far. Would that be OK?'

'Of course,' he said. 'If you just open that file there,' he pointed to the laptop screen, 'there's a couple of spread-sheets with the costings. And then a detailed breakdown of the planning for the night itself – tasks still outstanding are marked in red. Here, let me show you.' He pulled his seat closer to mine so we could both see the screen. There had been no recurrence of the weird moment from the pub, and neither of us had mentioned it, because there was nothing to mention, but I was somehow more aware of the physical presence of him these days. I moved slightly to the left to put a couple of inches' distance between us and we scrolled through the documents, jotting down ideas as we went.

By the time I next looked at the clock it was four thirty.

'Shit, I've got to go and collect Maisie,' I said, pulling on my coat. 'I'm not sure whether to leave Dad here or take him with me, back to an empty house.' The words caught in my throat and suddenly my eyes filled with tears. 'God,' I whispered. 'All the time I've been concentrating on how this is going to be for Mum. Moving into Bob's. Whether it's the right thing for *her*, and how we're going to smooth that transition for *her*. But Dad. Tonight's going to be so weird for him.'

Joe cautiously put both hands on my shoulders. 'You OK?' he said, and I nodded, shrugging him off as I wiped my eyes. 'Yes, I just… Maybe I'll get Maisie and then I'll come back here to collect Dad once Mum's had dinner – then he'll be happier and she'll be more settled. I'll do it in two stages.' I gave him a watery smile. 'That's a better plan.'

'Look, can I help in any way?' he said. 'I could drive your dad back later when I'm heading off?'

I paused, rifling through my handbag for the car keys, and looked up at him. 'Would you?' I said. 'You're sure? If he's happy with that then – well, yes, it would save me doing multiple journeys and…'

'Take some of the pressure off,' he said. 'Absolutely. It's no bother from my point of view as long as your dad's OK with it.'

'But you live in completely the opposite direction,' I said.

He sighed. 'Penny, just take the offer of help, OK? It's not a sign of weakness, or some kind of slur on your abilities to cope. I've said I'm very happy to do it. You wouldn't think twice if it was Tina or Veronica or Zahara offering.'

I nodded. He was right. I wouldn't. 'OK. Thank you so much. I'll go and check with Dad and then I'd better head straight off.'

'Sure. Tell him I'm fine to hang around as late as he wants. I've got plenty to be getting on with.'

Dad had brought Mum through to the residents' lounge after her art session and they were sitting together admiring her handiwork when I went in to relay the plan. They both seemed perfectly happy and I didn't allow myself to dwell on the presence of Mum's belongings in the room upstairs, or the fact that Dad would be walking out of here in a few hours with Joe, leaving his wife behind. 'Give me a call when you get back,' I said cheerfully. 'And I'll pop over.'

He smiled and nodded as I bent to kiss the top of Mum's head. 'And I'll see you tomorrow, Mum,' I said, just as brightly. 'Dad and I will bring some more of your things. Your recliner chair, one of the bedside tables, a few more pictures – we'll soon have that room looking beautiful.'

I kept the smile rigid on my face as I walked back out through the hall, briefly catching Joe's eye and giving him a cheery wave that fooled neither of us. It wasn't until I was in the car and pulling out of the lane that I allowed myself a glance over my shoulder to the space where Mum's wheelchair would usually be strapped securely in position. The emptiness was stark – sound bounced off the interior without Mum clad in her Max Mara coat to absorb it. I turned on the ancient radio to discover that one of her favourite songs was playing – one of the songs we'd been practising for the choir performance that I now wasn't entirely sure she'd be able to attend, or even want to. She might be completely institutionalised in two months' time. It was then I started crying properly.

By the time I pulled up to the school Mrs North was standing sentry by the back door. She glanced at her watch and was just about to greet me with the usual 'nice of you to finally grace us with your presence, Mrs Baker' kind of comment, when she caught sight of my face.

'Maisie,' she said. 'I'm just wondering whether I remembered to take those sheets of coloured card through to Badger class. Could you go and check for me?'

'I'm sorry I'm late,' I said as Maisie scampered off. 'I've just – uhm – I've just left Mum in the care home. And it's the first time it's been – well, this time it's probably permanent, so it's been a bit of a...'

I didn't get a chance to finish my sentence because Mrs North, in a move that astonished us both, pulled me into a hug. A rigid, slightly tense hug admittedly, but a hug nonetheless. Well, there was nothing else for it. I stood there and bawled my eyes out.

Chapter Twenty-Nine

Friday 9 June

It's been five weeks since Mum moved into Bob's Place, and I think we're through the worst. On that first Friday Joe was on hand to help us move the furniture in. I wouldn't have needed anyone else if it hadn't been for the recliner chair, which appears to weigh a similar amount to an armoured tank. It had taken both Sam and Tom half an hour to wrestle it into the disability vehicle earlier that morning, and any sadness I had felt about the emptiness of the car the previous evening was replaced by fears for its suspension on the return journey to Bob's with the floor weighted down so heavily Dad could barely get it over the speed bumps (I was following behind in my car similarly laden with books, pictures and toiletries).

Having independent transport meant that Dad could stay much later and then drive himself home. Tina told me he was there until nine o'clock that evening, sitting with Mum until she fell asleep. It's interesting how, now that Mum's safe and I don't need to worry about her quite as much, my anxieties have simply transferred to Dad – should he be driving late at night, is he lonely, is he eating properly now he doesn't have Mum to cater for? But I guess this is just part of life, and we've carried on in much the same routine since the first few days. Dad and I both drive over to Bob's Place separately, and now that I don't have to collect Mum I can be in work earlier, which means I often spend my lunch break with my parents. It's quite an unusual set-up and there are echoes of my childhood in this arrangement with us spending a lot of time under the same roof. When Rory comes to visit this sensation of being thrust back in time increases. Last week as we all sat out in the gardens enjoying the sunshine, Rory expounding on some theory of his own brilliance while I held Mum's hand and quietly ran through my personal list of worries in my head, it was like being twelve again.

It doesn't exactly feel normal yet. But it's OK. And to be honest, I know we're really lucky. I don't think there's anywhere else with this level of flexibility – the fact that Dad can still spend almost every waking moment in Mum's company despite no longer technically living under the same roof has helped him come to terms with the change. And Mum has fallen far fewer times since she's been at Bob's; in fact, I don't think she's fallen once. Because there's always someone to lend a hand if she's starting to slide out of the chair or if she's a bit wobbly getting to the shower.

I know it was the right decision but it's still strange, walking past my parents' bungalow, my hand pausing halfway to a wave before I remember there's nobody home. In that first week I'd picked Maisie up from school mid-afternoon with the intention of having our usual Wednesday visit to Granny's house and both of us real-ised as we turned the corner into our street that Granny didn't live there any more, and we weren't going to be popping in for a glass of squash because Grandad wasn't there either. My mother's presence in that bungalow had been what defined it as a home. Now, when I do drop in, it feels like an abandoned shell. Dad wants to be where Mum is, and she can't be there, so neither can he. Still, it's only bricks and mortar. What matters is that we've navigated that particular milestone.

And today, another milestone – Maisie's final primary school performance: *Alice in Wonderland*. There has been much fanfare and the casting has been contentious, as you'd imagine. The year six pupils tend to get the meatier roles in the summer term play, with year fives confined to the chorus. Thus, Eva is the Queen of Hearts, Darcy is Alice and Maisie is the White Rabbit. She's not thrilled about it. She wanted to be the Mad Hatter, but Leon was given this part and by all accounts has been hamming it up in spectacular style. But the biggest surprise is Darcy. Zahara said she's never given any indication of wanting a starring role in anything – Darcy's position in the friend-ship group, and indeed, within the class as a whole, has been *timid cast member – exit stage left*, and yet, here she is in her blonde wig and pinafore dress owning the stage like Liza Minnelli.

'I am gobsmacked,' said Zahara, who was sitting beside me. 'I had no idea she had it in her. Does that make me a bad parent?'

Hugh the Bastard, as I fondly refer to him, was sitting to her left. 'I've tried telling Darcy to be more confident,' he said loftily. 'She needs to push herself forward more. Hopefully today will prove my point.'

'It's funny, isn't it, Hugh,' I said. 'I can't imagine why Darcy, as a little girl, would be underconfident. Why she might feel that her role in life is to be relegated to the sidelines of a male-dominated world, or purely viewed from the male gaze. It's almost as if there had been some formative experience that had left her feeling insecure or uncertain about positioning herself as a strong, confident young woman.'

'Penny,' hissed Sam, who was sitting on my other side. 'Leave him alone. Now is not the time.'

'Hmmph,' I said, folding my hands into my lap and staring resolutely ahead while Zahara sniggered and Hugh fumed beside me.

'Oooh, I can see her!' said Sam, suddenly pointing to the right of the hall. 'Go, Maisie!'

Maisie, who was waiting in the wings (stock cupboard with a sheet hung as a curtain), turned her whiskered nose and rabbity ears towards her father and gave him a rictus grin of excitement and anxiety. In return Sam and I gave her a desperately uncool double thumbs up which we both knew she'd tell us off for later.

Tiggy leaned forward from her position three seats down. She was dressed in some ridiculously skimpy mesh top and mid-thigh shorts to show off her recently acquired tan from a week in the Seychelles (I know this because it had been ALL OVER Facebook to a point where it felt as though I had seen every possible combination of Tiggy emerging from an azure sea in a minuscule bikini that ever existed *#LuckyMe #Holibobs*).

'Hey there, Sam,' she said, giving my husband a coy little wave. 'Or should I call you *Daddy Rabbit*?' she nodded her head towards Maisie in her costume.

'Errr, no,' I muttered under my breath, 'because calling my husband *Daddy Rabbit* would be totally fucking weird and inappropriate.' I felt Zahara shaking with laughter beside me.

'I see the training's going well,' Tiggy continued, moving on from the coy little wave to the full appraising stare. 'Looking pretty buff!'

My eyebrows nearly shot off my forehead and I heard Joy snort behind me.

'Oh,' said Sam, blushing (yes, really, he was blushing). 'Uhm – thank you.'

'I've been following your progress on Facebook,' she said earnestly. 'Every single post. I really enjoy the updates.' (Simpering little laugh.) 'Always nicer to watch someone else exercising than to have to do it yourself!' (Another laugh.) 'Although I'm a bit of a runner too – for my sins!' (Comedy grimace.) 'Anyway, it's been fascinating to see the miles stack up, and all that ice swimming! I think one time the water was fifteen degrees?!'

'It was,' said Sam, bravely. I didn't want to point out that bathing in fifteen-degree water was not technically ice swimming.

'Well, I just wanted to say that I think what you're doing is absolutely marvellous. And all to raise money for charity. It's – well, it's fantastic. I said to John, we simply must sponsor him, darling, it's for a great cause, and it's all tax-deductible anyway, so look out for a large donation, Daddy Rabbit!'

'Well, gosh, that would be – great,' said Sam. I rarely see him tongue-tied but fair to say, he was now. I thought Tiggy had completed her blatant attempt to flirt with my husband, but not so. After another minute she leaned forward again.

'Are you sure you've got the best vantage point from that seat?' she said in a loud whisper. 'There's space next to me' – she glared at Lindi, who cast her eyes to the ground and shuffled into the row behind – 'if you want a better view.'

'A better view of her tits is what she means, Daddy Rabbit,' said Joy who was sitting behind us. 'How's Tiggy in the front row, anyway? Her daughter isn't even in the play.'

'She is,' I whispered. 'Have you not seen on Face-book – Rhiannon's the dormouse. It's all Tiggy's been blaring on about for the past few weeks, along with the Seychelles and her intimate acquaintance with the family of a convicted criminal, hashtag "keep our streets safe", hashtag "violence is not the answer" and hashtag "parents should lead by example".'

'She never said that?'

'Oh, but she did!'

Joy gave a low whistle. 'Jesus. The woman is a psycho-path.'

A sudden silence fell as Mrs North entered the hall and climbed the stairs to the stage (I have made this sound very grand – in reality we're talking two steps made of plywood).

'Ladies and gentlemen,' she announced, clapping her hands together. 'Boys and girls, mums and dads. Friends of St John's. Welcome to our annual school play.' There was the general murmur of an audience who don't know whether they are supposed to cheer or not. Mrs North continued unperturbed.

'This year we are performing *Alice in Wonderland*. The children have been working very hard over the past few months, and they are all very excited to share this with you. I have already seen the dress rehearsal and I guar-antee you are in for a treat! I think this might be the best performance we've ever staged.'

'She said that when Rex was in *The Wizard of Oz*,' Zahara murmured out of the side of her mouth as she looked directly ahead.

'She says it every single year,' I said, using the same ventriloquist's method of communication. 'So she's either lying or the amateur dramatic skills of St John's year six pupils really are improving at an exponential rate.'

'Ssshhh,' hissed Sam. He's a bit frightened of Mrs North. Aren't we all.

'Break a leg, darling!' whispered Tiggy very loudly in the direction of her daughter. 'You show those year sixes how it's done!' She turned slightly in her seat. 'Rhiannon's only in year five,' she said to the row behind her.

Mrs North gave her a hawkish stare. 'Glad to see everyone's feeling so enthusiastic,' she said. 'Can I ask that parents refrain from singling out individual children? A lot of hard work has gone into this performance, and it's very much a team effort. And as we say at St John's – there's no "i" in "team".'

'Oooh,' I gasped. 'Tiggy got burned!'

Suitably admonished, Tiggy stared down at her mesh top, cheeks ablaze.

'Now,' said Mrs North, 'all that remains is for me to hand over to our cast and crew. I give you *Alice's Adventures in Wonderland…*' She began the clapping and we all dutifully followed suit, trailing off as Darcy ran onto the stage and assumed the position of a sleeping Alice.

All went swimmingly until halfway through the first act when Alice, who'd just consumed the little cake labelled *Eat Me*, was growing and growing, bursting out of the rabbit's house (a very impressive plywood construction courtesy of Leon's dad, who owned a shed company). As Darcy's head popped out through the roof of the shed and a pair of fake arms shot out through the windows, there was a loud blast of *The Muppets* theme tune from my handbag. I stared resolutely ahead, trying to ignore my phone and praying that whoever was calling me would fall off the edge of a cliff or something, anything to stop the ludicrous noise. A murmur of disapproval rippled through the audience.

'Penny,' hissed Sam. 'That's your phone.'

'I KNOW,' I hissed back at him through gritted teeth.

'Turn. It. Off!' he said, staring straight ahead.

'I. Will!'

The action on stage had completely frozen at this point, Darcy's Alice and Maisie's White Rabbit unable to compete with the muppet chorus. Trying to maintain some shred of pretence that this wasn't my phone making the racket, that it wasn't Maisie Baker's mother who had yet again ignored the explicit instruction to turn mobiles to silent, the instruction that was uttered at the start of every school performance since time began (since phones began anyway), I inched forward in my seat and foraged around in my bag until I found the offending item and managed to switch it off. The fact that I did this without eyes on the device (I was staring resolutely forward in a complete denial of responsibility) was testament to my exceptional manual dexterity, but did anyone think to compliment me on that? No. They did not.

'Sorry,' I whispered, my cheeks burning hot enough to have lit up the Albert Hall, let alone St John's plywood stage. 'Sorry. So sorry.'

Darcy was still poised with her head poking out of the shed roof and Maisie was stood stock-still, her whiskers drooping to one side, unsure of whether to resume. I distinctly heard Tiggy say something about *spoiling it for everyone* and *won't someone PLEASE think of the children* (she might not have actually said this last bit but I could feel her vibes and they were not good).

'Thank you for the musical interlude, Mrs Baker,' Mrs North said, coming to the rescue of the cast by throwing me under the bus. 'May I take this opportunity to remind all parents, *again*, that mobiles are to be switched to silent. Now, come along, Alice!' She turned her attention back to the stage. 'What are you going to do now?'

It's possible I may have died for a few moments. Had an actual cardiac arrest from embarrassment. But Sam slid his hand over to mine and gave it a squeeze.

'Didn't that happen before,' he said quietly as the crew (year fours and Mrs Mabuse) changed the backdrop for the Mad Hatter's tea party scene.

I nodded forlornly. 'At Tom's nativity,' I said. 'When the three kings arrived. It was exactly the moment that Jacob Notley said, "We bring gifts of Cold, Frankenstein and Schloer". Although my ringtone was different then.'

'Europe's "The Final Countdown", as I recall?'

'That's the one,' I said. 'The tune was different, but the shame – the shame is the same.'

'Don't worry about it, you silly arse,' he said fondly, chuckling to himself. And bizarrely that made me feel a lot better.

An hour later, and we were all on our feet giving a standing ovation as our kids trooped onto the stage for their curtain call. The muppets' intrusion had been forgotten (it hadn't) and all was well. I didn't even begrudge Tiggy her rejoicing: Rhiannon had been a very good dormouse, and unlike her mother, she evidently knew not to try and upstage the other children. Maisie received a roar of approval and a deafening clap from her father, and a few tears from me, which she was mortified about, naturally. Especially as I cried in front of Cheshire Cat, George, who I think she quite likes. All was well until

I reached into my bag and turned my phone back on to see that I had two missed calls from Tina, one from Dad and one from Joe.

I called Dad as soon as I got outside.

'Nothing to worry about, Penelope,' he said briskly. 'Just your mother's had another one of her turns. We're in the ambulance now.'

'OK,' I said, wanting immediately to go and make an announcement in the school hall along the lines of 'See? It was an important call, and now you should all feel terrible for judging me because actually people were trying to tell me that my mother was being taken to hospital.' I didn't do this.

'Is she all right?' I asked, hearing the clanking rattle of the ambulance in the background.

'She's her usual self,' said Dad. 'Aren't you, Mary?' There was a pause. 'It's Penny,' he said loudly, enunciating each word in his distinctive military clip. 'Penny! She's asking if you're all right.'

Silence.

'She seems comfortable,' said Dad, returning back to me. 'Comfortable' is our code for, *I can't really tell how she's feeling because she's pretty unresponsive, but we know that's usual for her and she doesn't appear to be distressed or in pain but that's about as much as I can say.* The problem is that we both know Mum really well – we know what's normal for her. And we know she has these funny episodes. It's not like the choking in Snapeshill Park café. What Dad was describing was one of her little vacant periods where she's unresponsive for a while. We don't know what causes it but she generally comes round after an hour or so and is back to her old self.

'Rory's meeting us at the hospital,' said Dad. 'He's managed to swap his clinic with a colleague – says he wants to speak to the A&E consultant. Get a plan in place for the next time this happens.'

I ended the call with instructions to Dad to keep me informed and then, once Maisie had emerged from her dressing room (daaahling), the three of us walked home in the sunshine discussing the play. Dad sent me a reassuring text when they arrived at the hospital to let me know Mum had perked up (relatively speaking) and that Rory was 'making himself useful'. By the time we'd reached our house Tom was back from school and we found him in the sitting room, curtains drawn, glowering in front of the Xbox. He barely looked up when Maisie barrelled into the room, keen to share her amateur dramatic star turn.

'Tom!' said Sam sharply, pulling our son's headphones off his ears. 'Maisie's had her school play. She wants to tell you about it.'

'Oh, yeah, right,' mumbled Tom. 'Sorry, Maze. How was it?'

Maisie launched into a second-by-second account of the preceding two hours and Sam and I made our way into the kitchen.

'That's not like him,' said Sam as he put the kettle on. 'Do you think Tom just didn't hear us come home?'

'Sam,' I said, incredulous. 'That's exactly what Tom's been like for the past three months. What do you think I've been banging on about?'

He looked doubtful. 'Are you sure?' he asked, as if I'd been fabricating our son's low mood all this time.

'You haven't been here,' I said, trying and failing to keep the accusation out of my voice. 'I told you, he's been really low ever since he split up with Lauren. Anytime I ask him whether he's OK he shrugs. He's not engaging with me or Maisie at all. He's just really sad *all the time.*'

'Well, he's not been like that with me,' said Sam, stung. 'And I *have* been here. I've been back on the early train more often than not the past month or so.'

'Well, you're evidently knocking this parenting business out of the park then,' I said, shoving items into the dishwasher with a little more force than was necessary. 'Either that or you're simply not paying attention.' I slammed the dishwasher door. 'And when I was referring to your being *here*, I didn't just mean being in the building. I meant being *present*. You might come home a little earlier, but this ability you've discovered, whereby you can actually *catch* the early train, seems to have coincided nicely with your need to go straight out for a run or to the gym as soon as you are home. And if you're not out doing those things, you're thinking about them or talking about them. Or your calorie intake.' I paused, realising that there were tears on my hot cheeks.

'Pen,' said Sam gently. 'Are you OK? Is it your mum? Are you worrying about her?'

'No,' I said, miserably. 'I'm not. Dad says she's fine. She's in the hospital. She'll most likely be straight back out again in a few hours, same old, same old.' I sighed out a ragged breath. 'I'm just in a bad mood, that's all.'

He pursed his lips, unsure where to proceed with this admission. 'Would you like a cup of tea?' he asked eventually, voice full of trepidation.

'No,' I said, and forced out a 'thanks' as an afterthought. I ignored his hurt expression and left the kitchen, not knowing whether I was cross with him or with myself. I didn't really understand what I was upset about. This just kept happening recently. Tears, bursts of irrational anger. I'm sure if I asked Joy she'd say it was my depleted hormones, but I don't want to be defined by my oestrogen levels and I'm sick of everything being attributed to the menopause. Surely sometimes it's simply the business of holding shit together that feels a bit overwhelming for women my age. Not because of our hormones, but because of the various burdens we carry. It feels over-simplistic, and at times highly convenient, to blame the menopause for all of life's woes when the reality is that most women in their late forties or early fifties are in an unenviable position irrespective of their hormones.

Women like me are from a generation who had our children late in comparison to our parents and therefore find ourselves squashed into caring roles at both ends of the age spectrum. We are also a generation who were told we could have it all: the rewarding career, the gang of great mates, the doting husband and the happy brood of children. We therefore feel like a failure if we don't have these things – but are utterly exhausted if we do. Because however doting the husband, the bulk of work inside the home still falls to us. Taking care of the endless domestic arrangements, building relationships within the wider community, creating a safe and nurturing environ-ment for our family, being 'there' for every bloody indi-vidual who might possibly need us at any given moment – those tasks are firmly parked at the feet of middle-aged women, and no amount of oestrogen gel is going to get that shit done.

Having one parent in a care home, the other parent becoming increasingly frail, one daughter who could be throwing herself in front of a police car or being arrested as we speak, a depressed son who's struggling with rejection, a younger daughter who does still need me but won't for much longer, a business that's hanging in the balance, plus an ageing body, declining levels of fitness and, let's face it, dwindling desirability, I'd say this was enough to warrant the occasional meltdown. And that's what I seem to be having. The fact that I can't sleep and my internal thermostat is completely on the blink may be contributing to my problems, but I don't think it's entirely responsible for the way I'm feeling.

Life is responsible for that.

Chapter Thirty

Friday evening

Rory called later that evening to update me on the situation with Mum.

'Had a chat with the A&E consultant, Nigel,' he began. I had to stop myself eye-rolling at his casual matey ownership of every single medic involved in Mum's care and remember that it was actually useful in this scenario. 'We agreed that there was no point in admitting Mum to hospital, so I'm taking her and Dad back to Bob's Place now.'

'Have you called ahead to let them know?' I interrupted. 'Does Dad want to stay over? They can put a camp bed up in her room. I'll give Tina a ring now.'

'It's all sorted, Penny. Don't worry. And she's fine. They both are.'

'OK,' I said. 'Thanks.'

'Anyway, this chat I had with her consultant...'

'Nigel,' I said, helpfully.

'Yes. He's been quite clear that there isn't much we can do for Mum during one of these episodes. He suggested that it might be better, rather than blue-lighting her into the emergency department every time she's a bit vacant, that maybe we just let her have that little moment and recover in her own time, at home, at Bob's Place. No need for blood tests. No need for scans.'

'But what if it's a stroke or something?' I said, confused. 'How would we know if she doesn't go into hospital?'

'I think the key thing is what we would gain, or more to the point, what *she* would gain, from us knowing, even if it was a stroke,' Rory said. 'Her brain is already damaged, beyond repair. Us finding out on a scan that there's a bit more damage is not going to change her treatment, it's not going to alter what we do. So...'

'Why put her through it,' I finished for him.

'Exactly. She hates going into the scanner. She hates being in hospital. Nigel's point was that maybe we'd be better off avoiding the place altogether.'

'And you agree with him?'

'I do. And Dad does too. He sees that it's not in Mum's best interests to be carted off to hospital every couple of weeks. Not when there's nothing they can offer her.'

'OK. So, this is good news?' I said eventually.

'Well, it just means we've got a plan of care, a bit like when you have a Do Not Resuscitate order. You've got a few residents with those at Bob's Place, I'm imagining?'

'Yes, of course. OK. And does Mum have one? I don't think she does. She maybe should do?'

I could hear the shift in his breathing as he nodded. 'I think she should do. She'd never make it through a resuscitation attempt. We can ask her GP to come and talk it through with her and Dad. And you.'

'Yes,' I said. 'That would be good.' I paused. 'Rory, this all feels a bit – final? Like we're letting her slip away. We're allowing it somehow.'

'I see it more that we're *accepting* the situation,' he said. 'And we don't really have a choice. We can rail against it but what good would that do, other than exhaust us both? We've been having these final moments for years now.'

I nodded to myself. It was true. Mum's decline had felt like a series of small bereavements extending over a long period. This was simply another one. Just like her moving into Bob's Place. 'You're right,' I said. 'And thanks for having that conversation with the consultant. I know it will have helped Dad.'

'That's OK. It's my job. It's a bit easier for me.'

'Yeah – I don't know, Rory. Sometimes I think maybe it's actually *harder* for you. This whole thing. Because we all look to you for answers. And as you say, in this situation there aren't any answers.'

'Are you admitting that you value my opinion?' he said. I could hear he was smiling.

'God no,' I said. 'Consider that a momentary lapse in judgement.'

'Thought so. You didn't want to add anything about me being a great support, a tower of strength, anything like that?'

'Shut up, you idiot,' I said. 'Go and lie down before you hurt yourself.'

'Love you too,' he said. 'Smell you later, loser.'

–

It was close to midnight when my phone rang again and this time it was Tom. This was most peculiar. I wasn't sure that my son even knew how to use the call function on his phone, all his communication was done via text.

'Hi, darling,' I said as I answered. 'How's the party? Wait, we weren't supposed to be collecting you, were we? Your dad's already in bed and...' I looked down at my fluffy dressing gown and slippers. 'You're staying at Oliver's, yeah?'

'Mum,' he said. He sounded thoroughly miserable. 'Sorry. I tried Dad first but he's not picking up. I've been sick. Can you get me?'

'Oh, sweetheart! Of course. Wait, where are you?' I hadn't dropped him off.

'At Emily's house. I've been, oh God, I've made such a dick of myself...'

I heard the sound of his phone being wrestled off him and a familiar voice came down the line. 'Mrs Baker? It's Lauren.'

'Lauren! Oh – I – uhm. Is Tom OK?'

'Not really,' she said. 'He's been sick all over Emily's sofa. He's also – well, he's crying a lot and...'

'OK, thanks, Lauren,' I said, throwing a coat over my pyjamas and pulling on a pair of trainers. 'Can you just let me know where the party is?'

–

By the time Lauren had tracked down Emily for her postcode I was in the car. 'I'll be twenty minutes,' I said. 'Could you find one of his friends to stay with him until then?'

'Uhh, yeah, I guess... I can't see any of them...'

'Shgone,' I could hear Tom in the background. 'Shleft me.' It wasn't entirely clear whether he was referring to his friends having gone and left him or the ex-girlfriend I was currently speaking to.

'I'll sit with him,' Lauren said. She sounded a bit weary. 'I'll look out for your car.'

'Thank you.' I was genuinely grateful to her. She might be a double-crossing, two-timing cow-bag but she sounded significantly less drunk and more capable than my lovely boy at this moment in time.

I found Emily's house less via the satnav and more by following the trail of devastation that led halfway up her road. The density of drunken teenagers staggering around in mismatched gangs, veering into the road or snogging in bushes increased the closer I got, and the party house was easy to identify from the overlit windows and the bass thumping out of the front door. More bodies were littered across the front lawn, and I picked my way between them as an elderly gentleman leaned out of an upstairs window two houses down and shouted, 'I've called the police, you know! Public nuisance, this is!' in my general direction. I acknowledged him with a cheerful wave.

Tom appeared in the doorway flanked by Lauren and an older, bored-looking chap who on closer inspection bore a striking resemblance to the one I'd seen her snogging in town all those months ago. In an attempt to restore some of my son's dignity I greeted him as though my picking him up early (and covered in puke) had been the plan all along. Ignoring the vomit on his jumper and shoes, the tear-stained cheeks and the way he kept glaring furiously at Lauren's new boyfriend, I gestured with a thumb over my shoulder. 'Car's here,' I said. 'Let's go.' I nodded curtly at my son's ex and her new man. 'Nice to see you, Lauren,' I said. 'Say hello to your mum for me.'

'Thanks, Mrs Baker. I will. And I'm sorry about...' She gestured towards Tom – I wasn't sure if she meant sorry for the state of him, sorry for breaking up with him in such a callous manner, or sorry for ever going out with him, but I settled for a tight-lipped, 'It's OK,' which seemed to cover most bases.

When Tom veered off the path and into a group of vaping youths I slipped an arm around his back and basically hauled him to the car. Luckily everyone else at the party was evidently so wrecked that the sight of a pyjamaed, middle-aged woman went pretty much unnoticed and within minutes he was strapped into the passenger seat, an old carrier bag on his lap just in case.

'So,' I said as I swerved around a girl with heavy eyeliner and a crop top who was stood in the middle of the road. 'What happened?'

It seems that Tom had been enjoying the party up until about ten o'clock when Lauren had arrived, new man in tow, and things had taken a distinct turn for the worse. Tom had promptly fallen into the classic trap of 'I know what I'll do, I'll deal with this slightly awkward scenario by becoming intoxicated to the point of rambling incoherence. I'll tell all my friends who try and slow my drinking down that they don't understand and they can piss off, then I'll stumble over to my ex-girlfriend in tears and demand to know why she doesn't want me any more. I'll tell her that I was a great boyfriend and I'll ask how could she do this to me, and I'll let her know it doesn't matter because loads of other girls fancy me anyway. And then to prove what a great catch I am I'll try and punch her new boyfriend in the face, except I won't be able to see straight so I'll end up hitting the table lamp, and then I'll vomit over the sofa she's sitting on. Finally I'll start sobbing copiously, asking for her forgiveness, asking her boyfriend's forgiveness and generally make a massive tit of myself.' We've all been there – or a variation thereof. Don't deny it.

'Oh Tom,' I said, feeling the waves of humiliation rolling off him (accompanied by the distinctly tequila-and-gastric-acid-based scent of despair). 'I'm sure it wasn't that bad.'

'It absolutely was that bad,' he mumbled.

'Well, maybe not that many people were aware of what was going on...'

'There were at least thirty people in the room when I tried to punch him, and probably more when I was crying.'

'I expect the music would have covered most of the detail of what you were shouting, though?'

'But *she* heard me,' he said mournfully. 'Lauren heard it all. She wasn't even that drunk.' He groaned and leaned forward, head in his hands.

'Are you going to be sick again?' I checked my rear-view mirror and pulled into the nearest side street.

'No,' he said. 'I don't think so.' He sat back up and opened the passenger window. The cool breeze of a summer evening washed away some of the basement nightclub aroma. 'Why did she have to dump me, Mum?' His voice was small and accompanied by a sigh that carried the weight of world.

I unclipped my seat belt and leaned over, pulling him into my side. 'Oh, Tommy,' I said. 'I don't know. Sometimes there simply isn't an answer. People behave in odd ways.' I ruffled his hair. 'She still cares about you. She made sure you were OK and that you got home safely. She's not a bad person.'

He nodded sadly. 'I know.' Another heavy sigh. 'I said some pretty mean things to her. I feel bad about that, but then I just feel so sad – so much of the time.'

I let him cry it out for a few minutes, his face hot and sticky against my neck, his tears mingling with the ones leaking silently from my own eyes. There's nothing worse than witnessing the heartbreak of your own child, knowing that you can't make it better.

'You've got to move on, darling,' I said at last. 'This isn't doing you any good, wallowing in the past. You're seventeen. You've got...' (I almost said *your whole life ahead of you*, and thought better of it. Nobody wants to feel they're a cliché, even when they very obviously are.)

'I'll try,' he said. 'But what if I can't? What if she was the one? What if nobody else ever wants to go out with me?' His voice was wobbling. 'What if I never end up being happy and married like you and Dad are?'

'Oh Tommy, you will,' I said. 'I promise you will. You'll find someone you love, who loves you. Someone you want to spend the rest of your life with.'

As I was reeling off these platitudes there was a tiny part of me wondering whether my own relationship was robust enough to be held up as a matrimonial gold standard. Were Sam and I really *that* happy? Was I being disingenuous, allowing this illusion to persist? Maybe I should have said, 'Actually it's not all it's cracked up to be, wedded bliss – it's often bloody hard work. And most of the time we barely see each other. You might end up in a situation where every time your spouse opens their mouth you're inexplicably furious with them, and then you hate yourself. You might even end up exchanging a peculiar moment of chemistry with a work colleague and wondering idly about what might have been if you'd chosen a different path.' And then, of course, I felt a tidal wave of guilty recrimination wash over me. Not least because I was now wallowing in my own invented psychodrama instead of paying attention to my son.

'OK. Here's what you're going to do,' I said, sitting upright again. (My back was killing me from leaning at that angle, for one thing.) 'Tomorrow, you're going to send Lauren a brief message to thank her for looking out for you this evening and to say sorry for behaving the way you did. You will tell her that it won't happen again. However upset you are, however unfathomable it is to me that she would want to go out with anyone other than you, the girl needs to make her own mistakes without your interference, and you just need to be cool about it.'

He nodded. 'OK.'

'And then,' I said, clipping my seat belt back on and starting up the engine. 'Then you're going to delete her number from your phone and unfollow her on all your platforms and social media bits and bobs. You're going to do whatever is necessary to avoid a scenario where she feels you're spying on her, or where you end up making yourself miserable by messaging her drunkenly in a manner not dissimilar to tonight.'

'OK.'

'And then, you're going to message Emily, apologise profusely for vomiting in her house, and offer to pay for any dry cleaning and any damage to the table lamp.'

He gave a long, juddering exhalation as we pulled back out onto the main road, but he was nodding. We drove along in silence for a moment. The window remained open and there was absolutely no traffic, my lonely head-lights picking out moths and midges as we snaked through the winding streets back to the village.

'Thanks, Mum,' he said. And whether he was thanking me for collecting him, or cuddling him, or not telling him off, or just being there, it didn't matter. In that moment I felt like I'd got my boy back.

Chapter Thirty-One

Saturday 17 June

Today is Grace's graduation. The fruit of my loins is actually graduating from an actual university, and how on earth did I become so ancient? The sun was already high in the sky when we all crammed into the car, me in the back with Tom and Maisie, Dad in the front with Sam. Rory and Candice were meeting us there after the ceremony (it was only Sam, Dad and I allowed in the lecture theatre) and we had a table booked for lunch in a nearby restaurant. I think Grace really appreciates the full family entourage turning up (in fact, I think she hates it but she's the first of the grandchildren to graduate so she'll just have to suck it up – besides, Rory made so many jokes about whether I was sure it was a graduation ceremony and not a court hearing that I insisted he attend, just to see his niece holding a certificate to say she is definitely an upstanding member of the community).

After our big family meal, the plan was for Grace to return to her student house where she was staying until the lease expired in another week's time. I was hoping that either housemate Rania ('Burn the Establishment') would have found her own accommodation by then or at least Grace would have had an opportunity to discuss the *Rania staying at our house for the foreseeable future* plan with Sam, seeing as I hadn't had the chance, or the inclination, to mention it myself. The last time Sam and I had discussed Grace's plans (or lack of), it had boiled down to Sam saying we needed to encourage her to take responsibility for herself.

'She's an adult, Pen. I know she's still your baby but her being an independent member of society has always been the game plan, not some thirty-year-old still living in her childhood bedroom.'

I knew that, of course. I felt it too. But on the other hand, if our daughter needed somewhere to live and a bit of time to sort her head out, then the best place for that was at home. We could cross the other bridges when we came to them. To be honest, I felt that Sam was being a bit harsh and I was annoyed that by referring to her as *my* baby he was implying that if Grace *didn't* end up as a functioning adult it would be *my* fault. But this was an argument for another day – or more likely a postponed argument that would never take place, one that would instead silently seethe and roil behind my gritted teeth for a few months while it gave me a gastric ulcer.

Anyway, I digress – we were all very excited about the graduation and not in the least concerned with future careers or housing. The sun was shining and the whole family were together. Well, almost. The crush of car passengers on the journey down should have helped disguise the glaring omission of Mum, but in a way it just drew attention to it. Dad and I had pondered long and hard about the practicalities of taking her with us but concluded that we'd struggle to get her into the lecture theatre (and if she came then Dad was automatically excluded due to limited numbers). It was also questionable how well she'd tolerate the journey there and back, and whether she would gain any enjoyment from the restaurant when most of her food now had to be mashed to within an inch of its life to make it safe for her to swallow. It sounds hideously selfish, but I didn't want Grace's day ruined by Granny choking over her lunch, and I didn't honestly think Mum would enjoy the experience – although I may have persuaded myself of this fact to detract from the guilt. It's hard to objectively assess one's motivations in these scenarios, and I recommend not looking too closely. We decided Mum could stay at Bob's Place and Grace would come and visit her as soon as she returned next week.

Having made the decision didn't necessarily alleviate the sensation of there being something missing for pretty much the entire day. The journey over was spent worrying about the outfit I'd chosen (what does one wear to a daughter's graduation ceremony?) and wishing I could have sought Mum's advice or even remember what she had worn to mine. At the time of my graduation I hadn't been remotely interested in the presence of my parents, other than to give them a cursory wave as I sailed off to the pub afterwards armed with the cash they'd pressed into my hands before leaving. I hadn't stopped to think about whether this was a significant day for them – it was my day. And today was Grace's day. Three years of hard work culminating in a 2:1 Bachelor of Arts. It was a real achievement, and Sam and I squeezed each other's hands as we sat in the hall waiting for the name of our eldest child to be called out.

'How on earth did this happen?' whispered Sam in my ear. 'How is our little baby suddenly twenty-one years old and about to graduate?' (I notice she goes back to being *our* baby when Sam's feeling nostalgic.) 'Do you remember when she was really small and she used to go and hide in another room and then run back in a few seconds later, arms outstretched, all jazz hands like, "I'm here!" and we'd say, "Where on earth were you, Gracie? We missed you!" and she'd look so pleased with herself?'

'Seems like just yesterday she was sitting on my knee playing peekaboo,' said my Dad, who was seated on my other side. He looked a bit watery-eyed too.

'Oh, stop it, the pair of you,' I said, feeling the tight sensation of loss building in my throat.

'That Abba song came on the radio yesterday,' said Sam. '"Slipping Through My Fingers", the one you used to listen to all the time when Grace first left for university.'

'During my locked-in-a-cupboard-sobbing-and-eating-chocolate phase?'

'Was that a *phase*?' he said. 'So, it's over now?'

I jabbed him in the ribs.

After about an hour of politely clapping through all the other degree candidates, it was the turn of the Music and Psychology group (quite a niche combo). With a surname like Baker you're usually fairly early in the alphabetical roll call, and after Jennifer Ash and Gregor Asquith had returned to their seats it was our girl's turn. There may have been a considerable amount of weeping going on in our row, I couldn't possibly say for certain, but we all managed a cheery wave as Grace's eyes scanned the lecture theatre before she awkwardly scuttled off the stage clutching her piece of paper. Later we suggested we take her certificate home with us to keep it safe, not being entirely certain it would make it back to her student house in one piece given how much alcohol she put away at lunch. In fact, everyone was on good giggly form for the majority of the meal and we managed to get through four bottles of sparkling wine courtesy of a proud grandfather. Rory and Sam were both driving, so they didn't partake, but Grace, Tom, Dad and I all made the most of the occasion and there was a lot of uproarious laughter and sharing of silly stories, including one about Grace and Tom filling the paddling pool with emulsion paint and clambering in for a swim when they were little.

Tom has been a bit more like his old self in recent weeks. It seems that his apologetic phone call to Emily after throwing up on her parents' sofa resulted in a more prolonged exchange on various chat platforms and arranging to meet at another party (where he drank one bottle of cider before switching to water). His entire attitude to life seems to have lifted in response. It may be coincidence, and I do hope that his sense of self-worth isn't so precarious as to crash back into the doldrums if this tentative step towards 'hooking up' comes to nothing, but either way, it's nice to see him happier in himself. He's making much more of an effort with Maisie (and me), and his room smells a lot more pleasant now that the aftershave bombing campaign has recommenced after a four-month ceasefire. He might be in danger of overdoing it, though. The fug of pine and amber tones is now so dense at the top of the stairs that we can almost taste it, and Maisie complained yesterday that her eyes were burning when she was brushing her teeth in the neighbouring bathroom.

So I'm not sure whether it was due to inhaling the fumes of Tom's aftershave or the copious consumption of wine, but by the time we came to say goodbye to Grace I was back to the copious weeping.

'You're *definitely* coming home next week,' I slurred into her hair as I hugged her fiercely.

'Yes, Mum,' said Grace, her voice fond. She always has been able to handle her drink better than me. 'I mean, I have to come back. My lease runs out – so, you know. It's kind of a done deal.'

I nodded, still breathing in the scent of her, my little girl. 'I'm so proud of you, Gracie,' I whispered. 'So very proud of the wonderful human being you've become. So very, very, very proud.'

'Ye-es, OK Mum,' she said as she began to untangle herself from my grip. 'I know – and thank you. For lunch and everything.'

The word 'everything' was doing a bit of heavy lifting there, I reflected in the car on the way home. When you factored in the cost of paying for Grace to go to university, the rent, the living expenses, the transport, let alone the time, energy and effort poured into those years of raising a child to the verge of adulthood – it was a lot. It really was *everything*. Not for the first time, thoughts regarding my experience of parenting, specifically mothering, led to thoughts of my own parents and my own mother.

And her absence.

Chapter Thirty-Two

She's home now, my esteemed academic, and very much graduated, eldest daughter. It's embarrassing how happy I am to have her back and how reluctant I am to let her go again. As I said to Sam, Grace deserves a break after all the hard work she's put in, so we've agreed (I made him agree with me) that she doesn't need to even think about looking for work until September at the earliest. Tom meanwhile is out with Emily most evenings, and the academic and social pressures of sixth form seem to have receded into the background of impending school holidays and unlimited heavy petting. But while Tom's attention turns once again to romance and Grace's attention turns to, well, not very much from what I can gather, other than halting planetary destruction, Maisie's attention is very firmly focused on athletic glory. For today is St John's School Sports Day. Dah – dah – *dah*!!

To be honest, in the list of final primary school moments, sports day is perhaps the one I'm not too disappointed to relinquish. For a start, I can do without the constant terror of being called up for the Mums' Race. I managed to avoid it for most of Grace and Tom's school careers by virtue of being pregnant or having infant Maisie to look after, and the past few years I've pleaded various minor ailments or 'having to keep an eye on Granny' as excuses to avoid the humiliation of thudding along the track a mile behind the other mummies. But today I knew there was no getting out of it. I had Grace with me but I couldn't really argue that my twenty-one-year-old needed looking after, and as Maisie said, 'It's the last time you'll *ever* be able to do it, Mummy, so you really must.' And I couldn't argue with that.

By midday all the children had completed their various individual events as follows:

> *Running while balancing a bean bag on your head. Points deducted for holding onto said bean bag. Disqualification for any child charging into a rival and rugby tackling them to the floor (Oliver Jordan, year three).*

> *Running while batting a tennis ball up and down on a plastic racquet. Points deducted for simply ferrying the ball in the manner of a fried egg and not attempting to bounce it at all. Disqualification for headbutting the centre of the racquet so hard that you break the plastic strings, even if you were just doing it for a joke (Finlay Masters, year five).*

> *Hurdling over foam semicircular tubes that are so flimsy they fall over in a gentle breeze let alone when a lumping great ten-year-old clatters into them. Points deducted for accidentally stamping on Mrs North's hand when she tried to resurrect the fallen hurdles mid-race because a nearby parent sneezed too hard. Disqualification for any student who crossed lanes in order to strangle another contender with the foam tube (Adil Farooque, year four).*

Skipping. Points deducted for making no attempt to skip and simply dragging the rope behind your heels. Disqualification for anyone deliberately laying their own rope down across a neighbouring lane to act as a trip hazard for the next race (Eva Rossi, year six).

Long jump. Self-explanatory. Points deducted for landing in one of the ominous 'wet patches' of sand. Disqualification for producing one of the wet patches due to a combination of anxiety and too much orange cordial at breaktime (Arthur Simms, year one).

While I usually enjoy the spectacle of sporting endeavour, this year I was admittedly distracted. The other year group's events are always of less interest than those featuring your own child, obviously, but I also spent significantly less time cooing over the adorable reception kids in their tiny shorts and tiny T-shirts than I usually do – I'm clearly getting older/wiser/less broody/just *older*. In addition, despite my attempts to *#BeMindful*, *#LiveIn- TheMoment* and appreciate every element of this milestone day, I was haunted by the looming prospect of *my* race (*so* self-absorbed) and only really forced myself to pay attention when I was watching Maisie complete the obstacle course, which she lost.

'I don't even care,' she said defiantly, arms folded as she swaggered past the seated parents on her way back to her classmates in yellow bibs. 'These races are so lame anyway. *And* Lily went before the whistle blew. *And* she's a massive cheater – everyone says so.'

'That's not very sportsmanlike, Maisie,' I chided gently as I detached myself from the plastic chair I was welded to.

Grace had already moved to a shady area beneath a tree. 'It looked like Lily won fair and square, and it's not her fault you got stuck inside the hessian sack.'

'Well, you're just going to have to win the Mums' Race now,' she said, in a completely non-pressurising way.

'I don't think that's likely to happen, darling,' I said. 'Not unless everyone else pulls out at the last minute. But I'll do my best.'

'And that's all you can do, Mummy,' she said gravely. 'That's all any of us can do.'

Thus pep-talked, I made my sorry way to the far end of the field where parents were gathering with varying degrees of enthusiasm. Knowing that resistance was futile, I had duly strapped myself into a pair of Converse before I left the house this morning. I don't own any actual sports trainers other than my muddy dog-walking ones, unlike Tiggy, who pulled out what looked like a pair of running spikes from her lululemon sports bag a few moments before the race began.

'Are those allowed?' said Joy pointedly. She was loitering in the general vicinity of other parents but it was clear from her footwear (heels that kept sticking in the grass) and outfit (linen trouser suit) that she had no intention of participating in the race and was instead just about to sidle out of the sports day fun altogether and head over to the office.

'These?' said Tiggy. 'Oh, they're just a pair of Reuben's old sports shoes. I don't really go in for the high-performance gear. Leave that to the real athletes, I say!' She gave her tinkling laugh.

'Rhiannon did well in the skipping,' I said brightly. 'It was a shame about the rope getting caught on her ponytail, but she recovered well!'

'Yes. She has quite a knack. I'm not sure where she gets her coordination from,' (tinkly laugh), 'or her athletic figure!' (smoothing down the sides of her skin-tight Lycra). 'Who was the girl you were sitting with, Penny? The one in the dark and slightly foreboding outfit, lots of piercings, interesting hair?'

'That's my eldest daughter, Grace,' I said tightly. (I knew I shouldn't have brought up the ponytail skipping rope incident.)

'Oh, goodness. She's out of prison? That must be a relief.'

'She was never in prison, Tiggy,' I said patiently, knowing it would make not a jot of difference.

'She's got quite a distinctive look, hasn't she?' Tiggy lifted her immaculate heel to her immaculate buttock, presumably to stretch her immaculate quads. 'And are your parents here today? I always remember how funny it was a few years ago when your mum came and she was wearing that peculiar hat. She kept shouting things at the children and forgetting which one was Maisie, do you remember?'

'Uhm – no. They couldn't make it today. Mum's not been so well recently.'

'Oh dear.' Her mouth went through the motions of performative sympathy. 'Is she in hospital?'

'No, not in hospital.' (Leave it there, Penny.) 'No – she's actually in a care home now. She's in the one where I work – well, the one I sort of own.' (Why couldn't I stop giving this woman information?) 'She's – her dementia is now – it's quite bad and…' I trailed off, watching Tiggy's mouth now going through the contortions of performative shock at my callous disregard of the older generation. I steeled myself for the backlash. As expected, it was brutal.

'Gosh. You put her in a home?' The eyebrows were up. 'Well, that must have been a terribly hard decision, Penny. I must say I've always sworn to my mother that I'd never do that to her.'

'I think it's very important not to judge a situation unless you have direct experience of it, Tiggy, don't you?' Joy hove into view, seething with rage on my behalf. 'Nobody makes these decisions lightly, and Penny's mum has significant care needs.'

'Oh, yes.' Tiggy's voice was laden with false sympathy. 'It was obvious your mother wasn't quite right the last few times I've seen her, Penny. Such a terrible disease.' She stretched out her other quad. 'Still, I've always admired those cultures where the younger generation take care of the older ones, no matter what – everyone moves in together, muddling along. I suppose you're too busy really to look after your mum, what with everything going on with your daughter. I understand.' She did her little sad face again.

I just stood there gawping like a goldfish, sensing Joy preparing to unleash seven shades of hell beside me, but Tiggy clearly realised she was in imminent danger. Her attention was caught by a movement on the nearside of the track and she waved extravagantly.

'Lindi!' she shouted. 'LINDI! Thought I'd lost you! Could you look after my bag for a mo?' She turned back to me. 'Lovely to see you,' she said. And she was off.

Joy's face was a picture. 'That insufferable, sanctimonious cow,' she said. I could virtually see smoke coming out of her nostrils. 'Right! I'm going to *end* her, once and for all.'

That sounded ominous. Was Joy actually planning on *murdering* Tiggy? I know I've been tempted in the past, but…

'What are you…' I started, but Joy was already pulling off her heels and scanning the ranks of older children.

'Eva!' she called, spotting her daughter. 'Who has the biggest feet in your class?'

'Marcus Demetriou,' said Eva without pause. She pointed to a vast unit of a boy who looked like he played prop forward for Scunthorpe's first fifteen. 'Size six.'

'Could you ask if I might borrow his trainers?' said Joy. 'For the mothers' race.'

Eva pulled a face at the thought of wearing Marcus Demetriou's trainers for any reason, but she knew better than to question her mother. A few moments later Joy was pulling on Marcus's sweaty shoes and bouncing lightly on the balls of her feet.

'I'll knock the smile off that smug bitch's face,' she said, cracking her knuckles. 'I am going to WIPE THE FLOOR with her.'

Before I had a moment to say 'what about your trouser suit?', or 'but you hate the mothers' race as much as I do', or 'I thought you had a board meeting in an hour', the whistle blew and we were off, a sweaty, shiny, stumbling gaggle of mothers. It was soon apparent that the majority were there under duress and would be happy just to complete the event without disgracing themselves. I settled into a comfortable run (if there is such a thing), jostling between Anya Kowalski and Priti Raju, and soon it became obvious that nobody's attention was on us anyway. The real drama was occurring up front where Joy, fired up with righteous indignation and propelled by months of powerlifting, was steaming after Tiggy like a starving leopard who's just seen an injured gazelle. The rest of us could only watch in awe as Joy, linen suit billowing in her wake, closed the gap on Lycra-clad Tiggy in her running spikes.

As they neared the finish line it was neck and neck and the crowd were going wild with chants of 'Miss-is Ros-si! Miss-is Ros-si!' led by Eva, Maisie and a recently emboldened Darcy. Even Mrs North on the megaphone was sounding a bit breathy with the drama. And then, in slow motion, we saw Joy stumble, the toe of Marcus Demetriou's borrowed trainer catching in her trouser cuff. Tiggy glanced to her side, arms beginning to rise above her head in a victory cheer as the crowd held its collective breath… But Joy, ever the competitor, knew she was going down and somehow used her last ounce of strength in the foot that still had contact with the ground to propel herself forward, torso first, like they do in the Olympics. She ended up beating Tiggy by a boob and collapsed over the line, hands outstretched, breaking her wrist on the uneven turf.

'Well,' I said to Zahara and Grace as the ambulance doors closed on a triumphant Joy who was punching the air with her remaining good hand. 'There'll not be another St John's Sports Day quite like that one.' And I wiped a little tear from my eye as we made our way off the premises.

Chapter Thirty-Three

Friday 28 July

The Gala Performance

So, the end of term has come and gone. And I don't really want to talk about it, to be honest. Or at least, I don't want to wallow in it too much. It was sad, but I knew it would be. I think a part of me still believes that come September I'll be walking up that little hill to St John's with another one of my children. I've become completely institution-alised and can't really imagine anything else. God knows what happens to people when their children finish school altogether and there's no 'end of term' or 'summer holi-days' to mark their years into manageable chunks, no INSET days to fret over, no tests, no homework, no parent consultations… I'll cross that bridge when I come to it; relinquishing primary school is bad enough.

Maisie was fine. She thrives on drama, and managed to be appropriately emotional without becoming over-wrought. Leading up to the leavers' assembly, she had been badgering me about whether I thought I was going to cry. She and her friends seem to set a lot of store by how upset their mother gets in any given scenario, although I've never heard them comment on any fatherly blubbing; maybe they just never see that. Anyway, she kept telling me, 'Oh, Mrs North says all the mummies are going to be *a wreck*. They're going to be *in pieces* when we sing our final song. I won't tell you what it is. It's a surprise, but I bet you'll cry.'

The song was 'I Love My Mum'. Of course it was. But for the leavers' assembly the lyrics are altered to transform it into 'I Love My *School*' (clever). It works on many levels, that song. Endlessly adaptable.

'I love my school and my school loves me, more than I'll ever know. It's where I've come to learn and play, where I've come to grow' (last *ohhh* sustained until either a small child passes out or a parent cries, 'Stop! I can't take it any more!').

I didn't remind Maisie that this was not my assembly debut. I've already heard the adapted versions of 'I Love My Mum/Dad/School', and the surprise element is somewhat lost on me. No such emotional stunting from Joy, though. This was the first time she'd heard those particular lyrics, and it seemed to be them that tipped her over the edge. I have never seen Joy that upset, not even when she read Carrie Fisher's memoir and found out about the affair with Harrison Ford (although it's a close-run thing). When it came to saying goodbye to Mrs North and handing over the present we'd all chipped in to buy for her retirement, she starting sobbing again, and in a move that startled everyone, but particularly Mrs North, she grabbed hold of her and refused to let go, clamping her between the broken arm with the plaster cast and the one holding the orchid, and wailing into her rigid shoulder like a grieving widow. Joy broke off from sobbing occasionally, coming up for air to eulogise about the importance of early years education and how Evangeline would never forget the kindness and love shown by the staff at St John's, and that she wished more people understood just how essential teachers were, and had the pandemic taught us nothing? She continued in this vein for a solid five minutes until Eva, who had been equally taken aback but recovered her cool a little earlier than her mother, eventually went up on stage herself, prised Joy away from Mrs North and led her, still weeping, down the plywood steps to be comforted by Mrs Shan, the teaching assistant who works in the special educational needs unit.

Having recently benefited from the firm embrace of St John's scariest teacher myself, the day Mum moved into Bob's Place, I wasn't really in a position to criticise. Mrs North does have that natural air of authority that makes you feel it's safe to cry – like a benign prison warden. Or Angela Merkel. And when it came to my turn to take my leave of the woman who had been the only constant in my children's education to date, I too was a bit wobbly. We greeted each other like battle-hardened soldiers: a wry smile, a nod of recognition, a gulping sob (me), a proffered Kleenex tissue (her) and a promise to keep in touch, despite both of us knowing that this was incredibly unlikely. She gave Grace an enormous hug and wanted to hear all about her degree and her future plans, as well as how Tommy was getting on in sixth form.

It crossed my mind that I knew very little about Mrs North's family and yet she knows an awful lot about mine. It's funny how some people end up playing such a critical role in your life without you ever realising. I wonder how she feels about the many hundreds of children she's taught over the years, whether there are key moments that stick in her memory or whether the personalities of so many children just merge into one amorphous blob after a while. I guess she wouldn't tell me even if I asked; she'd say all the children she teaches are special and have a unique place in her heart, because that's the St John's Primary School way, and that's what the Department of Education and the board of governors would want her to say. Maybe Joy and I should take her out one evening, get her drunk, find out the truth. Or maybe it's better to preserve the illusion, for us as well as her. Either way, it's the end of an era, for Mrs North and for the Baker family.

I was talking to Sam about it a couple of nights ago – this weird combination of defined milestones that signify an ending, and the less well-defined but equally important landmarks. The last bedtime story, for example; you never know you're reading it. But then weeks go by and you realise that the child who couldn't get to sleep without a chapter of *Matilda* (complete with Mummy doing all the silly voices) can now settle themselves on their own, and would actually prefer to read their own very grown-up book, thank you very much, because *Matilda* is for little kids, and bedtime stories are for little kids too. Or the last time they hold your hand to cross the road – who remembers the date of that little bereavement? Nobody. But it happens. Suddenly they don't need to hold your hand (and usually you've got your hands full with another baby, or a dog, or a shopping trolley, or something amusing on your phone), and then one day they can cross the road without you even being there. One day they can (theoretically in the case of my kids) get into a car and drive it down said road ON THEIR OWN.

You never know which Christmas will be the last one where they believe in Santa, or when they're going to stop jumping in puddles for fun. You can't predict which will be the last television series you'll share together, exclaiming in horror as Jamil goes out of *Strictly Come*

Dancing, or declaring your collective astonishment that Clarence won *Bake Off* despite the collapse of his Showstopper. Suddenly that child is gone: they've either moved out of the house, or they've moved on to a different television series, or they don't really *do* mainstream television any more because they now *stream content over their phones* (or something equally incomprehensible).

Sam indulged my ramblings for a while, but he was only half listening, busy preparing his meals for the last days of carb-loading ahead of this weekend's triathlon. He also pointed out that a lot of supposed endings are nothing of the sort, citing Grace's 'leaving home' only to return again three years later, still unable to drive and barely acquainted with the washing machine. He jokes about her getting too comfortable, back in her old room and living off the Bank of Mum and Dad, but I know he loves having her back just as much as I do.

He set off for Scotland early this morning. I had been intending to wish him good luck but it was five o'clock and I hadn't slept a wink due to a combination of excitement and anxiety about tonight's performance, so I told myself I'd call him later when I had a chance. Although it was likely that I'd be pretty busy for the rest of the day – there was still much to organise. I knew that Joe had everything in hand. I also knew, from the trip we'd taken to the venue last week, that Sonja the events manager would be waiting for us, ready to do the final sound check and ensure that the technical equipment for the video streaming was working, but there is always that sense of nervous apprehension that something might go wrong, particularly when you're dealing with a group of people who between them have a set of quite complex needs.

Sixteen members of the choir were too frail to travel and they included Mum, but I'd managed to record something from each of them, even if it was just some percussion or a few la la la's. Many of our choir with more advanced dementia were no longer verbally communicative, but they still understood rhythm and tone; they still enjoyed the collaborative effort of music making, and I truly believed that every member of the group got something out of the sessions we ran almost daily. Mum certainly still enjoyed being in the room with everyone else, hearing their voices and contributing when she could. She particularly liked to sit next to Tina's grand piano while I played and would often rest her hands on the rim of the main body of the instrument to feel its vibrations. We encouraged our choir members who were hard of hearing to do the same, feeling the notes as they reverberated from the keys, down the strings, through the piano and into their fingertips. It made me think of that painting by Michelangelo, *The Creation of Adam* – where the very essence of life is communicated from one outstretched hand to another. Obviously, I wasn't casting myself as God in this context, but the idea that my fingers touched the keys that set off an entire cascade of sound to reach the hands of others seems a particularly pleasing way of communicating something deep and mysterious. And I've always been one for a whimsical notion.

As dawn broke this morning and the sun snuck around the edges of the curtains, I lay on my side of the bed and contemplated the plan for the next twenty-four hours. After lunch (and once I'd made sure that the kids were up and about – a lie-in during the school holidays was fair enough, but I expected them to be out of bed by the afternoon as a bare minimum), I was driving over to The Carlton and had been told I could check into my room from two o'clock. I had contemplated driving back tonight after the event – it was only an hour away – but Veronica suggested that I might want a drink or two after the performance, and it therefore made more sense to stay. Joe had also managed to secure us a deal on a group booking and anyway, the cost of the room was a fraction of the costs incurred by my husband for his triathlon weekend so I didn't feel too bad.

Once checked in I would go to the auditorium and run through the set list with the sound and lighting technicians. Sonja had assured me that she would be on hand if I needed anything. Joe would be focusing on the catering, ticketing, front of house and auction. He had also taken on much of the organisation around the performance itself, because once we started I would be up on stage with the choir, playing the accompaniment on one of The Carlton's lovely pianos, cueing in each section (this was often a challenge, as some of our choir members forgot whether they were altos or tenors and either missed their slot or joined in with both) and generally keeping the show on the road. I'd need Joe and Sonja to ensure that everything else was sorted. Veronica would also be milling around keeping an eye on things, although she and Gee had both paid the full price for their tickets (along with most of the rest of Sam's colleagues, who had two tables between them) so I wanted her to enjoy herself and not feel she was 'at work'.

The majority of the choir members would be arriving between five and six. We had hired two minibuses for those who were travelling alone, or with carers who couldn't drive, and everyone else was coming independently accompanied by family or friends. A dementia-friendly buffet would be provided for all of our singers, with an assortment of dishes and drinks taking into account everyone's specific dietary requirements as per the detailed information sent by Tina to The Carlton catering team (no green room rider could have been more thorough), so that nobody was going on stage hungry. From seven, the first guests would be arriving and taking their seats in the auditorium. At a quarter to eight Joe and Veronica would accompany our two celebrity guests on stage to give a brief introduction to the choir. Our celebs, Angharad and Miles, were both household names with illustrious careers in the music industry, and it's fair to say I was a little starstruck. They would be talking about the power of communal singing, the rise of choirs like ours and the particular importance of music as therapy. They would also allude to some of the prizes coming up in the auction after dinner. And then at eight o'clock they would walk off the stage, the curtain would go up and there I'd be, sitting behind the piano, flanked by fifty-seven singers of varying abilities and vocal ranges and backed by a wall of screens featuring our prerecorded performers.

Eight o'clock this bloody evening.

Showtime.

Gulp.

Chapter Thirty-Four

In the end it all passed in an absolute blur of nerves and adrenaline. I have performed on stage before, and this was not my first dementia choir outing, but it was easily the biggest and, as Maisie would call it, *the most epic*. The wall of screens flickering into life behind the choir gave the whole event something of an Eighties music video vibe and Nihal, who was my tech support for the night, crouching behind the curtain with his laptop, was able to time each clip perfectly to coincide with the appropriate song, no mean feat when our running time was all over the place. For example, by the time we got to Simon and Garfunkel's 'Cecilia' with all of its tambourine and marimba rattling, we were at least five minutes behind, but Nihal knew at exactly which moment the percussion came in, and lo and behold, there was eighty-five-year-old Sangita shaking her maracas on-screen, and a laughing ninety-two-year-old Arthur playing the tenor drum from his pressure-relieving electric bed back at Bob's Place.

The audience loved it. Really loved it. There was the perfect mix of live entertainment and quality performance with a smattering of (mostly intentional) comedy value. Some of our choir are really very talented musicians, a few with professional careers behind them, but all of them, without exception, love singing. And it was this that really came across. There is something about watching live music, something in the atmosphere at a gig, whether it be Madison Square Garden or the back room of The Woolpack pub, that cannot be recreated by downloading a song from the internet or hearing it over the radio. Some of the joy of the performance is communicated to the live audience. It's like I said before – Michelangelo's moment of electricity, sharing the spark, heaven speaking to earth. Live music does that. It connects people.

There were so many highlights for me: the rolling wave of noise generated by Bowie's 'Heroes' almost brought a tear to my eye (the addition of Dennis's grandson on the electric guitar for the opening bars really made it); Gertie's (somewhat unexpected) solo in the middle of 'Proud Mary'; the shuffling dance routine we'd worked out to accompany Pharrell Williams's 'Happy'; and the interwoven harmonies of Mama Cass's 'Dream A Little Dream Of Me' – the list is endless, really. But end it did, and by the time we'd bowed for our fourth ovation and exited the stage in a jumble of walking frames, wheelchairs and rollators, I was absolutely buzzing. God knows how Harry Styles and the like come down after a big show (roughly equivalent scale) – it's no wonder all these A-listers are hooked on pills and sleepers. I felt like the king of the world, mingling with our celebrity presenters, accepting praise for my keyboard skills from Krishnan, the comedian we'd booked to compere the auction, having Joe pull out a chair for me at the top table and bring me a glass of champagne...

'I feel bad that Tina's not here to see this,' I said, briefly distracted from my own stellar success by the omission.

'She wanted to stay with everyone at Bob's though,' said Veronica. 'It's not really her sort of thing any more.'

'But she used to love going to big corporate dos and society functions in the past,' I said, topping up my glass – that first drink slid down alarmingly fast. 'She's got a whole heap of stories about what happened during the Nineties that would make your hair curl. I think she and Bob ended up at one of the Downing Street parties once, the one with the Spice Girls. She used to love the champagne lifestyle.'

'But she used to go to all of those things *with Bob*. She talked to me about it once. Said it just wasn't the same, getting dressed up for a big night out, all the drinking and networking required. She doesn't get the same kick out of it without him – even something like this.'

I nodded. This made sense, and although Tina and I had never discussed it explicitly in those terms, I knew she missed her husband now just as much as she always had. 'I guess that figures. Bob's Place is the closest thing she's got to Bob himself. I'm glad she's back at home then, with all of our lovely performers. Didn't those remote screens work well?'

'Phenomenal,' said Joe. 'That was such a good idea of yours.'

'I think it was your idea,' I said. 'In fact I'm sure it was.'

'No.' He shook his head. 'Definitely you. It came from when you'd done the same during lockdown, do you remember telling me?'

I nodded, impressed he remembered the conversation that accurately. 'You're very good at not taking credit for things, Joe. It's pretty rare for a bloke.'

'It certainly is,' said Veronica. 'I can't count the number of times some jumped-up Eton schoolboy has stolen my ideas and rebranded them as his own.' She looked over my shoulder. 'Ahh – it looks as though the rest of our dinner companions are arriving. I'll go and make sure Gee's OK and then I'll be back.'

I followed her gaze. 'Oh. My. God!' I said. 'Angharad and Miles are staying?'

Joe smiled indulgently. 'They are,' he said. 'And they are sitting at our table.'

I stifled a scream of excitement because they were now within a metre of me and that would not have been cool. (Whereas my relentless stream of compliments and general gushing sycophancy that lasted the entire duration of dinner was the epitome of cool.)

A couple of hours later, and I was having the time of my life. The meal had finished (delicious). The auction was in full swing. Krishnan, the compere, was hilarious (and surprisingly good at identifying the high-rollers in the audience and gently poking fun at them until they parted with colossal amounts of cash). And I was drunkenly chatting to Angharad about her new role as a judge on ITV's *Great British Pianist* (a title one had to enunciate quite carefully).

'I had thought I might make a good professional musician,' I said, lurching in my chair. 'That, or a singer. Or anything really. Just famous.'

'Well, Bob's Place is sort of famous now,' she said gamely. She was wearing the kind of expression that goes with the territory of meeting superfans on a regular basis (I assume). 'And that's partly due to you and your amazing choir, Penny.'

'She says I'm famous.' I lurched back to whisper loudly in Joe's ear. '*Angharad* says I'm famous.' I sat bolt upright.

'Miles!' I shouted across the table. 'Do you think I'm famous?'

Poor man looked a little confused. He adjusted his glasses. 'Errrm, yes?' he said.

I gave Joe a meaningful look. 'See?'

On stage, Krishnan was telling some lengthy joke, the punchline of which just so happened to link directly to our last prize of the evening (a five-night stay at La Ronda, The Carlton's sister hotel in the Seychelles – I immediately thought of Tiggy).

'How much money do you think we've made?' I whispered (slightly more whisperingly than previous) to Joe as the bids came in.

'Depends,' he said, keeping an ear out for the final bid. 'But it's likely this last lot will take us over the two hundred thousand mark.'

'Pounds?' I said, stunned. 'Two hundred thousand pounds?'

He nodded, smiling broadly. 'Yes. Ticket sales were really good – lots of big businesses bought tables, many donated purely to sponsor the event, as you can see from the programme and the entrance hall. And then this auction has really topped it off. I mean, we've got to pay The Carlton, but they've given us excellent rates. Angharad and Miles have waived their fee, as has Krishnan up there.' He nodded towards the comedian. 'His aunt had dementia, apparently.' He turned to me. 'It's been a real eye-opener, actually, running this event. It's made me realise how many people's lives have been touched by the disease. How many thousands of people there are who want to invest and give something back to organisations like Bob's Place. The bigger picture from tonight isn't the money we've made running the event – it's the links we've made for the future. I've got a couple of meetings lined up with big investors in the next few weeks, many of whom are here. They've all got social investment funds and are looking for worthwhile projects to back.' He smiled at me. 'It's all good.'

'Wow.' I didn't know what else to say. I was so overwhelmed I just kept staring at Joe like he was some kind of miracle worker and completely missed the final bid and the enormous cheer that followed.

'I can't wait to tell Tina tomorrow,' I said. 'She'll be so hugely relieved.'

'She knows some of it already,' said Joe. 'I've kept her abreast of the money coming from ticket sales, as she asked.' He scanned my face, concerned for a moment. 'Whereas you just wanted to be informed if I looked like I was going over budget, that's right, isn't it?'

'Yes, absolutely. I wanted to concentrate on the choir and the music. I thought I'd leave the event in your capable hands.' I gave a little squeal of joy. 'And looks like I was right! God, I'm so glad we hired you!'

He beamed. 'I'm really glad you hired me too,' he said.

There was an odd moment where all the noise around us seemed to dial down a notch, fading quietly into the background as Joe and I smiled manically at each other, and then...

'I'm off for a dance,' announced Veronica from the other side of Joe. 'Anyone want to join me?'

Miles and Angharad bravely stood to accompany my formidable colleague to the dance floor where Kiss's 'Crazy Crazy Nights' was blasting out through the speakers. I raised my eyebrows.

'Check out Veronica and her celebrity dancing friends,' I said to Joe. 'These are crazy nights indeed!'

He laughed as we watched Veronica, arms aloft, shouting along to Gene Simmons's lyrics. 'You've got a nice working relationship, the three of you,' he said. 'Always seems very good-natured and harmonious. Not that common in most businesses.'

I nodded. 'Well, we are good-natured and harmonious women – especially me, I'm very harmonious.' I trilled off a scale of notes and then realised I sounded like a dick and stopped.

He laughed again and poured me another glass of champagne. I had no idea which bottle we were on now; they seemed to just keep arriving at our table. 'You are very talented,' he said. 'Musically.'

I rolled my eyes.

'I mean it! But, yeah, you and Tina and Veronica. Do you ever think how long that partnership is going to last?'

Whoa. That was me back down to earth with a bump. 'Way to kill the mood, Joe,' I said.

'Sorry.' He looked horrified. 'I didn't mean anything really significant,' he said in a rush. 'I just wondered whether you'd given any thought to succession planning and that sort of thing.'

'No. Not really. Tina's going to stay on as a trustee when she steps down as manager, so I think we'll stay as we are for the foreseeable.'

He nodded, thoughtful. 'Yes. You don't really want to mess too much with the formula you've got. I see that. I do wonder whether making changes to the business might be easier when Tina retires though. I think she's great. You know that. But she's too close to the organisation.' He topped up my glass again.

I watched the bubbles frothing around in my champagne for a moment as I mulled over his comment.

'Tina's the one who built Bob's Place from scratch,' I said. 'The ethos, the spirit of the place – it's all her.'

'But that's the problem,' he said gently. 'It was her baby, and now it's growing up. She's got to let it go.'

The unexpected metaphor for my own life suddenly felt a bit overwhelming. I sniffed as I took a gulp of my drink.

'Hey – are you OK?' Joe's voice was full of concern as he reached out and placed his hand on mine. 'Oh God, Penny. I didn't mean to upset you. I know how much Bob's Place means to you – and how much Tina means to you – gah! I'm sorry. I'm so sorry. I spoke out of turn…'

'No, no, it's fine,' I said, looking at his hand on top of mine for a moment before I withdrew it on the pretext of reaching for a water glass. 'I'm being a bit ridiculous – ignore me.'

'Well, I'm hardly likely to do that,' he said, giving me a strange look before glancing away.

'Now.' He pushed his chair back as he stood. 'I'm going to the bar. Do you want to join me, or get on the dance floor with that crazy bunch of A-listers?'

I laughed, the tension broken. 'I'll stay here for a minute and decide,' I said, suddenly wanting a moment alone. Time to process the events of an amazing few hours. I watched him as he crossed the vast dining room to the bar area and thought about what he'd said. It was true; there was no point in thinking things were going to stay the same forever. An element of succession planning was needed, and we'd all avoided the topic so far. I guess sometimes it takes an outsider to see what's required.

I allowed myself to daydream a future where I took more of a leadership role on the charity board, helping Bob's Place grow into a much more sustainable long-term business. Perhaps even branching out, heading up a franchise. There was no reason we couldn't replicate what we'd done locally elsewhere, and I knew I'd have Tina and Veronica's expertise and experience behind me every step of the way. It was something to consider and, in a way, this element of career possibility gave me a sense of freedom. I felt liberated. Like a window had opened on to a future where my children had left home and I could make choices about how to occupy my time without needing to defer to the colossal *list of things to do*, or the schedules of four other humans and one canine.

Every time I had thought about the kids leaving home prior to this point I had been overwhelmed with sadness, concerned about what I would do, how I would function, *what was I* if I wasn't actively being a mummy – but now I saw that there was a glimmer of possibility, a freedom in the loosening of that particular role. Of course, I'd always be a mother, I was defined by that probably more than anything else in my life. And I'd always be a wife and a daughter, a sister and a friend. But as the time spent absorbed and occupied by one role decreased, maybe there was an opportunity to be a little bit more of *me*?

Chapter Thirty-Five

We all ended up in Joe's suite when the bar closed: me, Veronica, even Krishnan, Angharad and Miles – it was like *Celebrity Big Brother*. In fact, I think I might have said that at one point, only to have everyone look a little embarrassed on my behalf. Joe had had the foresight to buy a bottle of brandy from the supermarket over the road, and between the six of us we got through most of it before people started peeling off back to their own rooms. Veronica was the first to go, claiming age and a possible twisted ankle from dancing to 'Jump Around'.

'I wonder if that's what House of Pain had in mind when they recorded it?' I mused to Joe, sloshing the ice cubes around my glass of brandy and Coke. 'Do you think they imagined that a sixty-four-year-old businesswoman whose usual preference of musical event is held at Glyndebourne would sustain an injury dancing to their track at a fundraiser for a dementia charity?'

'Probably not,' he conceded. 'Prob-ab-ly not.'

I stretched my feet out in front of me, turning my legs this way and that to admire the sparkly fabric of my dress as I sat on the floor. 'I think I might have lost a shoe,' I said, surprised.

'Was that before or after you suggested we break back into the auditorium so you could play "Rocket Man" on the piano?' Krishnan asked.

'After, I imagine.' I smiled winningly at him.

'Shame,' said Angharad. 'It was a great shoe. Lucky you've still got that one.' She pointed to my left foot where a silver high-top trainer remained. 'I've got to get back,' she said, looking at her watch. 'Shall we share a taxi?' She looked around at Miles and Krishnan.

They all promised to stay in touch and asked me to keep them updated about future fundraisers. I'm not sure that Angharad will necessarily want to follow up on my suggestion that we go out for dinner sometime to share stories about our respective dementia choirs, but I thought it was important to offer.

'You've got a new best mate there,' said Joe, chuckling to himself as the three of them left the room to go downstairs and wait for a taxi in reception. He looked at the bottle of brandy, tilting it to one side. 'We might as well finish this off,' he said. 'Shame to waste it.'

'It would be a shame,' I said. 'And we deserve it. We deserve all the good things!'

'We do?'

'We do.' I nodded emphatically. 'Because tonight was a giant success. A monster of an event!'

'A fundraising behemoth!' said Joe. He poured the last of the brandy into our glasses and raised his aloft. 'A toast! To Bob's Place!'

'To Bob's Place!' I held my own glass up to join his, my double vision meaning that I missed it by about ten centimetres. 'Whoops!' My drink sloshed a little over the edge onto the plush carpet of the suite.

'Wait right there,' said Joe, seeing I was about to start dabbing at the Coke and brandy stain with my sparkly dress (which was very lovely, as I may have mentioned, and should definitely not have been used in place of a dishcloth). He leapt up and pulled a sheaf of tissues out of the dispenser on the bedside table, crouching down beside me to blot the carpet. It briefly crossed my mind that if there was any spillage at home, whether animal, mineral or vegetable, it was always my responsibility to clear it up.

'You're very domesticated,' I said, impressed as I watched him pour a bit of water from the toothbrush mug that Angharad had been drinking out of onto the stain.

He peered up at me. 'What? Because I can throw tissues at a damp patch of flooring? I don't know as that's terribly domesticated.'

'Well, the bar's not very high.'

'That's not what you said when you were trying to clamber onto the one downstairs in order to give us your best Tina Turner.'

'Oh dear,' I said, hitting my forehead with the heel of my hand. 'Elton John and Tina Turner. I'm really giving it the full repertoire of impressions this evening, aren't I?'

Joe started singing the opening lines of 'Private Dancer' into an imaginary microphone. I joined him, but we soon realised we didn't know anything past the first verse, so we just made up a load of rubbish and delivered it in a Tina Turner style, falling about laughing at the lyrical mess we'd cobbled together.

'You're funny,' I said, leaning against him as I caught my breath from laughing. 'Funny old Joe.'

'Yup,' he said wryly. 'That's exactly how every bloke wants to be viewed by women. "Funny and old".'

'Oh, don't be silly,' I said, turning towards him. We were both still sitting on the carpet separated only by the spilled drink. 'You're not old. *I'm* old. I'm *really* old. Ancient. Decrepit.' I gave a heavy, melodramatic sigh. 'Past. My. Prime.'

Joe pulled a face. 'Don't do that.' He sounded annoyed.

'What?'

'When women do that "oh, I'm so haggard and physically repulsive" thing…'

'Hey, I didn't say I was *repulsive*!' I said, a little stung.

'No, but when women do that whole self-deprecating speech. It's like they're either fishing for compliments – which isn't you at all – or they genuinely have no idea how other people view them, how much people might value them. And that's just sad.'

'I'm not sad,' I said, feeling suddenly sad.

'It's sad when *really attractive* women don't understand how people – how *men* – see them.'

'That's because men *don't* see us,' I said, remembering the discussion with Joy. 'Women my age are invisible to men. We're stealth bombers,' I said, a little uncertain that I was recalling Joy's words verbatim.

'You're not a stealth bomber, Penny.' He laughed softly. 'And you're not invisible. I see you. I watch you.'

'In a creepy stalker way?' I said, confused.

'No. Sorry – that sounded… I meant in a normal grown-up way. I watch what you do. How you are around people. How you make other people feel.' He looked down at his hands. 'I'm *aware* of you. I'm *always* aware of you. Where you are. What you're doing,' he said with a sigh, resting his head back on the foot of the bed we were propped up against. 'It's like in the way you gradually notice something, the awareness creeps up on you, and then one day you realise that thing, that person, is something you want.'

He looked up at me again, his face inches from mine. And for one woozy moment I began to lean in. There was a ringing in my ears, the hum of alcohol in my veins, and a long-buried sensation returning to the surface, a memory of how it felt to be wanted, to be desired...

And then a phone rang, loud and insistent. We sprang apart, slightly dazed, both looking for our mobiles before we realised it was the hotel telephone, the one on the bedside table. Joe stood to answer it while I foraged around in my handbag.

'Shit,' I said as I found my mobile, switched off since six the previous evening. I'd been so scarred by my experience of interrupting proceedings at the St John's performance of *Alice in Wonderland* that I hadn't taken any chances with the dementia choir – I hadn't even risked Flight Mode. It had been properly switched off from the moment the choristers arrived, and after the performance I'd been on such a high that it simply hadn't crossed my mind to turn it back on again. It sounds pretty bad in hindsight, but my first thought had not been to phone or message Sam or the kids to tell them how the event had gone. I wanted to live in the moment, enjoy my brief but exhilarating time in the spotlight – and I'd let it go to my head. Now dimly aware of Joe's voice murmuring in the background, I switched my phone on and saw the messages and missed calls pinging through almost immediately.

'Penny,' called Joe, from across the room, the hotel phone receiver in his hand. 'You'd better take this. It's your husband.'

Chapter Thirty-Six

Saturday

'Pen!' Sam's voice was muffled. 'Thank God I've got hold of you. Are you OK?' There was no recrimination in his voice, no 'why the hell are you in some bloke's hotel room?'

'Sam? What is it? What's going on?'

'Oh, Pen... it's your mum.'

'What?' I said, still drunkenly trying to make the connection between what had just happened, *nearly* happened, with Joe, and the fact that I was now speaking to my husband, who was supposed to be tucked up in bed ahead of his triathlon... 'Where are you? Isn't today the...?'

'I've cancelled it, hon.' His voice was warm, crackly with the dodgy reception, but soothing and so familiar. 'Listen, it's your mum. She's not great. She had one of her episodes, early evening. I think your dad thought – well, Tina thought it too, and Rory... It just seemed like one of her normal things.'

'Yes,' I said faintly, aware that there was a 'but' hanging out there in the ether, suspended, ready to clatter down on my head.

'But then she didn't rally, like she usually does. She's still not really with it.'

'Is she dead?' My voice was robotic. I could see Joe perched awkwardly on the side of the desk. He looked worried. I turned away.

'No, sweetheart. No. But she's sick. Rory thinks... He thought it was best that we call you. He thinks she—' I could hear him take a deep breath. 'She might not have long left.'

There was a thud in my chest, that bit at the bottom of your ribs. It's got a funny name, that bit of cartilage. I remember Rory telling me what it was called once. But this thud, it was like a combination of nausea and pain, a cold, leaden feeling. A sudden realisation that I wasn't where I was needed. Separated from my entire family and... 'Oh Sam,' I whispered. 'I've got to get home.'

He was wonderful, my husband. Calm, rational, kind. He gave me the information I needed. Reassured me while telling me the truth. It seems that Rory had called him at around nine o'clock when he was unable to get hold of me. They'd discussed the situation. Debated what to do. Sam had told my brother that I would want to be at Bob's Place if there was even the remotest chance my mother was dying. He was right. Rory said he'd keep trying my mobile. Sam said I'd probably prefer to hear it from him. He was right. When he couldn't reach me on my mobile he'd hopped straight in the car and headed south, knowing that I'd want him to be home as soon as he could. To be with our kids. To be with my mum until I could get there. He did what I'd needed him to do. He knows me.

He knows exactly what I would want to happen in that situation. Even if we've never explicitly discussed a scenario where my mother is dying and he's in Scotland

and I'm too drunk to drive and sitting in a patch of brandy and Coke in a swanky hotel just outside London.

I was back in my room packing my bag moments later. Sam had been on the road for four hours by the time he'd called. He realised I probably had my phone off and didn't try me again until nearing midnight. When he still couldn't reach me, he ended up calling the hotel. They'd phoned my room. No answer. They'd put a shout out among the few remaining stragglers in the bar area. No answer. And then Sam had suggested they call Veronica's room. Thankfully she was back and able to blearily inform the hotel reception (and my husband) that I was likely to be in Joe Devlin's room. God knows what Sam must have thought. Anyway, the time it had taken to track me down meant that he was now only an hour away and could come and collect me. I lay on my bed for a while, wide-eyed and unable to focus before I realised it was pointless and made my way downstairs to wait in the hotel lobby. And then suddenly, in what seemed like both an eternity and no time at all, my husband was walking through the revolving doors and crossing the marble foyer and he was there. My Sam was there. And I was in his arms. And it was better – not right, but better.

He drove us straight to Bob's Place where Tina was standing, calm and patient at the doorway. 'I've just rustled up a batch of muffins,' she said. 'You'll be hungry. Come down when you're ready.' She gave me a cuddle. 'It's OK,' she said. 'You're going to be OK.'

Dad was sitting in the big recliner next to Mum's bed. Rory was there too. He rose from a chair in the corner and greeted us both with a brisk hug. He looked a little dishevelled, but otherwise fine. This is a man used to night-time reconnaissance missions and on-call bleeps.

This is a man who is also parenting small children, and we all know how that world has no respect for the boundaries of day and night. Dad, however, looked exhausted. Like a seventy-nine-year-old man who hasn't slept for twenty-four hours. Like a man whose wife is dying.

And Mum... she just sort of looked like Mum. I don't know what I was expecting – something more dramatic, I guess. But there she was, lying in her bed, looking at the ceiling. Unfocused. Tranquil. Not really there. Her usual expression when she's staring out of the window at something none of the rest of us can see. I guess maybe she's been living in this partial dreamworld for a while. Maybe the barrier between life and death is more porous when your brain has stopped functioning properly. Maybe this vague twilight existence is less frightening for her as a result. She certainly didn't seem troubled. Her breathing was a bit erratic but not particularly laboured. Her eyes were open but she didn't turn towards the sound of my voice as she usually would. I perched on the edge of her bed and picked up her hand, the skin papery soft, like a tissue you find in the pocket of a coat you've worn years earlier and long forgotten about.

'Mum,' I said. 'It's Penny.'

No response.

'Can she hear us, do you think?' I said, to nobody in particular.

'I don't know,' said Dad. 'Sometimes. She's comfortable at least.' We both smiled weakly at the shared code word.

'Is it a stroke? Shouldn't she be in hospital if she's *dying*?' I whispered the last word and was cross with myself for doing it. But maybe she could hear me and maybe she didn't know she was dying and the thought might frighten her.

'The out-of-hours GP is on his way,' said Rory. 'Dr Ormerod.'

'He's local,' I said. 'One of the partners at Highview. He knows Mum. That's nice.' I turned back to Mum. 'It's that nice chap coming to visit, Mum,' I said. 'The one you saw when you fell over by the pond and hurt your knee. He kept saying sorry about his cold hands, do you remember? And we said, cold hands, warm heart. Do you remember?'

There was a flicker at the corner of her mouth. She could hear me, I was sure of it.

'We'll chat with him,' continued Rory. 'But I think we'd need to ask ourselves what Mum would gain from being in hospital at this point.'

'If she's had a stroke then couldn't they treat her?' said Sam.

Rory gave a tired sigh. I could see that the burden of being the medical decision-maker in this context, when it was your own mother, was weighing heavily on him. 'I don't think they could,' he said. 'But we'll speak to the GP – see what he says.'

Sam nodded. There was a gentle tap at the door and Tina was there with a tray of mugs. 'Tea?' she said. 'The doctor's here.'

Dr Ormerod was wonderful and spoke with a quiet gravitas that we all found reassuring. Even Rory didn't feel the need to interject while the GP explained what could and couldn't be done for Mum now.

'We'll ask the palliative care team to pop in on Monday,' he said, speaking to Dad. 'Just to see if there's anything your wife needs in terms of symptom control. But it sounds as though she's being well looked after here. I know Bob's Place do a marvellous job with their residents.' He smiled at me and Tina.

'How long do you think…' I trailed off, not wanting to complete the sentence – the death sentence.

He shook his head. 'I really can't say. It could be hours, it could be days. She's in a light coma at the moment. She'll probably fluctuate in and out of consciousness, there may be some lucid periods…'

'That'll make a change, Mum!' I said, nudging her like I was in some Eighties comedy sketch show. 'Sorry – bit weird.'

Dr Ormerod gave me a benign smile of understanding. 'But if she continues to not eat or drink, then over time all the body's processes start to slow down until eventually…'

'They stop,' said Sam from the corner of the room. 'Sorry.' He looked at me. 'Bit weird.'

'But won't she be thirsty,' I said, 'if she's not drinking?' I was remembering the time I'd been nil by mouth after complications with Maisie's delivery and how the thirst had almost driven me insane, to the point where I was hallucinating about drinking out of the hospital toilets – which Sam said was a real marker of my desperation. 'Should she be on a drip, or something?'

'You can keep offering her drinks,' said the GP. 'If she's thirsty she'll have some sips of cool tea or water. But if she's not interested then don't feel you have to force it.'

'She struggles a bit with drinking,' my dad said. 'She's been coughing more the past few days, before this happened.'

The doctor nodded. 'Yes, so just be guided by her. Offer drinks but don't push it. If she wants to take a few sips then maybe sit her up a bit, but if her chest becomes a bit more rattly, don't worry.' He turned to Shilpa, one of our nurses. 'We can stop checking her oxygen sats,' he said, and she nodded.

'Do you want us to do any obs at all?'

'I don't think so.' He turned back to Dad. 'I think we can probably reduce the amount of interventions Mary has now. We won't be sticking thermometers in her ear or checking her blood pressure with the cuff.'

'But how will we know if she's getting better? Or worse?' said Dad, perplexed.

Dr Ormerod nodded slowly. 'I don't think she is going to get better, Gordon,' he said gently. 'Or get worse, as such. It's more that Mary's making a transition as she approaches the end. She's voting with her feet by not taking on food and fluids because her body's signalling that she doesn't need them any more.' He looked directly at my father. 'I think your wife is preparing to die.'

Chapter Thirty-Seven

Wednesday 2 August

My mum died today. What an odd sentence to write. I think I'll just retreat into practicalities while I describe this bit, if you don't mind. It's easier.

By the time Dr Ormerod left we were well into Saturday, and everyone looked shattered. Time had taken on that elastic quality where day and night have no meaning but those of us who were still very much in the land of the living were in need of some basics, like sustenance and sleep. Rory had to get home. He'd been on call the night before, so Candice had been looking after the kids on her own for two days and although the woman was formidable, and used to Rory being away for days at a time, there was a limit to how much one could manage alone in that scenario. We agreed that he would bring the whole family to visit later that afternoon and give the kids a chance to say goodbye. Sam suggested that he drive home to check on our kids now that dawn was breaking. I realised he had been on the road for over fifteen hours since he'd left our house at five the previous morning. He must be exhausted too.

'What about your triathlon?' I said as he made his way out of Mum's room promising to bring me some clothes and my toothbrush on his return. 'What about the sponsorship money and the...'

'Pen,' he interrupted me gently. 'It doesn't matter. I'll return it. It doesn't mean anything. What's the point in me raising money for dementia charities if I can't be with you when your own mother is dying from the disease?'

I nodded, my eyes full of tears. 'Sam,' I said, the image of what had happened with Joe popping suddenly into my head like an unwelcome visitor. 'After the show we all went back to...'

He wrapped his arms around me, his jaw resting against my temple. 'Pen,' he said. 'We'll talk later. Whatever it is, it's fine.' His breath was warm as he spoke into my hair and he kissed me on the cheek as he turned to leave. 'Try and get some sleep,' he said, knowing I wouldn't. 'You too, Gordon.' He looked at my dad and then at me. 'I'll bring the kids when I come back,' he said.

'I've missed them.' I gave a pathetic little sob – it had been less than a day since I'd seen them last. 'I've missed all of you.'

'I know,' he said. 'I love you.'

And he was gone.

–

We took it in turns after that first night. Dad stayed the whole time. I stayed when I could, but there was only one camp bed in Mum's room and we couldn't all move into Bob's Place, much as I'd have liked to. Rory came and went accompanied by a warm and affectionate Candice, an earnest MJ, nose in a book, and a belligerent Callum, who mainly wanted to play in the garden or throw things. Sam came and went, sometimes bringing all the kids

338

and sometimes just himself armed with a takeaway or an ovenproof dish of unidentifiable vegetables that Grace had prepared ('I think it's celeriac,' we'd whisper to each other, chewing seriously over each mouthful of stew, 'maybe fennel?' and, 'Is that an olive or a grape?'). Grace, despite her interesting culinary skills, was clearly stepping into the role of woman of the house in my absence. It didn't hurt as much as I thought it might. It felt right that she was making herself comfortable in my figurative shoes, moving one place further up the escalator of life, as the original woman of the house, my mother, reached the top of that moving stairway and glided off into the unknown. That's the thing about the crazy ride of living. You're stuck on it, right up until the moment you're not, and there's no refund if you didn't make the most of it; there's no running to the back of the queue and paying for another ticket to get back on again. Unless you're a Buddhist, I suppose.

Veronica and Joe organised the return of my car on Saturday afternoon (Gee drove it over to Bob's), and both popped their heads around Mum's door to say hello and check on how she was doing. They've assured me that they can cover my work between them while I'm on compassionate leave. 'For as long as you need,' said Joe. 'I'm here. I can pick up whichever jobs need doing.'

He hasn't mentioned what happened in his hotel room a few nights ago. Neither of us has. To be honest, since the moment with Sam where I almost blurted my guilty conscience out to my exhausted husband, I haven't really given it much thought. There are bigger fish to fry.

It's odd, this jumble of days, waiting for something to happen, hoping it won't, knowing it will, somehow wanting it to all be over while praying it never ends. It's a little like the hours before you give birth. That feeling in the delivery room as the contractions get closer and closer together and you know you're on the brink of something major but you also need to make sure you've paid for the parking and that someone's looking after the dog. Friends send messages: 'hope you're doing OK'; 'thinking of you'; 'how's it all going?' And what they mean is, 'has the baby arrived yet?' or in this instance, 'has your mother died yet?' The same messages at the beginning and then at the end.

We've all had our special moments with her. Periods spent alone in this room when the others have popped out, either to get some fresh air or to discreetly allow time for individual expressions of grief. Mine was yesterday. I had been idly flicking through a magazine as I sat beside Mum's bed – after all, we can't always be doing something significant and existential in the presence of death – and then she made a little noise, not one of distress, but a sort of dry swallow. The hospice nurses had told us about the importance of mouth care when they came on Monday (I sort of knew this from working here, but I guess it's been something our own nursing staff dealt with previously), and we have a couple of sealed oral care packs complete with a tiny plastic bowl, some sponge-tipped lollipop-type things (Callum tried to eat several when he was here), and a disposable toothbrush with fine bristles like those on a baby's. I moistened the sponge and wiped it carefully around Mum's lips, chatting to her as I squeezed a tiny speck of toothpaste onto the brush.

'Do you remember that dentist, Mum,' I said, drawing the brush across her teeth and then wiping it off with the sponge. 'The one with the awful breath and the worse bedside manner? She was terrifying, like she could spot plaque from across the waiting room. Like a human disclosing tablet. Odd things those tablets, weren't they? Tasted minging and made your mouth look like you'd been punched in the face. Not surprising we don't use them any more. Or maybe some people do.'

I prattled on in this fashion for a few minutes, and when I was satisfied that her mouth looked clean and less sticky I scooped a smudge of Vaseline onto my finger and smoothed it across her lips. Her skin was looking dry so I took some moisturiser, the same brand she'd always used, even when she'd forgotten what it was called, or even what it was for (I've had to stop her eating it more than once) and I rubbed it into her cheeks, across her forehead. Using my fingertips I smoothed the cream into the delicate skin around her eyes, and then dabbed some perfume on her neck and her wrists.

'Mmm, delicious!' I said as I leaned in to kiss her forehead. Just like she used to do when we were young, as if Rory and I were tasty little morsels. I knew that feeling with my own children when they'd been infants, their peachy cheeks and yeasty skin a sensory feast, a parenting smorgasbord.

She opened her eyes wide for a moment and her pupils fixed on mine. I held my breath, thinking she might be about to say something. But she didn't. She just held my gaze, unblinking, communicating something stronger than words could possibly have conveyed. A tear leaked its way out of the corner of her eye. I didn't know whether to attribute that to emotion or just a bit of biology, lacrimal ducts fulfilling their cleansing duties at the end of a lifetime. All the body's processes doing their thing right up to the end, a final hoorah, a literal last gasp.

'I love you,' I said.

Rory visited later that evening, and he, Dad and I sat around Mum's bed reminiscing about happier times until Dad finally dropped off to sleep in the recliner chair he'd positioned to be as close as possible to his wife.

'All those memories,' I said to Rory just before he left, during one of the quiet moments when the night staff had dimmed the corridor lighting and the vast mansion of Bob's Place was peaceful. 'It makes you realise how lucky we were. Parents who loved each other, a happy home to grow up in...'

'Sibling who wasn't a total pain in the arse,' he said, pulling on his coat. He had a longer drive than me to get home.

'Don't know as I'd go that far. But seriously – I think about some of my friends growing up, and they had such a difficult time of it compared to us. I sometimes wonder whether what's happened to Mum is fate's way of levelling the playing field. Like early-onset dementia is just our family's allocated portion of bad luck hitting later than everyone else's?'

'That's one way of looking at it,' he said. 'But honestly, one thing a career in medicine has taught me is that so much of life is completely arbitrary. There are some conditions you can take steps to avoid, but others come and bite you when you least expect it. There's no allocated portion of bad luck. You just get what you get – play the hand you're dealt as best you can.'

'Well, I think we've played this hand as well as we possibly could,' I said, looking down at Mum, whose face was peaceful in repose.

Rory put his arm around my shoulders. 'I think we have too.'

And we'd stood together for a moment, my brother and I, contemplating the strange twists and turns of life as the gentle but haphazard breathing of our mother punctuated the silence.

—

I left at around midnight with promises to return with breakfast, but a few hours after I'd crawled into bed next to Sam for a fitful sleep, I was woken by my mobile phone.

'Penny,' said my father. 'She's gone.'

'Oh!' I rubbed my bleary eyes, glanced at the clock feeling a sense of disappointment – I'd missed it.

'I missed it,' my dad said sadly. 'The moment she passed. I was in the bloody toilet. When I came back, she'd died.'

'Oh Dad,' I said, my voice tight with emotion while teetering on the edge of hysteria. 'Don't worry. Rory told us that might happen. And the Marie Curie nurses said so. People wait until the room is empty sometimes – it's like it gives them permission to leave.'

'Are you saying she was waiting for me to go to the bog? You mean it's what she would have wanted?' The hysteria was clearly contagious, or hereditary, or both.

'Well, she would have hated the idea that you were holding on,' I said. 'She always was a stickler for prompt toileting – and a regular bowel habit.'

He laughed. We were both laughing. About bodily functions. When the most important person in our lives had just died. It was so British that I half expected Noël Coward to pop up, comment on the weather, offer us a nice cup of tea, and write a farce about the whole thing.

Chapter Thirty-Eight

Thursday 10 August

'I went to see the GP today,' I said to Sam. We were clearing up after supper and the kids had taken Montmorency out for a long walk in the summer evening. Grace suggested they might end up at the pub and would that be OK for Maisie, and I had said that I didn't think Mandy or Vince would mind as long as they all stayed out in the beer garden.

'Given the circs,' said Grace.

'Given the circs.'

We're all taking advantage of the weirdly deferential behaviour that surrounds a grieving family. People have been so kind, and there's a sense of the community really drawing you near at times like this. Neighbours I haven't spoken to in years stop me in the butcher's and tell me how sorry they are that my mum has died. A death is relatable in the way that having a parent living with dementia simply isn't, and all the empathy and consideration I maybe needed five or six years ago has materialised now, after the event. A sort of retrospective, passive form of compassion.

I'm not being fair, of course. Many people demonstrated their care prior to Mum's death, and many in the village went above and beyond the call of neighbourly duty to help us in practical ways. Finding Mum when she went walkabout, and either calling me or steering her homeward. Assisting Dad when he couldn't get the wheelchair across the rutted path from the park, or when Mum suddenly expressed a desire to go to church but couldn't seem to navigate the pew situation. Kindly ignoring my frustrated shouts of 'For fuck's sake!' as I hauled the fourth load of soiled sheets in as many hours off my parents' washing line. So yes, I am being unfair. But I'm allowed to be. Because I'm grieving.

It's a week since Mum died, and I'm still existing in the strange limbo that I felt between coming back from The Carlton in the middle of the night, and the morning of her death. There are times when I burst into tears, times that I feel numb and moments of irrational anger, like yesterday when I couldn't get the dishwasher door to shut and I just slammed it repeatedly while screaming expletives until Sam came and manoeuvred me away. It was in this spirit of awareness about my erratic emotions that I went to see the doctor today. I have been putting it off, this conversation. The whole hot flush, tearful episodes, poor sleep and anxiety mess of it all. The menopause conversation. But now, at last, I have a bit of a gap in my schedule. Funny that it took losing an actual parent for me to find a window in my diary to look after my own health – really funny – really fucking hilarious (sorry – I warned you about the angry outbursts).

'I think I might need HRT or something,' I said to the GP this morning. She's new, or at least, I haven't seen her before. Youngish, brisk, with a heavy Eastern European accent. She reminded me of Katya, our art therapist at Bob's – the same sort of brusque empathy, although maybe that's me being racist just because they have the same intonations of speech.

'You have periods?' she said, typing something into her computer.

I explained the kamikaze nature of my menstrual cycle, the Russian roulette of my underwear choices (I didn't *say* Russian roulette in case *that* was racist) – the fact that the one day I choose to wear pale knickers is the day I can guarantee I'll have some sort of torrential bleed cascading down my thighs within moments of leaving the house, when for the six months preceding I've had absolutely nothing happening and have been using my sanitary towels to wedge open the shower room door instead.

'And the last time this happen?' she said, still typing. 'The last period.'

'About four months ago,' I said. 'And it only lasted a day. Prior to that it was probably another three months.'

'And you are' – she squinted at the screen – 'fifty in couple months.'

'Yes,' I said. 'Woohoo!'

She gave me a quizzical look. 'So, we say yes you are menopausal. Or at least perimenopausal.'

'Do I not need a test to confirm that?' I said, slightly alarmed to see her typing something so definitive into my notes. Probably a Do Not Resuscitate order to kick in the day after my fiftieth birthday.

'No,' she said. 'Blood test for other things maybe, but hormone levels are all over the party at the moment. They are useless.'

'OK.' Actually, Rory had said the same on the one occasion I had tentatively raised women's health matters with him (I don't make a habit of it, but Joy wanted a second opinion on something). After forty-five he said the blood tests aren't very helpful. Which I guess would be true if my useless hormones were indeed 'all over the party'.

'So we say, you are the right age and your periods are reducing – you are menopausal,' the GP said to me now, turning from the screen with a smile. 'We do not need a test to say yes, no, for this.'

'Right.'

'The question is you have symptoms and how is the best way to treat them,' she said.

I explained about the occasional hot flush I was still having at night, although we were currently experiencing a heatwave and maybe the sweats weren't actually as bad as they had been. I told her about feeling sad. I told her about my mother dying, about my children growing up, their various trials and tribulations. I told her about days when I was snappy and irritable, and days when I forgot which groceries I needed or where I'd left my phone. Was this brain fog, I wondered aloud? Were my sadness and volatility linked to my depleted hormones?

'Maybe,' she said, having listened patiently for a good fifteen minutes. I knew I was running over my time but her face gave nothing away. 'Some of these symptoms are perhaps menopause. And they might get better with HRT' (she pronounced it like one long word – 'aichartee'). 'But maybe some are to do with other things. Like your mother being dead' (oof). 'And your children shooting from the nest, yes? It is a difficult time. This time in life. But we can try HRT.'

'We can?' I was surprised. I'd been under the impression from Joy that I would have to wage a relentless campaign, a war of attrition on my local primary care services before I could get hold of the elixir of life that was a bottle of Oestrogel.

She shrugged. 'We can, yes. If you want to – and if we talk about possible risks – and you are happy.' She turned back to her computer, tapped something into the keyboard. 'But we may say also – HRT will not make your mother be not dead. It will not make your babies be babies again. It will not make you young woman. Yes?'

'I understand,' I said.

'I do not say this being patronising. I say this because I want to treat the right problem with the right medicine,' she said. 'And if the problem is grief, then HRT is not the right medicine, yes? If the problem is sad lonely nest, then HRT is not the answer. If the problem is life, then no medicine is cure.'

'It was like being in a consultation with that wood-pecker from *Bagpuss*,' I said to Sam now. 'Professor Yaffle, was it? Just coming out with her brutal wisdom and punchy diagnoses of the human condition.'

'Wow,' he said, sliding a glass of wine in my general direction.

'She was great,' I said. 'She's booked me a follow-up in two weeks, and she's happy to start me on HRT then if I want to, but she suggested I wait and see how I feel after Mum's funeral. Maybe a bit of distance from the grief will give me some clarity about which of my symp-toms are hormonal and which aren't. She also pointed out that while many women benefit from HRT, it's not for everyone. Menopause can cause symptoms, and those symptoms can be treated, *should* be treated – but it's not an illness in itself.'

'She does indeed sound wise,' said Sam. 'Do you think she should talk to Joy?'

'Now there's a conversation that would be worth hearing,' I laughed. 'Yes, the only time we had a bit of a communication issue was when she kept asking about my bajeena.'

'Bajeena?' He wrinkled up his nose in confusion.

'Yes. My reaction entirely. She kept asking whether I had any bajeena symptoms, pain, itching, dryness… It took me a while to realise she meant vagina.'

'Oh. Right.'

'Anyway. Once we'd got that cleared up, it was fine. She said I'd done the right thing coming to speak to her. She gave me some website addresses, British Menopause Society, Cruse Bereavement, that sort of thing. She signed me off work, and like I say, I'll see her in a couple of weeks. When this is all over.' I gestured around myself, not really clear what I was referring to.

'And it was useful?' said Sam carefully. 'Talking to her?'

'Yes. I should have done it months ago. There's just never the time.' I took a sip of my wine.

'Pen,' said Sam after a pause. 'I know life is tough at the moment. And I know this isn't about me. But are things OK? Between us, I mean?'

I took another sip of my wine. I still hadn't told him about Joe and the guilt was eating me up inside. Mum's death had pulled everything into focus, made me aware of my own mortality for one thing, hence the visit to the doctor's, but also showed me how important my family is. How, as this family gets older, it gets stronger rather than more fragile. I'm so grateful to Sam for all he has given me and I feel furious with myself for ever wavering in that. But I had to tell him.

'Nothing happened in the end,' I said, as I finished describing the events leading up to the almost-kiss.

'But you wanted it to?' he said quietly.

I considered this. I owed it to Sam to be completely honest. 'I don't know,' I said eventually. 'It was just a different sensation, for a while, to be wanted. To have someone see me. As a woman. Not as their mother or daughter or sister or business partner.'

'Or their wife,' he said.

I took a deep breath. I could see he was hurting and I knew that some of what I was saying didn't make sense. 'Without wishing to sound like a cliché, it was about me, not about you,' I said. 'I just felt like I was slipping away, becoming invisible. With the kids growing up, it felt like they didn't need me any more. It was like I was losing a sense of who I am. My purpose. What I'm for...'

'Do you not think I feel like that sometimes though, Pen?' He looked down at the table. 'Do you not think I feel sad about the kids getting so big, that I don't miss the days when they used to hang on my every word?'

I gave him a dubious look. '*Was* there a time when they used to hang on your every word?' I said, and he laughed.

'I should have realised that you were going through this too,' I said. 'But like I say, I'm trying to explain how *I* feel at the moment. Not about how I feel set in the context of how you, or any of the other people in my life, feel.'

'Understood,' he said. 'Fair point.'

'It's like there are so many things to worry about,' I said, trying to make sense of this as much for my benefit as for Sam's. 'So much in my head that I don't even know what to concentrate on any more. The kids and whether they are growing into good people, happy functional members of society – the kind of society we're offering them and how fucked up it is, so much hate and intolerance and misogyny, the kind of *world* we're offering them, sitting here twiddling our thumbs while the climate burns. And I feel so powerless. I think I was starting to go a bit mad with it all. And then Mum died – and I'm not using that as an excuse – I know what happened with Joe was before that. But her dementia, her decline, it's been so hard to watch, and to see Dad and the way he still loved her even though her illness was limiting his life just as much as hers. I guess part of me felt like, I don't know, like maybe his marriage had become a millstone – a curse rather than a blessing. Do you see? I didn't question the whole institution of marriage, but I feel like I saw its flaws.'

'But, do you still want to be married,' he said in a small voice. 'To me, I mean? Do you still want...'

'Yes! God, of course, yes.' I was as emphatic as I could be. 'I'm just trying to give you an insight into where my mind was a couple of weeks ago.'

There was a long pause before he spoke again. 'I'm not sure I needed quite that level of insight to be honest, Pen,' he said with a wobbly little smile.

'I *love* you,' I said. 'And I'm sorry. I screwed up. Or rather, I nearly screwed up. But this was about me sorting my own head out, and it's taken a while – you might say it's still a work-in-progress.'

He poured us both another glass of wine. 'I understand that I haven't been around that much this year,' he said. 'And maybe when I have been here, I've been a bit preoccupied. I guess I'm sorting my own head out too. It's just that my midlife crisis is more your standard male exercise-based one.' He sighed. 'I'm not surprised for one moment that Joe would find you attractive. You're amazing. And beautiful. And I love you so much. I'm sorry that I didn't tell you enough, or show you enough.'

'You have though,' I said, smiling through my tears. 'How you've been the past two weeks. How you knew what to say when I was drunk and stuck in a hotel an hour away and my mother was dying. How you knew the exact moment I'd need a cuddle on Grace's graduation day, and when Maisie finished primary school. How you remind me that this family is held together by us, not just me...' I pulled him towards me, my lovely Sam, and I kissed his lovely, grizzled face.

His mouth broke into a smile beneath my kisses and he squeezed me around the waist. 'So we're OK?' he said, a little uncertainly.

'We're OK,' I said.

Later, once the kids had returned and we were in bed, me lying beside him in my very thin pyjama shorts while the electric fan whined from the corner, he slid his arm around my waist and pulled me against him.

'And how *is* your bajeena?' he said, nonchalant as you like.

'Oh, arid,' I said, giggling. 'Dry and barren as the plains of the Mojave Desert, I expect. Perilous, probably. Beware all ye who enter here, et cetera.'

'Good thing I'm a very determined and well-equipped explorer then,' he said.

Chapter Thirty-Nine

The hearse arrived outside Dad's bungalow at a quarter to eleven, exactly as planned. Dad nodded as he glanced at his watch, always a stickler for timekeeping.

'Punctual,' he said. 'Ten forty-five. Good.'

'We love to see it,' Rory whispered in my ear and I giggled.

'Of course, it will depend on what the traffic's like on the ring road,' Dad continued. 'But we should make good time for the church.' He fell silent as the undertaker approached the front door and knocked softly with his gloved hand.

'Jeez, he must be boiling,' I whispered to Rory as I plucked the crepe of my black dress from the crepey skin of my damp cleavage.

We made our way silently to the polished car behind the hearse and the lead pallbearer bowed his head towards Mum's coffin before getting into the driver's seat.

'Should we have bowed?' I said, to nobody in particular. I turned to Rory. 'Are the family supposed to bow? Should we do it, like, every time we see the coffin, or is once enough?'

He shrugged. 'I don't know.'

'Have you got your speech?' I said. 'Dad, have you got tissues? I've got some in my bag – so, you know, if you need them then, uhm.' I fidgeted in my seat and made some comment about not being able to do my seat belt up. 'What are the odds of being involved in a collision when one is part of a funeral cortege,' I wondered aloud. 'Oh! There's Catherine from down the road. Should I wave, do you think? Does one wave from a funeral car?'

'Penelope.' My father rested his hand on mine which I noticed was jiggling and fidgeting in my lap like it had a mind of its own. 'Hush now.'

I clamped my lips together and nodded my head. Dad's hand stayed holding mine and Rory's came across to join them. I looked down at my lap as the car slowly began to move off. If I just concentrated on that jumble of hands, focused on breathing slowly in and out, then maybe I'd get through this bit of the day at least.

The sun was beating down on the car as we pulled to a stop outside the church. We eased ourselves out of the rear seats, the backs of my legs sticking to the polished leather. My handbag hung limply by my side and I peeked inside it to reassure myself that the speech was there. I'd only read it aloud once and that had been in the privacy of the bathroom at home. And I hadn't actually managed to finish speaking before the tears had started. It's very difficult to articulate when your throat is tight and the back of your nose feels like it's on fire. I just had to stave that feeling off for a little longer. Nobody would mind if I cried, I knew that. But I wanted to get through the speech first.

Rory and I had debated how to handle the eulogy and we both felt it was important not to gloss over Mum's dementia. It had been part of her life and ours. A constant companion, this past decade. So Rory had decided to talk about Mum's youth and early adulthood, the biographical details we'd got from Dad but didn't really have any first-hand knowledge of, and I would tackle her life as a mother and grandmother. Which meant I got the dementia bit. Dad said he just wanted to sit in his pew and think his thoughts and not to have to mess about with a lectern and cue cards and worrying about whether he'd got his reading glasses. I understood. He'd spent every moment of the past few years worrying over details, the minutiae of his and Mum's existence – did Mary have a temperature, was she able to eat that safely, were those socks too tight, would she be OK while he was in the bath… Today he just wanted to be like any regular chap paying his respects to his late wife of fifty-four years.

Sam and the kids were sitting in the front pew to the left of the church with Candice and her two behind them. I could feel the weight of their collective gaze, could imagine the red-rimmed eyes of Grace, the wobbling lip of Maisie, the hunched shoulders of Tom, but I couldn't look directly at them if I wanted to make it through the next ten minutes. The first hymn was 'Lord of All Hopefulness', and I could hear the sound swelling from the back of the church as the pews full of our dementia choir raised their voices to the rafters. I couldn't sing; my throat didn't seem to be working properly. But I listened to those voices and in some measure they soothed me. And then Rory was up. I didn't listen. I couldn't risk it. Instead I allowed my mind to wander, fixing on the last song I'd heard on the radio just before leaving for Dad's house. 'Happy Hour' by The Housemartins wouldn't be the standard choice for most people attending their own mother's funeral, but it was what my brain decided to give me.

And then Rory was standing at the end of the pew to allow me out and I was making my way up to the pulpit. I didn't allow myself to look out across the assembled guests until I'd finished reading. I tried to pace myself, speak slowly and clearly rather than rushing through to reach the end, but it was hard, especially when I was talking about Mum coming to live with us after Dad broke his hip. Those memories were so fresh in my mind. They'd marked a turning point in my relationship with my mother. A deeper understanding that had brought us closer. It was difficult not to lose myself in those moments, but eventually I reached the last paragraph, where I described Maisie's family tree project and the tatty piece of wrapping paper still tacked to our wall with evidence of all of Mum's roots and branches written across it. And then it was over.

I looked up briefly, taking in the faces of my friends: Zahara, Joy and Caz were all there; a few other school mums; Fizz and Clive, along with at least fifty members of our choir; Mandy from the pub; Tina, Veronica, Katya and Shilpa from work. Rory's friends were there too. I could see Dave, who he'd been at school with (and who I'd had a massive crush on) and Elijah from medical school. It was good of them to come. And of course there were friends of Dad's, from the golf course; from the army; a couple he and Mum used to go on holiday with before the dementia sabotaged travel to exotic locations; Dad's brother, Uncle Brian; cousin Nick and his wife. The church was full.

The rest of the service was relatively easy once I'd finished my speech. The hymns brought solace, belting them out, feeling the release of grief gusting from my lungs. And then the dementia choir sang Mum's favourite song, 'You Are My Sunshine', and everything got a bit blurry as I remembered her singing it to me as a small child. We filed out, following the coffin. Rory, Sam and Tom were pallbearers, so I held my father's hand in mine, the children flanking me on either side as we passed down the aisle.

Once outside, we stood beside a hole in the ground where the coffin was lowered. It didn't seem possible that my mother's body was in there. Frail and hollow. And dead. We'd decided eventually to bury her with her lovely coat – I think my father thought it was a frivolous notion – 'That's a good warm winter coat, Penelope – someone else might get good use out of that' – but I couldn't bear the thought of her being without it. The woman at the undertakers, whose kind hands arranged Mum's hair and painted her nails in the shade I requested, agreed. 'If she found joy wearing it in life,' she said to me, 'then why shouldn't she wear it now?'

I thought of that coat as they lowered her into the ground. How thrilled she'd been when I brought it round to their bungalow. How she had stroked the fabric and beamed at me. 'Beautiful,' she'd said, gazing up at my face, and I wasn't sure whether she was referring to the coat or to me. She'd never told me I was beautiful before, but dementia has a way of loosening the tongue, and maybe you always thought your own children were beautiful – it was part of the parenting contract. Sam was standing beside me, holding my hand – and *my* beautiful children, Grace, Tom and Maisie, had their arms around each other. There was a general sound of sniffing and shuffling, earth thudding onto the coffin, the bloody Housemartins still rattling around in my head. And the vicar said his bit as we stood politely watching the great circle of life complete another course.

After a time people began to shuffle away from the graveside with mutterings about being at the hall in time for the caterers, and did anyone know whether there was air conditioning, and I suppose not because you never really think you'll need it in this country, do you, and those sausage rolls will be getting a bit sweaty though, won't they, and best get a bit of a wiggle on and what a moving ceremony and wasn't it sad about, you know, and nice to see so many folks come to support the family and what a terrible disease it is…

Eventually it was just me and my dad. He came to stand by me and we looked over towards the cars where Sam was crouched low talking to Maisie. Fizz and Tina were ushering various members of the choir along the footpath in the direction of the village hall. Tom and Grace were shaking hands with the vicar, Rory had Callum on his hip and Candice was listening as MJ read out the names from the war memorial. As the sounds of their chatter filtered across the churchyard, the sun warmed our faces and my dad turned towards Mum's grave.

'Look at that, Mary,' he said, wiping a solitary tear from his eye. He pointed to me, to the family and friends beyond. 'Look at everything you made.'

Chapter Forty

Epilogue

Sunday 17 March the following year: Mother's Day

'Guess what?!' Zahara's voice came through the speaker.

'You're pregnant,' I said, indicating left.

'Fuck, no. I mean, God, can you imagine?'

'You're moving house,' I said, a leaden weight dropping suddenly into my stomach. 'Don't move house. Please never leave this village.'

'I shall not be leaving the Shire, young hobbit,' she said. 'No. We're getting a rescue dog!'

'Classic,' I said. 'Does it have all its legs? Is it one of those ones on wheels? Is it blind?'

'No. I don't think so. She's called Barbara and she's enormous.'

'Excellent, maybe she'll put Monty in his place.' (I've realised, somewhat belatedly, that by shortening Montmorency's name I sound slightly less of a dick when shouting it across the woods – but only slightly.)

We talked through the practicalities of dog ownership, whether she could borrow our crate, how Zahara's elderly cat and four gerbils would cope with the invasion of their territory (if they're anything like their owner, with complete equanimity, I suspect), and whether Raj was equally excited or just pretending in order to keep everyone happy. There is a real danger with those two that they just say yes to everything and everybody, right up until the moment they end up destitute. They were the same at their wedding last year, agreeing to everybody's requests no matter how unreasonable, because they were so happy to be getting married and wanted everyone to bask in the warmth of their love.

'It's all well and good,' Joy had said, 'but you can't have the aunt of the woman your ex-husband had an affair with sitting up at the top table just because apparently *her lumbago* means she can't use ordinary chairs. And honestly. Who puts a link to a goat farm in Sudan on their gift list?'

'It's what she wants, Joy,' I said firmly. 'And if the bride wants goats, then she shall have goats.'

And she did — have goats, I mean. Joy, Caz and I did what any self-respecting group of friends do — we each sponsored a goat as per the gift list while finding unique ways to treat Zahara and show her how special she was. Joy sourced a high-end caterer and brokered a deal that involved her paying the majority of the bill without Zahara ever realising; Caz made bunting, table-cloths, napkins and pretty much any other haberdashery-based item you could name, running them up on her sewing machine, and I managed to get hold of tickets for her and Raj to attend the opening night of this season's *Strictly Come Dancing* through my new celebrity contacts — Angharad's in the starting line-up this year but I am sworn to secrecy (although I have told Sam. And Zahara, obviously. And Joy. And Caz).

'Anyway, chick,' Zahara's voice filled the car again. 'Just wanted to wish you a Happy Mother's Day. I know it's a bit shit — first one since you lost your mum, and all that.'

'Yeah, I'm just on my way to the church to sort her flowers now,' I said, glancing at the arrangement I'd picked up from the florist on the seat beside me.

'Well, I'll let you get on. Stop in for a cuppa later if you fancy it. I've dropped a little something off on your doorstep.'

'Oh, you really didn't need to...'

'I know,' she said. 'But I'm thinking of you. Love, *love* you, Pea.'

'Love, *love* you, Zee.'

The call disconnected and I blew my nose, which was tricky when driving. Two minutes later, as I was making my slow way through town, another call came through. It was Grace.

'Tom's just going to stop in at the garage and get some of the devil's juice, but we'll be up at the church in ten minutes,' she said. 'Do you need anything? Looked like you were low on milk.'

'Yes, that would be great – two pints, please. Thanks, love. See you up there and tell Tom to...'

'Drive safely!' I heard him shout over the noise of his clanky engine. 'Will do, Mum.'

It's actually quite nice to have another driver in the family, and Grace is certainly making the most of it, bullying her brother into ferrying her around like a chauffeur when she comes up from London to visit. She's managed to find a job working for a mental health charity who do outreach with underrepresented communities (which Sam maintains is the most woke thing he's ever heard), and is doing a part-time Master's in music therapy at the Guildhall alongside the job, as well as singing in a band. She's living in a shared house with about forty other people and is always skint, but she's very happy and that's as much as you can wish for as regards your offspring, really. I'm hoping that she doesn't move any further afield than London, but as long as she stays in the country, it's fine. I can't cope with any other family members leaving the UK since Rory recently dropped the bombshell that he's moving the family to Australia to be nearer Candice's parents.

'She misses her mum so badly, Penny,' he said. 'And life as a doctor is way, way easier out there. Better pay, better conditions. Happy wife, happy life.'

I couldn't really argue with that, but I will miss him and miss watching the kids grow up so much.

'You'll just have to come and stay, like, all the time,' said Candice. And she's right. Yes, Maisie is still at school but I can see a future where Sam and I take some time out for travelling. It might be quite helpful to have family stationed on the other side of the world. A home-from-home. It also makes me smile to think that Mum's children will cover the globe in this way. She'll have a heritage reference point in two major continents – a diaspora. It's basically an empire, just with less slavery and/or devastation to indigenous populations.

Another more tangible part of Mum's legacy is in the early development stages as we look at franchise options for Bob's Place. The hope is that by next year a 'Mary's Place' will pop up in the neighbouring county. Talks are underway, and now that we have a blueprint for success with Bob's Place, I think we can consider rolling it out more widely. Tina and I have found the perfect location: an old lakeside hotel sitting in open countryside on the outskirts of a peaceful village. We'll be spending most of May there overseeing the initial build, safe in the knowledge that Bob's is being looked after by our care home manager Deepti, who started working for us in September – earlier than anticipated, due to our new staff crèche facilities which allow her more flexibility with her young family.

As well as being very popular with our staff, the crèche has also helped provide some financial stability for Bob's Place. The money we raised with the concert and auction gave us the platform to invest in our outbuildings, and we are now able to rent out the converted stable block to a local preschool. The revenue this generates provides us with the additional income to keep all the nice add-ons that distinguish Bob's Place from any other care home, but the arrangement has brought much more than basic financial security. Sharing the same geographical location means we often have little visitors using the facilities at Bob's Place, or residents of ours taking the short walk across the courtyard to join in a nursery rhyme singalong – a situation that seems beneficial regardless of age.

A significant amount of the improvement in our circumstances is of course down to Joe, who had the initial idea about renting the outbuildings, brought in the revenue to facilitate their conversion and managed to secure our charitable status, all during the short period of his fixed-term contract. I'm proud to say that I am now Penny Baker, CEO of a financially stable charitable trust, complete with board of trustees, and I am hugely grateful to Joe for all he did to help us achieve this position – securing the future of Bob's Place, my most favourite place in the world. He stays in touch and enjoys hearing how we're getting on, although his enquiries tend to go through Deepti now. His move to work on a contract with Riding for the Disabled came a little earlier than planned, but Veronica, Tina and I agreed he had fulfilled the brief and gave him a glowing reference. The two of us never mentioned what nearly happened at The Carlton, but on the day of his leaving party he came to find me in the gardens. He sat beside me on Ernest's Bench (most of our garden furniture is a legacy gift) and told me how much he'd enjoyed working with me. As he left he shook my hand, all businesslike, and then he said, 'Your husband is a lucky man. But I think he realises that.'

I think he probably does too. We're heading up to Scotland together in a couple of months, Sam and I. He's going to complete his triathlon a year later than planned, and then we're going to take a short break in the Highlands just mooching about, the two of us, while Tom looks after Maisie.

'It'll be like those first years after we got married,' he said, all excited about booking the accommodation and planning the tour.

'It won't,' I said. 'We're not in our twenties any more. But that's OK, and we're still going to have a brilliant time.'

Because we're not newlyweds. We've got a whole heap of marriage in our bunker – a family, a shared history, a legacy. We're not the same people we were when we first met. And that's exactly as it should be. We're stronger now. We know who we are and we're happy in our skins (even if they're a bit baggier than they used to be). I smile now as I remember the card he got me this morning along with my bunch of flowers (reasonably priced and sourced from the corner shop, judging by the cellophane, but still nice). Beneath the Happy Mother's Day caption he'd written, *Penny, you are one hot mother.* And that made me laugh. Because I am. Boiling hot most of the time, in spite of my dabbling with hormone patches.

He's there now, standing with Maisie and Dad in the road next to the churchyard, waving and gesticulating wildly like I don't know how to pull into a parking space. Grace and Tom pull in behind me, back from the petrol station and loaded up with the unnecessary groceries that always accompany such a trip. Sure enough…

'Got some Cadbury's Creme Eggs for later,' says Tom, beaming. He's so tall now, this little boy of mine. Taller than anyone else here. He'll be off in a few months, assuming he gets the grades he needs to fulfil his offer from Loughborough in August. But I remind myself I've done this before. I've experienced the gnawing emptiness of a child leaving home. And I survived. Grace came back. Changed, yes. They're never quite the same after that first term at university. But she came back nonetheless – and hopefully she'll keep returning, dipping into the family and out again as required.

My family grows, and as it grows it spreads out across the country. Just like Mum's family, spreading across the globe. I wonder who they will become, these people I've made? What will they achieve? Will they be happy? Maybe one day Sam and I will be grandparents. Speaking of which, I see Maisie take Dad's hand in hers as we walk over to Mum's grave. I point it out to Sam and he smiles, gives me a squeeze.

'Oh, hey, Pen,' he says, stopping suddenly. 'Come and have a look at this.' He steers me back towards his car. 'Zahara dropped it off a few minutes ago,' he says, opening the back seat and pulling out a large gift bag. 'I thought you'd like to see it.'

I reach into the tissue paper and pull out a mounted canvas. It's a montage of photographs and hand-drawn sketches, arranged with Zahara's eye for a pleasing aesthetic. There's me with Mum at the village fete; me heavily pregnant with Maisie, holding Tom's hand as I walk him to school; sitting with Joy in the pub garden a few years ago, laughing our heads off; and with Caz the day she got the all-clear after her chemo. There's a photo of me, Tina and Veronica when Bob's Place first opened, and another one from this year standing in the entrance hall pointing excitedly to the recently reinstated CQC Outstanding rating (*Up yours, Lorraine Rowbotham!* I wanted to shout when the woman herself conceded that we had ticked all the boxes and jumped through all the hoops). There's a picture of Rory standing beside me and the dog in a muddy field last Easter, and one of Grace's graduation, when I've clearly had too much alcohol. There's a photo of the dementia choir during our very first show, me sitting at the piano stool looking nervous as hell, as well as a picture from last year's gala performance where I look borderline hysterical. There are pictures of me with both my parents, with Sam and baby Maisie, one of the whole Andrews family and one of me and Zahara from her wedding day when I was matron of honour.

I am absolutely speechless, and I stand there for a moment, open-mouthed, taking in every detail, all the love that my wonderful friend has poured into this piece of work.

'She's really captured everything,' says Sam, beaming at my reaction, although he too has a tear in his eye. 'You are so many things to so many people.'

We look across the churchyard to where Dad, Grace, Tom and Maisie are gathering around Mum's grave, and then we look at each other. We don't say anything, because there is nothing more to say, but he smiles at me as he carefully rests the picture on the back seat of the car, and then he takes my hand and we walk to join the rest of the family.

A Letter from Nancy

Firstly, thank you lovely reader for buying or borrowing this book – especially if you are a man or a non-menopausal woman. Because *Hot Mother* is unashamedly a menopause novel and this might not be your usual oeuvre (if indeed menopause fiction can be considered an oeuvre – perhaps 'a dwindling supply of oeuvres' would be more appropriate). Anyway, all readers, irrespective of gender, age, and egg status are equally fabulous in my eyes, and the world needs people who are prepared to broaden their horizons and read widely – so, good for you for getting this far.

Whilst *Hot Mother* is written by a peri-menopausal woman and is hopefully relatable for others in a similar situation, it is not exclusively a book about menopause. Instead it is about a middle-aged woman, who happens to be menopausal, at the same time as getting on with all the other important business of living. Because menopause does not occur in isolation. It happens to women who are already pretty busy, thank you very much. It happens to women who are often still looking after children, running a household, running a business, caring for elderly relatives, carving out a career, and trying to be a good friend, a loving partner, and a fully functioning member of society. This is a lot to deal with even before the oestrogen level starts to drop.

With *Hot Mother* I wanted to put midlife and menopause in context. I also wanted to show it from different
perspectives with four women who are all experiencing middle age in their own individual ways. The
recent increase in public awareness around menopause is
welcome, and long overdue, but there remains an underlying confusion about what this time of life feels like
or looks like, and a fear amongst younger women about
what is in store for them. I worry that menopause may in
fact have become yet another stick to beat women with,
making them feel that they're simply *not doing it right*.

Hot Mother was written to show that there are many
ways to 'do' menopause. And all of them are OK; whether
you're a Joy, evangelical about HRT, testosterone gel and
powerlifting; a Zahara who prefers mindfulness and herbs;
a Caz whose options are limited by other risk factors; or
a Penny who's simply too busy looking after everyone
else to even think about her own health. The key thing
is choice and empowering women to make informed
decisions about their own bodies.

Hot Mother also builds on the themes of my previous
novel, *The Mother of All Problems* (if you haven't read it yet,
why the devil not?) where a younger Penny is struggling
to cope with life in the Sandwich Generation, and the
message remains the same – caring for other people is
hard, especially when their needs are pulling you in all
sorts of different directions. Losing a sense of yourself,
feeling invisible, questioning your role in life and your
ability to cope in this scenario is normal but not much
fun, and it's important that you take some time out to
look after yourself. Don't forget to put your own oxygen
mask on first, as the flight attendants say.

So, until the next time lovely readers, take care, look after yourselves, and if you want to do something really nice then leave a cheery book review on the website of your choice (ideally about *Hot Mother*). But even if you don't want to, or you hated the book, or you forget this sentence as soon as you've read it due to a bit of brain fog, don't worry – I still think you're wonderful.

Love Nancy xx

Acknowledgements

There are, as always, a whole heap of people to thank when it comes to bringing a book into the world and *Hot Mother* is no exception. Firstly, a huge bundle of gratitude must go to the team at Hera books headed up by the wonderful Keshini. Publishing with Hera has been an entirely collaborative process and a joy from start to finish. Jennie, my editor extraordinaire, who understands Penny and loves her almost as much as I do – you are an absolute dream to work with and I trust your judgement wholeheartedly. Thank you for shaping *Hot Mother* into a manageable beast from the hot mess of additional storylines, adopted siblings and country and western singers (although it would have been nice to keep the bit about Dolly Parton and Zahara's wedding). Kate, Thanhmai and the rest of the publicity team at Canelo, along with Digital Dan and her Tik-Tokkery, thank you for the magazine features, the proof copies, the interviews, posts and reels – you're all wonderful.

The writing community, both online and in person – you're all such a huge support. The Rumney's Chocolate Café gang, the Comedy Women in Print ladies and everyone who has read early copies, provided quotes and generally shown love to *Hot Mother* – thank you all. Equally, the friends who aren't writers (*yet*, in some cases) who have supported me through a turbulent period over the past couple of years; the Book Clubbers, Icy Dippers, Wives of Bath Quizzers and Buckingham Girls, plus Katie, Sophie and Charlotte, the fairy godmothers from afar – you are all absolute superstars, the hottest of mothers, and I love you dearly. Special thanks also must go to Cassie for persuading me to unleash Penny onto the world rather than letting her languish in a drawer; Heather, for coming up with the title for *Hot Mother*'s predecessor, *The Mother of All Problems*, thus saving me weeks of anguish; and Ange for buying about a hundred copies of every book I write.

And my family. My fabulous peachy family. To my husband, please know that *Hot Mother* is entirely a work of fiction and not a reflection of my thoughts regarding our marriage. You are a gorgeous human being, I adore you as much today as I did when we met all those years ago, and the spark is most definitely still there. My kids – watching you grow and become these amazing young people full of wit, warmth and character continues to be the greatest privilege of my life. I love you all so much.

My in-laws, who have all been so invested in my publishing journey, I cannot tell you how much it means to me. From sending photos when you've spotted one of my books out in the wild to buying up copies of every magazine featuring Nancy Peach's latest offering, attending launch events and generally banging the drum. It's much appreciated.

And finally, the original peach-tree. My parents and my sister. Losing Mum was hard and writing about Mary's death in this book brought much of that experience back. I, like Penny, have sometimes felt rootless without the grounding presence of a mother in recent years. But this tree remains strong due to the resilience, good humour and general tomfoolery of my dad, and the unshakeable, unbreakable bond between me and my sister. This book is for you, H. You are a superstar sibling and I am so very fortunate to have you as my constant companion through all the ups and downs of this bonkers old life.